THE MYSTERIOUS PRESS
ANNIVERSARY ANTHOLOGY

THE MYSTERIOUS PRESS

ANNIVERSARY ANTHOLOGY

CELEBRATING 25 YEARS

BY THE EDITORS OF MYSTERIOUS PRESS

Published by Warner Books

A Time Warner Company

Copyright © 2001 by The Mysterious Press
Contributions copyright: "Come Again?" © 2001 by Donald E. Westlake, "The Anniversary Waltz" © 2001 by Loren D. Estleman, "Inscrutable" © 2001 by DOJO, Inc., "The Usual Table" © 2001 by Peter Lovesey, "THEM!" © 2001 by William Marshall, "The Impostor" © 2001 by Marcia Muller, "Activity in the Flood Plain" © 2001 by Hui Corporation, "Sometimes Something Goes Wrong" © 2001 by Stuart Kaminsky, "Countess Kathleen" © 2001 by Jerome Charyn, "Instinct" © 2001 by Archer Mayor, "What's in a Name?" © 2001 by Margaret Maron, "Coming Around the Mountain" © 2001 by James Crumley, "Handle with Care" © 2001 by Marion Chesney, "The Mule Rustlers" © 2001 by Joe R. Lansdale, "Body Zone" © 2001 by Lindsey Davis, "Revision" © 2001 by Robert Greer, "Birdbath" © 2001 by Charlotte Carter, "High Maintenance" © 2001 by Beth Saulnier

All rights reserved.

 Mysterious Press books are published by Warner Books, Inc., 1271 Avenue of the Americas, New York, NY 10020.

Visit our Web site at www.twbookmark.com

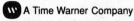 A Time Warner Company

The Mysterious Press name and logo are registered trademarks of Warner Books, Inc.
Book Design by Fearn Cutler
Printed in the United States of America
First Printing: May 2001
10 9 8 7 6 5 4 3 2 1

Library of Congress Cataloging-in-Publication Data
The Mysterious Press anniversary anthology : celebrating 25 years / by the editors of Mysterious Press.
    p. cm.
  ISBN 0-89296-739-0
  1. Detective and mystery stories, American. I. Mysterious Press.

PS648.D4 M8837 2001
813'.087208—dc21

00-068667

For all Mysterious authors:
The happy ones; and sad ones;
The sober and the silent ones;
The boisterous and glad ones;
The good ones—yes, the good ones too;
And all the lovely bad ones.

And for Susan, in gratitude

Cadfael looked back to the turning-point of his life, many years past. After all manner of journeying, fighting, endurance of heat and cold and hardship, after the pleasures and pains of experience, the sudden irresistible longing to turn about and withdraw into quietness remained a mystery. Not a retreat, certainly. Rather an emergence into light and certainty.

—Ellis Peters (1913–1995), *The Potter's Field*

"If I were either you or Mr. Vines," Leonard Deep said, "I'd get out of Durango as quickly as possible."

"Kelly and I're leaving on the evening of the fourth."

"Why not before?"

"We don't want to miss the parade," Vines said.

—Ross Thomas (1926–1995), *The Fourth Durango*

CONTENTS

INTRODUCTION

The Mysterious Press is twenty-five years old in 2001. And we've been here for sixteen of them.

Sixteen apiece, that is. We were both hired by Otto Penzler in June of 1985—Sara Ann as editor and Bill as managing editor—back when the Press was still in the old brownstone up the stairs from the Mysterious Bookshop on West 56th Street, behind Carnegie Hall and way, way over to the left.

The concept behind the Press, its reason for coming into existence, drummed into our heads in those salad days, is to proclaim that Great Crime Literature is Great Literature.* Creators of the best crime fiction are as deserving of respect and admiration as any "literary" author. Our goal as editors is to seek out, sign up, and nurture writers whose work— while featuring cops and private eyes and amateur sleuths— opens a window into the working of human nature. And, incidentally, provides a cracking good read.

Over the years, we've published dozens of crime novels we think are some of the best of the fin de siècle: *The Killjoy, Rough Cider, L.A. Confidential, The Good Policeman, The Bridesmaid, The New York Detective, Humans, 32 Cadillacs, Bootlegger's Daughter, The Mexican Tree Duck, Cranks and*

---

*"If detective stories are read with more exuberance than railway guides, it is certainly because they are more artistic."—G. K. Chesterton

Shadows, Wireless, One More River, The Yellow Room Conspiracy, Bellows Falls, Wolf in the Shadows, Life Itself, Ah, Treachery!, Never Street, The Bottoms ... these are a few of the books which ... well, we won't say "transcend the genre," due to our affection and respect for the genre ... but for which Mysterious Press will be remembered.

In 1990 Mysterious Press was bought outright by Warner Books, and we packed up and moved into a mighty midtown Manhattan skyscraper. This was also the year we were joined by Susan Richman, Queen of Publicists, whose inventive and enthusiastic effort has moved the Press and its authors ever more firmly into the limelight.

The three of us have had a marvelous time as the proud keepers of the Mysterious Press flame, and we look forward to continuing to publish the brightest of dark literature over the next twenty-five years.

Sara Ann Freed   William Malloy

FOREWORD

I t was sometime in the fall of 1975 when I decided that a publishing house entirely devoted to mystery fiction might be a good idea, and that I would create just such an entity.

For years I'd been reading and collecting mystery fiction first editions, and I helped write some books on the subject. My pet peeve (and one that remains to the present day) is that, even though the best mystery writers are among the most accomplished of all fiction writers working in the English language, not enough credit is given to them.

Admittedly, there are now fewer academic and literary snobs who look down their noses at the work of mystery writers, but there are still far too many who do not grasp that the best mystery fiction should be taught at the university level and deserves the front page of the *New York Times Book Review*. There is no less literary style, philosophic depth, and insight into human nature on the part of the top crime writers than there is among those regularly reviewed by the *New York Review of Books*. The intellectual seriousness of telling a story about the extremes of human passion and its consequences is at least the equal of a shocking stylistic dedication to the use of no punctuation or the moral lessons to be learned from sleeping with various members of the family.

This dedication to the excellence of crime fiction not merely as "escapist" (is there any decent fiction that isn't?) but as a serious mirror of the human condition became a major factor in the decision to start the Mysterious Press. I knew I couldn't single-handedly change the predilections of the reviewers and the academics, but I could at least take a small positive step in the elevation of mystery fiction by producing books that were worthy of their contents.

For the stepchild of publishing a quarter century ago, it was commonplace to produce mysteries on the cheapest possible paper, using pressed cardboard (instead of cloth) covers, and two-color dust jackets, while far less distinguished prose had nicely textured, acid-free paper, cloth, linen, or buckram bindings, and splendid full-color paintings to shout its existence to the world.

For collectors, I determined to make books that had previously been the province only of poets and authors of belles lettres: limited editions, numbered and signed by authors, with slipcases to preserve them. In the first years of the Mysterious Press, every book had a limited edition, and such talented artists as Steranko and Gahan Wilson provided full-color dust jacket art. A few times, I liked the art so much that I used it again as a frontispiece—that lovely throwback to nineteenth-century book production.

Having acquired the dedication to go along with the philosophy, I wasn't exactly sure what to do next. Some very good friends made modest investments so that there was working capital, and I went to the excellent but unjustly neglected Robert L. Fish (a three-time Edgar winner and author of the book on which *Bullitt* was based, among much else) and asked if he'd let me publish something of his, and we settled on a collection of stories about Kek Huuygens, Smuggler.

At the same time, having been a longtime Sherlock Holmes aficionado (and a member of the Baker Street Irregulars), I found an obscure parody cycle by Charles Todd from 1915–16 and put them together for a collection as well.

I now had two books in hand and went to the yellow pages to find a printer and a typesetter, hand-delivered the precious pages to the appropriate people, and in the course of time the cartons of books arrived at my apartment building in the Bronx. While I can now say that I ordered *only* 1,000 copies of each title, plus 250 limited edition copies, take my word for it that you have no idea how many books that is until you unload a truck and stack them in an already crowded apartment.

Bob Fish introduced me to his friend Robert Bloch, the author of *Psycho* and hundreds of other books and stories, who said, sure, I could publish one of his books. That's when I ran into trouble.

Now, to put this situation into perspective. I lived in a book-filled apartment and tried to earn a living as a freelance writer of books and magazine articles. This is a tough way to earn a living even if you have talent as a writer, which I do not. I paid the rent by making up in long hours what I lacked in skill.

There was no one to help with the running of a publishing company. I negotiated contracts, edited manuscripts, wrote flap copy and whatever advertising and publicity were needed, hired artists and designers for the dust jackets, and handled production, including buying paper and binding materials, proofreading and on and on.

Somehow, this was all possible until I published *The King of Terrors* by Bloch, the third Mysterious Press book. It was, by my terms at the time, a success. When few books were being sold, I could also handle packing books, typing the invoices, keeping the bank records straight, and hauling the books to the post office (though my brother was a huge help with that).

It was impossible to get secretarial help. ("Hello, would you send a Kelly girl to my apartment in the Bronx?") Besides, there was no room for a second person to work. I knew I needed to move into a larger space in Manhattan so that I could have an office and an assistant.

It quickly became apparent that I couldn't afford to rent space, so, after searching for many, many months, I bought (with a partner) the nice graystone building on West Fifty-sixth Street.

Now there was so much room I thought it would be great fun to open a bookshop in the building. I knew as much about running a bookshop as I'd known about running a publishing house, but, since ignorance hadn't stopped me once, I saw no need to let it stop me then.

Renovations began and proceeded quickly. Walls came down, walls went up, a spiral staircase was installed, and two mystery writer friends, Donald E. Westlake and Brian Garfield, together with my future wife, Carolyn, built the bookshelves. The Mysterious Bookshop opened on Friday the 13th of April 1979.

By now, slowly, the Mysterious Press had produced books by Isaac Asimov, Edward D. Hoch, Cornell Woolrich, Ellery Queen, Stanley Ellin, and the superb *Lew Archer, Private Investigator* by Ross Macdonald, a Mystery Guild selection, which had six printings and an introduction that was picked up and run on the front page of the *New York Times Book Review*. Even with that success the company was losing money until Stephen King gave me the chance to publish a limited, signed edition of *Cujo*, which sold out almost overnight and allowed us to pay our printing bills for two other books, keeping us afloat.

Running a bookshop, even an unsuccessful one (as it was in its early days), is pretty much a full-time job. So is being a freelance writer, as earnings from writing and some lecturing provided funds to keep the store alive. Running a publishing company, even one not making very much money, was yet another full-time job. My wife and I were thinking of closing it down when I had an unexpected visit to the bookshop one afternoon.

A very smart publishing entrepreneur sent his assistant to ask if I was interested in expanding the scope of my publishing house. If so, would I meet with her boss? Being no fool, I reckoned this couldn't be all bad and we met a few days later at 3:00 P.M. I know the time because I think it's rude to be late, and I didn't want to appear too eager and show up early, so I kept my eye on my watch and rang the bell at 3:00. Sharp. I was on the down elevator at 3:13, having shaken hands on an arrangement whereby money would be provided for additional staff, acquisition, production, and promotion of books. The deal was that he would get back his investment with first moneys received and then we'd share the profits fifty-fifty. Sounded pretty good to me.

We then needed to find a publisher who would distribute the books, which means a sales staff to sell them, a warehouse for storage, and a credit department that would collect the money owed.

After meeting with several of the largest houses, I decided I wanted to be with the smallish but very prestigious Farrar, Straus & Giroux. This decision goes back to the philosophical raison d'être of the house, giving mysteries the chance to be treated with the respect they deserved.

The first author who signed with me was Donald E. Westlake, one of the most talented, versatile, and (deservedly) praised writers of our time, a Grand Master of the Mystery Writers of America and Edgar winner in three different categories (novel, short story, and screenplay). Gregory Mcdonald soon followed suit, and so did Patricia Highsmith.

Things were looking pretty rosy until shortly before the first book was released, when the investor said he wanted to end the relationship, and when could he have his half of the losses? There it was, in our agreement: share profits *and* losses. It seems some tax shelter holes had closed and the deal was over. The losses at that moment looked to me like the combined national debt of four major European countries, but he made a very reasonable offer of a payout that could easily have taken the rest of my life but seemed fair to both of us.

Reasonable or not, my major emotional and intellectual response to this new situation was, of course, panic. First, I was in more debt than I could ever have imagined. Second, the Mysterious Press had already become a very good publishing house with a wonderful list of authors that had suddenly been flushed. Third, and a real reason for insomnia, many men and women who earned their living writing books had entrusted that living to *me*. Suddenly, some of the most talented mystery writers in America were going to be orphaned.

It was near Christmas 1983 when I called my friend and agent, Nat Sobel, partly as last resort but partly because I needed someone to whom I could tell this tale of woe, who would understand and, maybe, offer sympathy. Sympathy is not what happened.

"You've got a great company here," he said, "with great

authors. And it's a great idea—a publishing house devoted only to the best mystery fiction. I'll just get you another partner."

He made it sound so easy that I went home and told Carolyn our troubles were over and she nearly collapsed in my arms with relief and joy. Two months later Nat and I had lunch with the editor in chief of Warner Books, Bernard Schirr-Cliff, and his boss, Laurence J. Kirshbaum, president, and we shook hands on a deal after about fifteen minutes. On April 1 (April Fool's Day, as I like to remind people) we signed the contracts.

The first thing that Larry Kirshbaum asked after all the documents were signed convinced me that this was going to be a wonderful partnership. He didn't ask about projected income, or how many units we could move in the second year, or what additional profit centers did I envision beyond the sale of books. No. Larry asked me, "Who's your favorite writer? Who should we go after for the Mysterious Press list?"

Ross Thomas. No hesitation. The brilliant and versatile Thomas had never had the success he deserved and we felt we could help him achieve it. We did.

James Ellroy, the modern master of noir fiction, who had not found much of an audience with his first few books, then produced *The Black Dahlia*, which had numerous hardcover editions before making the *New York Times* best-seller list as a paperback.

In the next few years, such extraordinary authors as Ruth Rendell, P. D. James, Len Deighton, James Crumley, Ellis Peters, Aaron Elkins, Joe Gores, Marcia Muller, Eric Ambler, and Kingsley Amis produced books for the Mysterious Press as well. So did many other writers, also immensely talented, who have not had quite as much recognition. Yet.

It is not arrogance or hyperbole to say that the Mysterious Press has become the most distinguished publisher in history to be focused on mystery/crime/suspense fiction.

Success stories are team efforts, of course. The talented people at Warner Books struck me then, and still do (with some—but not too many—changes in the cast of characters), as the most intelligent, creative, and hardworking people in the world of publishing. It starts at the top, with Larry Kirshbaum (everybody's pick as the nicest man in publishing), and continues into the art department, the marketing and sales teams, production, and so on.

But it all really starts with the authors, and this book should be dedicated to them—for their talent as well as their courage and friendship in casting their lot with a publishing house that didn't have the grand tradition of a Scribner or Knopf or Viking or Random House.

This book is a monument to all those writers who lifted the Mysterious Press to its glorious success. I haven't been part of that history for more than a decade (Warner bought it in 1989), but it was time to let my baby go and leave its care to others.

—Otto Penzler
New York, July 2000

THE MYSTERIOUS PRESS
ANNIVERSARY ANTHOLOGY

DONALD E. WESTLAKE

Awarded the Mystery Writers of America's title of Grand Master in 1992, **Donald E. Westlake** began his writing career with *The Mercenaries* in 1960, which was nominated for the Edgar for Best First Novel. He has written dozens of novels over the past forty years, including, as Richard Stark, the Parker series of hard-boiled crime fiction. His Hollywood screenplays include *The Stepfather* and *The Grifters*, for which he received an Academy Award nomination. Boy Cartwright, the odious hero of the following story, made his debut in the novel *Trust Me on This* (1987).

FIRST MYSTERIOUS PRESS PUBLICATION:
LEVINE, 1984

COME AGAIN?

The fact that the state of Florida would give the odious Boy Cartwright a driver's license only shows that the state of Florida isn't as smart as it thinks it is. The vile Boy, execrable expatriate Englishman, handed this document across the rental-car counter at Gulfport-Biloxi Regional Airport and the gullible clerk there responded by giving him the keys to something called a Taurus, a kind of space capsule sans relief tube, which turned out on examination in the ghastly sunlight to be the same whorehouse red as the rental clerk's lipstick. Boy tossed his disreputable canvas ditty bag onto this machine's backseat, the Valium and champagne bottles within chattering comfortably together, and drove north.

This was not the sort of assignment the despicable Boy was used to. As by far the most shameless and tasteless, and therefore by far the best, reporter on the staff of the *Weekly Galaxy*, a supermarket tabloid that gives new meaning to the term degenerate, the debased Boy Cartwright was used to commanding teams of reporters on assignments at the very peak of the tabloid Alp: celebrity adultery, UFO sightings, sports heroes awash in recreational drugs. The Return of Laurena Layla—or, more accurately, her nonreturn, as it would ultimately prove—was a distinct comedown for Boy. Not an event, but the mere anniversary of an event. And not in Los Angeles or Las Vegas or Miami or any of the other centers of debauchery of the American celebrity world, but in Marmelay, Mississippi, in the muggiest, mildewiest, kudzuest nasal bowel of the Deep South, barely north of Biloxi and the Gulf, a town surrounded mostly by De Soto National Forest, named for a reprobate the *Weekly Galaxy* would have loved if he'd only been born four hundred and fifty years later.

There were two reasons why Boy had drawn this bottom-feeder assignment, all alone in America, the first being that he was in somewhat bad odor at the *Galaxy* at the moment, having not only failed to steal the private psychiatric records of sultry sci-fi-pic star Tanya Shonya from the Montana sanitarium where the auburn-tressed beauty was recovering from her latest doomed love affair, but having also, in the process, inadvertently blown the cover of another *Galaxy* staffer, Don Grove, a member of Boy's usual team, who had already been ensconced in that same sanitarium as a grief counselor. Don even now remained immured in a Montana quod among a lot of Caucasian cowboys, while the *Galaxy*'s lawyers negotiated reasonably with the state authorities, and Boy got stuck with Laurena Layla.

But that wasn't the only reason for this assignment. Twenty-two years earlier, when Boy Cartwright was freshly at the *Galaxy*, a whelp reporter (the *Galaxy* did not have cubs) with just enough experience on scabrous British tabloids to make him prime *Galaxy* material, just as despicable in those days but not yet as decayed, he had covered the trial of Laurena Layla, then a twenty-seven-year-old beauty, mistress of the Golden Church of Sha-Kay, a con that had taken millions from the credulous, which is, after all, what the credulous are for.

The core of the Golden Church of Sha-Kay had been the Gatherings, a sort of cross between a mass séance and a Rolling Stones world tour, which had taken place in stadiums and arenas wherever in rural America the boobs lay thick on the ground. With much use of swirling smoke and whirling robes, these Gatherings had featured music, blessings, visions, apocalyptic announcements, and a well-trained devoted staff, devoted to squeezing every buck possible from the attending faithful.

Also, for those gentlemen of discernment whose wealth *far* exceeded their brains, there had been private sessions attainable with Laurena Layla herself, from which strong men were known to have emerged goggle-eyed, begging for oysters.

What had drawn the younger but no less awful Boy Cartwright to Laurena Layla the first time was an ambitious Indiana D.A. with big eyes for the governorship (never got it) who, finding Laurena Layla in full frontal operation within his jurisdiction, had caused her to be arrested and put on trial as the con artist (and artiste) she was. The combination of sex, fame, and courtroom was as powerful an aphrodisiac for the *Galaxy* and its readers then as ever, so Boy, at that time a mere stripling in some other editor's crew, was among those dispatched to Muncie by Massa (Bruno DeMassi), then owner and publisher of the rag.

Boy's English accent, raffish charm, and suave indifference to putdowns had made him a natural to be assigned to make contact with the defendant herself, which he had been pleased to do, winning the lady over with bogus ID from the *Manchester Guardian*. His success had been so instantaneous and so total that he had bedded L.L. twice, the second time because neither of them could quite believe the first.

In the event, L.L. was found innocent, justice being blind, while Boy was unmasked as the scurrilous Galaxyite he in fact was, and he was sent packing with a flea in his ear and a high-heel print on his bum. However, she didn't come off at all badly in the *Galaxy*'s coverage of her trial and general notoriety, and in fact a bit later she sent him the briefest of thank-you notes with no return address.

That was not the last time Boy saw Laurena Layla, however. Two years after Muncie it was, and the memory of the all-night freight train whistles there was at last beginning to fade, when Laurena Layla hit the news again for an entirely different reason: She died. A distraught fan, a depressingly overweight woman with a home permanent, stabbed L.L. three times with a five-and-dime steak knife, all the thrusts fatal but fortunately none of them disfiguring; L.L. made a lovely corpse.

Which was lucky indeed, because it was Boy's assignment on that occasion to get the body in the box. Whenever a celebrity went down, it was *Galaxy* tradition to get, by hook or by crook (usually by crook), a photo of the recently departed lying in his or her casket during the final viewing. This photo would then appear, as large as physically possible, on the front page of the following week's *Galaxy*, in full if waxen color.

Attention, shoppers: Next to the cash register is an intimation of mortality, yours, cheap. See? Even people smarter, richer, prettier, and better smelling than you die, sooner or later; isn't that news worth a buck or two?

Getting the body in the box that time had been only moderately difficult. Though the Golden Church of Sha-

Kay headquarters in Marmelay—a sort of great gilded banana split of a building with a cross and a spire and a carillon and loudspeakers and floodlights and television broadcasting equipment on top—was well guarded by cult staff members, it had been child's play to Mickey Finn a staffer of the right size and heft, via a doctored Dr Pepper, borrow the fellow's golden robe, and slip into the Temple of Revelation during a staff shift change.

Briefly alone in the dusky room with the late L.L., Boy had paused above the well-remembered face and form, now inert as it had never been in life, supine there in the open gilded casket on its waist-high bier, amid golden candles, far too much incense, and a piped-in celestial choir oozing out what sounded suspiciously like "Camptown Races" at half speed. Camera in right hand, he had reached out his left to adjust the shoulder of that golden gown to reveal just a bit more cleavage, just especially for all those necrophiles out there in Galaxyland, then it was *pop* goes the picture and Boy was, so far as he knew, done with the lovely late lady forever.

But no. It seemed that, among the effects Laurena Layla had left behind, amid the marked decks, shaved dice, plastic fingernails, and John B. Anderson buttons, was a last will and testament, in which the lady had promised her followers a second act: "I shall Die untimely," she wrote (which everybody believes, of course), "but it shall not be a real Death. I shall Travel in that Other World, seeking Wisdom and the Way, and twenty years after my Departure, to the Day, I shall return to this Plane of Existence to share with You the Knowledge I have gained."

Twenty years. Tomorrow, the second Thursday in May, would be the twentieth anniversary of Laurena Layla's dusting, and an astonishing number of mouth-breathers really did expect her to appear among them, robes, smiles, cleavage, Wisdom, and all. Most if not all of those faithful were also faithful *Galaxy* readers, naturally, so here was Boy, pasty-faced, skeptical, sphacelated, Valium-enhanced, champagne-maintained, and withal utterly pleased with himself, even though this assignment was a bit of a comedown.

Here was the normally moribund crossroads of Marmelay, a town that had never quite recovered from the economic shock when the slave auction left, but today doing its best to make up all at once for a hundred and fifty years of hind teat. The three nearby motels had all quadrupled their rates, the two local diners had printed new menus, and the five taverns in the area were charging as though they'd just heard Prohibition was coming back. Many of the Sha-Kay faithful did their traveling in RVs, but they still had to eat, and the local grocers knew very well what *that* meant: move the decimal point one position to the right on every item in the store. The locals were staying home for a couple days.

Boy traveled this time as himself, a rare occurrence, though he had come prepared with the usual array of false identification just in case. He was also traveling solo, without even a photographer, since it wasn't expected he'd require a particularly large crew to record a nonevent: "Not appearing today in her Temple of Revelation in the charmingly sleepy village of Marmelay, Mississippi . . ."

So it was the truth Boy told the clerk at the Lest Ye Forget Motel, unnatural though that felt: "Boy Cartwright. The *Weekly Galaxy* made one's reservation, some days ago."

"You're a foreigner," the lad in the oversize raspberry jacket with the motel chain's logo on its lapel told him, and pointed at Boy as though Boy didn't already know where he was. "You're French!"

"Got it in one, dear," Boy agreed. "Just winged in from jolly old Paris to observe the festivities."

"Laurena Layla, you mean," the lad told him, solemn and excited all at once. Nodding, he said, "She's coming back, you know."

"So one has heard."

"Coming back tomorrow," the lad said, and sighed. "Eight o'clock tomorrow night."

"I believe that is the zshedule," Boy acknowledged, thinking how this youth could not have been born yet when Laurena Layla got herself perforated. How folly endures!

"Wish I could see it," the lad went on, "but the tickets is long gone. Long gone."

"Ah, tickets," Boy agreed. "Such valuable little things, at times. But as to one's room . . ."

"Oh, sure," the lad said, but then looked doubtful. "Was that a single room all by yourself?"

"For preference."

"For this time only," the lad informed him, speaking as by rote, "the management could give you a very special rate, if you was to move in with a family. Not a big family."

"Oh, but, dear," Boy said, "one has moved *out* from one's family. Too late to alter that, I'm afraid."

"So it's just a room by yourself," the lad said, and shrugged and said, "I'm supposed to ask, is all."

"And you did it very well," Boy assured him, then flinched as the lad abruptly reached under the counter between them, but then all he came up with was some sort of pamphlet or brochure. Offering this, he said, "You want a battlefield map?"

"Battlefield?" Boy's yellow spine shriveled. "Are there public disorders about?"

"Oh, not anymore," the lad promised, and pointed variously outward, saying, "Macunshah, Honey Ridge, Polk's Ferry, they're all just around here."

"Ah," Boy said, recollecting the local dogma, and now understanding the motel's name. "Your Civil War, you mean."

"The War Between the States," the lad promptly corrected him. He knew *that* much.

"Well, yes," Boy agreed. "One has heard it wasn't actually that civil."

■ ■ ■

In the event, Boy did share his room with a small family after all. In a local pub—*taa*-vin, in regional parlance—he ran across twins who'd been ten years old when their mother, having seen on TV the news of Laurena Layla's demise, had offed herself with a shotgun in an effort to follow her pastoress to that better world. (It had also seemed a good opportunity for her to get away from their father.) The twins, Ruby Mae and Ruby Jean, were thirty now, bouncing healthy girls, who had come to Marmelay on the off chance Mama would be coming back as well, presumably with her head restored. They were excited as all get-out at meeting an actual reporter from the *Weekly Galaxy*, their favorite and perhaps only reading, and there he was an Englishman, too! They just loved his accent, and he loved theirs.

"It's one P.M.," said the musical if impersonal voice in his ear.

Boy awoke, startled and enraged, to find himself holding a telephone to his head. Acid sunlight burned at the closed blinds covering the window. "Who the hell cares?" he snarled into the mouthpiece, which responded with a rendition of "Dixie" on steel drum.

Appalled, realizing he was in conversation with a *machine*, Boy slammed down the phone, looked around the room, which had been transmogrified overnight into a laundry's sorting area, and saw that he was alone. The twins had romped off somewhere, perhaps to buy their mother a welcome-home pair of cuddly slippers.

Just as well; Boy was feeling a bit shopworn this morning. Afternoon. And that had been the wake-up call he must have requested in an optimistic moment late last night. Most optimistic moments occur late at night, in fact; realism requires daylight.

. . .

Up close, the banana-split Temple of Revelation appeared to have been served on a Bakelite plate, which was actually the shiny blacktop parking area, an ebony halo broadly encircling the temple and now rapidly filling with RVs, tour buses, pickup trucks, and all the other transportations of choice of life's also-rans.

And they were arriving, in their droves. Whole families, in their Sunday best. Sweethearts, hand in hand. Retired oldsters, grinning shyly, made a bit slow and ponderous by today's early-bird special. Solitaries, some nervous and guarded in hoods and jackets too warm for the weather, others gaudily on the prowl, in sequins and vinyl. Folks walked by in clothing covered with words, everything from bowling teams and volunteer fire departments to commercial sports organizations and multinational corporations that had never given these people a penny. Men in denim, women in cot-

ton, children in polyester. Oh, if Currier and Ives were alive
in this moment!

Boy and the rental Taurus circled the blacktop, slalom-
ing slowly among the clusters of people walking from their
vehicles toward the admission gates. Show or no show, miracle or nix, revelation or fuggedabahdid, every one of them
would fork over their ten bucks at the temple gate, eight for
seniors, seven for children under six. Inside, there would be
more opportunities for donations, gifts, love offerings, and
so on, but all of that was optional. The ten-spot at the entrance was mandatory.

Everyone here was looking for a sign, in a way, and so
was Boy, but the sign he sought would say something like
VIP or PRESS or AUTHORIZED PERSONNEL ONLY. And yes, there
it was: MEDIA. How modern.

The media, in fact, were sparse in the roped-off section
of parking lot around to the side of the banana split, where
a second entrance spared the chosen few from consorting
with the rabble. Flashing his *Galaxy* ID at the golden-robed
guardian of the MEDIA section, driving in, Boy counted two
TV relay trucks, both local, plus perhaps half a dozen rentals
like his own. Leaving the Taurus, Boy humped onto his
shoulder the small canvas bag containing his tape recorder,
disposable camera, and a folder of the tear sheets of his earlier coverage of Laurena Layla, plus her truncated note of
gratitude, and hiked through the horrible humidity and sear-
ing sun to the blessed shade of the VIP entrance.

It took two golden-robers to verify his ID at this point, and
then he was directed to jess go awn in an keep tuh the leff.
He did so, and found himself in the same curving charcoal-
gray dim-lit corridor he'd traversed just twenty years ago when
he'd gotten the body in the box. Ah, memory.

Partway round, he was met by another fellow in a golden robe, next to a broad black closed metal door. "Press?" this fellow asked.

"Absolutely."

"Yes, sir," the fellow said, drew the door open, and ushered him in.

With the opening of the door, crowd noises became audible. Boy stepped through and found himself in a large opera box midway down the left side of the great oval hall that was the primary interior space of the temple. Raised above auditorium level, the box gave a fine view of the large echoing interior with its rows of golden plush seats, wide aisles, maroon carpets and walls, battalions of lights filling the high black ceiling, and the deep stage at the far end where L.L. used to give her sermons and where her choir and her dancer-acolytes once swirled their robes. The sect had continued all these years without its foundress, but not, Boy believed, as successfully as before.

The stage looked now as though set for some minimalist production of *King Lear*: bare, half-lit, wooden floor uncovered, gray back wall unlit, nothing visible except one large golden armchair in the exact center of the stage. The chair wasn't particularly illuminated, but Boy had no doubt it would be, if and when.

Below, the hall was more than half full, with the believers still streaming in. Sharing the box with Boy were the expected two camera crews and the expected scruffy journalists, the only oddity being that more of the journalists were female than male: four scruffy women and, with Boy, three scruffy men. Boy recognized a couple of his competitors and nodded distantly; they returned the favor. None of them was an ace like himself.

Ah, well. If only he'd succeeded in that Montana sanitarium. If only Don Grove were not now in a Montana pokey. If only Boy Cartwright didn't have to be present for this nothingness.

The con artists who ran Sha-Kay these days would no doubt produce some sort of light show, probably broadcast some old audiotapes of Laurena Layla, edited to sound as though she were addressing the rubes this very minute rather than more than twenty years ago. At the end of the day the suckers would wander off, very well fleeced and reasonably well satisfied, while the fleecers would have the admissions money, fifty or sixty thousand, plus whatever else they'd managed to pluck during the show.

Plus, of course, TV. This nonevent would be broadcast live on the Sha-Kay cable station, with a phone number prominent for the receipt of donations, all major credit cards accepted.

No, all of these people would be all right, but what about poor Boy Cartwright? Where was his *story*? "The nonappearance today in Marm—"

■　■　■

And there she was.

It was done well, Boy had to admit that. No floating down into view from above the stage, no thunderclaps and puffs of smoke while she emerged from a trapdoor behind the golden chair, no fanfare at all. She was simply *there*, striding in her shimmering golden robe down the wide central aisle from the rear of the hall, flanked by a pair of burly guardians to keep the faithful at bay, moving with the same self-confidence as always. Most of the people in the hall, including Boy, only became aware of her with the amplified sound of her first "Hosannas!"

That had always been her greeting to her flock, and here it was again. "Hosannas! Hosannas!" spoken firmly as she nodded to the attendees on both sides, her words miked to speakers throughout the hall that boomed them back as though her voice came from everywhere in the building at once.

It was the same voice. That was the first thing Boy caught. It was exactly the same voice he'd heard saying any number of things twenty years ago, *hosannas!* among them as well as *oh yes!* and *more more!*

She's lip-synching, he thought, to an old tape, but then he realized it was also the same body, sinuous within that robe. Yes, it was, long and lithe, the same body he well remembered. The same walk, almost a model's but earthier. The same pitch to the head, set of the shoulders, small hand gesture that wasn't quite a wave. And, hard to tell from up here, but it certainly looked like the same face.

But not twenty years older. The same age, or very close to the same age, twenty-seven, that Laurena Layla had been when the fan had given her that bad review. The same age, and in every other respect, so far as Boy could tell from this distance, the same woman.

It's a hologram, he told himself, but a hologram could not reach out to pat the shoulder of a dear old lady on the aisle, as this one now did, causing the dear old lady to faint dead away on the instant.

She's real, Boy thought. She's returned, by God.

A chill ran up his back as she ran lightly up the central stairs to the stage, the hairs rose on his neck, and he remembered all too clearly not the body in the box but the body two years before that, as alive as quicksilver.

She stopped, turned to face her people. Her smile was faintly sad, as it had always been. She spread her hands in a gesture that welcomed without quite embracing, as she always had. "Hosannas," she said, more quietly, and the thousands below thundered, "Hosannas!"

Boy stared. Gray sweat beaded on his gray forehead. His follicles itched, his clothing cramped him, his bones were gnarled and wretched.

"I have been away," Laurena Layla said, and smiled. "And now I have returned."

As the crowd screamed in delight, Boy took hold of himself—metaphorically. You are here, my lad, he reminded himself, because you do not believe in this crap. You do not believe in any of the crap. If you start coming all over goose bumps every time somebody rises from the dead, of what use will you be, old thing, to the dear old *Weekly Galaxy*?

Onstage, she, whoever she was, whatever she was, had gone into an old routine, feel-good mysticism, the basic tenets of Sha-Kay, but now delivered with the assurance of one who's been there and done that. The faithful gawped, the TV crews focused, the second-string stringers from the other tabs wrote furiously in their notebooks or extended their tape recorders toward the stage as though the voice were coming from there, and Boy decided it was time to get a little closer.

Everyone was mesmerized by the woman on the stage, or whatever that was on the stage. Unnoticed, Boy stepped backward and through the doorway to the hall.

Where the golden guardian remained, unfortunately. "Sir," he said, frowning, "were you going to leave already?"

"Just a little reconnoiter, dear," Boy assured him.

"I'm not supposed to let anybody past this point," the guardian explained, looking serious about it.

This was why Boy never went on duty without arming himself with, in his left trouser pocket, folded hundred-dollar bills. It was automatic now to slide hand in and C-note out, the while murmuring, "Just need a quieter location, dear. Those TV cameras foul my recorder."

The reason employees are so easy to suborn is that they're employees. They're only here in the first place because they're being paid for their time. Whatever the enterprise may be, they aren't connected to it by passion or ownership or any other compelling link. Under the circumstances, what is a bribe but another kind of wage?

Still, we all of us have an ass to protect. Hand hovering over the proffered bill, the guardian nevertheless said, "I don't want to get in any trouble here."

"Nothing to do with you, old thing," Boy assured him. "I came round the other way."

The bill disappeared, and then so did Boy, following the long curved hall toward the stage. More and more of the temple layout he remembered as he moved along. Farther along this hallway he would find that faintly sepulchral room where the body had been on display, placed there because crowd control would have been so much iffier out in the main auditorium.

That last time, Boy had had no reason to proceed past the viewing room, which in more normal circumstances would have been some kind of offstage prep area or green-room, but he knew it couldn't be far from there to the stage. Would he be closer then to *her*?

The likeness was so uncanny, dammit. Or perhaps it was so canny. In any event, this Laurena Layla, when close to people, kept moving, and when she stopped to speak she kept a distance from everyone else. Could she not be observed up close for long? If not, why not?

Though as Boy came around the curving hallway his left hand was already in his pocket, fondling another century, there was no guard on duty at the closed greenroom door; a surprise, but never question good fortune. In case the undoubted sentry was merely briefly away to answer mother's call, he hastened the last few yards, even though the brisk motion made his brain-walnut chafe uncomfortably against the shell of his skull.

The black door in the charcoal-gray wall opened soundlessly to his touch. He slipped through; he pulled the door shut behind him.

Well. It did look different without a coffin in the middle. Now it was merely a staging area, dim-lit, with the props and materials of cultish magic neatly shelved or stacked or hung, waiting for the next Call. A broad but low-ceilinged room, its irregular shape was probably caused by the architectural requirements of the stage and temple that surrounded it. That shape, with corners and crannies in odd shadowed places, had added to the eeriness when Boy and his Hasselblad had been in here twenty years ago, but now it all seemed quite benign, merely a kind of surrealistic locker room.

There. The closed door opposite, across the empty black floor. That was the route Boy had not taken last time, when the viewers of the remains had been herded through the main temple and over the stage, past many opportunities to show their sorrow and their continued devotion in a shall we say tangible way, before they were piloted past the dear departed, out the door Boy had just come in, and down the long hall to what at this moment had been converted into the VIP entrance.

After a quick glance left and right, reassuring himself he was alone and all the stray dim corners were empty, he crossed to that far door, cracked it just a jot, and peered one-eyed out at what looked like any backstage. Half a dozen technicians moved about. A hugely complex lightboard stretched away on the right, and beyond it yawned the stage, with Laurena Layla—or whoever—in profile out there, continuing her spiel.

She looked shorter from here, no doubt the effect of the high-ceilinged stage and all those lights. The golden chair still stood invitingly behind her, but she remained on her feet, pacing in front of the chair as she delivered her pitch.

How would it all end? Would she sit in the chair at last, then disappear in a puff of smoke? A trapdoor, then, which would make her devilish hard to intercept.

But Boy didn't think so. He thought they'd be likelier to repeat the understated eloquence of that arrival, that L.L. would simply walk off the stage as she'd simply walked onto it, disappear from public view, and come . . . here.

She would not be alone, he was sure of that. Determinedly alone onstage, once free of the suckers' gaze, she would surely be surrounded by her . . . acolytes? handlers?

Boy had his story now. Well, no, he didn't *have* it, but he knew what it was: the interview with the returned L.L. The *Galaxy* had treated any number of seers and mystics and time travelers and alien abductees with po-faced solemnity over the years, so surely this Layla would understand she was in safe hands when she was in the hands—as he certainly hoped she soon would be—of Boy Cartwright. The question was how to make her see his journal's usefulness to her before her people gave him the boot.

The old clippings; the thank-you note. Waggle those in front of her face, they'd at least slow down the proceedings long enough to give him an opportunity to swathe her in his moth-eaten charm. It had worked before.

His move at this point was to hide himself, somewhere in this room. This was where he was sure she would travel next, so he should conceal himself in here, watch how the scam proceeded, await his opportunity. *Snick,* he shut the stageward door, and, clutching his canvas bag between flaccid arm and trembling ribs, with its valuable cargo of clippings and thank-yous, he turned to suss the place out.

Any number of hiding places beckoned to him, shady nooks at the fringes of the room. Off to the right, in a cranny that was out of the way but not out of sight of either door, stood two long coatracks on wheels, the kind hosts set up for parties, these both bowed beneath the weight of many golden robes. Don one? At the very least, insert himself among them.

As he hurried toward that darkly gold-gleaming niche, a great crowd-roar arose behind him, triumphant yet respectful, gleeful yet awed. Just in time, he thought, and plunged among the robes.

Dark in here, and musty. Boy wriggled backward, looking for a position where he could see yet not be seen, and his heel hit the body.

He knew it, in that first instant. What his heel had backed into was not a sports bag full of laundry, not a sleeping cat, not a rolled-up futon. A body.

Boy squinched backward, wriggling his bum through the golden robes, while the crowd noise outside reached its crescendo and fell away. He found it agony to make this overworked body kneel, but Boy managed, clutching to many robes as he did so, listening to his knees do their firecracker imitations. Down at mezzanine level, he sagged onto his haunches while he pushed robe hems out of the way, enough to see . . .

Well. *This* one won't be coming back. In this dimness, the large stain across the back of the golden robe on the figure huddled on the floor looked black, but Boy knew that, in the light, it would be a gaudier hue. He felt no need to touch it, he knew what it was.

And who. The missing sentry.

I am not alone in here, Boy thought, and as he thought so he was not; the stageward door opened and voices entered, male and female.

Boy cringed. Not the best location, this, on one's knees at the side of a recently plucked corpse. Hands joining knees on the floor, he crawled away from the body through the robes until he could see the room.

Half a dozen people, all berobed, had crowded in, Laurena unmistakable among them, beautiful, imperious, and a bit sullen. The others, male and female, excited, chattered at her, but she paid them no attention, moving in a boneless undulation toward a small makeup table directly across the room from where Boy slunk. They followed, still relieving their tension with chatter, and she waved a slender forearm of dismissal without looking back.

"Leave her alone now."

This was said clearly through the babble by an older woman, silver-haired and bronze-faced in her golden robe, who stood behind the still-moving Laurena, faced the others, and said, "She needs to rest."

They all agreed, verbally and at length, while the older woman made shooing motions and Laurena sank into a sinuous recline on the stool at the makeup table. Boy, alert for any eruption at all from anywhere, trying to watch the action in front of him while still keeping an eye on every other nook and cranny in the entire room—a hopeless task—watched and waited and wondered when he could make his presence, and his news, known.

The older woman was at last succeeding in her efforts to clear the area. The others backed off, calling final praises and exhortations over their shoulders, oozing out of the room like a film in reverse that shows the smoke go back in the bottle. Boy gathered his limbs beneath him for the Herculean task of becoming once more upright, and the older woman said, "You were magnificent."

Laurena reached a languid arm forward to switch on the makeup lights, in which she gazed upon her astonishingly beautiful and pallid face, gleaming in the dim gray mirror. "What are they to me?" she asked, either to herself or the older woman.

"Your life," the older woman told her. "From now on."

Outside, the faithful had erupted into song, loud and clamorous. It probably wasn't, but it certainly sounded like, a speeded-up version of "We Shall Overcome."

Laurena closed her striking eyes and shook her head, "Leave me," she said.

Boy was astonished. An actual human being had said, "Leave me," just like a character in a vampire film. Perhaps this Laurena *was* from the beyond.

In any event, the line didn't work. Rather than leave her, the older woman said, "This next part is vital."

"I know, I know."

"You'll be just as wonderful, I know you will."

"Why wouldn't I be?" Laurena asked her. "I've trained for it long enough."

"Rest," the older woman urged. "I'll come back for you in fifteen minutes." And with that, at last, she was gone, leaving Laurena semi-alone, the raucous chorus surging when the door was open.

Boy lunged upward, grabbing for handholds among the robes, knees exploding like bags full of water. His first sentences were already clear in his mind, but as he staggered from concealment, hand up as though hailing a cab, movement flashed from off to his left.

Boy looked, and lunging from another hiding place, between himself and the stageward door, heaved a woman, middle-aged, depressingly overweight, in a home permanent, brandishing a stained steak knife from the five-and-ten like a homicidal whale.

Good God! Have they *both* come back? Is there hope for Ruby Mae and Ruby Jean's mom after all?

Laurena's makeup mirror was positioned so that it was the whale she saw in it first, not Boy. Turning, not afraid, still imperious, she leveled her remote gaze on the madwoman and said, "What are you?"

"You *know* who I am!" snarled the madwoman, answering the wrong question. "I'm here to finish what my mother started!"

And in that instant Boy knew everything. He knew that the roused chorus in the temple auditorium meant that cries for help would go for naught. He knew that escape past the madwoman out that door toward the stage was impossible. He knew that he himself could make a dash for the opposite door, the one by which he'd entered, but that Laurena, by the makeup table, would never make it.

But he knew even more. He knew the scam.

However, what he *didn't* know was what to do about it. Where, in all this, was poor Boy's story? Should he zip out the door, report the murders, have *that* scoop? Should he remain here, rescue the maiden without risk to himself and in hope of the usual reward, have *that* scoop (and reward)? (The "without risk to himself" part tended to make that plan Plan B.)

How old was she, *that* was the question, the most important question of all. Answer that one first.

"Dears, dears, dears," he announced in his plummiest voice, swanning forward like the emcee in *Cabaret*, "play nice, now, don't fight."

They both gaped at him. Like a tyro at the game arcade, the madwoman didn't know what to do when faced with two simultaneous targets. She hung there, flat-footed, one Supphose'd shin before the other, knife arm raised, looking now mostly like a reconstructed dinosaur at the museum, while Laurena gave him a stare of cool disbelief and said, "And who are y*ou*?"

"Oh, but, dear, you must remember me," Boy told her, talking very fast indeed to keep everybody off balance. "Dear old Boy, from the *Galaxy*, I still have your thank-you note, I've treasured it always, I brought it with me in my little bag here." Deciding it would be dangerous to reach into the bag—it might trigger some unfortunate response from the dinosaur—he hurtled on, saying, "Of course, dear Laurena, one had to see you again, after all this time, *report* our meeting, tell the world we—"

The penny dropped at last, and now she *was* shocked. "You're a *reporter*?"

"Oh, you do remember!" Boy exulted. "One *knew* you would!"

"You can't stop me!" the madwoman honked, as though she hadn't been stopped already.

But of course she could reactivate herself, couldn't she? Boy told her, "One did not have the pleasure of meeting your mother, dear, I'm sorry to say, but one did see her in custody and at the trial, and she certainly was forceful."

Whoops; wrong word. "And so am I!" cried the madwoman, and lumbered again toward Laurena.

"No no, wait wait wait!" cried Boy. "I wanted to ask you about your mother." As the madwoman had now halved the distance between herself and the shrinking Laurena, Boy felt an increasing urgency as he said, "I *wrote* about her, you know, in the *Weekly Galaxy*, you must have seen it."

That stopped her. Blinking at Boy, actually taking him in for the first time, a reluctant awe coming into her face and voice, she said, "The *Weekly Galaxy*?"

"Boy Cartwright, at your service," he announced with a smile and a bow he'd borrowed from Errol Flynn, who would not have recognized it. "And as a reporter," he assured her, "I assure you I am not here to alter the situation, but simply to observe. Madam, I will not stand in your way."

Laurena gawked at him. "You won't?"

"Good," the madwoman said, hefted her knife, and thudded another step forward.

"But *first*," Boy went hurriedly on, "I do so want to interview Laurena. Very briefly, I promise you."

They both blinked at him. The madwoman said, "Interview?"

"Two or three questions, no more, and I'm out of your way forever."

"But—" Laurena said.

Taking the madwoman's baffled silence for consent, Boy turned to Laurena. "The silver-haired party was your grandmother," he said.

Managing to find reserves of haughtiness somewhere within, Laurena froze him with a glare: "I am not giving *interviews.*"

"Oh, but, dear," Boy said, with a meaningful head nod toward the madwoman, "*this* exclusive interview you will grant, I just know you will, and I must begin, I'm sorry to say, with a personal question. Personal to *me.* I need to know how old you are. You *are* over twenty-one, aren't you?"

"What? Of course I—"

"Honest Injun?" Boy pressed. "One is not a bartender, dear, one has other reasons to need to know. I would guess you to be twenty-five? Twenty-six?" The change in her eyes told him he'd guessed right. "Ah, good," he said with honest relief.

"That's right," the madwoman said.

They both turned to her, having very nearly forgotten her for a few seconds, and she said, "People don't get older in heaven, do they?"

"No, they do not," Boy agreed.

Laurena said, "What *difference* does it make?"

"Well, if you were twenty-one, you see," he explained, "you'd be *my* daughter, which would very much complicate the situation."

"I have no idea what you're talking about," Laurena said, which meant, of course, that she had every idea what he was talking about.

Now he did dare a quick dip into his bag, and before the madwoman could react he'd brought out and shown her his audiocassette recorder. "Tools of the trade, dear," he explained. "No interview without the tape to back it up."

Laurena finally began to show signs of stress, saying, "What are you *doing*? She's got a knife, she's going to *kill* me!"

"Again, darling, yes," Boy said, switching on the machine, aiming it at her. "Just so soon as I leave, at the end of the interview." Because now at last he knew what his story was, he smiled upon her with as much fondness as if she *had* been his daughter—interesting quandary *that* would have been, in several ways—and said, "Of course, in your answers, you might remove our friend's *reason* for wanting to kill you all over again."

Growling, the madwoman bawled, "Nobody's going to stop me! I'm here to finish what my mother started!"

"Yes, of course, you are, dear," Boy agreed. "But what if your mother *did* finish the job?"

The madwoman frowned. "What do you mean? There's Laurena Layla right there!"

"Well, let's ask her about that," Boy suggested, and turned attention, face, and recorder to the young woman. "I must leave very soon," he pointed out. "I only hope, before I go, you will have said those words that will reassure this lovely lady that her mother did not fail, her mother is a success, she can be proud of her mother forever. Can't she, dear?"

Laurena stared helplessly from one to the other. It was clear she couldn't figure out which was the frying pan, which the fire.

To help her, Boy turned back to the madwoman. "You *do* trust the *Galaxy*, don't you?"

"Of course!"

"Whatever this dear child says to us," Boy promised, "you will read in the *Galaxy*. Trust me on this."

"I do," the madwoman said with great solemnity.

Turning to the other, Boy said, "Dear, five million readers are waiting to hear. How was it done? Who are you? Time's getting short, dear."

Laurena struggled to wrap her self-assurance around herself. "You won't leave," she said. "You couldn't."

"Too bad," Boy said with a shrug. "However, the story works just as well the other way." Turning, he took a step toward the hall door as the madwoman took a step forward.

"Wait!" cried the former Laurena Layla.

LOREN D. ESTLEMAN

Loren D. Estleman's Amos Walker novels have delighted dedicated readers of the classic private investigator tale ever since 1980's *Motor City Blue*. Estleman, born and raised in southeast Michigan, is also the author of award-winning western novels and a heralded crime series detailing the history of Detroit in the twentieth century, including *Edsel*, *Thunder City*, and the Edgar-nominated *Whiskey River*.

FIRST MYSTERIOUS PRESS PUBLICATION:
KILL ZONE, 1984

THE ANNIVERSARY
WALTZ

I caught up with Judd Lindauer in the Detroit Free Republic of Nicotine Abuse, otherwise known as the parking lot behind the Frank Murphy Hall of Justice. The flag is a black lung on a field of tobacco leaves.

A big man of sixty beginning to stoop to a mere six-six, Lindauer left a crowd of litigants and judges and changed hands on his cigar to shake my hand. He had on a blue suit with flared lapels and a tan suede yoke over a snap-front shirt secured with a string tie. As far as I knew he'd never been west of Kalamazoo except when tracking a jump on a hundred-grand bail. He was a bail bondsman and a bounty hunter and enjoyed looking the part.

"Remember me on this one, Amos," he said when we were out of earshot of the others. "There's miles of press in it if you tear this one off. That can't be bad for a one-man band like yours."

I said, "Maybe I'll buy you a drink when I know what it's about. All my service told me is you wanted to see me."

"That's all I told them." He lowered his voice to a reverberating boom. "It's Adelaide Dix."

"The trunk murderess?"

"If you believe the tabloids. Personally I don't think she

ever harmed a piece of luggage in her life, and I'm the one who went her bail."

"Which time? She escaped what, four times?"

"Four and a half. She got outside the wall up in Marquette six weeks after they transferred her from Jackson, but they kept that one out of the papers. They managed to hang on to her for two years after that; then she flushed herself down the sewer. That was eight years ago. Nobody's seen her since."

I plucked a Winston out of my pack and put it between my lips without lighting it. There was enough smoke drifting across the lot to cure a ham. "I heard she drowned in Lake Superior."

"I don't have any reason to doubt it. Superior never gives up its dead."

"So where is she?"

He handed me one of his cards, embossed in gold on white stock with a gold lariat in one corner. A telephone number was written on the back next to a name: G. Tolliver.

"The G stands for Geraldine," he said. "She's Adelaide's daughter. Her husband's Bert Tolliver, a building contractor. You get her, you get him too. But she does the talking. She says her mother's alive."

"Says to who, you? And why?"

"I put up bail when Adelaide got a new trial. She jumped—that was the first escape—and I brought her back. I flew with her from Denver to Detroit, first-class, no cuffs. I was the first person not to treat her like a tarantula. Geraldine was grateful. I'm the only member of the law enforcement community she thinks she can trust."

"Why tell anyone? Old lady getting too tough to care for?"

"Ask Geraldine. I didn't ask her any questions and I stopped her before she could give me any specific information. I'm an officer of the court; it's my license if I fail to report knowledge of a fugitive's whereabouts. I told her I was giving it to you and you're no gossip."

"I've got a license too," I said. "I didn't get this job drawing Sherlock Holmes off a matchbook."

"You've got the hot handle. What you do with it won't burn me." He blew a smoke ring big enough to snare me around the neck.

■ ■ ■

In 1985, Adelaide Dix had driven Iran-contra off the front pages when she was convicted of chopping up her second husband, packing him in an antique trunk, and stowing it in a corner of her Sterling Heights basement. A meter reader reported the smell and Adelaide got life. Her first escape while out on bail pending a new trial destroyed her defense; two more bought her a cell away up north in Marquette. She had an I.Q. of 160, fifty points higher than the average corrections officer, so another escape was inevitable. A set of size six footprints in the sand leading to Lake Superior convinced authorities she was dead, but that didn't prevent her from showing up at a McDonald's drive-through every couple of months with Elvis at the wheel.

A well-tended female voice, racheted a notch high for normal intercourse, provided an invitation and directions to a house in one of the newer suburbs, founded since white flight. It was a stack of trapezoidal boxes with passive solar windows—ornamental only in Michigan's cloudy climate—

tucked between hills in a tract named after a tree that had
been extinct in the area for three hundred years.

Geraldine Tolliver was small and compact, about twenty,
with short red hair and a tiny waist in a tailored shirt and
capri pants or whatever they're calling them this year. Her
husband, Bert, was heavily muscled and sunburned in a polo
shirt and khakis. He was a hand-mangler; two drinks and
he'd be pounding my back. I avoided the sofa in case he decided to sit within range and settled into an Eames knockoff with a Scotch and soda.

Mrs. Tolliver tasted her gin and tonic, set it down, and
never returned to it. "Mr. Lindauer says you're a man one
can confide in. Are you like a priest?"

"Only in that department."

"Honey, I think we'd better see some ID. We'd better see
some ID," Bert Tolliver told me, over the top of a whiskey
sour the size of a conga drum.

I showed them some ID.

"Mr. Walker, we need your word you'll tell no one about
this," the woman said. "Not even your wife. Things have a
way of getting back to Alvin Shrike. It's almost supernatural."

"I don't have a wife. Who's Alvin Shrike?"

"An icicle-pissing son of a bitch. Sorry, honey." Tolliver
sat back in the sofa and drank.

Mrs. Tolliver gave him the fisheye and finished what she'd
started to say. "Shrike's chief of police here. Bert's right about
the rest. He was an officer in Sterling Heights fifteen years
ago. The man my—the dead man in the trunk was his partner."

"That would be your father?"

"No. My father died of cancer when I was three months
old. George Dix was a good-looking brute and a drunk who

seduced my mother into marrying him and beat her up on a regular schedule. When he started in on me she did something about it."

"No one would argue with that."

"I don't remember much about that night. I remember he slapped me and the way my face was still burning when I woke up. When I was old enough to understand she told me she shot him with his service revolver. I have no doubt she'd have been acquitted if she'd stopped there. The dismemberment was a mistake."

"It usually is."

"She didn't want me to wake up and find a corpse in the house. She was temporarily insane, of course, but the jury rejected that. Calling her 'Adelaide the Axe' in the tabloids didn't help."

" 'Slice-and-Dice Dix,' " put in Tolliver.

She closed her eyes. "That too. There were others. Why do people take such delight in grisly details?"

"It's a dark old world," I said. "Have you heard from your mother?"

"Once a year for eight years." She got up, opened a drawer in a bleached oak table with a cordless telephone on top, and brought over a picture postcard. There was no message on the back, just a USPS postmark and the Tollivers' address block-printed with a black felt-tipped pen. It had been mailed last week. The picture on the other side was a color shot of Grand Traverse Bay.

"They always come before my birthday," Geraldine said. "Always a different scene, but always in Michigan. Mother's a native, but like so many she never got around to visiting the local vacation spots. We used to talk about going to all of them when she got out of prison. This is as close as we can come to that as long as Shrike's around."

I gave it back. "It's been fifteen years. Maybe he's put it behind him."

She shut the drawer on the postcard and stepped over to a window. "I want you to look at something."

When I joined her, she drew aside the curtain two inches. A gold Chrysler four-door was parked on the corner across the street. I could read the headline on the newspaper the driver had spread in front of his face.

"It isn't Shrike," she said. "Or maybe it is. The point is it doesn't have to be, as long as he runs the police department in this town. We have an escort every time we leave the house. I'd actually miss them if they weren't there."

"You could do a quarterback split and decoy him off."

"I'm sure there's a contingency plan. Anyway, where would we go? Mother's always been careful not to give any hints as to her whereabouts. You couldn't even prove in court she's the one who sends the cards. But I know."

We sat back down. I asked her what she wanted me to do.

"I want you to talk her into giving herself up. She can't run forever. I'm terrified someday I'll turn on the news and hear she's been shot down by Shrike or one of his officers. He said in court he wished Michigan would bring back the death penalty just for her."

"Traverse City's a good-size town. Even if it weren't, she's probably blown it by now, if she was ever there to begin with. You can buy postcards anywhere. I'd need a bigger comb than Shrike's got and I'd have to start in Little America."

"No, you wouldn't. She'll be at the cemetery in Sterling Heights the day after tomorrow."

. . .

I looked from her to Tolliver, who was watching me over his glass like someone who'd heard the joke before and was waiting to see the reaction. I disappointed him. I sipped Scotch and soda and said, "What time? I'm going to a ball game that night."

Geraldine shook her head. "I can't tell you that because I don't know. The day after tomorrow is my parents' twenty-fifth wedding anniversary. It'll be their anniversary all day."

I was starting to get it. "That's where your father's buried? What makes you think she'll show?"

"Because when my father got sick and needed hope, my mother promised him they'd be together on their silver anniversary. She keeps her promises. And she never forgets a date." She tilted her head toward the drawer containing the postcard. "By now that officer outside has radioed in your license number and knows who you are, but I assume you're experienced in discouraging people from following you. We're not. We'd lead Shrike right to her."

"Okay, the Tigers can lose without me in the bleachers. My fee's five hundred for the day."

Tolliver made himself useful and put down his drink and wrote me a check. His wife took the back off a picture frame from the fireplace mantel and handed me a photo of a handsome middle-aged woman with sharply intelligent eyes. "That's the latest we have. It was taken nine years ago. Every Christmas the inmates got to put on civilian clothes and pose for a professional photographer."

I got up and slid it into my inside breast pocket along with the folded check. "It wouldn't be an honest five hundred if I didn't tell you it's wasted. If your mother keeps that promise she isn't as smart as I'd heard, even if she's alive. Anyone could be sending you those postcards as a sick gag. You don't know who knows about your conversations."

"Thank you, Mr. Walker," Geraldine said. "It isn't wasted."

I went out and stopped to light a cigarette before getting into the car, because I needed it and because it let me get another look at the driver of the gold Chrysler. He was still reading the Lively Arts section, committing the opera times to memory.

I put five blocks behind me before I spotted the tail. Same make, different color, fresh from Dispatch. You didn't get to be chief of anyone's police by sitting around growing your whiskers.

. . .

The outer-office buzzer caught me thinking the next morning about climbing up and dumping the fly wings out of the bowl fixture above my desk. I decided they wouldn't be any deader an hour later, and opened the door for a square party a couple of inches below my height in a stiff gray suit with his tie snugged up to a chin that had begun to double and shards of silver glittering in his sandy crew cut. He looked like an unmarked car.

"I'm going out on a limb," I said. "Chief Shrike?"

"That obvious?" He smiled with his bottom teeth only and took my hand. His was one even Bert Tolliver couldn't mangle.

"Just the cop part. I was expecting the rest." I showed him the chair. He put his hands in his pockets and stayed where he was.

"What's a Detroit private cop got doing with Adelaide Dix's daughter?"

I put my hands in my own pockets. It was like looking in a mirror from ten years in the future, if I didn't hurry up and take violin lessons. "Lizzie Borden was taken. What color's your Chrysler?"

"Blue. That was me, all right. I figured you were wise. You know that was my marriage Adelaide broke up with her set of Ginsus. Best partner I ever had. He saved my ass six ways from Sunday."

"Sundays he kicked his wife's."

"He had a temper. Lots of guys slap their women around. Lots of women don't cut them into easily manageable pieces and put them up like preserves."

"She's in a lake."

"I don't think so. Why go that direction? Once you're over the wall you got directions up the ass."

"So she drowned herself."

"She could've stopped her clock inside. Why go over the wall at all? She walked backwards in her own footprints and she's been walking ever since. Her daughter knows it. She just don't know where she is. That's why she hired you. I knew she'd crack if I leaned on her long enough."

"I'm looking for a hit-and-run vehicle. Hers was on the list."

"She told me you're working for her."

I laughed in his face.

He turned deep copper right up to his cropped hair. His hands came out fists. "I can pull you in right now as a material witness."

"To what? A drowning? She's dead. Marquette thinks it, the governor thinks it, the FBI thinks it, and so does the secretary who filled out the legal declaration of death. You're a one-man Flat Earth Society, Shrike."

"Wrong. There's three others. Adelaide Dix knows she's alive. So does Geraldine Tolliver. So do you. And I'm going to be on you like flies on a carp till you walk me right up to her."

After he left, I looked up at the dead wings in the fixture, but I didn't go after them. I appreciated the company.

．　．　．

I spent the rest of that day with Alvin Shrike.

The blue Chrysler was with me when I wheeled my bucket out of its slot and it stayed three lengths behind except when it looked like I might lose it in traffic. It followed me around seventeen corners, across a vacant lot, and down both sides of a divided street as well as up and over the divider itself. Either he was one hungry fly or I was a pretty ripe carp. After we got both our cars washed on West Grand River I could see I would have to get rid of the horses.

I parked where the trucks go into the *Free Press*, where I could get a nice safe tow to the police garage, cut through the thundering pressroom on foot, and went out the front entrance past a surprised security guard. He probably did a double take when Shrike went out right behind. I thought I'd shaken the tail when I skipped across Washington directly in front of the streetcar, but when I stopped sprinting a couple of hundred yards later and looked behind me, he was legging his way along Fort. I got lucky and caught a cab two blocks over; Shrike got lucky too and flashed his badge at a motorist who turned out to be a solid citizen and they trailed me clear to Redford.

We had supper at a chain place with license plates and other assorted junk on the walls. I sent him a bottle of beer, which he drank without even lifting it in acknowledgment.

We had a moment when we both called for cabs from adjacent pay telephones, but by then I was getting tired and couldn't raise a chuckle. I reached over and pushed down the lifter on his, breaking his connection. "Why don't we just share mine? All I'm going is home."

"I don't tip cabbies," he said. "You want to, go ahead."

When the Redtop came, I got in first. He pushed in fast in case I tried to jerk the door shut. I hit him with everything I had; he was hard for a desk cop, but his forward momentum helped and he sagged against me like a sack of ball bearings. I worked the door handle on my side and slid out from underneath him.

"Take my friend to the Wayne County Airport," I told the driver.

"Where's his luggage?" He was a big Jamaican with gold teeth.

"He doesn't have any. He's going to a nudist camp."

After the cab left I hightailed it to a Shell station, called another cab, and took it to my reporter friend Barry Stackpole's place to borrow his car. He has an artificial leg and the hand controls took getting used to, but they got me to a motel in Sterling Heights.

I wasn't taking chances. In the room I set the radio clock for 11:30 and called for a wake-up in case it wasn't working. If I were on the run from the law—which I was, but my situation was variant—and I had to be somewhere tomorrow, I'd pick one minute past midnight. Before I caught some sleep I laid my Chief's Special on the floor in front of the door so I wouldn't forget it when I left. I was meeting Adelaide the Axe, and I hadn't thought to ask her daughter if she liked surprises.

■ ■ ■

At one minute past midnight I was leaning against the cool marble wall of a mausoleum in the Sterling Heights cemetery, wanting a cigarette and jerking my head around every time a nighthawk squirrel scampered up a tree. The temperature had dropped steeply after nightfall and there was a light ground mist rolling among the headstones like the dry ice in a Dracula movie. It and the squirrels were the only things that moved until dawn, by which time my back ached from standing and the clothes I'd had on for twenty-four hours felt like wet burlap. When it was light enough to burn tobacco I moved under a tree where the branches would break up the smoke. That was when I spotted Alvin Shrike striding between the posts that flanked the entrance to the cemetery.

He'd gotten it out of Geraldine Tolliver somehow, or more likely Bert, who seemed closer to the type who succumbed to the oldest kind of police persuasion. It had taken all night, and he'd started out mad; his face was the deep copper I'd seen earlier and his feet pounded dust out of the gravel path. There was a purple mark on his jaw left by my knuckles and his tie was no longer snug.

"Shrike."

His head swiveled in my direction. He saw my gun and stopped, his flush draining away, the pro adjusting to a familiar situation. His bottom teeth showed in that werewolf grin.

"Drop the weapon!"

This time I swiveled. The uniformed cop was a pro too. I hadn't known he existed until I saw him leveling a sniper's rifle at me across the top of the iron fence that enclosed the grounds. I dropped the Chief's Special and raised my hands. Shrike got his piece out and pulled me away from the tree and threw me up against the mausoleum and frisked and cuffed me in less time than it takes to tell.

"Aiding and abetting a fugitive and officer assault," he said. "If one don't stick the other will."

"What'd you do to the Tollivers?" The cuffs were cutting off circulation to my fingers. I worked them. I didn't want to forget how to make a fist.

"He'll be sucking his lunch through a straw for a while, but he'll live. Usually those muscle boys bend easy, but he did better than expected. Geraldine's the one who talked, to save him the rest of his teeth. She loves her old lady, but Bert was there and so was I. Okay, Kennedy. Put him in the car and be invisible."

Kennedy was tall and black and carried his rifle at rest as if it weighed no more than a cardboard roll. Fingers like pliers closed around my biceps and we walked out the entrance. The car, another unmarked Chrysler, was parked down the street in the shade of a tall hedge. One fender of Shrike's blue Chrysler or another just like it showed around the corner.

"Why two cars?" I asked.

"Shut up." Kennedy shoved me into the backseat of the one by the hedge and got in behind the wheel, leaning his rifle against the door on the passenger's side.

After we'd sat long enough he got talkative. "Chief said two cars. I don't ask how come."

I didn't like it. But there wasn't one thing about the way the day was starting out that I did like.

A quiet cemetery will draw some visitors even on a weekday. Half a dozen people came and went over the next several hours, including two couples. Nobody looked like Adelaide Dix in the picture in my pocket.

She came at high noon.

It was either a bonehead play or diabolically smart. She wasn't even in disguise, unless you counted the quietly tailored dress and simple hairstyle. She looked older than her picture, older than she was, but not as if she'd been eating and sleeping in ratty motels for eight years. She had a job and had probably arranged identification papers that would pass quick inspection. I decided on diabolically smart.

Until that day.

In front of the entrance she stopped and looked around, looked directly at us. But we were too far away and the shade was too deep to see inside the car. Still she went on looking for a minute before she entered the cemetery. She was carrying long-stemmed yellow flowers wrapped in silver paper.

"She's coming, Chief." Kennedy had his microphone in his hand and an old front-and-profile mug of Adelaide Dix taped to the dashboard.

"Okay. Cover the gate." Shrike's voice from a handheld radio sounded thin and tight.

Kennedy hung up the mike and got out with his rifle. He positioned himself on the side of the car opposite the cemetery entrance, bumping the roof a couple of times as he leveled the long gun.

When Adelaide walked out five minutes later with her hands behind her and Shrike's hand on her shoulder, I took my fingers out of the seat cushion and worked blood back into them. The woman's face was pale but calmer than the chief's. His bottom-teeth smile was a rictus. He walked her right past us and around the corner and came back a minute later alone.

"Take this character's piece and lose it in the system."

He smacked my gun into Kennedy's palm. "I'll see you back in the barn."

"Great work, Chief. She give you any heartache?"

"Tame as a kitten. No trunks close by."

He still sounded wound up tight. Most cops talk lazy after an arrest. The adrenaline leaks out fast once the job's done.

Two cars.

"Kennedy!" I shouted. "Go with him. If he gets in that car alone with her she'll never make it to the station alive."

"Get him the hell out of here," Shrike said. "Mirandize the son of a bitch and throw him in Holding. Throw him hard."

"Two cars, Kennedy! No witnesses. Think about it."

"Shut up, you. See you there, Chief." Kennedy got back in and put up his rifle. Shrike walked back around the corner. The blue fender swung away from the curb and was gone.

. . .

No charges were filed against me because the arresting officer never appeared. After twenty-four hours they got around to letting me go and I got my gun back finally at the end of a long strip of red tape.

Neither Adelaide the Axe nor Alvin Shrike made it to the police station. They found the blue Chrysler parked on a quiet residential street in Sterling Heights with a bullet from Shrike's revolver embedded in the backseat, clotted with his blood. No one could figure out what he'd been doing in the backseat to begin with. He wasn't around to tell whatever story he'd cooked up, and I wasn't asked. It had to happen close so he could say he shot her during a struggle for the gun. Only he forgot she'd outmaneuvered more than one cop and a couple of hundred prison guards.

Adelaide Dix wasn't seen again in Sterling Heights or anywhere else. It hasn't been a year yet, so Geraldine Tolliver hasn't gotten any more postcards.

When the cops searched the rest of the car, they found Chief Shrike. In the trunk.

JOE GORES

Born in Minnesota, **Joe Gores** served in the U.S. Army and was educated at Notre Dame and Stanford. He has worked as a laborer, truck driver, carnival roustabout, gymnasium instructor, auto auctioneer, logger in Alaska, and English teacher in Africa. For twelve years he was a private investigator in San Francisco. He has won Edgar Allan Poe awards for Best First Novel, Best Short Story, and Best Episodic Teleplay, as well as being twice nominated for the Best Novel Edgar (1986's *Come Morning* and 1992's *32 Cadillacs*). Gores introduced the men and women of Dan Kearny Associates in 1972's *Dead Skip*.

FIRST MYSTERIOUS PRESS PUBLICATION:
COME MORNING, 1986

INSCRUTABLE

Knuckles Colucci wasn't known as Knuckles because they dragged on the ground when he walked. Far from it. Oh, his jaws were blue enough, his nose was Roman, his eyes were mean, his lips had that Capone twist. But he was physically slight, not bulky. So while maturing into a classic Mafia soldier, and then graduating to Armani suits and Ferragamo shoes—which he invariably wore with parrot-bright aloha shirts—Knuckles needed some sort of physical edge. Thus the habit, in his youth, of carrying a set of brass knuckles as an equalizer.

Those days were long past. Now Knuckles was a frightener. He never demanded of some poor fool the vigorish due a local loan shark. He never broke knees or cut off thumbs. He wasn't an enforcer. He *warned* people. Once.

If the warning was ignored, he killed them.

On this particular Wednesday he had flown first-class from Detroit to San Francisco. A boring flight because today would be just a warning. He walked through the jammed, noisy, jostling airline terminal and down two escalators. The first took him past the luggage area, where he had no luggage to pick up. He never brought anything more lethal than sinus breath onto any of the numerous commercial flights that his profession demanded. He'd taken three falls in his thirty-nine years. If he took another he wouldn't get up again, so he wasn't about to take it.

The next escalator took him to a long slow moving walkway. In the underground parking garage a bright-eyed kid in his twenties fell into step with him on the angle-striped pedestrian walk.

"Nice flight?" Knuckles merely grunted. The kid handed him a set of Lexus keys. "The red one," he said, and turned off to lose himself among the endless rows of cars.

The Lexus was nestled between a hulking sullen SUV and some sort of canary-yellow Oldsmobile convertible. Knuckles pulled on thin rubber surgeon's gloves, unlocked the door, got in. There was a black violin case on the passenger seat. He unsnapped it, raised the lid, looked inside, grinned thinly, closed and resnapped it. He set it upright in the bucket seat and snugged the seat belt about it, then followed the EXIT signs out of the labyrinth. His nose was already tingling from the exhaust fumes trapped in the garage. Too many freaking people. Kill 'em all.

. . .

"I need a frozen Milky Way," said Larry Ballard.

He was a tall athletic blond man in his early thirties, with a surfer's tan, and a hawk nose and cold blue eyes that just saved his face from true male beauty. He was also a repo man for Daniel Kearny Associates at 340 Eleventh Street in San Francisco.

"Nobody needs a frozen Milky Way," Bart Heslip pointed out.

He too was very well conditioned, early thirties, shorter, thicker, plum black, and with the shaved head currently in favor among African American males. After winning thirty-nine out of forty pro fights, he had quit the ring to become a repo man for DKA.

"I've been working out really hard," explained Ballard. "My blood-sugar level is way down."

"We can't have you going hypoglycemic before you win that black belt," said Heslip. "Ray Chong's it is—*after* you take me back to my car in Pacific Heights."

. . .

Above the door of the narrow Eleventh Street storefront sandwiched between a tire repair shop and an auto supply store run by Persians in turbans was the legend PEKING GROCERY STORE—CHINESE DELICACIES in English letters and Chinese characters.

The owner, Ray Chong Fat, was anything but. Ray was skinny and stooped, with a thin face, not much chin, a long upper lip, and lank black hair. As always, he wore a highly starched white shirt, the cuffs rolled up two turns over his skinny wrists, the collar two sizes too big for his scrawny neck.

Ray was a widower with seven, count 'em, *seven* daughters. And not even one lousy little son. One daughter in grad school, two in college, two in high school, one in elementary school, one just about to enter kindergarten. Seven daughters meant a lot of expenses, which meant a lot of hard work for Ray.

But he was satisfied man, whistling tunelessly to himself as he stocked the shelves with assorted cans of exotic fruit: rambutan canned with pineapple; soursops; jackfruit in syrup; and of course Chinese lychees.

The rest of the narrow store was jammed with Chinese yams and cabbage; mandarins and mangoes and pawpaws and star fruit; dried and salted squid; frozen ducks and fish, frozen candy bars and ice cream bars, green tea and chow mein noodles and dried rice noodles and sweet rice candies, all redolent with the smell of strange spices. The shelves in the back room bulged with rental videos, all in Chinese and most shot in Hong Kong. Romance and martial arts were the favorites.

The front door jangled its little bell. The familiar salt-and-pepper team from down the street came in.

"Hey, got riddle," exclaimed Ray in his high-pitched singsong voice. "Why Chinese so smart?"

"I don't know, Ray," said Ballard. "Why are they?"

"No blondes." Ray went off into gales of high hee-hee-hee-hee laughter. Heslip shook his shaved head.

"It's what I always tell you, Larry. Inscrutable."

Two jokes and a riddle later, they headed for the door. A slight man was getting a violin case out of a red Lexus when they emerged. Ballard waved the frozen Milky Way after him.

"Not my idea of the third violin at the symphony."

"Maybe it isn't a violin in the case," chuckled Bart.

■ ■ ■

The bell tinkled. A short swarthy man with a nose as big as a parrot's was coming up the aisle toward Ray. The man wore a very expensive suit and carried a violin case. Ray wreathed his lean face in a welcoming smile full of prominent teeth.

"Yessir, yessir, help you, sir?"

"Yeah, you freaking slope, you can help me," said Knuckles.

Ray Chong Fat's eyes became flat and stupid.

"No savvy," he said.

Knuckles set his violin case on the counter.

"Know what I hear? I hear some Chinaman is running an unsanctioned Asian card club for the really high rollers in this town once or twice a month, on the weekends."

"No savvy," said Ray Chong Fat.

"I hear this freaking Chink's got a game planned this weekend. I hear a certain gentleman in the South Bay don't like that shit, get my drift?"

"No savvy." A drop of sweat ran down Ray Chong Fat's nose.

Knuckles Colucci unsnapped the violin case. He opened it. "Take a look at that," he said.

Ray Chong Fat looked into the case. He paled.

"Yeah, you savvy that okay, slope," said Knuckles. He closed the case, resnapped it, waggled a finger under Ray's nose. "Don't do it no more," he said.

. . .

"I need a beer," said Bart Heslip.

It was 9:30 that same night and he and Ballard, working in tandem, had scored two repos each.

"Nobody needs a beer," Larry Ballard pointed out.

"This is thirsty work."

"Okay. Ray'll be open for another half hour at least."

But Ray Chong Fat's store had the CLOSED sign out, even though light still glowed from the back room. They rapped on the glass and rattled the door. In this neighborhood, even DKA had alarms on the doors and heavy mesh screens on the ground-floor windows. Ray had neither.

"How many years have we been coming here and he's never been closed before ten o'clock?" asked Ballard.

Bart said softly, "Maybe it *wasn't* a violin."

Ray's door was no proof against their lockpicks. They were halfway down the length of the store when the door of the back room opened and Ray came out. Even in the dim light he looked drawn and wasted.

"Go 'way! We closed."

"After you tell us what's wrong."

Over green tea and delicate almond cakes in the video room they got the story out of him. The little man with his threats and the violin case with anything but a violin inside.

"It's easy," said Bart. "Just cancel the game."

"Two year ago, number three daughter real sick, 'member?"

"We remember." They had gotten up a cash donation at DKA.

"Go to Chinese Benevolent Association, borrow money. Lots of money." He opened his arms wide. "Big interest."

"Not so benevolent?" suggested Bart.

Ray nodded morosely, sipped tea. They ate almond cakes.

"Man come, say I gotta run weekend Asian card club to pay off loan. If I won't, he say they do things to my daughters."

"They needed a front," said Larry. "At least the loan—"

"Never get loan paid off. Only pay off interest."

"You know the guy with the violin case?" asked Bart.

Ray shook his head vigorously.

"Know who *sent* the guy with the violin case?"

"Somebody in South Bay." Ray started wringing his hands with the theatricality of true emotion. "What I do?"

"You hold the game and save your daughters," said Ballard.

"Then man with violin come back and kill me."

The two repo men looked at one another.

"No," said Heslip.

. . .

"Why is sex like insurance?" asked Rosenkrantz.

"The older you are, the more it costs," said Guildenstern.

"Their jokes are worse than Ray's," said Bart Heslip.

It was six A.M. Thursday. He and Larry were with the
two bulky SFPD homicide cops in the upstairs conference
room at DKA where they had total privacy because nobody
could get up the stairs without making noise. The cops had
insisted on this since they were outside department regs just
being there.

Rosenkrantz was bald as Kojak and Guildenstern had
hair that looked fake but wasn't. It was rumored in the department that even their wives called them by their nick-
names.

When they did good cop/bad cop, Guildenstern was always the bad cop. He had the eyes for it. He said, "You
guys been talking for ten minutes and you ain't given us
anything we'd be ashamed to tell our mothers."

"Only thing could embarrass your mothers is that they
are your mothers," said Heslip.

Guildenstern looked at Rosenkrantz. "He being pro-
found?"

"Just nifty," said Rosenkrantz.

"Just careful," said Ballard. "If you try to take down the
game, our guy's family gets hit."

"And if he holds the game, he gets hit. We got that part
of it." Rosenkrantz was suddenly angry. "The mayor and the

D.A. are always telling us there ain't any Mafia in San Francisco. Asian gangs fighting for power, maybe. Chicano gangs fighting over turf, perhaps. Black gangs fighting over drug money and rap music, could be. But—"

"But no Mafia action," said Guildenstern. "These days, local guys who are connected have only bookkeepers on their payroll. They need something done, they make a call and somebody gets on a plane out of Chicago or Detroit or even Cleveland."

Rosenkrantz took it up. "The threatener picks up his hardware at the airport on the way in, does what he does, leaves his hardware at the airport on the way out. We got a lot of names and reputations, but we can't get nothing on nobody."

"You're saying the guy with the violin case isn't local?"

"Tell us about him," suggested Rosenkrantz.

They did. The cops exchanged glances.

"Knuckles Colucci out of Detroit," said Guildenstern.

"Mean as a snake," said Rosenkrantz.

"Call the undertaker for your pal," said Guildenstern.

"Who hired him?"

The two big cops heaved themselves to their feet. "South Bay? Let us worry about that," they said almost in unison.

"Who runs the Chinese Benevolent Association?"

"Let us worry about that, too."

"You'll let us know when Colucci leaves home again?"

Rosenkrantz said, "What's the most important question to ask a woman if you're interested in safe sex?"

"What time does your husband get home?" said Guildenstern.

. . .

Larry and Bart descended the back stairs to the big back office that office manager Giselle Marc shared with the mainframe computer and the teenage girls who sent out legal notices and dun letters after school. Giselle was a tall, lithe blonde in her early thirties whose brains were even better than her long and wicked legs. This early she was alone in the office.

"Well?" asked Ballard.

"Every word," said Giselle with an almost urchin grin. She held up the tape recorder she'd had plugged into the intercom that Heslip, at her suggestion, had left open in the conference room. "Was that a yes or a no on Colucci from those guys?"

"A yes," said Ballard. "No, there'd have been no joke."

"If you think you're leaving me out of this, you're crazy."

"Never crossed our minds," fibbed Heslip.

They had been listening to the tape for about ten minutes when behind them O'B said, "Ahem."

Patrick Michael O'Bannon, in his early fifties, with guileless blue eyes in a leathery drinker's face splattered with freckles, was devious as a two-headed snake. He was also the best repo man around save Kearny himself. He pulled up a chair and sat down.

"Now, you got a couple of holes in your plan . . ."

None of them thought about letting Dan Kearny, their boss, in on things. He'd just say no, then he'd take over their operation and run it himself. He did it every time.

■ ■ ■

The Chinese Benevolent Association was up a flight of creaky wooden stairs from an aged Buddhist temple on Old Chinatown Lane, a little stub of an alley just below Stockton

Street. There was nothing to tempt the casual tourist or, indeed, any Caucasian to try the street door. It just bore a set of Chinese characters that spelled out God knew what.

Yet on this particular Thursday midday two bulky white men came tramping up the stairs and into the reception room. It was hung with bright silk tapestries and there were delicate carved ivory figurines on inlaid tables. There was a hint of incense on the air. On the walls were numerous photos of association leaders shaking hands with local and national politicians.

A pert, pretty Chinese girl was making her fingers fly over the keyboard of a very modern computer. She looked up when they entered, finding a smile for them.

"May I help you?"

When they just walked past her toward the door in the back wall, she dove for the buzzer under her desk. But by then they were already into the next room, where a white-haired Chinese gentleman sat behind a desk arranged so no window overlooked it. A heavyset thug was coming out of his chair on their side of the desk even as he reached for his armpit.

Guildenstern put a big hand on the man's face and pushed. He pushed with stunning, unexpected strength. The thug went backward over his chair. Rosenkrantz was holding out his badge for the older gentleman to see.

"Rosenkrantz and Guildenstern, SFPD Homicide," he said.

The old man spoke sharply in Mandarin. The thug righted his chair, sat back down, and ceased to exist for them.

"Mr. Li?" asked Rosenkrantz.

"I am Fong Li," admitted the white-haired man gravely.

His English was accented but elegant. He had a long narrow lined face with a thin aristocratic nose. His eyes were dark but benevolent, like his association. In any country of the world, in any race, at any time, he would have been a patriarch.

Rosenkrantz sat on a corner of the desk. "Ray Chong Fat."

"Ah so," said Fong Li, much as Ray Chong said, "No savvy."

"Guy came around and threatened him with death if he held your Asian card game this weekend."

"I am desolated that I have no information of this event for the honored gentlemen," said Fong Li.

Guildenstern turned from a table under the window with a delicate Chinese urn in one paw. "This one of them Ming vases?"

Fong Li went very still. He said very softly, "I can make inquiries and discover whether this game of which you illustrious gentlemen speak might be canceled."

"We don't want it canceled," said Rosenkrantz.

Surprise actually flitted across the Chinese man's august features. "Then I am sure that Mr. Chong Fat need not run—"

"We want Ray to run it this weekend," said Guildenstern.

Sudden comprehension illuminated Fong Li's face. "Ah so," he said again, with a very different inflection.

"But after this weekend, he don't have to ever run another one," said Rosenkrantz. "And he don't owe you any money. The books are balanced, the slate is wiped clean. Anything ever happens to him, or his daughters, anything at all . . ."

Fong Li bowed gracefully. "This insignificant person would not wish to insult such brilliant men as yourselves, but—"

"I said we were Homicide. We don't care about gambling."

A delighted Fong Li beamed. Rosenkrantz stood. Guildenstern carefully set the Ming urn back on the table.

"Nice vase," he said, making the word rhyme with "base."

. . .

Two-Ton Tony Marino took his nickname from the heavyweight boxer Two-Ton Tony Galento, who had once gotten himself creamed by Joe Louis. Tony didn't weigh quite two tons, but even so he was built like a watermelon. When the phone rang in his Detroit office on the following Monday afternoon, he picked up without hesitation: The place was swept twice daily for bugs.

"Yeah, Marino."

"Tony. Leone in San Francisco. The *scemo* Chinaman held the game last Saturday night. So Knuckles'll have to come back out." Leone gave a sudden gross chuckle. "Blood on the chop suey by Wednesday, right?"

They said laconic good-byes and hung up. Tony was a little offended. Leone had no real class. You didn't say things like that. Things got done, bing bang boom, they were over. Nothing personal, you never talked about them before or after.

He dialed the phone. When a machine answered, he told it, "Knuckles, on Wednesday you gotta make that West Coast delivery."

. . .

Shoehorned with the technician into the closed van parked on a side street in the South Bay town of Milpitas near the Summitpointe Golf Course, Guildenstern asked Rosenkrantz, "What's the leading sexually transmitted disease among yuppies?"

"Headaches," said Rosenkrantz.

"I think that's what we'll be giving our boy Leone."

"I especially liked the part about blood on the chop suey."

"Conspiracy to commit?" suggested Guildenstern.

"At least," agreed Rosenkrantz.

· · ·

It was Wednesday again, and Knuckles was flying first-class from Detroit to San Francisco. He was feeling good. No dry run today. The real thing. At SFO he went through the jammed, noisy, jostling terminal and down the two sets of escalators to the moving walkway. As he started along the angle-striped pedestrian walkway in the vast echoing underground garage, a tall elegant blonde with breathtaking thighs fell into step with him.

"Nice flight?" she asked. Her voice was soft, caressing.

"My name is Knuckles Drop-Your-Pants," Knuckles said with his most winning smile. She handed him a set of keys.

"The gold Allante," she said, and was gone among the endless rows of cars before he could think up another zinger.

He sighed, pulled on his thin rubber gloves, unlocked the Allante, got in. He knew damn well he would never be able to buy anything like that in his entire life. The black violin case was on the passenger seat. He unsnapped it and raised the lid. Yeah.

But as he was setting it upright on the bucket seat there

was a knock on the window. The blonde. She had a cell phone up to her ear and was gesturing at him to roll down the window.

"Open the trunk." As she spoke she reached through the open window for the instrument case. "Hurry, there's no time."

She tossed the case into the trunk, slammed the lid, came back to slide into the front seat next to him.

"Terrorist bomb threat. They're searching all the cars with single men in them, so our only chance is to get you and that hardware out of here before they bottle up the garage." When he did nothing, she yelled angrily at him, "*Move it!*"

Knuckles had no experience of a woman like this. He put the car in gear, followed the arrows toward the exit as if on automatic. Just before the ramp down to the ticket booths, a hard-eyed red-haired man in his fifties stepped out in front of the car and held up a badge wallet with a freckle-splotched hand. He came around to Knuckles' side of the Allante.

"FBI. We're going to have to take a look in your trunk."

"You got a warrant?" demanded the suddenly strident blonde. "This is harassment! My husband has just picked me up from a seven-hour flight and I'm not going to have you getting filthy pleasure from pawing through my under-wear looking for drugs."

"It isn't . . ." The redhead stopped and sighed and stepped back. "And they wonder why," he muttered under his breath. He gestured wearily. "On through, the pair of you."

Once they were on the exit road from the airport, she told Knuckles to pull over at the Standard station. She got out.

"Open the trunk. I'll get your case for you." She recited a phone number. "Remember it."

She retrieved the violin case, slammed the trunk lid, put the case back in the car, and finally leaned in his open window.

"If the heat's still on here at the airport when you're finished, call me and report," she told him.

This was the kind of thing Knuckles understood. He'd make damn sure the heat would still be on at the airport.

"If it is, maybe you and me can—"

"Sure. Whatever you want, Knuckles. Leone said to treat you right." She gave him a suddenly wicked, even a debauched smile. "You'll be staying over at my place."

A freaking dream come true. Yeah! Do the Chink, call the blonde, then do her. All night. Paradise on a platter. In a feather bed, rather.

. . .

Knuckles turned the dead-bolt knob on the front door and flipped the OPEN sign over to CLOSED. Only when he was going down the aisle did he see that there were a couple of customers with the dead man. On the killing ground that was how he always thought of his prey: the dead man.

One customer was a tall blond guy with a hawk nose, the other a shorter, wider jig with a shaved head. Sexual excitement rippled through Knuckles. His first triple-header! Tonight he'd give that freaking blonde a ride she'd *never* forget.

All three men were eating ice cream cones, for Chrissake! Goddamn pansies, maybe. He set his violin case on the counter.

"I told you I'd be back," he said roguishly to the Chink.

He opened the case, reached in. "The back room. All of you."

"Or?" said the jig.

"Or this," said Knuckles, and brought up from the violin case—a violin. He gaped down at it.

The Chink stuck an ice cream cone into his left eye. He yelled and clawed at the icy mess, and the white guy kicked him explosively in the balls. Pain shot through his entire being. As he coiled down on himself, mouth strained open in a rictus of pain, the black guy caught him with a terrific right cross that knocked three teeth right out of his head.

. . .

Knuckles Colucci came around sitting behind the wheel of the gold Allante in a no-parking zone at SFO's domestic terminal. His savaged mouth was bleeding and his groin was pure pain. Beside him on the other bucket seat was the violin case.

It was the blond bitch who had made the switch, of course. She'd had a second violin case in the trunk, and after the redheaded federal agent had been bluffed out . . . No! Not an agent. Part of the con. He'd been hidden by a pillar from the ticket-takers in the booths. No terrorist bomb. Nothing. But *why*?

Later for that. Get out of here, fast. He somehow pulled himself together enough to reach for the ignition keys.

There were no ignition keys.

Both front doors opened. Two hulking men, one bald and the other with a thatch of sandy hair, peered in at him.

"Knuckles Colucci, you are under arrest for attempted murder," said the bald one. He was opening the violin case.

"With a freakin' violin?" asked Knuckles hoarsely.

"No, with this," beamed the bald man. His hand came out with a stubby machine pistol wearing a silencer as long as it was. "Looks to me like an Ingram M11 using a .380 ACP. Heard it was your weapon of choice, Knuckles, 'cause it'll just fit in a violin case. Frilled barrel with a wire screen, a baffle—"

"And two spirals to decelerate the gases so the gun doesn't make any noise at all," said the one with hair, slipping the cuffs on the dazed Knuckles' wrists.

The bald one put his nose down and sniffed. "It's been fired, too. The report I got said he shot up the Chinaman's place pretty bad . . ."

"You know, Knuckles," said the other one, shaking his head, "you're a real birdbrain, aren't you?"

. . .

All five of them were feasting at the House of Prime Rib on Van Ness Avenue. It just seemed the kind of occasion to saw at slabs of blood-rare beef two inches thick and to hell with diets and cholesterol and a size six dress.

Ballard raised his glass. "To Ray. For shooting up his own grocery store."

"All that fun, and it's covered by insurance," said Bart.

"You make a hell of a Feeb," Giselle was saying to O'B.

O'B pulled down the lower lid of his right eye. "And you make a hell of a con woman. You hit him with everything all at once, never gave him a moment to think . . ."

They all drank. O'B, who was facing the door, gestured. Rosenkrantz and Guildenstern were threading their way through the tables. They came up and looked over the company with benevolence. Rosenkrantz spoke first.

"Hear about the blonde who got an AM radio?"

"It took her a month to figure out she could play it at night," said his partner.

Giselle, as the only blond woman present, said, "What's SFPD Homicide's version of the Miranda warning?"

"You have the right to remain dead," said Larry Ballard.

"Have a seat, gents," suggested Bart Heslip.

Guildenstern shook his head and chuckled.

"We got an all-nighter going. Knuckles is in a cage downtown and squawking like a parrot, trying to get a deal. He's giving us everything he ever knew about anybody in the mob."

"Witness relocation?" asked Giselle.

"Four-time loser? No chance. We don't need him anyway. The feds are busting Two-Ton Tony back in Detroit right now—he took the conspiracy across state lines. He can buy the local heat but he can't buy the feds. He's going down."

"Leone?" asked Bart.

"We got him on tape talking about blood and chop suey. He'll get a five-spot at Q, be out in two—but by then somebody'll have eaten his lunch down there in the South Bay."

Ray Chong Fat asked almost timidly, "Mr. Li?"

Guildenstern said, "What do you call someone who's half-Apache and half-Chinese?"

"Ugh-Li," said Rosenkrantz. He clapped Ray on the shoulder. "Seems he made a bookkeeping mistake. You're all paid up with him forever, and you don't have to run any more games."

Ray looked at him for a long time. There was a great deal in the look. Then he said, "Chinaboy cook at dude ranch. One ranch hand, every day he come in, say, 'What's fo' dinner?' Chinaboy say, 'Flied lice.' Pretty soon, ranch hand always asking, 'Flied lice? You got flied lice fo' dinner?' Every day. So Chinaboy get book, study English. Next time ranch hand come in, say, 'Flied lice? Flied lice?' Chinaboy say, 'We have a very great sufficiency of fried rice— you plick!' "

Rosenkrantz beamed down at the others.

"What d'you think he means by that?" he asked.

"If you stand by the river long enough," said Ballard, "the body of your enemy will float by."

"Huh?" said Rosenkrantz.

PETER LOVESEY

Peter Lovesey, born in Middlesex, England, began his writing career with the Cribb and Thackeray series of Victorian mysteries. He has published more than twenty books, including the Bertie, Prince of Wales, and Peter Diamond novels. He has twice been nominated for the Edgar for Best Novel: for 1987's *Rough Cider* and 1995's *The Summons*. He received the Cartier Diamond Dagger for Lifetime Achievement from the British Crime Writers' Association in 2000.

FIRST MYSTERIOUS PRESS PUBLICATION:
ROUGH CIDER, 1987

THE USUAL TABLE

Two weeks after Ella and Gavin opened their restaurant on Bodmin Moor they heard someone say there would be shooting for the next three weeks on Harrowbridge Hill, just up the lane. Bad news. When they bought the business no one mentioned military exercises or field sports in the area. You can't serve relaxing meals to the sound of gunfire. Mercifully it turned out that the only sounds were a call for action followed by actors speaking lines. They were shooting a film. And even better news followed. The American film star Mikki Rivers spotted the restaurant sign and decided she would risk a meal there one evening. Danny Pitt, the director, made a reservation for two.

"Mikki Rivers! Brilliant!" said Gavin. "What a stroke of luck."

"It is *the* Mikki Rivers, is it?" said Ella, feeling both excited and terrified.

"We couldn't ask for a better endorsement," said Gavin. "Everyone for miles around is going to know she ate here."

"Please God she likes it," said Ella. "The menu is a bit thin."

"They'll know it isn't the Ritz. A limited choice, maybe, but what we serve is second to none."

Gavin didn't lack confidence. He was a trained chef, and a good one. The restaurant was tiny, just two rooms in a private house. You knocked at the front door, hung your coat in the hall, and drank aperitifs in the small space in front of the bay window. But each item on the menu was *cordon bleu.*

Mikki Rivers came in on Wednesday evening with Danny Pitt. A photographer from the *Cornishman* got a shot of her stepping out of the Porsche in her mink. Ella was worried that Mikki would object to being photographed, but she gave her wide-screen smile and said she was used to far worse from the paparazzi.

They had the table closest to the log fire and everything was perfect. They ordered champagne and Gavin's special, the roast duck and black cherry sauce, and said it was the best meal they'd had since they arrived. At the end, Mikki Rivers said she wanted to come back Saturday.

She meant it. Danny Pitt made the booking before they left. Mikki's photo was on the front page of the *Cornishman* with the comment "I'll be back Saturday. Try and keep me away!" By midmorning on the day the paper appeared, every table was reserved. The phone rang through the day. Gavin and Ella could have filled their little restaurant five times over.

"We're made. It's a dream start," said Gavin.

"I hope they won't all gawp at her," said Ella.

"Not when they see the food you put in front of them. This is our chance, Ellie. Can you cope, or shall we hire an extra waitress for the evening?"

"If you can cook all by yourself, I'm sure I can manage my part."

They opened at seven on Saturday evening. Mikki Rivers didn't arrive until later, thank goodness, because there was a problem with some other customers, who had booked in the ominous name of Hellings.

"There must be a mistake."

"What's that, madam?" Ella asked with proper concern.

"Some people are sitting at our usual table in the conservatory."

Ella had never seen them before. She remembered with an effort that the restaurant had been in business for some years before she and Gavin took over.

"The con— which, madam?"

"Conservatory. Out there."

"Oh, the sunroom."

"It's the conservatory. It's always been the conservatory."

"I didn't know that," Ella said humbly. "We haven't been here long."

"If you had," said the woman, a senior citizen with three rows of paste pearls that lent symmetry to the triple bags under her heavily made-up eyes, "you would know that we always have that table for our anniversary dinner."

"They'll have to move," said her companion in a combative voice. This burly man with a red bow tie looked uncomfortable in his suit. His weather-beaten face suggested he'd worked outdoors most of his life.

Desperate as Ella felt, she knew she must humor these people and get them settled before her star guest arrived. "Did you say it's your anniversary? Congratulations. Is it a special one?"

"They're all special to Wilf and me," said the woman. "Actually, this is the thirteenth. We come every year."

"And sit at our usual table," added Wilf. He wasn't to be sidetracked. "We're not sitting anywhere else."

"We asked for our usual table when we booked," said the

woman. "That's the whole point of coming here, that table. There are better restaurants, with better food and better service, but that table has associations."

And Wilf chimed in, "So will you tell those people to move their arses, or shall I?"

Fortunately he'd lowered his voice. Normally if you took the trouble to listen you could hear anything anyone said in the tiny rooms. How tempted Ella was to show the door to this obnoxious pair. On any other evening, she would have risked it.

She glanced across at the young couple sitting in the sunroom. They were still looking at the menu. They might be persuaded to move. They appeared amenable.

"Listen," she said to Wilf Hellings and his lady, "I'm sure we can sort this out. Please have an aperitif with our compliments, while I speak to my husband."

"You can stuff your aperitif," Wilf told her. "We want action, not farting around."

Ella went into the kitchen and told Gavin about these appalling people. He was terribly busy cooking whitebait for starters. "Who took the booking? Did they mention a special table?"

"Does it matter who took the booking?" Ella said. "The point is, we'll have a riot if they don't get that table. Mikki Rivers could arrive any minute."

Gavin pulled the pan from the flame. "I'll speak to the people in the sunroom, then." He moved off at speed.

Happily—and with the bribe of a bottle of Chablis, courtesy of the management—the young couple were willing to move.

So the Hellings, the customers from hell, took possession

of their usual table. Ella handed them the menu just as Mikki Rivers and her companion Danny Pitt drove up.

"So pleased to be back in your wonderful restaurant," said Mikki as she slipped out of the mink. She was in a gorgeous glittery top and black skirt slashed to the hip.

"We're a little busier than last time," said Ella apologetically.

"No problem," said Danny Pitt. He winked. "Good to see fine cooking appreciated."

"If it *is* the cooking."

Ella showed them to their table by the fireplace and left them with the menu while she took other orders.

"Give me the wine list," said Wilf Hellings when she reached him. "The drinks are on Gus this evening."

"The whole meal's on Gus," said his companion, giggling.

"He's got no choice, has he?" said Wilf.

"Gus was my husband," the woman explained to Ella. "I still have his money in the bank."

"*Is* your husband," Wilf corrected her. "In theory, anyway."

Ella didn't show it, but her fury at these obnoxious people increased. They'd made a scene because they were supposed to be celebrating their thirteenth anniversary. And now it appeared they weren't even married.

"He disappeared one day," said the woman. "Gus, my so-called better half, vanished."

"Sank without trace," said Wilf, and for no obvious reason threw back his head and guffawed, and the woman joined in.

All of this was audible to anyone who cared to listen.

The woman's piercing laughter must have got through to those with no interest in listening.

"He was a pig," she said of her husband. "You couldn't have brought him to a place like this."

"You wouldn't need to. He never left it," Wilf said in a cryptic aside, and earned another shriek.

"I wouldn't want him back," she said. "I don't mind spending his money, though."

Ella glanced nervously toward the table by the fire. Thankfully Mikki Rivers and her escort seemed to be oblivious of all this.

Wilf glanced at the wine list. "Got anything unusual in your cellar?"

This won the customary hoot of amusement from his companion.

"Everything we stock is on the list, sir. Perhaps you'd like a little longer to make up your mind."

"What's on the menu?" the woman asked.

Ella went through the specials.

"Now tell us in plain English," Wilf said.

Ella knew he was winding her up, testing her, trying to find her breaking point. In her time as a waitress she'd never met anyone so unpleasant.

The woman said to Ella, "Come here, love. No, really close. I want to whisper something in your ear."

She wasn't sure if she wanted to get any closer, but she had to appear friendly, so she dipped her head and heard the woman say, "Play along with him and you'll get a socking great tip."

The tip was the last thing on her mind, but she gritted her teeth and explained what each dish consisted of.

"Right," said Wilf. "I'll have the pie."

"And would you care for a starter?"

"Just a big portion of fish pie and plenty of veg. I've had you for my starter, had you over a barrel, and very tasty it was. Might have some more before the evening's through."

The woman shook with mirth. "He's a wicked man. Don't take any notice. I'll have the pie as well."

In the kitchen, Ella told Gavin, "Two *saumon en croûte*, and I feel like spitting in them. Those people in the sunroom are horrible."

"Don't let them get to you."

"It's all right for you. You don't have to speak to them."

"Better change their knives and forks if they're having the salmon."

"Oh, God, yes."

Probably her state of mind had something to do with the fumble she made with the cutlery at the Hellings's table. A fish knife slipped from her hand and dropped on the floor.

"Watch it!" said Wilf at once. "Careful of my floor."

"Careful of your floor," his companion said, simpering at him. "It's not much of a floor if a fish knife cracks it."

"Six inches of hardcore and six inches of concrete," said Wilf.

"Mostly hardcore, anyway," she said, nudging him as if they had some private joke.

Ellie picked up the knife and said, "I'll get you another."

"And a bottle of house white," said Wilf.

"Mean bastard," said his lady.

When Ella returned with the knife and the wine, the woman said, "You must be wondering what Wilf was on about, talking about his floor as if he owned it. You see, he's a builder. He built this conservatory thirteen years back."

"You must have seen my name on the trucks in big red

letters. Hellings," said Wilf with pride. He addressed this re-
mark to the room in general, turning to see if anyone responded, and several nodded their heads to humor him.
There was general interest in what was being said.

"He's very well known," said the woman, pitching her
voice higher to involve more of the diners. "This building
was my home, see, before it was a restaurant. I lived here
with Gus, my lawful wedded pain in the arse. He always
wanted a conservatory, and we weren't short of money, Gus
being a garage owner, so we got the planning permission
and hired the best builder in West Cornwall, and that was
Wilf."

"That's why I called it my floor just now," said Wilf, looking around the room. "I built it, but it belongs to Pearl
really."

"And Gus," said the woman now revealed as Pearl.

"Specially Gus," said Wilf, and got a giggle from Pearl.

Ella went to Mikki Rivers's table and took their order.
The film star still seemed perfectly at ease, faintly amused
by what she and everyone else had overheard in the last few
minutes.

In the kitchen, Ella passed on the orders to Gavin and
updated him on what had been said. "That woman with
Hellings lived here, apparently," she told Gavin. "This was
her house."

"If it was," said Gavin, "she's still the owner. We lease it
through the agents, but it's owned by some company with a
woman as managing director. Must be her."

"The husband left her, and I'm not surprised. He disappeared thirteen years ago, after Wilf Hellings built the sunroom for them. She seems to have taken a fancy to her
builder and moved in with him."

Gavin said, "Their salmon is ready. Got your tray?" He transferred the food to the plates. "Be nice to them, Ellie. I know it's difficult."

She carried the tray to the table with extreme care and set the plates in front of them.

"Right," said Wilf. "Let's see if the cooking is up to standard. The trouble with salmon is the bones."

"It's filleted," Ella assured him.

"Better be. There's nothing worse than finding bones when you don't expect them, eh, Pearl?"

"Shut up, you old fool," Pearl scolded him, half-smiling, and blushing, too.

"Relax," said Wilf. "I wouldn't embarrass you. We've been coming all these years and I've never said a word out of turn, have I?"

"He's not used to eating out," Pearl told Ella. "We have this anniversary meal once a year, and that's enough for him."

"The anniversary of the day her husband Gus disappeared," said Wilf, and once again he had the attention of just about everyone in the room, including Mikki Rivers. "He was a toerag, was Gus. Treated her like something the dog dragged in. I saw it at first hand when I got the job here, building the conservatory. How long was I working here, Pearl—six, seven, eight weeks? I say it myself, I'm a master builder. He knew he was hiring the top man around. It was purpose-built, this conservatory, not one of those ready-made things that let in the damp. As I say, I saw him knock her around."

Pearl said, "You don't have to go into details, Wilf."

"He was a rich bastard and he thought that gave him the right to do as he liked," Wilf pressed on relentlessly, pouring himself more of the house wine. "She would have put up with it, wouldn't you, Pearl, if I hadn't come on the scene? She didn't know he was seeing other women."

While Wilf regaled the room with Gus's deplorable behavior, Ella did her best to take the orders and serve the meals. It was difficult to get anyone's full attention. Even Gavin had the kitchen door open and was trying to listen. "Do you think they bumped off the husband?" he asked Ella when she came to collect some meals.

"They wouldn't talk like this if they had."

"It could be the wine talking. Maybe this anniversary of theirs is the anniversary of the murder."

"What a gruesome idea."

"They're a gruesome pair."

"That's true." She picked up her tray and took another order out.

In the sunroom Wilf was saying in his carrying voice, "It all came to a head one Saturday morning thirteen years ago. I'd just finished digging the foundations, right here where I'm sitting. Backbreaking work. Pearl said she'd make me a coffee, and I don't turn down good offers from the ladies. We got talking, as you do, and I happened to mention I'd seen Gus the night before in the Jamaica Inn with a gorgeous redhead. Now, I swear I wasn't making trouble. I wouldn't have said a word about it—except I thought this girlie had to be his daughter. She was so much younger than old Gus, you see."

His story was interrupted by the doorbell, but like all good raconteurs, Wilf turned it to advantage.

"The front door opens, and in walks the man himself— Gus. He doesn't ring the bell, it's true, 'cause he's got a key, hasn't he? Just walks in. He's obviously been on the job all night. Looks a wreck. No prizes for guessing where he spent the night. They say it's really comfortable up there, and the cooked breakfasts are out of this world. Pearl asks the old stallion where he's been, and he tells her to shut up asking questions and get him a black coffee—and I decide it's time to get back to my foundations. I know when to make myself scarce. The trouble is, Pearl asks me to stay. She wants him in the dock, with me as witness for the prosecution. Isn't that a fact, Pearl? Am I telling it right?"

"You shouldn't be telling it at all," said Pearl, getting a word in at last. "People come here for a nice meal. They don't want to hear about my two-timing husband."

"They want to know what happened."

"It's no business of theirs."

"They're interested."

"Shut up and eat your dinner. And I don't think you should have any more of that wine. You're not used to it."

So for an interval, Wilf was gagged.

Back in the kitchen, Ella asked Gavin, "Did you go to the door just now?"

"Yes. Just some customer who came in at lunchtime and thought he left his umbrella."

"You let him look for it?"

"And missed part of the story. Where did Gus spend the night?"

"The Jamaica Inn, with a redhead half his age."

"I'm even more convinced they murdered him."

"What would they have done with the body?" asked Ella.

Occasionally two people who know each other intimately have the same thought at precisely the same time. In this instance, the shared thought was so horrific that neither spoke. Ella gasped and Gavin stared.

Finally Ella said, "The foundations."

Gavin, pulling himself together, said, "You'd better take the dessert trolley round."

Mikki Rivers opted for the raspberry mousse. She said the food had been delicious again.

Ella said, "I just hope you weren't disturbed by the loud-mouth in the sunroom."

Mikki said, "We adored it. What a strange couple. We're dying to hear the end of the story."

Feeling slightly more relaxed, Ella pushed the dessert trolley into the sunroom.

Wilf Hellings put up two hands defensively. "Don't bring it over here. We're supposed to be dieting."

"It's tempting, though," said Pearl.

"If you fancy something, go ahead," said Wilf. "You won't get another crack at it till next time the anniversary comes around."

"I'd better not. Why don't you settle up now?"

"A coffee, perhaps?" Ella suggested.

They shook their heads.

From the other room, Danny Pitt spoke up. "Before you go, would you mind telling us what happened between you and Gus, the lady's husband?"

There were murmurs of support from all around the room.

Wilf looked at Pearl, who shrugged.

"There isn't much more I can tell you," said Wilf. "He called me a liar and I called him a rat and soon after that he disappeared. Who knows where he ended up? Someone suggested he may have gone down under, and there could be some truth in that." He paused and looked at the floor, milking the line for all it was worth.

Pearl began to giggle again.

"Anyway, it cemented our relationship."

Pearl found this uncontrollably funny.

"I don't think he'll surface now," added Wilf. "So we come here once a year and sit here at our usual table and have a meal on Gus, and, do you know, we feel quite close to him?"

Soon after, they paid their bill in cash and left. Ella got a ten-pound tip. The money was unimportant. Her suspicions meant she would never feel comfortable in the house again.

Which didn't matter, as it turned out, because she and Gavin left soon after, even though the police convinced them that the story of the missing husband had been just a clever con. It was the bad publicity over the stolen mink coat that did for them.

WILLIAM MARSHALL

William Marshall, born in Australia, has lived and traveled all over the world. He has worked as a playwright, journalist, proofreader, morgue attendant, and as a teacher in an Irish prison. He is the author of numerous police novels, including the Hong Kong–based Yellowthread Street series, the Manila Bay books, and two novels featuring Detective Virgil Tillman of 1884's New York City police.

FIRST MYSTERIOUS PRESS PUBLICATION:
FROGMOUTH, 1987

THEM!

Hong Kong is an island of some thirty square miles in the South China Sea facing the Kowloon and New Territories areas of continental China, until 1997 under British colonial administration, but now returned to China as an SAR, a Special Administrative Region under the old British-style judicial system of the Rule of Law and its own totally semi-independent system of naked and unbridled capitalism gone mad. The climate is generally subtropical, with hot, humid summers and heavy rainfall. The population of Hong Kong and the surrounding areas at any one time, including tourists and visitors, is in excess of seven and a half million people.

Hong Bay is on the southern side of the island, doesn't seem to belong to anyone and never did, has no rules or system at all, and the tourist brochures advise you not to go there after dark.

In the Detectives' Room of the Yellowthread Street police station at 6:15 A.M., someone stuck his head in through the door and said loudly in bad English, "Government Bug Man!"

He'd been called worse. Sitting at his desk catching up on his paperwork in the deserted room, Detective Senior Inspector O'Yee said back in even badder English, "Fuck off!"

His paperwork catching-up consisted of going through the morning's newspaper for a movie to take his family to that evening to mark the twenty-fifth year of his service in the Hong Kong police, something celebratory, something nice. Something like him—half Chinese and half Irish American—in Cantonese with English subtitles, or the other way around. Something like . . .

BIO-ZOMBIE
With Jordan Chan Siu-chan

FORBIDDEN CITY COP
With Vincent Kok Tak-chui

RAPED BY AN ANGEL 2
With . . .

Presumably nobody. Or, at least, the paper didn't want to say.

YOUNG AND DANGEROUS
With Jordan Chan Siu-chan

Him again. And just in case you didn't care for a steady diet of violence, coarseness, and pure nonstop sex and martial arts:

NOW YOU DIE

With what read like the entire roll call of a dozen Shaolin temples full of murderous monks.

Or, and God alone knew what this one was really about:

GOD OF COOKERY
With Stephen Chow Sing-chi

Or as a double feature with that great and enduring family favorite

SCREW YOU!! AND THEN I TAKE YOUR HEAD!

O'Yee said in hopeless exasperation, "Holy shit! Isn't there anything decent on anywhere anymore?"

He was still at the door. The Government Bug Man, wearing the standard street maniac's uniform of frayed baggy anorak and wild look, said, shaking his head, "No, not you. Me. The Government Bug Man." He pointed twice to the center button on his coat so O'Yee would know who he was pointing at. "I'm here to do a long and detailed report on vermin infestation at this station before it's all refurbished and repainted in the police corporate colors of blue and gray." He looked like a Chinese version of the thin, bespectacled guy who had played the Mad Scientist in the old *Jet Jackson, Flying Commando* series on TV. What was his name? Tut? Sock? Something Greek. O'Yee, like all middle-aged men, giving up on the modern world and retreating back to his childhood, said to himself, "Aristotle Jones."

O'Yee said, "We haven't got any infestation. Try North Point."

"I have. I did them a week ago. They didn't have any either. They've already started the repainting."

He was carrying a leather holdall with what looked like a radio direction finder sticking out of it. He reached into it and took out a camera. The Government Bug Man said, "I won't disturb you in your important work. I just need a

picture of a bug or two and I'll be out of your way." He
seemed very anxious. The Government Bug Man said, "Just
a little bug'll do. A termite. Maybe a louse." He shrugged
hopefully. "The odd cockroach or two? The dirt-common
Blatta orientalis? Maybe a migratory pair of *Blattella ger-
manicus?*"

"No. Sorry."

"Spiders?" The Government Bug Man said with a sudden gleam in his eyes, "A tarantula maybe? 'A Monster Spider! A Crawling Terror 100 Feet High! A Creature from Hell
with Enough Poison in Its Fangs to Wipe Out an Entire
City!'"

O'Yee said, brightening up, "1955. *Tarantula!* With John
Agar and Mara Corday."

The Government Bug Man said, "Right. That was a good
movie."

It was. Except for John Agar, who acted as if he had been
carved out of oak.

O'Yee said, "He married Shirley Temple, didn't he? John
Agar?"

"So I believe." The Government Bug Man said with another shrug, "It didn't last."

What did? He looked at the Government Bug Man and
wondered how old he was. O'Yee said, "I'm sorry. We just
don't have anything for you."

"Nobody does. You're the last. Even the station out on
the old leper colony on Lantao Island didn't have anything.
Everything's just too clean now. There's nothing left for the
bugs to infest. Everything these days is all plastic and synthetics. There just aren't good old-fashioned enduring things
like wood or lead or copper or brick dust for them to eat
anymore, so in the end they all just curl up and die."

He knew the feeling.

The Government Bug Man said, "Very sad."

It was.

He was a lot older than he looked, maybe close to retirement age. The Government Bug Man said, shaking his head, "I've been in bugs all my life. And now they've all gone."

Sic transit gloria mundi. O'Yee said sympathetically, "Sorry. We're just totally bug-free here."

He sighed. The Government Bug Man said, "I used to go to all the old insect movies when I started out in bugs." He thought for a moment. "And all the old creature and monster ones too, not just for the insects and the creatures and the monsters but for the people in them too. People were good in them." He looked hard at O'Yee for a moment as if he wondered just how much the man knew about the real world. "Did you know that in *Creature from the Black Lagoon,* even after the creature had devoured people and attacked people and hauled the lady off in its arms into its lair, the hero, Richard Carlson, wouldn't let the creature be shot in the back because it wasn't right and because the creature also had its own right to live?" The Government Bug Man said as if he had said it a hundred times before and been met by a hundred blank stares back, "Does that tell you anything about the way things used to be?"

It told him that there would have been something else for him to take his family to other than *Raped by an Angel 2.*

"And in *The Day the Earth Stood Still,* Klaatu the spaceman and Gort the robot don't come down in their spaceship to destroy Earth, they come to save it!" He was getting warmed up. "Understanding, you see! Thought, compassion, decency—not just bang, bang, screw, screw, bang, bang!"

His eyes blazed momentarily with anger. "Not all plastic and synthetic and steel and glass, but wood and natural products teeming with life—food and sustenance for all our insect friends! A time when people were heroes, when they were worth something, when they weren't just thrown on the scrapheap! A time when—" He paused, on the edge of the final treason. "A time when government offices and police stations weren't painted in corporate colors designed by some twelve-year-old with a computer! When individuality and hard work and conscientiousness and honor counted!"

O'Yee said, "Right." He looked at his watch.

The Government Bug Man said, "*Them!*" At the door, gripping his hands into fists, his eyes gleaming with fire, the Government Bug Man said fiercely, "'THEM! A Horror Horde of Crawl-and-Crush Giant Ants Crawling out of the Earth from Mile-Deep Catacombs!'" He drew a breath. "'Kill One and Two Take Its Place!'" The Government Bug Man howled as a warning to anyone who might listen, "Them! *Them! THEM!!*"

The Government Bug Man said desperately, "I can't be silent anymore! Even if they send me to jail for the rest of my life for it, I have to say it! The Chinese cobalt bomb tests of the seventies . . . *Something went terribly wrong, and, just like in the movie, they created an entire race of huge murderous ants six foot long from head to tail, and now, three generations later, they're all on their way down here—down here to Hong Kong—to kill and destroy us all!*"

. . .

. . . He thought he'd just let him chat happily away for another twenty-five minutes or so, and then, when half a dozen Uniformed came in downstairs for the change of shift, have them bundle him up and take him off to the nearest rubber room.

Or, failing that, if Uniformed were late, shoot him.

O'Yee said pleasantly, opening his top desk drawer where his gun was, "Really?"

In a single bound, the Government Bug Man hurled himself across the room and threw himself into the chair opposite him.

The Government Bug Man said, "Yes! Yes!" He was released, free. He didn't care anymore. All his little bug friends were dead, and his life was over anyway.

The Government Bug Man said fiercely, "I know here in Hong Kong we're only independent at the continuing pleasure of our real masters in Beijing, but there are some things—Science, Saving the World—that go beyond national and geopolitical boundaries and must—*must*—see the light of day!" He leaned forward and didn't drop his voice. "*Them!* was just a movie, but *These!* are real!"

Oh, God! And *Him!* was a raving lunatic!

O'Yee said softly, steeling himself for the fastest quickdrawer draw in the history of the world, "Right!"

The Government Bug Man, touched as a tick, said in that desperately sincere voice all tick-touched madmen seemed to acquire to go with the gleam in the eyes and the fixed stare, "No one will admit it officially of course, but, even as we speak, all over China, the ants are mutating, getting bigger, more ravenous, traveling, moving—eating, destroying, taking over, becoming the Master Race! injecting, poisoning, killing—" He leaned in even closer. "The Great Northern Chinese Famine of '86—the ants! The terrible Central Provinces Floods of '92—the ants!" He glanced around the room in case, secreted somewhere in the wall, there was a spy from Conspiracy Central writing it all down to hold against him. "The mass criminal executions in Shanghai in '97—people who tried to talk about the ants! The war games off the coast of Taiwan in 2000—depth-charging swimming ants! Big ones! Even further mutated! Atomic ants that can swim! Nuclear, glowing ants! Ants that can—"

Oh, Lord! O'Yee, nodding nonstop like a wobble-headed celluloid figurine in the rear window of a car, said, "Right! Right! Right!" Why didn't he carry his gun in a shoulder holster like other cops? Just because he hadn't even fired the thing on the range for over eighteen months didn't mean he shouldn't have worn it all the time and had it with him all the time and slept with it and taken it to the bathroom with him, and, and, and—

"Huge, ever-growing, ever stronger giant *Ants.*"

Where the hell was goddamned Uniform? Where the hell was anyone? O'Yee, nodding even harder, said, "—Wow!"

"They move in tunnels, old tunnels, you know. Or in sewer pipes, or in old basements . . ."

O'Yee said, "Right!"

"Or down dark corridors. Or, in the night, in the darkness . . ."

O'Yee said helpfully, "Making a funny sort of high-pitched whistling sound." He'd seen the movie too, when he was about six, but it really hadn't scared him the way it had scared all the other kids in the movie house that day and by the time he was twelve or thirteen he was almost over it completely. O'Yee said, "And eating sugar."

The Government Bug Man said, "Right. Ha-ha! Sugar . . ." The Government Bug Man, cocking his head to one side and narrowing his eyes, asked quietly, "Just how much Chinese sugar have you seen for sale lately?" He said, nodding to himself, "Hmm? Hmm?" He glanced again to the wall where the spy was. "Or, even more lately, Chinese *bread?* Or Chinese *meat?* Or even more recently—in the last few weeks or *so*—Chinese *illegal immigrants?*" He leaped to his feet so quickly O'Yee felt his heart stop. The Government Bug Man, flinging his arms around, warned the world, "And now they're coming here! And no one can stop them! And unless I can do something to save it, the human race is doomed! *Doomed!*"

Okay. Time to shoot him. He'd given Uniformed more than enough time to be punctual, and obviously, they just weren't going to behave responsibly and clock in on time when they were supposed to, and so now, as usual, he was going to have to do everything himself and—O'Yee, reaching into the drawer for his gun, said, just full of conversation and vocabulary, "Right! Right—!"

On his feet, waving his arms around, the Government Bug Man said in a gasp, "The horror! The horror!" The Government Bug Man, abruptly stopping in midwave, said aghast, "The smell! The smell!"

It was formalin.

From nowhere, suddenly the odor of it was everywhere in the room.

The Government Bug Man, pointing, waving, spinning, yelled, "The door! At the door!"

Standing there, looking in at them, there was a giant ant at least two foot long from head to tail, and, judging by the way it kept snapping its mandrils and making an angry whistling sound, as hungry and vicious as hell.

. . .

"Gun. Gun! *Gun!*" O'Yee's brain, making things simple for him, yelled as he reached for the thing so quickly not even

kind-hearted Richard Carlson or anyone else could have
stopped him from blasting the thing in the back, the front,
the side, or anywhere else where there was a target, "Get
gun!" Grabbing at it, hauling it out, almost tearing the skin
off his knuckles as it stuck for a moment on the top of the
drawer, he was over the desk in an instant, colliding in midair
with the Government Bug Man as the Government Bug Man
collided with him and they both interlocked in midair and
hit the floor together.

O'Yee, disentangling himself, yelled, "Look out! Get out
of the way! Get out of the line of—"

"No! No!" He was all arms and legs. The Government
Bug Man, holding him back, getting entwined with him,
falling over with him, yelled in a panic, "No! No! *No! Don't
shoot it! Don't—*"

Oh, God, he was some sort of Friend of the Bugs, or—
O'Yee, fighting to get free as at the door the ant reared up
for a second and then turned to flee, shrieked as the Government Bug Man grabbed for his bag and pulled out the
end of the radio direction finder. "Get out of my way! Get
out of my way!"

"You fool!" The Government Bug Man, still pulling at
the device, yelled, "Didn't you see the movie? Don't you
know anything? Don't you know bullets just bounce off them?
Don't you know the only way to destroy them is to—"

It wasn't a radio direction finder at all. It was a miniature flamethrower.

O'Yee said in horror, "Oh, my God!"

The Government Bug Man, lighting it up with a roar,
yelled as both he and the giant ant disappeared out the door
and raced down the corridor for the back stairs. "—is to burn
them! Burn them! *Burn them!!*"

. . .

"Get a picture of it!" The Government Bug Man, flinging his camera back over his shoulder at O'Yee as he, like the ant, reached the end of the corridor and high-dived down the back stairs to the old Evidence Room, shrieked as an order, "Forget the gun! Take the camera! Get a picture of it before I light it up!" He was making a heavy thumping, breathing, puffing noise as he ran. Either that or his flame-thrower was. The Government Bug Man, hitting the floor at the bottom of the stairs in a combat crouch with the flame darting in and out from the nozzle of the thing like a dragon's breath, demanded, "Where'd it go? Where'd it go?" He got to the end of the passageway at the bottom of the stairs and pulled at a mesh door blocking the way. The Government Bug Man yelled, "What's this? What's in here? What's behind this door?" He puffed and lit the entire door up in a roar of flame.

O'Yee yelled back, "The old Evidence Room!"

"Tunnels?"

"No!" O'Yee said. "No!" O'Yee yelled in terror as the Government Bug Man stepped back preparatory to turning the metal mesh gate into a wall of lava. "Paper! It's full of paper!"

"Ah-ha!"

"—all piled up on top of each other in stacks and lines and—" O'Yee said in a gasp, "Oh my God—!"

"*Tunnels!*"

Where the hell was Uniformed? What the hell was Uniformed doing while a giant baby ant was charging about the place whistling and formaling, and—? And if that was a baby ant, where the hell were Mommy and Daddy and Uncle

Giant Ant, and—? O'Yee, freezing with terror as the Government Bug Man kicked the mesh door open with a bang, said in horror, "My God! They've eaten Uniformed!"

He was a second behind the Government Bug Man, reaching for the light switch.

The light switch didn't go *click!* It went *clumph.*

O'Yee yelled as a warning, "They've eaten the wiring! There's no light in here!"

He didn't need it. In a blast of flame, the Government Bug Man turned on the sun.

The Government Bug Man shrieked as something black and horrible scuttled across the room and halted momentarily to one side of a mountain of papers, "There! There!" Still holding the burning flamethrower, he turned and with a single shove propelled O'Yee ahead of him. "Quick! Get a photo before I burn it to nothingness!"

"It's gone!"

It had. All that was left was just a terrible stink of formalin. O'Yee, fumbling with the camera and the gun, trying to remember which one was which, yelled, "Where is it? Where's it gone?"

Then there was a sudden whistling sound, another stink of formalin, and the thing came out in a rush, ran over his shoes, and went behind him.

Not so awful a moment until the Government Bug Man turned back with the flamethrower.

O'Yee, hitting the ground as a blast of fire went over the top of him, shrieked, "Oh, my God! *Oh, my God!*"

All he had wanted to do was go to the movies. At that moment, anything would have done. O'Yee, twisting and rolling to get away from the flames, yelled, "Don't! Don't! You'll burn the whole place down to the ground!" O'Yee, looking up in midroll and finding himself looking directly into the eyes of a giant ant snapping and gnashing its mandrils at nose level, shrieked, "*Aaaarggghhh!*"

"Get a photo!"

That was odd. About to be denosed, eaten, and then incinerated, O'Yee thought he had heard someone say, "Get a photo." Then, and he knew he had gone mad, he thought he heard someone tell him which f-stop to use for the available light conditions. O'Yee, still rolling as the ant went after him, yelled, "What? *What?* Are you out of your mind? *Burn it! BURN IT!*"

Any moment, still rolling, he was going to roll over all the eaten skeletons of Uniformed. O'Yee, rolling, ducking, weaving, squirming, lashing out at the ant in a tangle of camera, strap, and gun, howled to the Government Bug Man, "Kill it! *Kill it!*"

"Photo! Get the photo! I have to have a photo to show them!"

In *Them!*, he recalled, they had had to have a photo too. The photo, when it was developed later by someone else, was of an ant eating the photographer. O'Yee, losing his scientific objectivity as the ant reared up on its hindquarters with a terrible buzzing sound and waved its arms around for a waiter to bring a knife and fork to its table, screamed to the Government Bug Man, "Burn it! Kill it! Destroy it! *Slaughter it!*"

"Photo!"

"Exterminate it!"

"Photo!"

O'Yee shrieked, "*KILL IT!*"

Ah-ha! Gun. Ah-ha, *gun, gun, gun.* O'Yee, fumbling and yanking at the mass of straps and camera and gun in his hand, trying to pick out the right one, yelled, "Shoot! Kill! *Shoot!*" And then, as the ant reared even higher, then with a buzzing sound suddenly turned in a complete circle, the Government Bug Man, filthy anorak, still burning flame-thrower, and all, was on top of him, wrestling for the gun and camera and screaming at him, pointing to the ant.

The ant, still making buzzing sounds, was running around in little circles snapping its mandrils.

He was crazy. He was a madman. He was the sort of madman from all the old bug pictures where the madman wanted to keep the bug alive for scientific research and was sure—absolutely certain—that it wouldn't breed again to be in Bug Film 2, but it always did, and when he was a kid, when he had seen *Them!*—and O'Yee had never admitted it to anyone before this, not even himself—he had wet himself in terror in the movie house and for years later he had had nightmares and—and—O'Yee, getting his camera free and clubbing at the Government Bug Man with it, yelled, "No! No!" All he had ever wanted to do was see a nice movie. O'Yee, whacking the Government Bug Man on the flamethrower and lighting the whole place up like a scene from hell as the weapon hit the ground with a thud, roared, "No! No! Goodness and decency are bad! Violence is good!" Staring down at the barrel of the flame-licking incinerator, smashing the camera to pieces and getting his gun up and pointing it in the Government Bug Man's face, O'Yee shrieked with all semblance of civilization gone, "Get out of my way or I'll blow your fucking face off!" The ant had stopped running around in circles. O'Yee, getting a bead on it, yelled, "I've got it! I've got it! I've got it—"

"*No!!*" He was a maniac. Throwing himself back on O'Yee

and flailing at him, the Government Bug Man howled at the top of his voice, *"No! Don't shoot it! Don't—"*

O happy day. O long and guaranteed continuing life to be. He shot it.

O'Yee said as the ant disappeared in a blast of flame and smoke and bullet, "Aaahh . . ."

The Government Bug Man, suddenly releasing him, said sadly, "Ohh . . ."

It was dead. Lying there, blown apart, it was naught but a . . .

. . . but a pile of clockwork and radio-controlled servos and little electric motors and batteries.

O'Yee, gazing at the ant in the light of the still burning flamethrower on the ground, said, "What the—"

He looked at the Government Bug Man.

The Government Bug Man looked at him

In that moment, someone needed to say something.

The Government Bug Man said something.

The Government Bug Man, full of eloquence, said sheepishly, "Um . . . *oops!*"

■ ■ ■

Back in the Detectives' Room, O'Yee was still hopping, raving mad, mad as a loon. Loon-looming above the Government Bug Man as he slumped down in a chair and tried to make himself small, O'Yee roared, "You scared the shit out of me!"

"I'm sorry." He knew he was in trouble. The Government Bug Man, trying to get even smaller, getting older and smaller by the moment, trying hard for total invisibility, said without looking up, "I'm sorry."

"Sorry doesn't do it!" Down there, he had almost wet

himself again. O'Yee, totally bereft of pity, roared even louder, "I'm not six anymore, I'm middle-aged and I can't take this sort of thing anymore!" He still had the gun in his hand. For some reason, even though he wanted to put it back in the drawer, he couldn't get his fingers to open around it and let it go. O'Yee, waving it around like a cheerleader's pom-pom, yelled, "I could have shot you down there!" Damn gun, it was stuck to his hand. O'Yee yelled, "This isn't some sort of 1950s movie where the good guys always win out— this is the real world where people get *killed!*" O'Yee, unable to stop shouting, shouted, "You're not allowed to get away with this sort of stuff anymore! It isn't—it just isn't *allowed!*" O'Yee, trying to shake the gun off, roared, "It's all the new world of the new century, see? Of the new millennium! It's all corporate colors and *Raped by an Angel 2,* and, and—" He finally got the gun loose and rammed it back in the open drawer. (It gave him time to check the front of his pants. Thank God, they were dry.) O'Yee, counting them off on his fingers, said, "You're gone for so many offenses you won't see the light of day for the rest of your life! You're gone for, just for starters, for—"

He didn't know. He genuinely didn't know. The Government Bug Man asked mildly, "For what?"

"One, possession of a flamethrower! Two, use of a flamethrower! Three, throwing a flame from a flamethrower! Four, attempted arson with a flamethrower! Five, using a flamethrower under false pretenses!" And that was just the flamethrower. He switched to his other hand. "Not to mention attempted grievous bodily harm with a flamethrower, simple assault with a flamethrower!" He was up to finger two on hand two, or was it three? "Plus a few other minor little things like attempted murder, fraud, causing alarm, at-

tempted destruction of a government building, and—and—"
O'Yee, getting to his last finger, said as the clincher, "Tampering with police electricity supply and theft of a lightbulb!"

The Government Bug Man said from his gnome-chair, "I didn't do that. The bulb must have gone out by itself."

All right. O'Yee, putting that finger up again, said, "And the attempted incineration of evidence, to wit, one radio-controlled and clockwork giant ant."

The Government Bug Man said mildly, "I thought if you got a picture of it before I flamed it—"

He needed another hand. O'Yee said, "And manufacture and operation of a noxious insect for the purpose of financial gain!"

"I just wanted my job back!" The Government Bug Man, suddenly sitting up straight in the chair, said as if he had said it before but nobody had listened, "I just wanted my job back! I just wanted to see out my last few years before retirement in the company of my insects! I just wanted to go into my office for a few more years longer and see all my insects up there on the walls in their cases and laid out in their drawers for just a little bit longer before I was—" His eyes filled with tears. "Before I was bottom-lined and number-crunched in your horrible, nasty little new world and told, because everything was plastic and steel and synthetics, that I wasn't needed anymore and that my entire life's work was all going to be bundled up and destroyed and the whole Government Bug Department closed down to make way for an extension to the government computer room!"

He was the Creature from the Black Lagoon staggering back into the black lagoon mortally wounded.

He wasn't even that. His lagoon had been drained and

there was nowhere for him to stagger back to. The Government Bug Man said with tears running down his face, "I just thought if there was a photo of something that—" The Government Bug Man said, "Taken by someone—someone powerful who represented everything that was modern, like you, then—" His lagoon hadn't just been drained, it had been turned into a parking lot. The Government Bug Man said hopelessly, "Nobody comes down in their spaceship in movies with their robot to save the world anymore. All anyone does these days is send you an e-mail to destroy it."

Or *Rape an Angel 2,* or—

O'Yee said full of anger, "No one makes movies like that anymore! That's yesterday! Today is—"

He knew what today was. The Government Bug Man nodded.

"That's all gone! It's all—" O'Yee said, "For Christ's sake! I could have shot you down there!"

Or *screwed you!! And then taken your head!* O'Yee said desperately, "For Christ's sake! Don't you realize there aren't any heroes left in the world anymore? Or monsters or giant ants or spacemen, or—"

"No." The Government Bug Man, looking up, said sadly, "You're right. They don't make movies like that anymore. Good movies. Movies you could take your family to and not feel embarrassed. Good movies where people had kindness and compassion for even the lowest crawling thing, where in the last reel, even though he'd eaten people and mutilated people, the hero, Richard Carlson, still wouldn't let the creature be shot because that wasn't the compassionate thing to do, and because—"

Forbidden City Cop!

Now you die!!

. . . God of Cookery . . . ?

There weren't any good movies anymore. Nothing to look up to, to be inspired by, to model your life on. All the heroes were gone, all the people with kindness and compassion and thought for what it might be like to be someone else—even a monster—to be inside their body and feel what they felt.

He knew. As the Government Bug Man had told him, he was someone powerful who represented everything that was modern.

The Government Bug Man's eyes, as O'Yee looked down at him, were full of tears. He was disappearing in the chair, getting smaller, turning to dust.

Heroes.

Good people.

Compassion.

Kindness. Understanding.

He was right. Like the old movies, they were all gone, things from the past.

He had run out of fingers. All he had left were his two open hands. For a moment he held them out. O'Yee said as a once and one-time-only offer, *"Fleas!"*

"What?"

"Fleas! I'll accept fleas!" Getting both his hands on the Government Bug Man's shoulders and hauling him out of the chair to stand up straight, O'Yee said, shaking the man back and forth to bring him back to life, "Fleas! Ordinary, normal-sized, nonatomic, common or garden-variety fleas! I'll accept a plague of fleas! Have you got any fleas?"

"Yes! Lots!"

"Don't shoot! He's had enough! Let him live!" Richard Carlson in *Creature from the Black Lagoon.* O'Yee said a

moment before he pushed the Government Bug Man out into the corridor and closed the door of the Detectives' Room behind him, "Come back in an hour or so with your fleas. And bring another camera!"

Twenty-five years as a cop. It was a hell of a long time.

Going back toward his desk to look through the paper one last time for something decent to take his family to that evening, he wondered, in all that time, if he had ever done anything worthwhile, anything good.

MARCIA MULLER

Born in Detroit, **Marcia Muller** has lived in northern California for over thirty years. She began her writing career in journalism, switching to fiction in 1977 with the publication of *Edwin of the Iron Shoes*, the first novel to feature San Francisco private investigator Sharon McCone. Sharon has now appeared in twenty-one novels and two collections of short stories. In 1994 Muller received the Lifetime Achievement Award for her contribution to the genre from the Private Eye Writers of America.

FIRST MYSTERIOUS PRESS PUBLICATION:
EYE OF THE STORM, 1988

THE IMPOSTOR

The house was in Daly City, a suburb abutting San Francisco to the south, which had been developed with an eye for practicality rather than style. There was nothing to distinguish this dwelling from its neighbors to either side: All were beige stucco with a garage on the ground floor, a picture window above, and stairs to the front door rising on the right. But inside, the resemblance to a conventional suburban home stopped.

For one thing, the living room was full of balloons that bobbed and stirred on the breeze that followed me inside. Gold lamé balloons, no less. Costumes in satin and sequins and velvet were crammed onto a rack in the foyer. Gigantic bags of confetti were stuffed behind the sofa; a rubber octopus leered from one corner; mouthwatering aromas emanated from the kitchen. In the cramped office to which my new client, Barbara Baldwin, led me, the computer screen showed a spreadsheet with substantial totals.

Baldwin cleared the screen and shut the machine off while motioning me toward a chair. She was a short, plump woman with frizzy red hair that looked as if it could radiate sparks; laugh lines around her mouth suggested she smiled often, but right now her brow was creased in a frown.

She said, "Thanks for taking the time to drive down here, Ms. McCone. We've got a huge party at the Hyatt Regency tonight, and they've requested a triple order of our Wildest Dreams canapés. Plus my partner's down with the flu, and I'm waiting for confirmation that the strolling minstrels will actually show up this time, and—Well, I'm sure you don't want to hear about my problems. Not those particular ones, at least."

When she'd called to request McCone Investigations' services, Barbara Baldwin had explained that Wildest Dreams Productions were professional party planners who assumed responsibility for coordinating large corporate events. Apparently that included preparing hors d'oeuvres and corralling straying minstrels. I'd done some checking on the firm after I'd talked with her and been impressed: In five years Baldwin and her partner, Melanie Katz, had gone from a shoestring operation that catered neighborhood children's parties to a company that did more than two million dollars' business annually, and they kept their profit margin wide by continuing to work out of Baldwin's home so she could keep tabs on her young children—one of whom had been seated on a carousel horse watching TV cartoons when I'd entered. The kids loved the party props, my client had explained.

Now I said, "You mentioned a problem of a serious nature."

"Yes. Have you heard of Raffles?"

"You mean where you buy a ticket and—"

"No, it's a name. The alias of a man here in San Francisco, after the gentleman burglar of English literature. No one knows his identity, what he does for a living, or what he looks like. He's a party crasher by avocation."

"Unusual hobby. I take it he's crashed parties you've planned."

She rolled her eyes. "He's crashed *everybody's* parties. The man's an absolute master at it. They say he's in his late twenties, has a good social background, but his family lost its money and position a number of years ago. He regards it as a game to slip into the important corporate parties or upper-crust benefits, wine and dine himself, hobnob with celebrities and the rich, then slip out undetected. And he always leaves an engraved card with just the one word on it—Raffles."

"Does he wear disguises to keep from being identified?"

"Only a veneer of charm and good breeding. He's probably a familiar face to the people he encounters on the social circuit, and they don't identify him as a notorious crasher because his mannerisms and appearance make him seem to be one of them. He may even introduce himself by an aristocratic-sounding name."

I finished making a few notes and asked, "Do you have much trouble with crashers?"

"Yes and no. There's a hard core of about a hundred of them in the city who regard it as a kind of sport. They're young, semi-affluent, not very well connected socially, but with aspirations. And relatively harmless. Most of the time they're easy for the security staff to spot: They're not dressed exactly right; they make pigs of themselves at the buffet table and the bar; they don't appear to know anybody. When the guards corner them and ask them to leave, they go without protest. But lately they're becoming more sophisticated and skilled, and there's also been some theft."

"What kind of theft?"

"Oh, expensive party favors. Crystal. Silver cutlery. We're insured against loss, of course, but now—"

A woman in a clown's costume burst into the room. "It's

too tight!" she wailed. "If I try to juggle in this I'll pop my buttons!"

Baldwin sighed. "Call Dress You and explain the problem. Tell them to give you another or make alterations on this one."

"At the last minute?"

"They'll do it. God knows we throw enough business their way."

The woman nodded and left.

Baldwin looked at me and asked, "Where was I?"

"There's been some theft."

"Ah, yes. But that's minor, compared to the Raffles problem. He's sent us a note indicating he has special plans for a party we've organized for this coming Saturday." She took a cream vellum envelope from her desk drawer and passed it over to me.

The typewritten address was that of Wildest Dreams' post office box. I slipped a card from it, saw "Raffles" spelled out in raised lettering. Beneath he'd typed a single line: "I will honor the Colossus.com party with my presence and take action that will astonish you."

"What's Colossus-dot-com?" I asked.

"A big new client. They're one of the hottest dot-coms in Multimedia Gulch, and the party's to commemorate the third anniversary of their founding. The partners, David Keith and Preston Freeman, are both Stanford graduates, under thirty, and about to become very, very rich when the company goes public. We've rented the entire Bakker Mansion on Octavia Street. Ordered the best champagne, liquors, caviar, seafood, filet mignon. The entertainment is big-name. If the party goes well, more business of this type is sure to come our way, and our kids will someday be able to afford the colleges of their choice. But if it doesn't . . ." She shuddered.

I asked, "Do you have any idea what this astonishing action that Raffles promises might be?"

"I can't begin to guess."

"Is there any reason this Raffles would want to ruin you or your partner?"

"As far as I know, he's never set eyes on either of us. We don't interact with the guests—legitimate *or* crashers—at our events."

"Do either of you know anyone who fits his profile?"

"Well, the hosts of the parties we plan. But they're mostly A-list, high-visibility people."

"Has the security staff at one of your events ever roughed up a crasher?"

"God, no! They're told to be discreet so as not to upset the guests. And the crashers don't want a scene, either."

"Okay, now: What exactly do you want me to do? McCone Investigations isn't a security firm, although we have good connections in that area. I can refer you—"

"We're not concerned about security for the event," Barbara Baldwin said. "We want you to identify Raffles and prevent him from ruining the party—and *us*."

• • •

I drove back to Pier 24½ on San Francisco's Embarcadero, a renovated structure in the shadow of the Bay Bridge where my agency occupies half the second story. Instead of following the iron catwalk to my office at the far end, I went the other way and stopped in to see Charlotte Keim, my best operative in the financial area. Keim, a Texas transplant in her twenties, was at her desk, twirling a lock of curly brunette hair around her index finger as she frowned at her computer screen.

"Shar!" she exclaimed. "This data from the new client you assigned me is driving me crazy. Somebody's been fiddling with his accounts like a musician at a barn dance, but I can't figure how."

I glanced at the meaningless columns of numbers on the screen. "If you're hoping for input, you're talking to the wrong person. Even Humphrey would be more helpful." Humphrey was the Boston fern that sat atop her file cabinet.

"Yeah, I know." She swiveled away from the offending figures. "So what's up?"

"Have you heard of an outfit called Colossus-dot-com?"

"Who hasn't? Well, you, of course. They're an on-line service that provides fitness information, helps you tailor your exercise and diet programs to your specific needs and then track how they're working. Company's been around a few years now, and they're planning to float an initial public offering of their stock soon, although it's been delayed twice now. Probably, like a lot of the dot-coms, they look better on paper than they do in fact."

"You know either of the founders?"

"Pres Freeman and Dave Keith? Sure. Oddly enough, I used to date Pres. The two of them make a strange pair. Never agreed on which direction the company was going to take from day one. Dave's really into making money; Pres saw them as bringing proper health and fitness to the masses. Dave invested most of the start-up money, so he wanted to call all the shots. Around the time I was seeing Pres, they had a major blowup and Dave tried to force him out. That would've ruined Pres; he's always been on shaky financial ground. But I guess they smoothed things over, and the IPO will finally go forward."

"You still see Pres?"

"Around, sometimes. We didn't date long. The man's a health nut and a food snob. It drove him crazy when I'd eat pork rinds and drink bourbon and Dr Pepper."

I stared at her.

"Right." Keim nodded. "The man doesn't know what's *good*."

■ ■ ■

When I got to my office I realized there was something else I should have asked Keim and went back along the catwalk. There I found her with her arms around my tall blond nephew, Mick Savage, who had both his hands on her ass. I cleared my throat and they pulled apart, flushing.

"Office romances," I said, shaking my head in mock disapproval. Mick and Charlotte had been living together for a while now, and I was pleased with the way she'd domesticated my younger sister's wild son.

"Actually, she was sexually harassing me," he said.

"Good for her. Listen, have either of you ever crashed a party? I don't mean some beer bust, but a genuine upscale party?"

They exchanged glances.

"I'm asking because I've got a case involving a crasher."

"Well . . ." Charlotte said. "Yeah, we have."

"But not often," Mick added.

"Tell me how you did it."

"First off," he said, "you've got to find out what kind of event it is, then dress to fit in. The first party we crashed was at the St. Francis Yacht Club, and security wasn't so hot.

We just breezed through the door, had a couple of free cocktails and some canapés, and slipped out when we saw one of the guards watching us. The second time we got booted out of the Mark Hopkins ballroom before we even finished our first drinks. And the third time finished us." He shook his head ruefully.

Charlotte laughed. "That time was a benefit for charity at this mansion in Pacific Heights. We wanted to go because a lot of celebrities would be attending. I started talking to a couple on the sidewalk, complimenting the woman on her dress, and the people on the door thought we were with them and let us in without asking for our invitation. And the place was full of celebrities, huh, Mick?"

"Yeah. One of whom was Dad." My former brother-in-law, country music superstar Ricky Savage, lived in the city.

"What did he do?"

"Pointed us out to one of the security people, who escorted us to the door."

I smiled. Ricky must've loved the opportunity to put in his place the son who had given him more than a fair share of trouble. "So what's the appeal of crashing?" I asked.

"The challenge. The thrill of getting away with something. The really great food and drinks. Being around people you only read about in the papers."

"Like your own father."

"Well . . ."

"You ever hear of a crasher who calls himself Raffles?"

"He's legendary."

"Any idea who he is?"

"Nobody knows."

"Know anybody who could give me a lead on him?"

Mick shook his head and glanced at Charlotte. She said,

"I think somebody interviewed him a while back, in that new on-line magazine called *Soiree*. The reporter might be able to help you."

I had a suspicion who that reporter would be. J.D. Smith, my old friend and former *Chronicle* reporter, had recently crossed over into the world of electronic journalism. J.D., who—in whatever medium—always managed to get the most interesting assignments.

■ ■ ■

"Haven't you ever heard of reporters protecting their sources?" J.D. said.

"Oh, come on." I cradled the phone against my shoulder and shifted in my chair so I had a better view of the excursion boats passing on the bay. "I'm not asking you to reveal the identity of someone who's given you information on matters of national security. This is a guy who sneaks into parties, for God's sake."

"The confidentiality rule applies across the board."

"Since when did you become so principled?"

"Since when did you become so *un*principled?"

Impasse. "Okay, let me tell you what your buddy Raffles has been up to lately." I explained about his note to Wildest Dreams Productions.

"So?" J.D. said. "'Astonish' isn't a word that necessarily implies trouble."

"It doesn't imply lack thereof, either. At least not in that context."

"Look, Shar, I can't help you."

"I think you can. Why don't you call Raffles, tell him I want to talk with him about his plans?"

"I suppose I *could* put the ball in his court."

"Of course you can. And if you do, I'll consider your debt canceled."

"Debt? What debt?"

"You remember an evening three years ago when you announced there wasn't a cop within ten blocks, right before you started breaking into that sleazy lawyer's office? And the officer who was parked across the street watching you happened to be a friend of mine?"

"Jesus! I pay and pay—"

"And pay. Call the man, J.D."

■ ■ ■

There's usually a bite to April nights in San Francisco—and most nights at any other time of the year—but on this one the air was balmy. When the phone rang I was sitting on the backyard deck of my small earthquake cottage, glass of wine at hand. I picked up and a cultured male voice said, "Ms. McCone, this is Raffles. J.D. Smith suggested I call you."

"Thanks for phoning so quickly. I'd like to set up a meeting."

"I'm afraid that's impossible. I never allow anyone to learn my true identity."

"What about J.D.?"

"That's different. We're old friends."

"I can promise you the same confidentiality J.D. did."

"That's not the point. What if you were to encounter me while on the social circuit? You'd recognize me, perhaps give me away."

"I'm not likely to attend the same parties as you do," I said dryly. "My name doesn't appear on anybody's A list."

He hesitated. "It's not really necessary we meet, Ms. McCone. The reason I called is to assure you that I'm not

the one who sent that note to Wildest Dreams Productions.
I have no stationery like you described to J.D., only the calling cards. Both, of course, can be made up at any copy shop.
Someone has usurped my good name, and it makes me
angry. When you identify the individual, I'd appreciate you
letting me know who he is."

Of course he would say that. "I'm not sure I believe you."

"And I can understand why you wouldn't. But think of
it: Writing a note to forewarn someone that I plan to crash
a party would be self-defeating. And, frankly, this particular
fete is not on a par with the events I favor. Dot-commers
don't interest me, except when I can get in on an IPO. And
I've heard rumors that Colossus can't get theirs off the ground."

"You forget—the note was addressed to Wildest Dreams."

"I've never heard of them. I don't concern myself with
the little people behind the scenes; it's the rich and powerful who count, and I intend to number among them one
day."

He was vain, and vanity could be played upon. "So what
should be done about this impostor?"

"As I said, when you identify—"

"By then he may already have taken his 'astonishing' action. It'll be too late to save your reputation."

Silence.

"If you really care about exposing this impostor, Raffles,
I have a suggestion . . ."

■   ■   ■

For the rest of the week I delved into the lives of Barbara
Baldwin and Melanie Katz, attempting to identify someone
with a reason to want to ruin them. I had extensive conversations with both women, talked with Baldwin's former hus-

band and two of Katz's former boyfriends, plus three dissatisfied clients and the owner of a rival party-planning company who felt Wildest Dreams had lured clients away from her in an unethical manner. None of the leads got me anywhere, but during our talks I did pick up on certain tensions between the partners.

Baldwin: "Melanie gets sick a lot, and I end up with most of the responsibility heaped on me. And I'm the one who's inconvenienced, because the office is here in my house and all the party crap gets delivered to me."

Katz: "Barbara wants to make the majority of the decisions, even though this is supposed to be an equal partnership, because she invested more money initially."

Baldwin: "Mel doesn't understand business and cost control. If I let her have her way, we'd be bankrupt within six months."

Katz: "Barb is looking to make a ton of money, and lots of times she cuts corners. We can't agree on what the company is supposed to be about. I know she'd like to buy me out, but I've got two kids to support and no other skills. Even if she paid me a good price I'd probably end up broke in a few years."

It made me glad I'd never taken in a partner.

■ ■ ■

On the night of the Colossus.com party I opened my door to a tall, slender stranger in his late twenties, with aristocratic features and finely styled dark hair. He wore a tuxedo and highly polished shoes and—when he saw me—a frown.

"No!" he exclaimed. "Absolutely not!"

I'd been extending my hand to him, but now I withdrew it and stepped back, amazed at receiving such a greeting from someone I'd never laid eyes on before. The man who called himself Raffles strode into my front hall.

"This will never do," he announced.

"What?"

"Just look at you!" He gestured dramatically from my head to my toes.

I glanced down at the red velvet dress that I always trotted out for special occasions.

"The key to dressing for these events," he said, "is understatement. Not red. Not velvet. Not short skirt, garnet earrings, or cleavage. Especially not cleavage. Where is your closet?"

Dumbstruck, I pointed toward the rear of the house.

Raffles grabbed my hand and dragged me through my sitting room and kitchen to the bedroom, where he threw open the closet door and started pawing through what could loosely be termed my wardrobe.

"No," he muttered. "No. No. Certainly not. Never!"

I watched him, turning the phrase "psychological abuse" over in my mind.

"Ahah!" he said triumphantly. "Here it is!"

The garment he brandished at me was a twenty-some-year-old black dress that I'd bought for the funeral of my godmother and never had on since. I'd saved it in case any of the other pious, proper individuals in my life died.

"Put this on," Raffles told me, brushing dust from its shoulders. "Where is your jewelry?"

Still taken aback, I pointed mutely to the box on the bureau. He rummaged through it and produced a pearl necklace and earrings that had been a college graduation present from my parents. I'd seldom worn them.

"These are appropriate. Now, shoes . . ." He glared down

at my T-straps. "Don't you have any black pumps that are simple and elegant?"

As a matter of fact I did: Ferragamos, my one extravagant purchase of the past decade. I went to the closet and held them up for his inspection.

He sighed with relief.

I shooed him out of the bedroom so I could change.

• • •

"That was a novel experience," Raffles said.

"What was?"

"Presenting a bona fide invitation to get into a party."

We were standing in the foyer of the Bakker Mansion, a twenty-room Queen Anne Victorian that had once been a private residence and now belonged to a historical foundation which rented it out for special events. Formally attired partygoers deposited their coats at the checkroom, then moved through the archway to the front parlor, where a sting quartet played. Others carried flutes of champagne and plates piled high with delicacies from the buffet in the dining room. Still others ascended the wide staircase to explore the second-story rooms or to check out the big-name entertainment on the third floor. Raffles kept his eyes on the door, scrutinizing each arrival.

"I'm not sure I like being a legitimate guest," he said.

"Well, after tonight you can go back to your wicked ways."

"They're not really wicked—ah!"

"What?"

"That couple."

They were in their twenties and dressed simply but stylishly. The man said to the woman who was collecting invitations, "My mother's here, and she was supposed to meet us at the door, but we're late and I guess she got tired of waiting."

"I'm sorry, sir, but I can't—"

"Oh, there she is. Mom!" He waved toward the living room. A woman there waved back. The invitation taker glanced her way, but turned toward the couple before the woman frowned, not recognizing them. The couple was admitted immediately.

"Not bad," Raffles said. "For amateur crashers."

A few minutes later an elegantly dressed man appeared and began apologizing for having forgotten his invitation. When the woman said she couldn't admit him without it, he beamed. "My lucky day! Now I get to go home and veg out in front of the tube. Of course, my department manager'll be furious."

The woman hesitated, considering possible repercussions, then passed him through.

"Smooth," Raffles commented.

Within the next half hour he identified three more lone male crashers and then, as the flow of arrivals ebbed, we began drifting through the crowd, keeping tabs on them. In the middle parlor, Raffles spotted a heavyset man of around thirty, who was already beginning to show the effects of too much of the good life, downing champagne and holding court for a circle of admirers.

"Dave Keith," he said. "Just the man to tell me about that IPO. Watch this." He went up to the man and put a hand on his shoulder. "Great party, Dave."

Keith turned, trying to mask his confusion at not being able to place Raffles.

Raffles said, "Amory Thayer, Stanford, ninety-six." He

drew me forward. "And this is Buffy Millhouse, of the Boston branch of the family."

Keith nodded and shook hands with both of us. "So what've you been doing since graduation, Amory?"

"This and that. Venture capital, investments. I've heard good things about Colossus-dot-com. When's your IPO?"

"Not for a while, unfortunately. I've got to . . . do a bit of reorganizing before that happens. You thinking of buying in?"

"Definitely."

Dave Keith's eyes warmed. "Well, splendid. You and I will ride the bubble all the way to the top."

"That we will. Great seeing you, Dave. We'll circulate now."

When we were out of Keith's earshot I said, "*Buffy?* Do I look like a Buffy?"

Raffles studied me. "Perhaps of the vampire-slayer type."

"Oh, thanks. While you were showing off back there, were you also keeping an eye on those crashers?"

"Yes. The fellow who said he wanted to veg out in front of the tube is over by the bar. The couple with the nonexistent mom are stuffing themselves at the buffet."

"And I can see the other three, but security's closing in on one of them."

"Well, that makes our job easier. Ah, I see Preston Freeman. Let's say hello to the other half of the team."

Freeman was the opposite of his partner: He had the lean physique of a mountain biker and was standing alone near the fireplace, looking ill at ease and sipping at what appeared to be mineral water. When Raffles introduced himself as Amory Thayer, Stanford '96, Freeman regarded him with open bewilderment. Even after Raffles introduced me and complimented him on the anniversary party, Keith's partner seemed uncomfortable. I couldn't imagine such a man dating Charlotte Keim.

Raffles said, "I was just talking to Dave, and he indicated your IPO's been delayed."

Freeman looked at him for a moment, then nodded. "Yes, delayed." He glanced around the room at his guests and put on a smile that fit him about as well as his obviously rented formal wear. After an awkward silence he said, "Would you excuse me, please? I need to speak with the caterers."

Raffles watched him walk toward the staircase, then said to me, "He has the social graces of a turnip."

"Well, a lot of these high-tech people don't relate very well."

"I suppose not. Ah, there goes our well-stuffed couple. They're being shown the door."

"That leaves three men who arrived alone. Your impostor could be any one of them."

"My odds are on the fellow who said he wanted to veg out. He's almost as smooth as I." He glanced around. "They're all in the vicinity of the buffet."

"And so's Dave Keith, helping himself to Wildest Dreams canapés and jumbo prawns. At least one of the partners is enjoying the party."

As I watched, a waiter went up to Keith and handed him an envelope. I heard him say, "This was just delivered by messenger." Keith ripped it open, read the message, and frowned. Then he set his plate down and excused himself to the people he was talking with. He headed for the staircase.

"Damn!" Raffles exclaimed softly. "Security just apprehended my prime suspect."

I glanced toward the door, saw the crasher being quietly escorted out.

"Damn!" Raffles repeated. "I wanted to tell that impostor what I thought of him for appropriating my good name. He was using me for his own purposes, and I'd like to know—"

"Be quiet." I'd begun to feel a peculiar uneasiness. Words and phrases that I'd heard over the past few days were filtering through my mind.

At odds about the direction . . . invested more money initially . . . call all the shots . . . looking to make a ton of money . . . buy out . . . force out . . . end up broke . . . on shaky financial ground . . . do a bit of reorganizing . . . IPO . . .

Partners, complaining about partners.

"That wasn't your impostor," I told Raffles. "And Wildest Dreams isn't his target. And you don't go upstairs to talk with the caterers."

"What? What does all that have to do with—"

I hurried to the staircase, pulling him along with me.

Upstairs the rooms glowed with light and guests wandered from one to another, stopping to exclaim over the exquisite decor and costly artworks. From the third floor came the percussive beat of a well-known rock band. I scanned the hallway, saw that a door at its far end was closed, a handwritten PRIVATE sign taped below a brass plaque that said "Renoir Room." I ran to it, threw it open.

Preston Freeman stood on a chair in front of the fireplace, about to lift off the painting that hung above the mantel. Dave Keith lay on the floor, blood oozing from his head. A stained poker leaned against the hearth.

Freeman heard me come in and turned, nearly losing his balance. His face froze in shock.

Raffles stepped up behind me. I said, "There's your impostor."

Freeman leaped from the chair and scrambled toward the door, but Raffles intercepted him and dragged him down. Freeman tried to knee him in the groin, then aimed a kick at my shin as I rushed to help. His foot connected solidly; my leg gave and I fell smack on top of both of them. We flailed around—a many-limbed creature intent on destroying itself—until I got Freeman's arms pinned. Raffles squirmed out from under us, glared at Freeman's inert form, and sat on him.

In the struggle one of us had torn Freeman's jacket pocket. A card and a note protruded from it, the card engraved with the word "Raffles." I took out the note by its edges so as not to smear any fingerprints and read: "Mr. Keith: Meet me in the Renoir Room. I have important information about Mr. Freeman that will clear the way for you buying him out of Colossus.com. A Potential Investor."

I set down the note and closed the door against the crowd that had gathered outside, then said to Freeman, "You were taking the Renoir down so it would look as if your partner was killed when he surprised a burglar. You planned to take away the note and leave Raffles' card in order to implicate him."

Raffles' face darkened with anger. "And I wouldn't have *dared* come forward to proclaim my innocence because there would be too much evidence against me. Besides, why would I? No one knows who I am. But now they will." He grabbed Freeman by the hair and thumped his head against the floor. "Damn you! You've spoiled everything!"

Freeman groaned and muttered something.

"What?" Raffles thumped his head again.

"He told me there wouldn't be any IPO. He wanted me out of the company. But his buyout offer was so low I couldn't have lived a year on it. I was counting on that IPO. I've got debts, big ones. To the kind of people who don't forgive money owed."

Gambling debts, I thought, and almost felt sorry for him.

Behind me Dave Keith moaned and stirred. I went over and helped him sit up. His being alive didn't surprise me; scalp wounds always seem worse than they are because they bleed a lot, and when I'd first seen him I'd noticed the rise and fall of his chest.

It surprised Freeman, though. He turned his head, conflicting emotions passing over his face. Probably relieved that he wouldn't be charged with murder and sick because Keith would be able to testify against him.

Dave Keith stared groggily at his partner for a moment, then said, "Happy anniversary, Pres, you son of a bitch."

ED MCBAIN

Ed McBain is one of the most illustrious names in crime fiction, the creator of the men and women of the 87th Precinct, the greatest sustained series of police novels ever published. Under his real name, Evan Hunter, he has had a long and successful writing career, including the best-selling *The Blackboard Jungle* and the screenplay for Hitchcock's *The Birds*. In 1986 Hunter/McBain became a Grand Master of the Mystery Writers of America, and in 1998 he became the only American ever to receive the British Crime Writers Association's Diamond Dagger Award for lifetime achievement.

FIRST MYSTERIOUS PRESS PUBLICATION:
MCBAIN'S LADIES, 1988

ACTIVITY IN THE FLOOD PLAIN

I moved to East Hadley, Connecticut, because I wanted to get away from memories of the big bad city and a woman named Anita Lopez, who used to pose for me. I am a portrait painter.

At least, that's how I earn my living. My other paintings rarely sell. Anita was the model for twenty canvases with the collective title *The Mayagüez Suite*. I chose the title because Anita herself was from Mayagüez, which is in Puerto Rico. All twenty abstract paintings showed Anita magnificently nude. I was halfway through the twenty-first canvas when she informed me she was pregnant with the child of the short-order cook at Epstein's Deli, around the corner from where I lived and painted in Manhattan. She told me Max— his name was Max Goldberg—was going to marry her and take her to Israel with him. She told me he was going to open his own delicatessen in Tel Aviv. I gave her the half-finished canvas—there was still a lot of work to be done on the breasts—as an engagement present. Then I began look-ing for a house in Connecticut.

The house I found was on the banks of the Pasquetuck River. In the Pequot Indian language, Pasquetuck means "White Man Drown in Shallow Water." I told that to the real estate agent who sold me the house, but she didn't laugh. Actually, I have no idea what Pasquetuck means in Pequot or any other Indian language. Anita once told me, in Spanish, that I had no sense of humor. This was before she met Max, whose riotous sense of humor extended to taking a Puerto Rican girl to live in Tel Aviv. But the river that runs past my land is indeed a shallow one, especially during the hot summer months when rain is scarce. It was difficult to imagine the land ever flooding. In fact, when I bought the house, I didn't know my meager two acres were in the so-called flood plain. Arthur Manning was the first person to inform me of this fact.

Arthur was a Westport architect who'd been recommended to me by a sculptor I knew in Manhattan. Arthur told me he was very impressed with my work. Arthur told me he might even ask me to paint his wife's portrait one day. Meanwhile, he warned me that architectural fees for residential alterations usually came to at least 20 percent of the building costs. To design and supervise the construction of a heated, well-lighted fifteen-by-twenty-foot extension at the rear of my house, Arthur was charging me an hourly rate of $125 for his services, plus $50 an hour for drafting fees. He told me that my little studio room overlooking the river would cost me something like $50,000 to $75,000 before all was said and done.

"Your land is in a flood plain," he said. "But that shouldn't be a problem."

He was smoking a pipe. He looked like an architect in a film from the fifties. Blond hair, a somewhat pudgy face, cheeks ruddy from the sudden September chill outside. I had bought the house and moved into it in July, two weeks after Anita Lopez left for the Holy Land. I had hoped to have the extension built before Christmas, but it was already September and I was just hearing about a flood plain.

"What does that mean?" I asked. "A flood plain?"

"It means that no regulated activity—as defined in the Public Inland Wetland and Watercourse Act of the State of Connecticut—shall be permitted in any area designated as wetlands."

"Wetlands," I said.

"Wetlands," Arthur said, and nodded almost reverently.

"And what exactly are wetlands?"

"Wetlands are established areas whose natural and indigenous character is preserved by law," Arthur said. "They can't be encroached upon for any use that would alter the natural character of the land."

"How would my little studio alter . . . ?"

"Your house is within the hundred-year flood plain. That's an area that's expected to be flooded every hundred years."

"*Expected?*"

"Yes. As calculated by records and charts. There are people who figure all the computations and permutations."

"If it floods only every hundred years," I said, "who gives a damn?"

"They do."

"Who's they?"

"East Hadley's Planning and Zoning Board. But don't worry," Arthur said, puffing on his pipe. "I foresee no difficulties."

. . .

Smoking was forbidden in the East Hadley Town Hall offices, on the second floor of which was located the hearing room in which the Planning and Zoning Board held its regular meeting every Monday night. Three weeks ago, Arthur had submitted his application to the board. Tonight, there was to be a public hearing on it. In addition to our business, the three-man, two-woman board would be addressing three other matters: a modification of conditions for something called the Graham Subdivision, Phase I; a discussion of and decision on conditions for the eleven-lot subdivision called the Graham Subdivision, Phase II; and a discussion of and decision on conditions for the nine-lot subdivision called the Orleans Subdivision.

It seemed to me, and I said so to Arthur, that a mere fifteen-by-twenty-foot extension at the back of an artist's house was hardly in the same commercial league as these big-time subdivisions, and I didn't see why we had to go through all this red tape to get a goddamn permit. He agreed with me.

"*But*," he said, "you have the misfortune of being in the flood plain, and these people at P&Z take their jobs very seriously. They're only an appointed body, Jamie, but their power is absolute. You can't so much as belch in the flood plain without their permission. The problem is they're all laypeople who aren't sure of the issues relating to the federal mandate from FEMA, the Federal Emergency Management Agency that controls *all* flood plain and floodway activity in the United States."

"In other words, they're well-meaning jackasses," I said.

"Not even well-meaning," Arthur said. "I sometimes think they're opposed to *any* sort of development in the flood plain. Simply because they don't really *know* what's good or what's bad for the environment. Even Cassandra Howell isn't as knowledgeable as she appears to be, believe me."

"Who's Cassandra Howell?"

"Chairperson of the board. She merely *acts* as if she knows where the body's buried. That doesn't mean she has the faintest idea of what the federal mandates require. None of them do. They're just a pack of amateurs infatuated with the scent of their own perfume."

At that moment, Cassandra Howell walked into the room.

You have to understand that I was used to big city girls with their big city looks and their big city ways. Cassandra seemed to me the personification of all things wonderfully suburban. Thirty-three years old, maybe thirty-four, she was tall and supple and brimming with good cheer and autumn-spanked beauty. Her smile was as wide as my river. She was wearing a pleated brown woolen skirt, and brown panty hose, and brown loafers, and a russet-colored turtleneck sweater. Her hair was cut short, as black as a raven's wing.

Arthur leaned closer to me.

"Her husband left her five years ago," he whispered. "Got up one morning, ran off, and was never heard from since. I understand she's a trifle bitter about it."

I sat spellbound, listening as she presented our application to the rest of the board. Her voice sounded like buttered rum.

"We are asked to consider an application for a one-story, fifteen-by-twenty-foot addition in an area which is within the footprint of an existing deck," she said. "The deck will be demolished to make way for the addition."

She was pacing back and forth before the long table at which the one other woman and the three men on the board sat listening attentively. In the audience, seated on uncomfortable folding chairs similar to the one I myself sat upon, were the bored attorneys and contractors representing the three subdivision developers applying for permission to go ahead with their doubtless multimillion-dollar projects.

"Footing work will be necessary for the addition," Cassandra said. "This will require digging. The addition will allow expansion of the existing kitchen and dining area, and it will be approximately eighty feet from the Pasquetuck River. The space between the addition and the river is a combination of lawn and an area vegetated with mature trees and saplings. The lawn slopes slightly downgradient near the house and is flat to the edge of the river. The owner of the property is a portrait painter who plans to use the proposed extension as a studio."

She turned to look out over the audience, as if trying to locate me. Our eyes met. My heart stopped. She turned back to the table again.

"The house and addition are within the hundred-year flood plain," she said. "A flood-zone development permit is required for such activity in the flood plain. It is my recommendation that the board walk the site this coming Saturday in order to assist it in making a decision on petitioner's application to build in the flood plain."

She looked out at the audience again, her eyes grazing mine, walked back to the table, dropped her sheaf of notes on it, and then polled the members of the board.

It was agreed that they would meet on my property at eight A.M. this coming Saturday, the fourteenth day of October.

■ ■ ■

I was up at the crack of dawn.

I had been advised by Arthur not to interfere with the work of the board. Let them wander the property at will, do not offer them guidance or advice, just stay out of their way. But I showered and shaved and dressed myself in country threads from L.L. Bean, corduroy trousers and a red flannel shirt, wide black suspenders and ankle-hugging boots. I watched from an upstairs window as they traipsed down to the river and then walked back to the house, pacing off distances, talking animatedly among themselves. Cassandra was wearing gray slacks, the bottoms of which were tucked into shin-high yellow boots. She wore a yellow scarf over her coal-black hair. She wore a short black car coat. She had on no makeup, not even a trace of lipstick. She looked fresh and beautiful and serious and intent as she considered distances and elevations and God knows what else with the other board members. I waited until the rest of them had piled into their cars and were already leaving the property. Then I came out of the house and walked to her just as she was opening the door on the driver's side of her Jeep.

"Miss Howell?" I said.

She turned. Eyes as dark as a Gypsy dancer's, glowing in the bright October sun. A blue jay shrieked across the lawn, scaring me half to death.

"I'm Jamie Larson. I'm the petitioner," I said, and shrugged in what I thought was a boyishly charming manner. This sometimes worked with big city girls. But this was the country.

"How do you do, Mr. Larson?" she said.

I was holding out my hand to her, but she didn't take it. I yanked it back. Put it in my pocket.

"Would you like to come in for a cup of coffee?" I asked. "Take the chill off?"

She was staring at me. Studying my face, searching my eyes. Only the fate of the entire universe hung in the balance.

"Yes, I think I might," she said. And smiled.

. . .

Outside, squirrels rattled through fallen leaves. A lawn sumptuously green after heavy September rains sparkled in the bright golden sunshine. The leaves kept falling, twisting on the mildest of autumn breezes. We sat at the kitchen table sipping coffee, talking about how beautiful it was here by the river, how tranquil, how seemingly removed from everyday troubles and concerns.

"I used to live in this house, you know," she said.

I looked at her.

"Yes," she said, and nodded. "When Michael and I first moved to East Hadley, eight years ago. My husband," she explained.

"I didn't realize that."

"Yes," she said. "I know this house well."

"Would you like to walk through it?"

"Well . . ."

"Please," I said. "You must be curious."

"I must admit I am," she said.

"Come then," I said. "Bring your coffee."

I took her into the living room with its huge walk-in fireplace dating back to the 1800s, and she looked around appraisingly and commented that the bookcases had been moved, and I said the Carters—the family from whom I'd bought the house—had probably done that. She said nothing to this, merely nodded and kept looking at the bookcases as if trying to remember them in their previous location. We went upstairs then, into an area that used to be one large bedroom, but which the Carters had divided into two smaller rooms to accommodate their two children. She told me they'd mentioned they were going to do that when they were still considering buying the house.

"They used to drive up every weekend from New York,"

she said. "I never thought they were serious. I thought they were just enjoying the countryside."

"When was that?" I asked.

"I sold it to them four years ago," she said. "I don't really see two bedrooms as an improvement over the original, do you?"

"Well, I guess the renovation was necessary," I said.

"But this used to be a *huge* guest room," she said, and opened her dark eyes wide. "There were windows all along the front here, overlooking the gardens. I had gardens everywhere," she said, somewhat wistfully. "I loved those gardens so much."

"People change things to suit their needs," I said.

"I suppose," she said, and I wondered immediately if I'd said the wrong thing. Would she now begin thinking that here was another city slicker moving into the house she'd lived in and nurtured, only to make changes that would not be improvements over the original?

"Where do you paint now?" she asked.

"In the dining room," I said. "Until I get my studio."

"Can't you paint up here?"

"Well, I use models, you know. I like to keep the upstairs of the house private."

"Are you a good painter, Mr. Larson?"

"There's a big demand for my portrait work," I said. "As for the *other* paintings . . . well . . . I do those to please myself, I suppose. Would you like to see some of them?"

"Yes, I would," she said.

I took her out to the garage where I had racked my most recent work, the twenty abstract nudes premised on the voluptuous figure and form of the former Anita Lopez, now Anita Goldberg, a housewife and resident of Tel Aviv. "I call them

The Mayagüez Suite," I said, and showed her the first of
them, which represented Anita lying on her side like an oda-
lisque nude descending a staircase horizontally.

"Why, it's beautiful!" she said.

"Would you like to have dinner with me next Saturday
night?" I asked.

"Why, yes," she said, "that might be nice." And smiled.

• • •

Arthur received the letter from the board three days after they
walked my property. It read:

> *Dear Mr. Manning:*
>
> In the opinion of East Hadley's Planning and Zoning
> Board, your proposed plans for expansion of the Larson
> house located in the floodway and flood plain may have
> serious implications downstream. We are therefore ask-
> ing that you submit for our further study and considera-
> tion a topographic survey prepared to Class T-2
> topographic standards, depicting contours at one-foot in-
> tervals, physical improvements, trees twelve inches or
> larger in diameter, wetlands (delineated by a certified soil
> scientist), 100-year flood line (from FEMA mapping) and
> location of the Pasquetuck River. All surveys shall be pre-
> pared in compliance with Sections 20-300b-1 through 20-
> 300b-20 of the Regulations of Connecticut State Agencies.
>
> When we are in receipt of this material, we shall
> promptly schedule another appearance before the board.

The letter was signed by Cassandra Howell, Chairperson.

• • •

"The topographic surveys will cost you between three and four thousand dollars," Arthur told me. "Plus the soil scientist's fee, which won't be as high. Maybe twenty-five hundred or so."

"The whole damn *addition* won't cost more than seventy-five thousand!" I said.

"They're fighting a war of attrition," Arthur said. "They're hoping if they make it difficult enough, you'll simply pack your tent and go away."

"I just got here," I said. "Order the surveys, Arthur."

"Why don't you just paint in your upstairs bedroom?" he suggested.

"Because I don't want my subjects roaming all over the house," I said. "Order the damn surveys."

. . .

My first subject in the town of East Hadley, Connecticut, was an eighty-year-old woman named Hannah Peabody, whose grandchildren had ordered her portrait. I had a difficult time getting her to sit still because all Hannah wanted to do was talk all the time. Or else get up to pee. Hannah peed almost as much as she talked. I had set up a temporary studio in what should have been the dining room, and which would go back to being merely that once the extension was completed. If ever the extension got *started*. If ever the board granted us a permit.

The light was excellent here in the dining room, and the location had the added advantage of being close to the powder room near the entry. Hannah would pop up every five minutes or so and come back some five minutes later, settling again into the chair I'd set up near the bank of windows. When Hannah wasn't peeing, she was talking. I tried to get some painting done in between times.

It was Hannah who told me a little bit about Cassandra Howell's husband who had run away. I welcomed the information; our dinner date was for this coming Saturday night.

"You never would've thought what happened would've happened," Hannah said. "They seemed so much in love. But one day, Michael just upped and left. Like the old joke, you know? Man goes to the grocery store for a pack of cigarettes, never comes back. You'd have thought they were so happy together. But you can't ever tell what's going on in a marriage, can you?"

"Is that really what happened?" I asked. "He went to the grocery store one day . . ."

"Well, no, that's the old *joke*. You don't have much of a sense of humor, do you? What *actually* happened is Michael walked himself to town one afternoon and took either a bus or a train to God knows where, never did get in touch with Cassandra to let her know where he was or what he was doing. Just disappeared from sight. Men do that sometimes, you know. Men are peculiar sometimes. Cassandra sold the house a year or so later. You probably bought it from the Carters, didn't you?"

"Yes," I said. "Why'd she sell it?"

"Bad memories here, I guess. Man leaving her and all. A woman can get used to a lot of things, but not a man leaving her. That's the one thing a woman can't abide. Although, in Cassandra's case, you'd have thought . . ."

Hannah closed her mouth.

"Better get some painting done here, don't you think?" she said.

. . .

To my enormous surprise, there was a little French bistro in East Hadley. To my greater surprise, the food there was really very good. It was Cassandra who originally recommended the place—which I found a bit awkward, to tell the truth, but I was after all new in town and she didn't seem at all embarrassed making the suggestion so why get all macho about it?

The place was very romantic. I considered it a good sign that she'd recommended a romantic place. I considered it a further good sign that she was dressed like a wicked big city girl in very high heels and a sophisticated little black dress fashioned to reveal breasts I hadn't expected to be quite so sumptuous and legs I hadn't suspected to be quite so shapely.

The waiter welcomed her like a cousin from Provence. He told me his name was Henri, and recommended a burgundy that cost sixty-eight dollars, which I figured was reasonable if the wine was truly as excellent as he said it was.

We sipped the wine by candlelight. It *was* truly excellent. Edith Piaf oozed from hidden speakers. Cassandra's eyes were sparkling. She told me again how much she'd loved the paintings in *The Mayagüez Suite*, and I told her the long sad story of my ill-fated romance with Anita Lopez who had run off with a delicatesseur and was now Anita Goldberg. She looked at me through the burning candles. I thought for a moment she would lean across the table and kiss me.

Instead, she said, "Why don't you paint *me* sometime?"

"Sure," I said, "I'd be happy to. What sort of portrait were you thinking of?"

"Actually," she said, "I was thinking of a nude."

. . .

On the Monday following our dinner date, East Hadley's P&Z Board informed us that the surveys and soil analysis—which together had cost me a mere $6,500—were insufficient for them to make a decision on the proposed addition. They were now asking for an engineer's flood-rise report, based on generally accepted engineering formulae and computing the expected rise in the hundred-year flood elevation due to the construction of a proposed fifteen-by-twenty-foot addition within the flood plain. They also wished a cross section cut through the proposed addition to clearly demonstrate the effect of the addition in relation to the entire flood plain.

"I'd like to say something," I said, and got to my feet. "I'm James Larson, it's my property and my house we've been discussing here since September."

"Sit down, Jamie," Arthur whispered.

"I can understand the Board's reluctance to grant permission for any building that might adversely affect the environment," I said, "but . . ."

"Sit *down*," he whispered again.

". . . I don't intend building a fast-food joint or a bowling alley on the Pasquetuck. We're talking about a fifteen-by-twenty-foot extension here, a studio for a working artist, eighty *feet* from the river, and so far it's taken us almost two full months—this is almost the end of October already—to get a simple building permit. Meanwhile, this board has cost me close to eight thousand dollars in legal and other professional fees, and I'm *still* painting in my dining room!"

The room went silent. I looked at the members of the board sitting behind their long table on the platform. Cassandra's eyes met mine. She seemed hurt, as if I'd attacked her, personally, when of course I hadn't. Ellen Krieg, the other woman on the board, was in her fifties. She appeared embarrassed by my outburst. Two of the men seemed amused. The third man, bald and wearing a heavy cardigan sweater, stared out at me for a moment, and then said, "I'm Jerry Addison. I must say I tend to agree with you, Mr. Larson. I suppose at times we do seem like a five-star chamber here. The truth is we don't always agree, even among ourselves, but we do try to get the job done."

"I just don't understand this excessive *caution*," I said. "I don't know what this engineer's report will cost me . . ."

"You can figure another three thousand dollars," Arthur said, loud enough for everyone to hear.

"Well, there you are," I said. "The longer this thing drags on . . ."

"Believe me," Addison said, "there are some of us on this board who've been trying to expedite your permit."

"Well, I hope you'll reach a decision soon. If this were New York . . ."

"But it isn't, you see," Cassandra said all at once.

"*If* it were, you'd be staring at a lawsuit."

"Oh Jesus," Arthur whispered.

"Which is just what I'm trying to *avoid* here!" Cassandra said.

"Why don't we just grant the damn permit?" Addison said. "We've studied the plans, we've walked . . ."

"What happens fifty years from now?" Cassandra said. "What happens if we grant this permit, and Mr. Larson tears down the deck, and digs his footings, and puts up his proposed studio—and there's a flood?"

"Oh, for God's sake, Cassandra," Ellen Krieg said. "There won't be any flood, and you know it!"

"What if his studio gets washed away in a flood . . ."

"The river's only three feet deep on his property," one of the men on the board said.

"What if his studio gets carried downstream?" Cassandra insisted.

"No such thing has happened in the past two hundred years!" Addison shouted.

"What if his studio crashes into somebody's living room? What if those downstream people sue the town of East Hadley? Are your children or your children's children going to pay the damages?"

The room went silent.

"Mr. Larson," Cassandra said, "we've asked for an engineer's report. When we receive it, we'll consider your application further." She turned away. "Are the lawyers for DBD Partners Land Tech present?" she asked.

"We're here, Madam Chairperson," a man in a striped suit said, leaping to his feet.

"Are you ready to discuss the proposed lot-line changes for the Farm Hill Road subdivision? Those would be the six lots off Sleepy Hollow Lane."

"We are."

I was still standing.

Cassandra's dark eyes met mine. Locked with mine. There was something like a warning in them.

"Was there anything else, Mr. Larson?" she asked.

"Not right this minute," I said.

"Then thank you," she said, dismissing me.

The next day she called to ask when she might start posing for me.

On Saturday, I painted her nude for the first time.

And went to bed with her that very same day.

. . .

"It would seem to me," she said, "that you'd *cherish* the privacy of an upstairs studio."

"How do you figure that?"

We were in my bedroom. On my bed. We were both naked. Half an hour ago, Cassandra had been lying nude on a divan downstairs, posing for me. Now we were in each other's arms.

"I'm assuming I'm not the first model to find her way into your bed . . ."

"Cassandra . . ."

"Please, we're both grown-ups. What I'm saying is that it would surely be more convenient—and less expensive in the long run—to convert one of these upstairs bedrooms into a studio. Then you wouldn't have to tear up the house again . . ."

"I haven't torn it up before."

"Well, the Carters moved those bookcases and converted the guest room . . ."

"To suit their needs," I reminded her.

"It seems to me *your* needs would be satisfied by simply . . ."

"My needs would be satisfied by kissing you right this minute," I said.

"Why are you being so stubborn?" she asked.

"What is it?" I asked. "Have you decided *never* to grant the permit? Are you breaking the news to me gently? Is that it?"

"No, that isn't it," she said. "Anyway, it's not *my* decision alone to make. There are five of us on the board, you know. And by the way, it's unethical of you to ask the *Chairperson* of the board a question like that when she's nude in your bed."

"Naked in my bed," I said. "When you were downstairs

on the divan, you were nude. Up here in my bed, you're naked."

"I fail to see the difference."

"Which is why you fail to see the difference between a studio and a bedroom."

"I don't know why you insist on making things so difficult," she said, and sighed deeply. "Why don't you just paint upstairs here, and kiss me the way you said you would?"

"I'll kiss you," I said, "but I won't paint upstairs here."

■ ■ ■

On Monday evening, November 13, Mr. Samuel McReady of McReady Engineering in New Canaan presented his report to the board. McReady was a tall, white-haired man in his late fifties, I guessed. There was a no-nonsense air about him as he faced the long table behind which sat the heart-stoppingly beautiful Cassandra Howell and the four board members.

"McReady Engineering Associates was retained by Arthur Manning, Architect," he said, "to provide flood-plain computations for a proposed addition to an existing dwelling at 87 Sector Road in the town of East Hadley, Connecticut . . ."

I knew what was in his report. This was hardly suspenseful to me. Cassandra knew what was in it, too. She had been leafing ahead through the typewritten pages as he spoke.

"Based on our computations," McReady said, "the predicted increase in flood elevation due to the decreased flood storage volume within the site is zero point zero zero six feet. That's approximately one-sixteenth of an inch. It is our opinion that this computed rise is negligible."

He looked at the table where the board sat.

He nodded his head for emphasis.

"It is clear," he said, "that the proposed addition lies in

the flow shadow of the existing house. The existing house is what defines the hydraulic limitation of the existing flood plain, and the proposed addition will do nothing to alter that capacity. In brief, there will be no adverse effect on flooding due to this proposal. Moreover, it is the conclusion of this report and the opinions of this office that the construction of the proposed addition will have no adverse impacts to the adjoining property owners."

He looked up at the table again.

"Thank you," he said.

"Thank you, Mr. McReady," Cassandra said. "We'll take your report into consideration when making our decision. Was that all for this evening, Mr. Manning?"

Arthur nodded, and was waving away any further discussion. When I got to my feet, he sighed deeply. I was certain the board could hear him all the way up there on the platform.

"Madam Chairperson," I said, "I would merely like to ask that we now bring this matter to a climax as swiftly as possible."

"That is surely a consummation devoutly to be wished," Cassandra said, and smiled, and lowered her eyes to the pages on the table before her.

I painted her again that Saturday, and on Monday morning, Arthur received another letter from the board.

Dear Mr. Manning:

I am sorry to report that East Hadley's Planning and Zoning Board is still of the opinion that your proposed plans for expansion of the Larson house may have serious implications downstream. We are asking, therefore, that you review the plans with the State of Connecticut's

Department of Environmental Protection. We have this date mailed the original of the enclosed letter to Mr. Franklin Garth, Director of Inland Water Resources in Hartford. Please contact him at your convenience.

The letter to Hartford read:

Dear Mr. Garth:

The above referenced application is before East Hadley's Planning and Zoning Board. It proposes construction in the floodway.

Because the applicant is insistent, we would appreciate the DEP reviewing the plans and sending us your comments.

Thank you for your consideration.

Both letters were signed by Cassandra Howell, Chairperson.

· · ·

It began snowing two days before Thanksgiving.

I asked Ralph, the man who plowed my driveway, to shovel off all the walks and the back deck as well. He was a man in his late sixties, weathered and gnarled, and it was a bitterly cold day. Along around eleven, while he was still working out there, I invited him in for a cup of coffee. We sat at the kitchen table, steam rising from the mugs, fat lazy flakes still falling from the sky.

"I hear you'll be putting on another room," he said.

"Well, if we ever get a permit," I told him.

"Will you be planting gardens again?"

"I'm not much of a gardener," I said.

"The Howells had the prettiest gardens," he said. "Ran from the back of the house here almost halfway down to the river. There's good sun this side of the house, you know. Them gardens were really something."

"What happened to them?"

"She tore 'em out after Mr. Howell left. Guess she didn't want anything reminded her of him. Put in a lawn and a deck instead—well, the one I'm shoveling clear of snow today. This was some five years ago," he said. "Before the Carters bought the place."

"Did she need a permit for the deck?" I asked.

I was making a joke. If the chairperson of East Hadley's Planning and Zoning Board, a known pain in the ass when it came to granting permits for any activity in the flood plain, was *herself* considering the construction of a—well, I guess you had to be there.

"Don't suppose she did," Ralph said. "The deck being directly at ground level and all. But who knows how they figure these things? I sure don't."

"I don't, either," I said. "Why'd he leave her, anyway, would you know?"

"Mr. Howell? Well, he always did have an eye for the ladies, you know."

"You think another woman was involved, is that it?"

"Man just ups and leaves without a tip of the hat, I'd say Churchy La Flame, yes."

"Is that what he did? Just walked out one day?"

"So the story goes," Ralph said.

"Walked over to the railroad station . . ."

"Or the bus terminal, whichever."

"Hopped a train to Nebraska or Kentucky, huh?"

"Or River City Junction, Iowa. Wherever."

"With another woman."

"Could be."

"So she tore up all her gardens . . ."

"Is what she done."

". . . and built herself a deck."

"Same one right outside the windows here. Was my cousin Rollie and his crew put it in. Took 'em most of three weeks to finish the job, a good solid deck." He drained his coffee cup, set it back on the table. "Which I better get out there and finish shoveling," he said, "'fore another two inches accumulates. Thanks for the coffee, Mr. Larson."

"Thanks for the good talk," I said.

■ ■ ■

Cassandra called me the very next day.

"May I come over?" she said.

"Yes," I said.

"Now?" she said.

"Whenever," I said.

She arrived ten minutes later. She was wearing a bulky green turtleneck sweater and a heavy woolen skirt to match, the black car coat over them, a long striped college-boy muffler trailing. She was grinning from ear to ear as she climbed down out of the Jeep. Her short black hair danced in a fierce wind that blew off the river. We kissed.

"I have something for you," she said, and took an envelope from her tote bag. The return address on it was:

STATE OF CONNECTICUT

DEPARTMENT OF ENVIRONMENTAL PROTECTION

BUREAU OF WATER MANAGEMENT

"Read it," she said, and handed the envelope to me. I unfolded the single sheet of paper inside it. The letter was addressed to Ms. Cassandra Howell.

Dear Ms. Howell:

I am in receipt of your letter to Mr. Garth of the Inland Water Resources Division of the Connecticut Department of Environmental Protection. Your letter references the plans for work within the flood plain portion of the Pasquetuck River in East Hadley as mapped by FEMA and the National Flood Insurance Program Floodway Maps.

The most critical part of the plan includes the installation of a 15' x 20' addition to the existing house structure. This addition is located on the south side of the existing structure, which happens to be on the downstream side of the structure as this river is flowing from north to south at this location. This addition is also located in the flowline "shadow" of the structure.

Construction within such a flowline-shadow area rarely affects water surface profiles. For this reason, an engineer reviewing the placement of the addition does not always have to perform a detailed hydraulic analysis in order to prove that the addition causes no adverse hydraulic impacts.

Mr. Samuel McReady, P.E., states in his hydraulic report that the addition lies within the shadow of the existing structure. I agree with Mr. McReady's conclusion.

In short, this construction will not affect river hydraulics in this section of the river.

If you have any additional questions, please feel free to contact me.

The letter was signed by Jason L. Carpenter III, Supervising Civil Engineer.

"Congratulations," Cassandra said, and kissed me again. "Want to go away together for Thanksgiving?"

. . .

I called Arthur with the good news. He told me Cassandra had already called to say our petition would undoubtedly be approved at the Monday meeting after Thanksgiving, and that we could start demolishing the deck and digging the ground for our footings as soon as we had the signed piece of paper in our hands.

That Wednesday night, Cassandra and I left for a little inn in Vermont. The flood plain seemed very far away. We shopped antiques stores and drank mulled cider. We ice-skated on a pond behind the inn and took long walks in a countryside crackling with color. We made love at night in an eaved and shuttered room and slept under down comforters.

In bed on our last night there, cradled in my arms, the wind whistling in the trees outside, she lay awake for a very long while.

"What is it?" I asked.

"A favor."

"Name it."

"Withdraw your application."

"What do you mean? It's about to be *granted.*"

"Please withdraw it, Jamie. You don't need that studio. You can paint somewhere else in the house."

The room was silent except for the sound of the insistent wind.

"I don't understand," I said.

"I'll lose the chair," she said. "They'll vote Jerry Addison in as chairman."

"Why would they do that?"

"It was my idea to go to Hartford. Jerry resisted it, he was in favor of granting you the permit all along. But I had to protect the board, don't you see? I wanted to have a higher authority to quote if ever there was any trouble downstream. I didn't want the board to be sued later on."

"But Hartford *okayed* my proposal. I don't see . . ."

"That's just the point. Jerry will use that to prove I was being overly cautious. Wasting everyone's time. An unsuitable chairperson. But if you withdraw your application . . ."

"You can't ask me to do that."

"I am asking you. The board will think I was right all along. They'll think *you* were the one wasting our time."

"But I wasn't."

"It's what they'll think."

"But I *wasn't* wasting anyone's time. I *wanted* that studio, I *still* want it. I'm a working artist. I need a space where I can work. Cassandra, you can't really be asking me to get involved in the petty politics of . . ."

"I don't want to lose that chair," she said.

"I'm sorry. I can't do it."

"Okay, thank you," she said, and rolled away from me.

In a little while, I heard her even breathing and knew she was asleep.

I lay awake for most of the night.

. . .

In the morning, she seemed to have forgotten the harsh words we'd exchanged the night before. We made love in sunlight streaming through the dormer windows. We had breakfast at eleven and then packed our bags and drove leisurely down back roads, stopping at antiques shops and apple stands, discovering town fairs along the way. We did not get back to Connecticut until just before dinner. We ate dinner by candlelight in the dining room of my house, where my paints and easels still stood against one wall.

On Monday evening, November 27, Jerome Addison, the P&Z Board member who'd favored granting me a permit all along, moved that the application of James Larson to conduct a regulated activity in an inland wetland and/or watercourse area located at 87 Sector Road as proposed and shown on a plan dated August 11 and revised August 23, be approved. The motion was seconded by Ellen Krieg and was carried unanimously.

All that following week, I painted Cassandra Howell in the nude.

On Monday morning, she left town as suddenly as her husband had.

■ ■ ■

Every weekday morning, the East Hadley *Herald* ran a report titled "The East Hadley Police Blotter." Among the crimes reported on Tuesday morning, December 5, the day after demolition of my deck began, were the following:

> Two stone statues were reportedly stolen from a residence on Carlyle Street. The two-foot statues of a pig and a dog were stolen separately over the weekend from the front lawn. They are valued at $175 and $250.

Workmen digging footings for an extension to a house on Sector Road reported finding a human skeleton buried some four feet deep. Both workmen are from Brazil and do not speak good English, police said, so an interpreter was brought to the scene to help translate.

A resident on Littlejohn Avenue reported a Compaq laptop and a Datacom computer test cable stolen from a GMC truck parked in the driveway Sunday night. The computer is valued at . . .

On Thursday morning, December 7, the police in Wichita, Kansas, telephoned the police in East Hadley, Connecticut, to say they had arrested a woman driving a Jeep over the posted speed limit on the interstate, and that her driver's license identified her as the fugitive named in East Hadley's all-points bulletin.

Cassandra Howell was returned to Connecticut the very next day, to answer charges of first-degree murder. It seemed that a dental chart obtained from a Dr. Nathan Neuberger, who used to be Michael Howell's orthodontist, matched the teeth on the skeleton the Brazilians had found under my deck.

■   ■   ■

Since the only cells in town were the two small holding cells at the back of the police station, Cassandra was moved to the county jail over at the county seat. It was there that I went to visit her shortly before Christmas.

She looked pale in her gray prison threads. She wore no makeup, but then she rarely had. She said she was happy I was there. I told her I hoped she didn't think I *wanted* those two Brazilian workmen to find the skeleton under my deck . . .

"Well, *my* deck, to be more accurate," she said, and smiled. "Since I was the one who had it built five years ago."

"What I mean . . . if I'd have known . . ."

"Yes, but of course, you didn't."

"Why'd you kill him, Cassandra?"

"Well, maybe because the son of a bitch was cheating on me, hmm?" she said, and smiled again, and I remembered her smiling up at me that day she accepted my invitation to come in for a cup of coffee. "It got to be too much, Jamie. So one night I confronted him, and he admitted it, and I picked up a bread knife from the kitchen counter . . ."

I could not imagine her picking up a bread knife.

". . . and stabbed him," she said.

I could not imagine her stabbing anyone.

"I buried him at the back of the house," she said, and nodded with a finality that was chilling. "Dug up all the gardens so nobody'd think to question the fresh earth. I loved those gardens so much. But then . . ."

She hesitated.

"I loved *him* so much, too," she said, and nodded again.

The cell went silent. She sat on the edge of her cot like a child in a gray school uniform, her hands folded in her lap, her dark head bent. She did not look up at me. I wanted to see her eyes, but she did not look up. "I had the deck built afterward," she said. "I never in a million years expected anyone would tear it down and go digging for him."

She looked up suddenly. Her eyes were brimming with tears.

"But then you came along, didn't you, Jamie? You and your dear innocent need for a studio."

"Cassandra . . ."

"I'm sorry I had to fight your application so hard," she said. "But I knew if it was ever granted, they'd start digging." She smiled again. Tears were streaming down her face, but she was smiling. "I'm so sorry," she said. "Please forgive me, Jamie. I don't want you to think I deceived you. I wasn't trying to bribe you, Jamie."

"I never thought you were."

"I went to bed with you because you made me feel beautiful and desirable, and I hadn't felt that way in a long while. Not to bribe you, Jamie." She reached out and took my hand. "Was I a good model?" she asked.

"You were a wonderful model," I said.

"Better than Anita Lopez?"

"Better than anyone."

"If only we'd met . . ." she started.

She shook her head.

"But then . . ."

She shook her head again.

"I'm sorry," she said.

. . .

I have lived in that house for a year and a half now.

I have never sold the eight paintings I did of Cassandra Howell, nor have I ever painted another nude. All I do now is portrait work.

Every time it rains, I wonder if the property will be flooded.

Maybe that's why I work in one of the upstairs bedrooms, and not in the new studio at the back of the house.

STUART M. KAMINSKY

Stuart M. Kaminsky won the Edgar Award for Best Novel for A *Cold Red Sunrise*. He writes four quite different and successful mystery series: the Toby Peters historical private eye novels, the Abe Lieberman detective series, the Lew Fonesca mysteries, and the Porfiry Rostnikov police novels. He also authored two original *Rockford Files* novels. He has written forty published novels, thirty-five published short stories, and four produced screenplays.

FIRST MYSTERIOUS PRESS PUBLICATION:
BURIED CAESARS, 1989

SOMETIMES SOMETHING GOES WRONG

You sure?"

Beemer looked at Pryor and said, "I'm sure. One year ago. This day. That jewelry store. It's in my book."

Pryor was short, thin, nervous. Dustin Hoffman on some kind of speed produced by his own body. His face was flat, scarred from too many losses in the ring for too many years. He was stupid. Born that way. Punches to the head hadn't made his I.Q. rise. But Pryor did what he was told and Beemer liked telling Pryor what to do. Talking to Pryor was like thinking out loud.

"One year ago. In your book," Pryor said, looking at the jewelry store through the car window.

"In my book," Beemer said, patting the right pocket of his black zipper jacket.

"And this is . . . ? I mean, where we are?"

"Northbrook. It's a suburb of Chicago," said Beemer patiently.

Pryor nodded as if he understood. He didn't really, but if Beemer said so, it must be so. He looked at Beemer, who sat behind the wheel, his eyes fixed on the door of the jewelry store. Beemer was broad-shouldered, well built from three years with the weights in Stateville and keeping it up when he was outside. He was nearing fifty, blue eyes, short, razor haircut, gray-black hair. He looked like a linebacker, a short linebacker. Beemer had never played football. He had robbed two Cincinnati Bengals once outside a bar, but that was the closest he got to the real thing. Didn't watch sports on the tube. In prison he had read, wore glasses. Classics. For over a year. Dickens. Hemingway. Steinbeck. Shakespeare. Freud. Shaw, Irwin, and George Bernard. Then one year to the day he started, Beemer stopped reading. Beemer kept track of time.

Now, Beemer liked to keep moving. Buy clothes, eat well, stay in classy hotels when he could. Beemer was putting the cash away for the day he'd feel like retiring. He couldn't imagine that day.

"Tell me again why we're hitting it exactly a year after we hit it before," Pryor said.

Beemer checked his watch. Dusk. Almost closing time. The couple who owned and ran the place were always the last ones in the mall besides the Chinese restaurant to close. On one side of the jewelry store, Gortman's Jewelry and Fine Watches, was a storefront insurance office. State Farm. Frederick White the agent. He had locked up and gone home. On the other side, Himmell's Gifts. Stuff that looked like it would break if you touched it in the window. Glassy-looking birds and horses. Glassy, not classy. Beemer liked touching real class, like really thin glass wineglasses. If he settled down, he'd buy a few, have a drink every night, run his finger around the rim and make that ringing sound. He didn't know how to do that. He'd learn.

"What?"

"Why are we here again?" Pryor asked.

"Anniversary. Our first big score. Good luck. Maybe. It just feels right."

"What did we get last time?"

The small strip mall was almost empty now. Maybe four cars if you didn't count the eight parked all the way down at the end by the Chinese restaurant. Beemer could take or leave Chinese food, but he liked the buffet idea. Thai food. That was his choice. Tonight they'd have Thai. Tomorrow they'd take the watches, bracelets, rings to Walter on Polk Street. Walter would look everything over, make an offer. Beemer would take it. Thai food. That was the ticket.

"We got six thousand last time," Beemer said. "Five minutes' work. Six thousand dollars. More than a thousand a minute."

"More than a thousand a minute," Pryor echoed.

"Celebration," said Beemer. "This is a celebration. Back where our good luck started."

"Back light went out," Pryor said, looking at the jewelry store.

"We're moving," Beemer answered, getting quickly out of the car.

They moved right toward the door. Beemer had a Glock. His treasure. Read about it in a spy story in a magazine. Had to have it. Pryor had a piece-of-crap street gun with tape on the handle. Revolver. Six or eight shots. Piece of crap but a bullet from it would hurt going in and might never come out. People didn't care. You put a gun in their face they didn't care if it was precision or zip. They knew it could blow out their lights.

Beemer glanced at Pryor, keeping pace at his side. Pryor had dressed up for the job. He had gone through his bag at the motel, asked Beemer what he should wear. Always asked Beemer. Asked him if he should brush his teeth. Well, maybe not quite, but asked him almost everything. The distance to the moon. Could eating Equal really give you cancer. Beemer always had an answer. Quick, ready. Right or wrong. He had an answer.

Pryor was wearing blue slacks and a Tommy Hilfiger blue pullover short-sleeved shirt. He had brushed his hair, polished his shoes. He was ready. Ugly and ready.

Just as the couple inside turned off their light Beemer opened the door and pulled out his gun. Pryor did the same. They didn't wear masks. Artist's sketches were for shit. Ski masks itched. Sometimes Beemer wore dark glasses. That's if they were working the day. Sometimes he had a Band-Aid on his cheek. Let them remember that or the fake mole he got from Gibson's Magic Shop in Fayetteville, North Carolina. That was a bad hit. No more magic shops. He had scooped up a shopping bag of tricks and practical jokes. Fake dog shit. Fake snot you could hang from your nose. He threw it all away. Kept the mole though. Didn't have it on now.

"Don't move," he said.

The couple didn't move. The man was younger than Beemer by a decade. Average height. He had grown a beard in the last year. Looked older. Wearing a zipper jacket. Blue. Beemer's was black. Beemer's favorite colors were black and white. That was the way he liked things. The woman was blond, somewhere in her thirties, sort of pretty, too thin for Beemer's tastes. Pryor remembered the women. He never touched them but he remembered and talked about them at night in the hotels or motels. Stealing from good-looking women was a high for Pryor. That and good kosher hot dogs. Chicago was always good for hot dogs if you knew where to go. Beemer knew. On the way back, they'd stop at a place he knew on Dempster. Make Pryor happy. Sit and eat a big kosher or two, lots of fries, ketchup, onions, hot peppers. Let Pryor talk about the woman.

She looked different. She was wearing a green dress. She was pregnant. That was it.

"No," she said.

"Yes," said Beemer. "You know what to do. Stand quiet. No alarms. No crying. Nothing stupid. Boy or a girl?"

Pryor was behind the glass counters, opening them quickly, shoveling, clinking, into the Barnes & Noble bag he had taken from his back pocket. There was a picture of Sigmund Freud on the bag. Sigmund Freud was watching Beemer. Beemer wondered what Freud was thinking.

"Boy or girl?" Beemer repeated. "You know if it's going to be a boy or a girl?"

"Girl," said the man.

"You got a name picked out?"

"Melissa," said the woman.

Beemer shook his head and said, "Too . . . I don't know . . . too what everybody else is doing. Something simple. Joan. Molly. Agnes. The simple is different. Hurry it up," he called to Pryor.

"Hurry it up, right," Pryor answered, moving faster, the B&N bag bulging, Freud looking a little plump and not so serious now.

"We'll think about it," the man said.

Beemer didn't think so.

"Why us?" the woman said. Anger. Tears were coming. "Why do you keep coming back to us?"

"Only the second time," said Beemer. "Anniversary. One year ago today. Did you forget?"

"I remembered," said the man, moving to his wife and putting his arm around her.

"We won't be back," Beemer said as Pryor moved across the carpeting to the second showcase.

"It doesn't matter," said the man. "After this we won't be able to get insurance."

"Sorry," said Beemer. "How's business been?"

"Slow," said the man with a shrug. The pregnant woman's eyes were closed.

Pryor scooped.

"You make any of this stuff?" Beemer asked, looking around. "Last time there were some gold things, little animals, shapes, birds, fish, bears. Little."

"I made those," the man said.

"See any little animals, gold?" Beemer called to Pryor.

"Don't know," said Pryor. "Just scooping. Wait. Yeah, I see some."

Beemer looked at his watch. He remembered where he got it. Right here. One year ago. He held up the watch to show the man and woman.

"Recognize it?" he said.

The man nodded.

"Keeps great time," said Beemer. "Class."

"You have good taste," the man said.

"Thanks," said Beemer, ignoring the sarcasm. The man had a right. He was being robbed. He was going out of business. This was a going-out-of-business nonsale. The man wasn't old. He could start again, work for someone else. He made nice little gold animals. He was going to be a father. The watch told Beemer that they had been here four minutes.

"Let's go," he called to Pryor.

"One more minute. Two more. Should I look in the back?"

Beemer hesitated.

"Anything back there?" Beemer asked the man.

The man didn't answer.

"Forget it," he called to Pryor. "We've got enough."

Pryor came out from behind the case. B&N bag bulging. More than they got the last time. Then Pryor tripped. It happens. Pryor tripped. The bag fell on the floor. Gold and time went flying, a snow or rain of gold and silver, platinum and rings. And Pryor's gun went off as he fell.

The bullet hit the man in the back. The woman screamed. The man went to his knees. His teeth were clenched. Nice white teeth. Beemer wondered if such nice white teeth could be real. The woman went down with the man, trying to hold him up.

Pryor looked at them, looked at Beemer, and started to throw things back in the bag. Wait. That wasn't Freud. Beemer tried to remember who it was. Not Freud. George Bernard Shaw. It was George Bernard Shaw with wrinkled brow who looked up at Beemer, displeased.

"An accident," Beemer told the woman, who was holding her husband, who now bit his lower lip hard. Blood from the bite. Beemer didn't want to know what the man's back looked like or where the bullet had traveled inside his body. "Call an ambulance, Nine one one. We never shot anybody before. An accident."

It was more than five minutes now. Pryor was breathing hard trying to get everything. On his knees, scampering like a crazy dog.

"Put the gun away," Beemer said. "Use both hands. Hurry up. These people need a doctor."

Pryor nodded, put the gun in his pocket, and gathered glittering crops. The man had fallen, collapsed on his back.

The woman looked up at Beemer, crying. Beemer didn't want her to lose her baby.

"He have insurance?" he asked.

She looked at him, bewildered.

"Life insurance?" Beemer explained.

"Done," said Pryor with a smile. His teeth were small, yellow.

The woman didn't answer the question. Pryor ran to the door. He didn't look back at what he had done.

"Nine one one," Beemer said, backing out of the store.

Pryor looked both ways and headed for the car. Beemer was a foot out the door. He turned and went back in.

"Sorry," he said. "It was an accident."

"Get out," the woman screamed. "Go away. Go away. Go away."

She started to get up. Maybe she was crazy enough to attack him. Maybe Beemer would have to shoot her. He didn't think he could shoot a pregnant woman.

"Joan," he said, stepping outside again. "Joan's a good name. Think about it. Consider it."

"Get out," the woman screamed.

Beemer got out. Pryor was already in the car. Beemer ran. Some people were coming out of the Chinese restaurant. Two guys in baseball hats. From this distance, about forty yards, they looked like truckers. There weren't any trucks in the lot. They were looking right at Beemer. Beemer realized he was holding his gun. Beemer could hear the woman screaming. The truckers could probably hear her too. He ran to the car, got behind the wheel. Pryor couldn't drive, never learned, never tried.

Beemer shot out of the parking lot. They'd need another car. Not a problem. Night. Good neighborhood. In and gone in something not too new. Dump it. No prints. Later buy a five-year-old GEO, Honda, something like that. Legal. In Beemer's name.

"We got a lot," Pryor said happily.

"You shot that guy," Beemer said, staying inside the speed limit, heading for the expressway. "He might die."

"What?" asked Pryor.

"You shot that man," Beemer repeated, passing a guy in a blue BMW. The guy was smoking a cigarette. Beemer didn't smoke. He made Pryor stop when they'd gotten together. Inside. In Stateville, he was in a cell with two guys who smoked. Smell had been everywhere. On Beemer's clothes. On the pages of his books.

People killed themselves. Alcohol, drugs, smoking, eating crap that told the blood going to their heart that this was their territory now and there was no way they were getting by without surgery.

"People stink," said Beemer.

Pryor was poking through the bag. He nodded in agreement. He was smiling.

"What if he dies?" Beemer said.

"Who?"

"The guy you shot," said Beemer. "Shot full of holes by someone she knows."

The expressway was straight ahead. Beemer could see the stoplight, the big green sign.

"I don't know her," Pryor said. "Never saw her before."

"One year ago," Beemer said.

"So? We don't go back. The guy dies. Everybody dies. You said so," Pryor said, feeling proud of himself, holding G. B. Shaw to his bosom. "We stopping for hot dogs? That place you said? Kosher. Juicy."

"I don't feel like hot dogs," said Beemer.

He turned onto the expressway, headed south toward Chicago. Jammed. Rush hour. Line from here to forever. Moving maybe five, ten miles an hour. Beemer turned on the radio and looked in the rearview mirror. Cars were lined up behind him. A long showroom of whatever you might want. Lights on, creeping, crawling. Should have stayed off the expressway. Too late now. Listen to the news, music, voices that made sense besides his own. An insulting talk show host would be fine.

"More than we got last time," Pryor said happily.

"Yeah," said Beemer.

"A couple of hot dogs would be good," said Pryor. "Celebrate."

"Celebrate what?"

"Anniversary. We've got a present."

Pryor held up the bag. It looked heavy. Beemer grunted. What the hell. They had to eat.

"Hot dogs," Beemer said.

"Yup," said Pryor.

Traffic crawled. The car in front of Beemer had a bumper sticker: DON'T BLAME ME. I VOTED LIBERTARIAN.

What the hell was that? Libertarian. Beemer willed the cars to move. He couldn't do magic. A voice on the radio said something about Syria. Syria didn't exist for Beemer. Syria, Lebanon, Israel, Bosnia. You name it. It didn't really exist. Nothing existed. No place existed until it was right there to be touched, looked at, held up with a Glock in your hand.

Gluck, gluck, gluck, gluck, gluck.

Beemer heard it over the sound of running engines and a horn here and there from someone in a hurry to get somewhere in a hurry. He looked up. Helicopter. Traffic watch from a radio or television station? No. It was low. Cops. The truckers from the Chinese restaurant? Still digesting their fried wonton when they went to their radios or a pay phone or a cell phone or pulled out a rocket.

Cops were looking for a certain car. Must be hundreds, thousands out here. Find Waldo, only harder. Beemer looked in his rearview mirror. No flashing lights. He looked up the embankment to his right. Access drive. The tops of cars. No lights flashing. No uniforms dashing. No dogs barking. Just *gluck, gluck, gluck.* Then a light. Pure white circle down on the cars in front. Sweeping right to left, left to right. Pryor had no clue. He was lost in Rolexes and dreams of french fries.

Did the light linger on them? Imagination? Maybe. Description from the hot-and-sour-soup-belching truckers? Description from the lady with the baby she was going to name Melissa when Joan would have been better? Joan had been Beemer's mother's name. He hadn't suggested it lightly.

So they had his description. Stocky guy with short gray hair, about fifty, wearing a black zipper jacket. Skinny guy carrying a canvas bag filled with goodies. A jackpot piñata, a heist from St. Nick.

Traffic moved, not wisely or well, but it moved, inched. Music of another time. Tony Bennett? No, hell no. Johnny Mathis singing "Chances Are." Should have been Tommy Edwards.

"Let's go. Let's go," Beemer whispered to the car ahead.

"Huh?" aked Pryor.

"There's a cop in a helicopter up there," Beemer said, moving forward as if he were on the roller-coaster ride creeping toward the top where they would plunge straight down into despair and black air. "I think he's looking for us."

Pryor looked at him and then rolled down his window to stick his head out before Beemer could stop him.

"Stop that shit," Beemer shouted, pulling the skinny dryness inside.

"I saw it," said Pryor.

"Did he see you?"

"No one waved or nothing," said Pryor. "There he goes."

The helicopter roared forward low, ahead of them. Should he take the next exit? Stay in the crowd? And then the traffic started to move a little faster. Not fast, mind you, but it was moving now. Maybe twenty miles an hour. Actually nineteen, but close enough. Beemer decided to grit it out. He turned off the radio.

They made it to Dempster in thirty-five minutes and headed east, toward Lake Michigan. No helicopter. It was still early. Too early for an easy car swap, but it couldn't be helped. Helicopters. He searched this way and that, let his instincts take over at a street across from a park. Three-story apartment buildings. Lots of traffic. He drove in a block. Cars on both sides, some facing the wrong way.

"What are we doing?" asked Pryor.

"*We* are doing nothing," Beemer said. "*I* am looking for a car. I steal cars. I rob stores. I don't shoot people. I show my gun. They show respect. You show that piece of shit in your pocket, trip over thin air, and shoot a guy in the back."

"Accident," said Pryor.

"My ass," said Beemer. And then, "That one."

He was looking at a gray Nissan a couple of years old parked under a big tree with branches sticking out over the street. No traffic. Dead-end street.

"Wipe it down," Beemer ordered, parking the car and getting out.

Pryor started wiping the car for prints. First inside. Then outside. By the time he was done, Beemer had the Nissan humming. Pryor got in the passenger seat, his bag on his lap, going on a vacation. All he needed was a beach and a towel.

They hit the hot dog place fifteen minutes later. They followed the smell and went in. There was a line. Soft poppy-seed buns. Kosher dogs. Big slices of new pickle. Salty brown fries. They were in line. Two women in front of them were talking. A mother and daughter. Both wearing shorts and showing stomach. Pryor looked back at the door. He could see the Nissan. The bag was in the trunk with George Bernard Shaw standing guard.

The woman and the girl were talking about Paris. Plaster of? Texas? Europe? Somebody they knew? Nice voices. Beemer tried to remember when he had last been with a woman. Not that long ago. Two months? Amarillo? Las Vegas? Moline, Illinois?

It was their turn. The kid in the white apron behind the counter wiped his hands and said, "What can I do for you?"

You can bring back the dead, thought Beemer. You can make us invisible. You can teleport us to my Aunt Elaine's in Corpus Christi.

"You can give us each a hot dog with the works," Beemer said.

"Two for me," said Pryor. "And fries."

"Two for both of us. Lots of mustard. Grilled onions. Tomatoes. Cokes. Diet for me. Regular for him."

The mother and daughter were sitting on stools still talking about Paris and eating.

"You got a phone?" Beemer asked, paying for their order.

"Back there," said the kid, taking the money.

"I'm going back there to call Walter. Find us a seat where we can watch the car."

Pryor nodded and moved to the pickup line. Beemer went back there to make the call. The phone was next to the toilet. He used the toilet first and looked at himself in the mirror. He didn't look good. Decidedly.

He filled the sink with water, cold water, and plunged his face in. Maybe the sink was dirty? Least of his worries. He pulled his head out and looked at himself. Dripping-wet reflection. The world hadn't changed. He dried his face and hands and went to the phone. He had a calling card, AT&T. He called Walter. The conversation went like this.

"Walter? I've got goods."

"Jewelry store?"

"It matter?"

"Matters. Cops moved fast. Man's in the hospital maybe dying. Church deacon or something. A saint. All over television with descriptions of two dummies I thought I might recognize."

"Goods are goods," said Beemer.

"These goods could make a man an accessory maybe to murder. Keep your goods. Take them who knows where. Get out of town before it's too late, my dear. You know what I'm saying?"

"Walter, be reasonable."

"My middle name is 'reasonable.' It should be 'careful' but it's 'reasonable.' I'm hanging up. I don't know who you are. I think you got the wrong number."

He hung up. Beemer looked at the phone and thought. St. Louis. There was a guy, Tanner, in St.Louis. No, East

St. Louis. A black guy who'd treat them fair for their goods. They'd check out of the motel and head for St. Louis. Not enough money, without selling the goods or going to the bank, to get a new car. They'd have to drive the Nissan, slow and easy. All night. Get to Tanner first thing in the morning when the sun was coming up through the Arch.

Beemer went down the narrow corridor. Cardboard boxes made it narrower. When he got to the counter, the mother and daughter were still eating and talking and drinking. Lots of people were. Standing at the counters or sitting on high stools with red seats that swirled. Smelled fantastic. Things would be all right. Pryor had a place by the window where he could watch the car. He had finished one hot dog and was working on another. Beemer inched in next to him.

"We're going to St. Louis," he said behind a wall of other conversations.

"Okay," said Pryor, mustard on his nose. No questions. Just "Okay."

Then it happened. It always happens. Shit always happens. A cop car, black and white, pulled into the lot outside the hot dog place. It was a narrow lot. The cops were moving slowly. Were they looking for a space and a quick burger or hot dog? Were they looking for a stolen Nissan?

The cops stopped next to the Nissan.

"No," moaned Pryor.

Beemer grabbed the little guy's arm. The cops turned toward the hot dog shop window. Beemer looked at the wall, ate his dog, and ate slowly, his heart going mad. Maybe he'd die now of a heart attack. Why not? His father had died on a Washington, D.C., subway just like that.

Pryor was openly watching the cops move toward them.

"Don't look at them," Beemer whispered. "Look at me. Talk. Say something. Smile. I'll nod. Say anything."

"Are they coming for us?" asked Pryor, working on his second dog.

"You've got mustard on your nose. You want to go down with mustard on your nose? You want to be a joke on the ten o'clock news?"

Beemer took a napkin and wiped Pryor's nose as the cops came in the door and looked around.

"Reach in your pocket," said Beemer. "Take out your gun. I'm going to do the same. Aim it at the cops. Don't shoot. Don't speak. If they pull out their guns, just drop yours. It'll be over and we can go pray that the guy you shot doesn't die."

"I don't pray," said Pryor as the cops, both young and in uniform, moved through the line of customers down the middle of the shop, hands on holstered guns.

Beemer turned and so did Pryor. Guns out, aimed. Butch and Sundance. A John Woo movie.

"Hold it," shouted Beemer.

Oh God, I pissed in my pants. Half an hour to the motel. Maybe twenty years to life to the motel.

The cops stopped, hands still on their holsters. The place went dead. Someone screamed. The mother or the daughter, who had stopped talking about Paris.

"Let's go," said Beemer.

Pryor reached back for the last half of his hot dog and his little greasy bag of fries.

"Is that a Glock?" asked the kid behind the counter.

"It's a Glock," said Beemer.

"Cool gun," said the kid.

The cops didn't speak. Beemer didn't say anything more.

He and Pryor made it to the door, backed away across the parking lot watching the cops watching them. The cops wouldn't shoot. Too many people.

"Get in," Beemer said.

Pryor got in the car. Beemer reached back to open the driver-side door. Hard to keep his gun level and open the door. He did it, got in, started the car, and looked in the rearview. The cops were coming out, guns drawn. There was a barrier in front of him, low, a couple of inches, painted red. Beemer gunned forward over the barrier. Hell, it wasn't his car. He thought there was just enough room to get between a white minivan and an old convertible who-knows-what.

The cops were saying something. Beemer wasn't listening. He had pissed in his pants and he expected to die of a heart attack. He listened for some telltale sign. The underbody of the Nissan caught the red barrier, scraped, and roared over. Beemer glanced toward Pryor, who had the window open and was leaning out, his piece-of-crap gun in his hand. Pryor fired as Beemer made it between minivan and convertible, taking some paint off both sides of the Nissan in the process.

Pryor fired as Beemer hit the street. Beemer heard the hot dog shop's window shatter. They wouldn't be welcome here in the near future. Then came another shot as Beemer turned right. This one went through Pryor's face. He was dead, hanging out the window. Beemer floored the Nissan. He could hear Pryor's head bouncing on the door.

The cops were going for their car, making calls, and Pryor's head was bouncing like something out of the jungle on the door. Beemer made a hard right down a semidark street. He pulled to the curb, reached past Pryor, and opened the door. It swung open, Pryor draped over it. Beemer grabbed the dead man's shirt, pulled him back through the window, and pushed the body out the door. Then he reached over to close the door. Pryor was looking up at him with three eyes, one of them brand-new.

Beemer drove. There were lights behind him now, a block back. Sirens. He turned left, wove around. No idea where he was. No one to talk to. Just me and my radio.

Who knows how many minutes later he came to a street called Oakton and headed east, for Sheridan Road, Lake Shore Drive, Lake Michigan.

People passed in cars. He passed people walking. People looked at him. The bloody door. That was it. Pryor had marked him. No time to stop and clean it up. Not on the street. He hit Sheridan Road and looked for a place to turn, found it. Little dead end. Black on white sign: "No Swimming." A park.

He pulled in between a couple of cars he didn't look at, popped the trunk lock, and got out. There was nothing in the trunk but the bag of jewelry. He dumped it all into the trunk, picked up the empty canvas bag, closed the trunk, and went looking for water.

Families were having late picnics. Couples were walking. Beemer found a fountain. He soaked George Bernard Shaw and brought him dripping back to the Nissan, where he worked on the bloody car door. It streaked. He worked, turned the canvas bag. Scrubbed. He went back for more water, wrung the bloody water from the bag. Worked again. Gunga Din. Fetch water. Clean up. Three trips and it was done.

George Bernard Shaw was angry. His face was red under the parking lot lights.

Beemer opened the trunk and threw the bag in. When he turned, he saw the cop car coming down the street. Only one way in the lot. Only one way out. The same way. He grabbed six or seven watches and some little golden animals and shoved them in his pockets quickly. Then he moved into the park, off the path, toward the rocks. Last stand? Glock on the rocks? Couldn't be. It couldn't end like this. He was caught between a cop and a hard place. Funny. Couldn't laugh though. He hurried on, looking back to see the cop car enter the little lot.

Beemer found the rocks. Kids were crawling over them. Big rocks. Beyond them the night and the lake like an ocean of darkness, end of the world. Nothingness. He climbed out and down.

Three teenagers or college kids, male, watched him make his way down toward the water.

Stop looking at me, he willed. Go back to playing with yourselves, telling lies, and being stupid. Just don't look at me. Beemer crouched down behind a rock, the water touching his shoes.

He had no plan. Water and rocks. Pockets full of not much. Crawl along the rocks. Get out. Find a car. Drive to the motel. Get to St. Louis. Tanner might give him a few hundred, maybe more, for what he had. Start again, find a new Pryor to replace the prior Pryor, a Pryor without a gun. Beemer knew he couldn't be alone.

"You see a man out here?" He heard a voice through the sound of the waves.

"Down there," came a slightly younger voice.

Beemer couldn't swim. Give up or keep going. He kept going. A flashlight beam from above now. Another from the direction he had come.

"Stop right there. Turn around and come back the way you came," said a voice.

"He's armed," said another voice.

"Take out your gun and hold it by the barrel. Now."

Beemer considered. He took out the Glock. Great gun. Took it out slowly, looked up, and decided it was all a what-the-hell life anyway. He grabbed the gun by the handle, holding on to the rock with one hand. He aimed toward the flashlight above him.

Before he could fire he heard a shot, felt the pain, fell backward. His head hit a jutting rock. The rock hurt more than the bullet that tore at his stomach. But the water, the cold water, was worst of all.

"Can you get to him, Dave?" someone called.

"I'm trying."

Beemer was floating on his back, bobbing in the black waves. I can float, he thought, looking at the flashlight. Float out to some little sailboat, climb on, get away.

He bobbed further away. Pain gone cold.

"Can't reach him."

"Shit. He's floating out. Call it in."

Footsteps. Beemer looked up. Beyond the light aimed at his eyes, he could see people in a line looking down at him as he floated further and further from the shore into the blackness. He considered waving to them. He looked for the moon and stars. They weren't there.

Maybe the anniversary hit hadn't been such a good idea.

He closed his eyes and thought that he had never fired his Glock, never fired any gun. That would be a regret if they didn't save him. That would be a regret if they did. It was a damned good gun.

Beemer fell asleep. Either that or he died.

JEROME CHARYN

Born in the Bronx, New York, **Jerome Charyn** attended Columbia University and was founding editor of the *Dutton Review* and the executive editor of *Fiction*. In 1996 he was named an Officier des Arts et des Lettres by the French minister of culture. Dividing his time between Paris and New York, Charyn has written more than thirty novels, including ten chronicles of the New York City police commissioner/mayor/vice-presidential candidate Isaac Sidel, introduced in 1975's *Blue Eyes*.

FIRST MYSTERIOUS PRESS PUBLICATION:
THE GOOD POLICEMAN, 1990

COUNTESS KATHLEEN

His campaign headquarters was a white castle on Seventy-third and Broadway, the Ansonia, where Caruso and Toscanini had once lived, where Babe Ruth had practiced his swings on the castle's wide marble landings, where Arnold Rothstein had kept his blond mistress, Inez, in an apartment with octagonal windows, the same windows that Isaac had. He was the party's choice for V.P., ten times more popular than his own running mate, Michael Storm, and President Cottonwood. The country loved a candidate with a Glock in his pants, a kind of drugstore cowboy, a brawler who was willing to take on Cottonwood and the whole Republican machine.

But the Big Guy was grim around the mouth. He could no longer campaign with Marianna Storm, Michael's twelve-year-old daughter, who was known as the little first lady. Tim Seligman said she was taboo. The party's chief strategist had banned her from Isaac's entourage, and Isaac turned on Tim, threatened to boycott his own campaign.

"Isaac, it's war out there. The bombs are flying. Do you want to ruin that little girl? The Republicans are concocting a very tall tale. Unless Marianna vanishes, they'll accuse you of having a Lolita complex."

"What Lolita?"

"Isaac, it's a smear. They're talking pedophilia."

Isaac wanted to jump on the Metroliner, capture the White House, and rip out Calder Cottonwood's tongue. The Secret Service tried to stop him. The boss of Isaac's detail, Martin Boyle, had to beg the Big Guy.

"Sir, will you promise to behave?"

"Not until I strangle Cottonwood."

"Then we'll have to hold you here until kingdom come."

"Perfect. I won't have to campaign."

But the Big Guy campaigned in spite of himself. A lunatic called Dennis Cohen, a gunman who'd grown up on the Lower East Side with Sidel, who'd gone to Seward Park High with him, and whom Isaac had arrested several times when he was the commish, decided to take revenge. He stormed the white castle, shot up Isaac's octagonal windows, almost killed Martin Boyle, and Isaac, with all the reluctant bile in his heart, glocked the mad gunman, Dennis Cohen, his former high school friend . . . and his popularity leaped twenty points in the polls.

Isaac had to sit shivah for Dennis, do his seven days of mourning. He wouldn't return messages from Tim Seligman, Michael, or that prick, President Cottonwood. He sat on an old wooden crate, in a ripped overcoat, the visible sign of his grief. The telephone rang on his second day of mourning. Martin Boyle picked up the phone.

"I'm inconsolable," Isaac said. "I can't talk to anybody . . . not even God."

"What about Marianna Storm?"

Isaac grabbed the receiver. "Marianna, are you there?"

"I miss you, Uncle Isaac. *Monstrously.*"

The Big Guy sobbed in his torn coat.

"Couldn't we have lunch, Marianna? I'll wear a disguise."

"And wreck your future? . . . I'm Lolita, the little fire-bomb. I can't even bake you a batch of cookies. Mr. Seligman says people might call it provocative. You aren't hurt, are you? That gunman . . ."

"I wasn't even scratched."

"We won't be able to talk until the election. This is the last time."

"But where are you? In Miami with Michael? Where?"

Isaac heard a click. Someone had cut off Marianna. He returned to his wooden box. But he couldn't grieve too long. There was a gala the Big Guy had to attend in his own honor, after the seventh day of mourning, at the Salmagundi Club on lower Fifth Avenue. The candidate had to meet with Democratic donors who were financing his campaign. But he'd need an escort. He couldn't come alone. He'd hurt his glamour, his mystique . . .

Seligman visited the castle while Isaac was sitting shivah. There were still bullet holes in the walls where Dennis Cohen had left his signature.

"It's idiotic, Isaac. A gunman out of your past. That cocksucker could have destroyed all our plans with a single bullet . . . you're a hero."

"I didn't enjoy whacking him. We were in the chess club together at Seward Park. I was much more of a delinquent than Dennis Cohen."

"Ah, but you got into line, and Dennis didn't. You joined the police, went right up the ladder."

"With the help of half a dozen rabbis. The NYPD is almost as political as the White House."

"And what did Dennis's rabbis get him? Right into the grave."

"Don't mock him. He had a mean mother, and his dad nearly beat him to death."

"Then I'll cry for Dennis, and I'll sit on your crate, but what about the Salmagundi Club? I can get Kim Basinger. Or some other Hollywood babe. Give me a short list. I'll see what I can do."

"My list is shorter than that. The little first lady is what I want."

Seligman didn't even bother to groan. "That's great. Marianna Storm. We'll lose every fucking donor. You'll end up in the garbage can . . . and she wouldn't agree to go with you. Should I call her, Isaac?"

"You put poison in her head."

"That's what campaigning is all about. Guerrilla warfare. Well, should we ask Basinger or Meryl Streep?"

"I'm a cop," Isaac said. "I wouldn't blend in with an American beauty. What about Rebecca Karp?"

This time Seligman did groan. The former mayor, Becky Karp, was in a mental ward on Staten Island. "She's crazier than Dennis Cohen. She'll start stripping in front of the donors . . . Rebecca is out."

Seligman disappeared. Isaac whistled to himself. He'd won his little war. He'd arrive at Salmagundi with the Secret Service and no other escort.

He wanted to wear a secondhand suit from the barrels of Orchard Street. But he couldn't behave like a brat. He'd come in black tie and tails. Boyle brushed Isaac's dinner jacket, and the Democrats' own housekeeper ironed Isaac's tie. He stared at his own image in the mirror, looked like a cockatoo. Ah, if he couldn't have Marianna, he wanted Rothstein's mistress, Inez, whose presence seemed to haunt the Ansonia. She had platinum hair in the pictures Isaac had seen of her, had spent a month or so at Smith College, in Massachusetts, according to all the legends. Inez. Did she dream of A.R. under the octagonal windows, dance the "tulip" or the "froggy bottom"? But Rothstein wasn't a dancing man. He lived at Lindy's, took his meals at Broadway's own cafeteria, placed his bets between bites of Lindy's cheesecake, which mesmerized you, destroyed your desire for anything else in the world. Coffee and cheesecake were Arnold's only nourishment. And if he was out of town, attending to one of his thoroughbreds, he had Lindy's deliver the cheesecake. The driver's bill was a fortune . . .

He whistled while he got into the limo with Martin Boyle. There was a woman waiting in the backseat. Sidel wasn't blind. It was Countess Kathleen, the wife he'd never bothered to divorce. She was five years older than the Big Guy. He'd married her when he was nineteen, and it was the countess who had connections with the NYPD, who helped haul him up that strictly Irish ladder. He'd never have become commish without her.

She was sixty, but her long separation from Isaac must have nurtured Kathleen. She had the same red hair Isaac remembered. He was a sucker for redheads.

She wore a black gown, and barely had a mark on her throat. She'd gone into the Florida swamps, found spectacular real estate, had become a millionairess, while Isaac couldn't keep a penny in the bank. He gave the cash he had on hand to whatever pauper was around.

The Big Guy was suspicious. How had Tim coaxed her away from the swamps? She shook Boyle's hand. "I heard about that ordeal with the gunman. I hope you're taking care of my hubby."

"I'm not your hubby," Isaac said.

"Did you bring me a corsage?"

"What corsage? How the hell could I have known you'd be here?"

"It's our fortieth. Did you forget?"

"Fortieth?"

"Wedding anniversary. We were married on this same day, forty years ago."

"That's impossible. I wouldn't have . . ."

"Wouldn't have what? You're such a romantic, darling . . . Mr. Boyle, do you know the emblem of a couple's fortieth anniversary?"

"Is it coral, ma'am . . . or pearl?"

"It's ruby, Mr. Boyle."

"Like the color of your hair."

The countess laughed. "You're a charmer . . . there are no rubies in my hair."

"I'm not going to the Salmagundi," Isaac said.

"And disappoint the Democrats?"

"But you're a Republican. I read that somewhere."

"I cross over from time to time. And I've made an exception in your case, even though Michael's a thief."

"Did Seligman bribe you, did he pay you to come?"

"No, darling. I paid him . . . I wanted to spend the first day of our ruby year together."

"It's a trick, Boyle. Stop the car."

"They're expecting us, Mr. President."

"See how loyal he is to you," the countess said. "He knows that you're going to win . . . and that Michael will have to resign right after his inauguration. That will make me mistress of the White House."

"Tim has been feeding you a lot of crap."

"It wasn't Tim. Actually, it was Bull Latham."

Latham was director of the FBI, and Isaac could no longer

tell if Bull was sleeping with the Democrats, the Republicans . . . or both.

"You haven't even asked about Marilyn."

"Oh, she's your daughter, Isaac. You raised her. That's why she gives you such a hard time. You're the one she should have married. How many husbands has she had? Nine or ten?"

"But she's happy now. She's married to Joe Barbarossa."

"One of your loyal thugs. Believe me, Isaac, you aren't very far from her bed."

He wanted to slap her, this countess of the swamps, but they'd arrived at the Salmagundi Club, and how would it have looked if Isaac the Brave battled with his lost wife at the beginning of their ruby year?

He stepped out of the limo, opened Kathleen's door, and they climbed up the steps of Salmagundi with Martin Boyle in their wake. Six Secret Service men were already inside. It was an art club, but he couldn't recognize the art on the walls. He longed for one of Paul Klee's harpooners or pirate ships, and all he got were portraits of Manhattan without a moment of madness.

Salmagundi was packed with Isaac's admirers. They crept around him, gazed at Kathleen. The Big Guy didn't dodge their curiosity. He introduced the countess as his wife.

"We've been separated," he said. "But this is our anniversary."

The reporters clung to Kathleen, the wife who'd come out of the swamps. But she didn't betray Isaac. She would listen to questions and smile like the Salmagundi's own red-haired Mona Lisa.

"I'm here to help."

That's all she had to say. But Isaac knew that vultures

would descend upon Kathleen, pick at the bones of her past, and piece together a lovely little "sound bite" about Kathleen of Marble Hill and the Everglades. And Isaac would have to live with their fable.

He spotted Tim Seligman with a glass of champagne. He spun Tim around and brought him into a private closet.

"That's grand," Isaac said. "That's lovely. Can you imagine what the press will do to us? They'll have a field day. I would have been much better off with all the Lolitas in the world. Did the FBI find her for you, Tim?"

"She didn't need finding. We've known about her for years."

"And suddenly you wake up Cinderella and bring her to the ball."

"Isaac, we had to interview her. We couldn't take the chance. And that's when she volunteered . . . to come up north and be with you."

"At the Salmagundi Club."

"It was providence, pure luck. How could we have known that the gala would coincide with your fortieth anniversary?"

"Why? Did Bull Latham neglect to tell you a little more about our marriage?"

"This has nothing to do with Bull. We had our own people."

"And you don't think the Republicans bought her off?"

"Isaac, she's too rich to be bought. That's a fact. She could finance half our campaign out of her own pocket."

"But she could still be working for Calder and the Bull."

"The Bull's with us. He's on our side."

"In your dreams," Isaac said. "He's Cottonwood's man. And he's behind her visit. They had to drop the Lolita baloney . . . Calder's sleeping with Kathleen."

"He's impotent."

"That's only your guess, Tim. He might just be hiding his dick from the Democratic Party."

"Then what can we do?"

"Wait. Until Calder makes his move."

"Isaac, are you fond of the missus? We could always have her meet with an accident. Nothing major. Just enough to keep her quiet."

He rushed at Tim, but the party strategist knocked him to the floor. Isaac cursed himself. He must have been sleepwalking. He'd forgotten how to brawl.

Tim helped him to his feet, and they returned to the ballroom.

Kathleen was surrounded by reporters and Democrats. Isaac felt a curious tug toward her, this redhead who'd jump-started his career and then left him to raise Marilyn the Wild.

But it was time for Isaac to sing for his supper, even if there was no supper at the Salmagundi Club, just champagne and strawberries and a light buffet. The Big Guy had become a politician. He revealed his Glock, talked about Social Security and taxes, the downward spiral of public education, the widening war on drugs, white-collar crime.

"I won't shag flies. I'll fight for the young, the aged, the poor."

But the Big Guy had begun to dream of something else, not the countess and who her real employers were, not Tim Seligman and his Democratic tricks, not even of Marianna, but the late Dennis Cohen. Why had Dennis tracked him to the Ansonia? He could have fitted Isaac out months and months ago when he didn't have to deal with the complications of a castle. Had Bull Latham whispered in Dennis's ear? Isaac had sat across a chess table from Dennis, they'd traded queens, massacred each other's army of little men. That was almost as intimate as having a wife . . .

Kathleen rode back to the white castle with Sidel. It was inevitable. Man and wife made love. It felt like another dream, with a bit of passion and loneliness. She rose in the middle of the night, got dressed, and took the early bird back to Miami.

"Are you Calder's girl?" he asked, just before she left.

She smiled. Isaac's Mona Lisa.

"Even if I were, darling, what could it possibly mean? He doesn't have a pecker. And you'll be the next inhabitant of the White House, not Michael Storm. And how would it look if I deserted my husband?"

She'd sucked at his mouth. His tongue bled from such a deep kiss. And then she was gone. The Countess Kathleen.

ARCHER MAYOR

Archer Mayor lives in a Vermont village, where he is town constable. He writes full-time and volunteers as a firefighter/EMT. He has lived all over the United States, Canada, and Europe, variously employed as a scholarly editor, a researcher for Time-Life Books, a political advance man, a theater photographer, a newspaper writer/editor, a lab technician for *Paris-Match* in France, and a medical illustrator. He introduced his Brattleboro-based cop Joe Gunther, hero of eleven novels to date, in 1988's *Open Season*, after having written two scholarly history books.

FIRST MYSTERIOUS PRESS PUBLICATION:
SCENT OF EVIL, 1992

INSTINCT

The snow hitting the windshield reminded me of an old movie, as if two guys on ladders were just off camera, pouring confetti out of barrels onto the hood of my car. Except that the effect in real life was more stressful than in a theater. The snow was heavy and thick, dry enough that I didn't need the wipers, but so incessant I was starting to think it might never stop. My eyes strained to see into the black night beyond the dizzying white vortex until they felt ready to fall out of my head.

Despite the warnings on the radio earlier, I'd decided to drive home, and compounded the folly by taking the back way through heavily forested hills—ensuring that if I had a wreck, no one would find me until next spring.

Now, one hour and a mere ten miles into the trip, I had doggedly reached the point where continuing would cost me no more than turning back, which, the way my hands and shoulders were aching, was a definite mixed blessing.

All the more so because one irony of my position was that despite its peril, it was also curiously sedating. The car's heater belied the freezing cold outside, the snow had created a carpet beneath so thick and sound-absorbent as to make the trip virtually silent, and the serried trees, flickering by in the dim half-arc of my headlights, enhanced the sensation of being encased in a protective cocoon. It was hard to fight the feeling that if I just stayed put for another hour or two, this insulated capsule would deliver me home entirely on its own.

It led to a temptation, lulled as I was by the mesmerizing wash of white static against the windshield, to simply let my hands drop from the steering wheel.

Until I saw a man—young, pale-faced, eyes wide with fright—loom up out of the darkness like an onrushing meteor, and flash by in an instant mere inches from the car.

With a surprised shout, I hit the brakes, fought the resulting skid, struggling to stay on the road, and ended up with my headlights staring at a tree trunk not three feet away.

"Jesus," I said to myself, craning over my shoulder to confirm what I'd seen. For a moment, there was nothing besides darkness and snow. Then, emerging into the harsh red glow of my brake lights, a thin figure shimmered into view like a blood-soaked ghost.

In the decades I'd been a cop, facing hazards large and small, I'd rarely experienced the irrational fear I felt right then—a visceral, heart-stopping, utter conviction that my life was about to end.

And then the man passed out of the red light, came up alongside the car's passenger side, and rapped on the window with his gloved hand like any other pedestrian in need of help. He looked to be in his mid-twenties.

"Hello?"

I leaned over and opened the door, trying not to show my relief. "Get in. What the hell're you doing out here?"

"My car's in the ditch about a mile back," he said, half falling into the seat in a small flurry of snow and a gust of frigid air. He slammed the door and banged his hands together between his knees. "God almighty. I thought I'd had it." His voice was high and nervous.

I began straightening the car in the road. "You need to go back to your vehicle for anything? Were you alone?"

"Yeah, yeah. I just want to get somewhere warm. I can find the car in the morning."

I hit the mileage counter button on the dash and started rolling again. "When we reach the next town, you can use a pay phone and tell the police how many miles back you went off the road. Might be hard to find otherwise."

"I don't care."

The sudden flatness in his tone made me glance at him — and see the black hole of a gun barrel pointed at me.

I kept driving, knowing that was my best defense, and stifled the urge to tell him I was a cop, figuring that might get me killed even sooner. "What is this?" I asked instead.

"I want your car. Pull over."

His voice had now graduated to trembling.

I gave him another quick look. In the anemic green glow from the dash lights, he looked gaunt and sickly, his eyes hollow with fear, his lips pressed tight. Despite the cold he'd just left, a sheen of sweat glimmered on his forehead, just under his wool watch cap.

I picked up speed slightly. "Throw the gun out the window first."

He was plainly bewildered by this. "What? You're crazy. Stop the car or I'll kill you."

There was no certainty I was right. This was purely a gut reaction. But his panic encouraged me to keep pushing. I just hoped I wouldn't betray my own fear. "You mean you'll kill us both. I *am* driving this thing. Figure it out."

In my peripheral vision, I saw him work his mouth soundlessly a couple of times. Since keeping on the road hadn't gotten any easier, I decided to try ending the debate by re-thinking my initial strategy.

"Not only that, but you'd be killing a cop—Brattleboro P.D.—Lieutenant Joe Gunther."

I'd anticipated a couple of possibilities, only one of them good, but not what he did next.

He hit me on the side of the head with his gun barrel and grabbed the steering wheel.

The results were predictable, although I was surprised to see them unfold in slow motion, just as in the cliché. As I watched in a dizzying haze of pain, the view before the wind-shield flashed between darkness and the nearby trees as we spun around in circles, until there was a solid thump from beneath us, a brief sensation of weightlessness, and our en-tire world pitched forward. Just before the lights went out completely, I felt the other side of my head smack sharply against the doorpost.

．　．　．

I woke up to his slapping me, and anxiously muttering, "Come on, mister. Wake up. Jesus. Come on, come on, come on."

I raised a hand to protect my cheek from further abuse. So much for wanting me dead.

The young man's face was inches from my own, peering at me as if searching for enlightenment. "You okay?"

I closed my eyes, dizzy enough already, and took men-tal stock of my body parts. "I guess."

"We crashed."

That brought me completely back. I opened my eyes. "No kidding."

He pulled away, apparently satisfied I'd recovered. "I got your gun, so don't try anything."

I resisted pointing out the idiocy of that statement, choosing instead to control my inner fury at ending up in this situation—which was only exacerbated by not knowing how I could have avoided it.

I looked around. The dash lights were still burning feebly, giving the car's interior a subaquatic appearance. Encouraging this image, all the windows were inky black, we were pitched nose-down as in a sinking submarine, and there wasn't a sound to be heard outside.

"How long have I been out?" I asked him.

"A few seconds. Your head hurt?"

Like the straight man in a comedy team, I thought. I didn't play along, sensing in him someone seriously out of his depth—almost in need of help. "I'll live," I told him. "What's your next move? Shoot me and turn the car into a bobsled?"

He looked pained by that, and glanced down at the gun still in his hand. "I'm sorry."

I extended an open palm to him. "Then give me the hardware and let's see if we can sort this out."

Wrong move. He withdrew until his back was pressed against the passenger-side door, the gun held higher, if no more steadily. "No way. My only chance is to get the hell out of here."

"And you're going to do that . . . how?"

He smacked the back of his head twice against the window and howled at the roof, his body trembling in frustration.

"What's your name?" I asked him suddenly.

He stared at me for a moment. "Roger Blake."

"What did you do, Roger? Why the gun?"

He leaned forward, his eyes feverish with intensity. "I didn't do anything. But that won't matter. My ass is grass anyway. I might just as well have killed her."

"Who?" I asked quietly.

His shoulders slumped and he stared into the darkness beyond the windshield. "It doesn't matter."

I could have snatched the gun from him, the way he was holding it—or I could have tried. But the risks of tussling over a loaded weapon in such tight quarters were looking far worse than just maintaining the status quo. I'd spent my entire adult life dealing with people like Roger Blake, many of them innocents, guilty or not. True victims of circumstance, they tended to live their lives by reaction alone, either making or avoiding decisions without thought of consequence. I didn't know what he had or hadn't done— I was pretty sure he was at a loss for what to do now.

Which is where I thought I could help us both.

"Roger, first rule of survival in something like this is to stay with the car, clear the tailpipe, and run the heater every quarter hour or so to keep from freezing."

"Okay." It was pitched halfway between a statement and a question.

"Can I see if the motor'll turn over?"

His face cleared slightly at the possibility of at least one certitude. "Sure."

Unfortunately, it didn't last. The starter cranked several times, but it was obviously without hope.

"I shoulda known," he said mournfully. "Now what?"

I shrugged. "It's a bad storm—could last awhile. Long enough to kill us if we stay here. I'd sooner risk walking back up the road. We might lose a few body parts to frostbite, but I think we'd make it. It's only about ten miles to town."

He sighed, and rubbed his forehead as if fighting a migraine. "We don't have to do that," he admitted.

I sensed what he meant. "You know somewhere closer?"

He spoke as if the words caused him pain. "There's a place near here, about a mile."

"You didn't put your car in a ditch?"

"At the foot of the driveway." He seemed ready to say more, but then closed his mouth.

It was starting to get cold in the car, but I wanted to take advantage of the almost confessional setting to pry him further open.

"You must've been pushing it hard."

"No shit," he said, more to himself than to me.

"What happened, Roger?"

He brought his eyes reluctantly to mine. "What do you care? You're not taking me in. We'll go back there to survive this"—he waved his hand at the storm—"but then you're getting hog-tied and I'm disappearing."

"Why, if you didn't do it?"

He stared at me, startled. On one level, it was just an old cop trick—making the suspect think you believe him. But there was that nagging something about this man that made me think I might be right, too.

"Who's the woman we'll think you killed?" I asked.

"Jenny Mayhew, my ex-girlfriend. And I didn't do it."

"Who did?"

He was back to staring out into space. "I don't know."

Now, I thought, was the time. "Take me there," I told him.

His voice regained some of its artificial strength and he

waved the gun again. "Okay, but I'll shoot you if you try anything. I'm not kidding around."

"I know," I reassured him, content that he had no idea who was out to control whom.

It took some doing to open the doors against the piled-up snow outside, and even more to get back up to the deserted roadway. I'd taken a flashlight from the backseat, but its effect was little better than my headlights had been earlier. Still, it did pick out the trees by the roadside and thereby the direction we had to follow.

That we did largely in silence, since the snow's depth made for hard going. Also, the cold was intense, and although there was no measurable wind, the bite of frigid air in the nostrils and lungs had a numbing effect. Heavy, quiet snowfalls worked like incubators anyway, muffling enough of the surrounding world to where one's breathing and heartbeat were finally the only life signs left. You ended up staring at your shadowy, blurred feet, watching their endlessly repetitive movement without any sense of progress. I had no trouble believing that soldiers could sleep on the march in similar circumstances—they simply yielded to the same intoxicants they'd been exposed to as sleepy infants—their own regular, rhythmic, biological patterns combined with the metronome of a parent's steady gait, walking in circles in the middle of the night, trying to soothe a fussy babe in arms.

Roger Blake was behind me through all this—his gun trained on me as I kept the light on the snow ahead—out of sight and eventually out of mind. I was startled when his voice suddenly intruded like a slamming door in the middle of a dream. "Here it is. Turn right."

There was a subtle break in the wall of silent, white-shrouded trees—a driveway barely wider than a track. Once along it about fifteen feet, we came across a heavily blanketed pickup truck, tilted drunkenly to one side as if taking a nap.

"Up ahead," Blake informed me dully. "About a hundred yards."

I saw the lights first, hovering like two dim fireflies beside one another. I was very cold by now, and tired, and chose to see in those small blotches of yellow the warmth and comfort I was seeking, regardless of what else it offered. Slowly, I was rewarded with the emergence of a small, one-story cabin, two lighted windows bracketing a front door, accompanied by the scent of woodsmoke in the air.

There was also something else. The building looked vaguely familiar, its image scratching feebly at some memory long buried. I just couldn't bring it back fully to mind.

I stumbled up the narrow front steps and paused with my hand on the doorknob. "Okay?"

Despite his effort to get here, Blake was hesitant, reminding me of the same effort he'd made to get away. I could appreciate the irony, but I sensed all he felt was dread.

"I suppose."

For no reason I could immediately grasp, I responded to what I felt he wasn't saying. "It's okay. You're not alone this time."

He didn't answer. I opened the door and stepped into the light.

The cabin's embrace was such a relief from what we'd been slogging through for the past hour that all we did initially was stand there, the door closed behind us, and let the heat from the woodstove soak through our snow-covered clothing. Finally, as if the same process were thawing my brain, I began to consider my predicament.

So, apparently, did Blake.

He prodded me in the back with his gun. "Go sit in that armchair over there so I can tie you up."

We were standing in a small, square living room with a kitchenette lining its far wall, next to a door I assumed led to a back bedroom. The place didn't smell too clean, was roughly furnished, and looked like a sampler for a building supplies outlet, its walls composed of an impressive and mismatched assortment of either unfinished Sheetrock or wood panels ranging from fake mahogany to plastic-coated bamboo. The lamps on the walls were all kerosene fueled, and I recognized that both the slightly rusty fridge and the countertop cooking unit were gas fired. A woodstove squatted in the middle of the plywood floor, and now that I'd been here for a few minutes, I realized it was all but out.

I shook my head to Blake's request. "Show me the body first."

"What?"

"You told me you didn't do it. You going to throw away the best chance you have to prove that? I'm a trained investigator."

"Why would you want to help me?" he asked. "I threatened to kill you."

"It's not about helping you. If you didn't do it, somebody else did. He's the guy I want."

He thought about that for a moment, but then pointed to the chair again. "Forget it. You're just trying to mess me up. Put your butt over there."

I shrugged. "Which tells me all your 'I didn't do it' crap was just that."

He half raised his hand to either hit me or ward me off like an evil spirit. "What the hell do you know? You son of a bitch."

I stared at his wide, bewildered eyes without comment.

After a long moment of suspended animation, he slowly capitulated, and said in a near whisper, "She's in the bedroom."

Now that I could move, I didn't move. "Tell me what happened tonight."

"Nothing," he said sulkily. "I came to see her, I found her dead, I left."

I pointed at the gun in his hand. "What about that?"

He looked at it as if I'd just put it there. "It's hers. I took it 'cause I knew I was screwed."

"Why'd you come here in the first place? You said she was your *ex*-girlfriend."

He actually hung his head like a kid, reinforcing the notion that I could probably just snatch the gun away. If I'd still been interested.

"I just wanted to see her."

"At night? In the middle of a storm?"

"Yeah," he admitted simply.

Perhaps more than anything he'd said or done so far, that one comment—and the complex of feelings behind it—made me believe him.

"Who broke off the affair?" I asked.

"She did." I could barely hear him in the silent house.

"Why?"

"I hit her."

I didn't respond, his response settling like an all-too-familiar cold stone in my chest. He looked up at that, his expression pleading. "I know it was wrong. I was drunk and pissed off. I told her I was sorry. But she threw me out and had a restraining order put on me."

"That still in force?"

He began getting worked up again. "Hell, yeah. Why do you think I tried to run for it? I know what this looks like. I'm a guy with no job, a drinking problem, I got a history of beating my girlfriend, and now she's dead. This ain't rocket science. I even have a record with you guys—assault and battery. Perfect, huh?"

"When was that?" I asked quickly.

He stopped with his mouth half open. "What? I don't know. Five years ago. I got into a fight with some guy—broke his nose."

A silence fell between us. I took advantage of it to move toward the bedroom door. He watched me, obviously wondering whether to stop me. I tried heading him off before he could decide.

"Okay," I said authoritatively. "I'll check this out. Don't move around more than you have to. I don't want you messing up any potential evidence."

I reached the door and twisted the knob, pushing it open. The room beyond had one wall lamp burning. There was a double bed, a rickety chest of drawers, a night table made from a crate. Sprawled across the bed was a young woman, blond, fully clothed in jeans and a work shirt. She lay on her back, with her arms flung out to both sides. Her face was bruised and bloody, and her neck was twisted at an unnatural angle. I checked for a pulse, despite the obvious lack of need.

She was already cold, her fingers and jaw stiffening.

I straightened and simply looked at her for a moment, wondering how and if she might have avoided ending up like this—and wondering, too, how many times I'd gazed at the bodies of dead young women in the past and asked myself the same question.

I heard a ragged sob behind me and saw Roger in the doorway, tentatively looking in. "This the way you found her?"

"Yeah," he murmured, his eyes welling up.

"You didn't try to revive her at all? Take her pulse?"

"I half picked her up—lifted her head. But I knew she was dead."

"How?"

He flinched, wiped his nose. "Look at her, man."

"How?" I repeated, almost resentful of his sorrow.

"She was cold. And her neck . . ." He didn't finish.

"Let's see your hands."

He shook his head, but only in resignation. Still holding the gun, he pulled off his gloves, saying, "That's what I mean. I'm up shit creek. I knew it's the first thing you people would do."

I studied his right hand. "How'd you cut your knuckles?"

"You're not going to believe me."

"Not if you don't tell me."

"I punched the wall in my apartment. I was pissed, I was lonely. It was just before I came out here to talk to her."

I nodded. He was right about the circumstantial evidence. It made for a strong case. "Let's go back to the other room," I suggested.

He led the way, his back to me, the gun dangling by his side.

"Sit," I told him, pointing to a chair while I opened the stove and fed a couple of pieces of wood into it from a nearby box.

At last, I settled into the armchair he'd wanted me in from the start.

"Now what?" he asked, having apparently given up trying to be in charge.

"Tell me about Jenny," I said. "When did you two break it off?"

He was sitting slumped in his chair, the gun held loosely between his knees. "A month and a half ago."

"This her house?"

"Yeah. I mean she rents it, but she's been here a couple of years."

"What's she been up to this last month? Any new boyfriends?"

His expression soured. "I guess. She got around."

"Is that what you fought about?"

"That and other things. I don't guess I was too good there, either . . . and there was the drinking . . . I can't believe she's dead . . ." His voice trailed off.

I scanned the room from where I was sitting. "Where's her cat?"

His brow furrowed. "Cat? I don't know. How did you know . . . ?"

I pointed to a smudge on the edge of the refrigerator door, about a foot up from the floor. "My girlfriend used to have cats," I explained. "They rub their scent glands on corners like that—it leaves a stain after a while. Besides, there's hair on all the furniture."

"I don't know," he answered. "It's an indoor cat. It's always here."

I got up and began walking around the room, checking into corners, under a chest, behind a closet door. I repeated the same routine in the bedroom, with similar results. Signs of the cat were plentiful and recent, including some half-eaten moist food in a bowl. But the animal itself was missing.

I stood for a moment on the threshold between both rooms, my eyes traveling from where Jenny lay on the bed to the front door, trying to reconstruct what had happened. I finally approached the woodstove again and crouched next to it.

"What?" Roger asked from his seat.

"Looks like blood on the corner here," I said. "And a few drops on the floor. It's hard to see mixed in with the burn marks."

I rose and crossed to the front door, buttoning my coat and pulling my flashlight out of my pocket.

Roger sat forward, alarmed, and pointed the gun at me as if he'd just discovered it there. "Where're you going?"

"Outside to look around," I answered, pointedly not looking at him. "If you can find another light, you can help."

He rose and began searching the cabinets in the kitchenette, shoving the pistol into his waistband. I left him to it and stepped outside.

It was still snowing, but just barely, and visibility was much improved. I stood on the top step and played the light's halo around me in ever-widening arcs, hoping reality would confirm what was in my mind's eye.

I found it just as Roger opened the door behind me.

"Wait there," I told him, and stepped carefully into the fresh snow by the side of the steps. I walked about fifteen feet out in a straight line, to where the flashlight beam had revealed a slight, oblong depression in the powdery surface. There I reached down gingerly, found what I was looking for after a few seconds of groping around, and extracted the frozen-stiff body of a small gray cat.

"Holy Jesus," Roger said from the steps. "That's it. How'd you figure that out?"

I returned to the house and stepped past him into the living room. "Educated guess," I told him. "Did Jenny keep any plastic bags around?"

He closed the door and walked over to the counter with the gas burner on it, pulling open a few drawers until he found what he was after. "Are bread wrappers okay?"

"They'll do. And show me where she kept her personal papers."

I examined the cat before he gave me the bags, which I then used to carefully and completely wrap up the animal's stiff legs and head.

Roger had approached a small school desk in the meantime, and now lifted its lid to reveal a jumble of bills, letters, and junk mail. "This is the only place I know that she kept stuff."

I sat before the desk and began sorting through its contents. Ten minutes later, I discovered why the cabin had seemed so familiar to me earlier. Satisfied, I placed several documents in my pocket and looked up at him, pointing to his belt as I did so. "You don't want to carry a gun that way. Could mess you up if it went off."

He looked embarrassed and laid his hand on the weapon's wooden butt. "Damn. I didn't think of that."

He hesitated a moment before gingerly pulling the pistol free and handing it to me, almost apologetically, along with my own gun from inside his coat. "I guess maybe you should keep these."

I took them both and put them away, suppressing a paradoxical mixture of relief and anger as I did. "Yeah—maybe."

After a telling pause, he asked, "What happens now?"

"That's a loaded question, Roger," I admitted, the anger just barely riffling the surface. "Technically, you've committed some pretty serious crimes—assaulting a police officer, reckless endangerment, kidnapping. We could even pile on your putting my car in the ditch. None of which even touches the young woman in the next room and how she ended up dead. You can't be accused of being overly smart."

He didn't deny any of it. All the turmoil, frustration, and anxiety that had fueled him earlier seemed to have dissipated into simple lethargy. "I know."

I stood up. "That having been said, I think we should hitch a ride on the first plow truck that comes through here and deliver you home." I leaned forward slightly so that our eyes were just a foot apart. "With one understanding."

The uncertain relief on his face was palpable. "What?"

"You stay put there. If this works out the way I think it will, you might be asked to tell the prosecutor or a judge about how you came here and found Jenny dead, and then stopped me for help on the road, but that should be it. Jenny's killer will be behind bars and there'll be no reason for anyone to know what else you did tonight."

"You'd do that?" He sounded incredulous.

I took hold of his shoulder and squeezed hard. "Yeah. But if you do me dirt—disappear, act stupid, anything at all—I'll make sure you go to jail. Understood?"

He nodded once, his eyes wide and clear. "Yes, sir."

. . .

Two days later, I climbed the staircase of an old, red brick throwback to the industrial era that had been cut up into dozens of tiny, dark, airless apartments overlooking Main Street on one side and the railroad tracks on the other. It was a toss-up about which was the preferable location, given the distinctly different but equally jarring noise levels emanating from both.

Roger Blake lived over the street, and answered at the first knock.

"Hi, Lieutenant," he said, his nervousness making him awkward and shy. "How're ya doin'?"

"I'm doing fine," I answered. "More to the point, so are you. You won't have to talk to a judge after all. The man who killed Jenny confessed."

"How?" he blurted, straightening with a start. "Who was it?"

I stepped past him uninvited and walked into the one-room apartment, drawn by the sun pouring in through the dusty window opposite the door. I stood next to it, feeling the heat on my face, along with an unexpected resurgence of the mixed emotions I'd felt when last in this man's company.

"Her landlord," I answered him. "When I went through her papers that night, I saw she was behind in the rent. He'd written her a letter that if she didn't pay up, he'd come by personally to collect what she owed him—one way or the other. I knew the guy, as it turns out. I couldn't put my finger on it when you and I were there, but I'd been in that cabin years ago to interview him about a sexual assault. Given that, I figured he'd done what he'd promised her he would, probably just before the storm broke, considering how long she'd been dead."

Roger was standing behind me. In the window's reflection, I could see him shaking his head. "Wow—that's incredible. I mean, everything pointed to me. You really saved my butt, just on a hunch."

I turned to face him, his gratitude raising my ire. "Not really. The cat's head had been smashed against the corner of the stove. No reason to have done that unless it had hassled the killer first. You didn't have any scratches, nor did Jenny's body, and there were traces of skin in the cat's claws."

"The landlord?"

I nodded. "His hand was not only all scratched up, but bruised from hitting Jenny. DNA analysis will bear it all out, but the confession should stand in any case. You were just in the wrong place at the wrong time—and you acted like a jerk."

Now it was Roger's turn to stare contemplatively out the window. "I thought I didn't have any choice."

"You didn't think at all," I corrected him, my voice tightening with a simmering anger I was surprised I couldn't control. "You just made assumptions, and sold everyone short, including yourself."

"I knew how it would look . . ."

"You had no idea," I interrupted, and pointed to a hole in the wall next to his rumpled bed. "That where you messed up your hand?"

He nodded.

"Punching the wall in rage against Jenny, just before you set out in midstorm to confront her?"

He was utterly still, seemingly frozen by my tone of voice.

"What were you going to do, Roger, if you hadn't found her dead? You didn't stop somewhere to bring her flowers, did you?"

"I wasn't gonna kill her," he whispered.

I moved closer to him, forcing him to look at me, a professional lifetime of pent-up resentment and frustration pushing to find expression. "The landlord didn't set out to kill her, either. But he'd hit women before, just like you hit Jenny that once. She didn't put up with it from you, and she wasn't going to take it from him. The only difference was that he didn't take no for an answer. He was farther down the road than you are, Roger, but it's still the same road. And as sure as I'm standing here, you'll end up in the same place."

He didn't say a word, not surprisingly, but his uncomprehending silence triggered a burst of pure rage in my brain, like a single electrical spark from an overloaded fuse. I smacked his forehead with the heel of my hand, hard enough to send him staggering a step or two backward. He stared at me, openmouthed, his hands at his sides.

"Focus on that fine line, Roger. Stop feeling so goddamned sorry for yourself and think about what you're doing when you're doing it. Is that too much to ask? From one human being to another?"

He blinked a couple of times. "No."

In control once more, I crossed over to the front door and stepped out into the hallway, turning to look back at him. "I hope not."

But I knew it was just a matter of time.

MARGARET MARON

Margaret Maron grew up near Raleigh, North Carolina, but for many years lived in Brooklyn, New York, where she drew her inspiration for her series about Lieutenant Sigrid Harald of the NYPD. When she returned to her North Carolina roots with her artist husband, she created the award-winning Deborah Knott series based on her own background. Knott's first appearance, in 1992's *Bootlegger's Daughter*, earned four top awards of the mystery world—the Edgar, the Anthony, the Agatha, and the Macavity—an unprecedented feat.

FIRST MYSTERIOUS PRESS PUBLICATION:
BOOTLEGGER'S DAUGHTER, 1992

WHAT'S IN A NAME?

It was a *Romeo and Juliet* love story.

Literally.

The Possum Creek Players staged a farcical version of Shakespeare's classic play last year—and yes, I agree that Shakespeare shouldn't be subjected to the desecrations of modern slang and modern levels of morality, but this was a very witty adaptation written to celebrate the four-hundredth anniversary of the play's original performance. Although the first half was played for laughs, the direction was such that by the end, we had segued fully into the original version, language and all. The audience, which had come for the laughs, found themselves totally involved, and there wasn't a dry eye in the house when Juliet, arising from her drugged "death" to find that Romeo has killed himself, commits suicide herself.

No laughs. Pure Shakespeare.

Romeo and Juliet were played by a couple of semiprofessionals with Equity cards, but the rest of the cast was drawn from stagestruck amateurs around the area. I myself played Lady Capulet, and before you picture me in gray wig and greasepaint wrinkles, remember that she was only fourteen when Juliet was born, if you can believe the lines Shakespeare has her speak. Friar Laurence was played by Paul Archdale, a Dobbs attorney with a thick shock of white hair;

and Marian Wilder, who owns a boarding stable between Dobbs and Cotton Grove, played Juliet's nurse.

It was lust at first sight.

But this *is* the Bible Belt and while the belt may have loosened a bit over the last few years, single women still can't let it all hang out. Not when they give riding lessons to impressionable children with straitlaced mothers. Nevertheless, courthouse gossip had Marian's little green pickup nosed under his carport, flank-to-flank with his silver BMW, six nights out of seven. His golden retriever immediately bonded with her fox terrier and the two dogs could be seen riding in her truck or romping together in the pasture almost every day.

Paul's taste usually runs to entry-level paralegals in flowery dresses, but he seemed to enjoy the novelty of a roll in the hay with someone who pitches hay for a living and who was his own age for a change.

Marian Wilder is widowed and childless and a lovely earthy woman with a heart as big as one of her horses. She wears her dark wavy hair clipped short and is letting it go gray. Her strong chin and determined nose are softened by deep blue eyes rimmed in long sooty lashes. Her laugh bubbles up in her throat like a brook that chuckles over smooth stones. It was clear to me what Paul saw in her, but I couldn't understand what she saw in him. He's a showboating egotist who never met a mirror he didn't love. It's impossible for him to pass any reflective surface without checking to see that his silk tie is perfectly knotted or to smooth his prematurely white hair with a beautifully manicured hand.

Marian cuts her own hair, probably hasn't had a manicure in twenty years, and prefers denim to silk.

With Paul's short attention span and voracious appetite,

I expected the novelty to wear off before we finished rehearsals. But no, a month after we closed the play, I heard that he had been seen pricing diamonds at the Jewel Chest on North Main. My friend Portland, whose law offices are in the same building as Paul's, said he'd even asked her where she and Avery went on their honeymoon.

"You think it's possible Paul Archdale could love somebody besides himself?" she asked doubtfully.

"Do pigs fly?" I said. "Get real."

. . .

It came as no surprise when I heard that the affair had ended scarcely three months after it began. What *was* a surprise—and much snickered over behind Paul's well-tailored back—is that Marian was the one who did the dumping. It was a first for Paul, and not something he was treating as a life-enhancing learning experience, according to my sources (any resemblance between said sources and partners in his own firm being purely coincidental).

None of this would have concerned me personally except that shortly after the breakup, Marian Wilder appeared in my courtroom before the first case was called. When I gave her permission to approach the bench, she came up, leaned in so that we wouldn't be overheard, and begged me to sign a restraining order against Paul.

"He hurt you?" I asked, keeping my own voice low. "Threatened to kill you?"

"Not me," she said, and her deep blue eyes filled with sudden tears. "Junebug."

The only Junebug in my memory banks was my brother Herman's granddaughter, born in the month of June and a real cutie, hence the nickname. I hardly thought Paul Arch-dale was any danger to a four-year-old living in Charlotte.

"His golden retriever," Marian explained. "He's going to have her put down."

"You want me to restrain him from having his own dog put to sleep?"

"He knows how much I love her and this is his way of getting back at me for ditching him."

It was too early in the morning and I'd had only two cups of coffee. "Let me get this straight. Paul's mad at you, so he's going to kill his own dog for revenge?"

"He doesn't give a flying flip about her." Marian spoke so sharply that my clerk looked up curiously from her com-puter screen and a couple of lawyers sitting in the jury box paused in their whispered conversation. She glared at them and they immediately dropped their eyes.

"She was a legacy from an old lady that he conned the same way he conned me."

In passionate whispers, Marian explained that Junebug had originally belonged to an elderly client, to whom Paul was assigned when she outlived the senior partner in his firm. She and her late husband had met at Duke and the bulk of their fortune was in trust to the university, but as she grew older, the interest accumulated faster than she could spend it and she found herself with a spare hundred thou-sand or so that wasn't already earmarked. Widowed and child-less, she had poured all her love into her pets, a couple of ancient cats and a golden retriever puppy; and when she de-veloped congestive heart failure, it had distressed her that they might be left homeless. Enter Paul, who shared her dis-tress and guess what? Damned if he didn't seem to love her pets almost as much as she did.

"I think Paul hoped she'd leave him a bundle outright, but instead, she made him their guardian and left him six thousand a year for as long as they lived with him. The two cats died before she did, but Junie was still a pup."

"He's going to put her down and give up six thousand a year?"

"He says that's just chump change for him these days. The real reason he's doing it is because he knows how much it'll hurt me. When he was begging me not to leave him, I made the mistake of saying that I'd already stayed two weeks longer than I would have because of Junie. She loves me more right now than she ever loved him. And why not? I took her out of that fenced-in yard. I let her romp all over my pastures and bridle trails. She and my dog are like littermates. You can't let him kill her! Please?"

Her eyes filled again and a tear spilled over onto her neat blue chambray shirt.

"I'm surprised he found a vet that'll put a healthy dog down for no real reason," I said as I clicked on my laptop computer and started looking for case law and precedents.

"He says Junie bit him. That's the only way he can get Gene to agree to this."

"Gene Adams?" Dr. Gene Adams takes care of Hambone, my Aunt Zell's beagle, and had, despite his basic shyness, played the Prince of Verona in our production of *Romeo and Juliet*.

Marian nodded. "I told Gene he had to be lying. Everybody knows how sweet-tempered goldens are. No way she's a biter, but Gene says there's nothing he can do about it. He says that if he won't put her to sleep, Paul's threatened to just shoot Junie himself. They're going to do it at four this afternoon."

I pulled up the text of North Carolina's cruelty to animals statute and rapidly scrolled through, skim-reading as I went. The gist was that should any person "maliciously torture, mutilate, maim, cruelly beat, disfigure, poison, or kill" an animal, that person would be guilty of a Class I felony. The word "maliciously" was defined as "an act committed intentionally and with malice or bad motive." Marian could swear on the Bible that these words exactly described Paul's true motive for killing his dog. Unfortunately, the law had several exemptions and one of them allowed "the lawful destruction of any animal for the purposes of protecting the public, other animals, property, or the public health."

Paul didn't have to prove that the dog had bitten him. His word was enough. The law doesn't try to understand *why* a dog bites; it only assigns liability when it does.

"I'm sorry," I told Marian. "Unless there's something in the original owner's will, there's no legal way to restrain him."

"The will?" she breathed, hope spreading across her face.

"If she was a resident of Colleton County, it'll be on file here at the courthouse," I said.

Marian had no idea of the date, but she did remember the woman's name and I told her I'd look it up during my lunch break.

"If there's nothing there, could you just talk to him?" she implored. "He respects you. I saw how he went out of his way to be nice to you during the play."

I was amused. For such a competent businesswoman, Marian Wilder could be extremely naive. Of course Paul Archdale was nice to me. Most attorneys are. Judges are supposed to be objective, their decisions unaffected by personalities. But judges are also human, and when a ruling for your client could literally go either way, best not to have been rude or disrespectful to the judge.

If Paul's dog were a pit bull or rottweiler, I might not have interfered. But this was a golden, for pete's sake, probably the least prone to biting in the whole canine family. Against my will, I heard myself say, "Okay. I'll talk to him."

■ ■ ■

Easier said than done as it turned out. Paul was supposed to try a case in front of me later that morning, but the charges against his client had been dropped and the hearing canceled.

Down in the county clerk's office, I found Louisa Ripley Ferncliff's emended will with no trouble and was bemused to see that she must have been smarter than Paul could have wished because she'd figured out a retriever's average life expectancy and put a sunset clause into the bequest. It expired this very year. How nice for him. Put a guilt trip on Marian when he was probably going to dump the dog anyway now that she was no longer worth six thousand a year to him.

I called over to his office and was told that he'd be out for the rest of the day. A machine answered his home phone. I left a message, but wasn't hopeful he'd get it in time.

Court finished at 3:40 and Marian was waiting for me in chambers.

"Was there anything in the will to stop him?" she asked.

"Sorry," I said.

"Well, what did he say when you talked to him?"

"I didn't," I told her. "I couldn't get in touch with him."

She looked aghast. "And they're going to do it in twenty

minutes! You've got to come with me to Gene's. Talk him out of it. Please?"

It was only six minutes across the river to Gene Adams's clinic. Marian was so agitated I made her follow my car instead of tearing over through red lights. When we got there, Paul and Junebug were the only ones in the waiting room. As soon as she spotted Marian, that beautiful animal stood up and started wagging her tail happily. Paul had to double his hold on her leash to keep her from rushing over. Marian immediately knelt down beside her and started petting the dog, who nuzzled her with touching enthusiasm.

Paul seemed surprised to see me.

"You here to pick up an animal, Judge?" he asked, reaching out to shake my hand.

"Not exactly." I kept his hand in mine and said in my most coaxing tones, "I came to ask you to rethink what you're about to do. Is it really necessary to put this dog to sleep? I read Mrs. Ferncliff's will and I know the dog's annuity expires this year, so couldn't you just give her to Marian? Let her go live at the stable?"

"And maybe have her bite one of the children who go to ride there?" he asked with matching earnestness. "I'd have it on my conscience for life if one of those kids had to have stitches in their face."

"Goldens aren't natural biters," I argued. "Surely it was an aberration."

He hesitated. After all, I *am* a judge and he's an ambitious attorney.

Unfortunately, Marian picked that minute to look up from the dog. "Liar! She never bit you. You're only doing this because I dumped you."

Paul's lips tightened and he gave Junebug's leash a vicious tug just as Gene Adams opened the door to his examining room.

The dog yelped and looked at Paul reproachfully but he didn't notice.

"Sorry, Judge," he said. "But the only thing to do with a biter is put it down."

Oblivious to its fate, the condemned dog had gone back to nuzzling Marian's hand, tail thumping happily against the tiled floor. Marian was openly weeping now and Gene was clearly distressed by her unhappiness, yet was too shy to offer a consoling hug. Paul tried to look sad but I could see malice in his eyes when Gene said, "Are you sure this is really necessary, Paul?"

"The damn dog bit me. It's my public duty."

So he had read the statute, too.

"What are you going to do with her?" Marian asked. "Afterwards, I mean."

That was clearly something Paul hadn't given thought to.

"I can dispose of the body, if you wish," Gene offered. His words were for Paul, but his eyes were on Marian and I suddenly realized that Paul wasn't the only one who'd fallen for her during the run of our play.

"No!" Marian said fiercely. "Let me bury her out at the stable. She was so happy there. Please, Paul! You can't say no to this."

Actually, he probably would have had I not been standing there.

"If that's what you want, then, of course," he said, as if bestowing an enormous favor.

The injection wasn't something I wanted to watch, but Marian dragged me inside. Gene rummaged through his file cabinet and came up empty-handed.

"I don't know where my secretary keeps the releases," he told Paul. "But here." He quickly scribbled some phrases onto a pad. "Just sign and date this and we'll get started."

Paul signed impatiently without reading, then stood back as Gene lifted Junebug onto a table and weighed her so he could compute the correct dosage.

While Marian scratched her ears and whispered sweet sad words of good-bye, he filled a syringe with pentobarbital and inserted the needle so gently that Junebug didn't flinch. A few moments later, the dog gave a big sigh and lay down. Her eyes closed, her body relaxed, her breathing slowed. Quicker than I expected, Gene covered the dog's body with a disposable paper sheet.

"So how much do I owe you?" Paul asked, reaching for his wallet and bringing it back to a commercial transaction.

"Nothing," Gene answered brusquely. "I don't charge for putting an animal to sleep like this."

"Well, okay, then," said Paul. "Thanks."

There was a moment of awkwardness as he tried to figure out the protocol of leave-taking after an execution.

Gene ignored his outstretched hand. "One more thing, Archdale."

"Yeah?"

"If you decide to get another animal, find yourself a different vet."

Except for the lines Shakespeare had provided, none of us had ever heard this big shy man speak so forcefully. Paul glowered and left in a huff, but Marian reached out and touched his arm.

"Thank you, Gene."

He turned bright pink and said, "I'll carry her out for you."

I followed them to the truck and Marian had him lay the body on the passenger seat in the cab.

As he closed the door, Gene gathered his nerve and said, "I'm finished here for the day. How about I come on out and dig her grave for you."

"You don't have to do that," Marian said.

"I want to."

"Okay, then. Thanks. And thank you, too, Deborah, for trying." With tears stinging her eyes again, she gave us both impulsive hugs and drove off toward her stable.

Well, I thought, looking at Gene's face, one good thing might yet come out of this unhappy little episode.

■ ■ ■

Less than a week passed before I heard that Gene had located another female golden for Marian through one of the breed's rescue shelters. Once again her terrier had someone to romp with and people began to wonder—okay, I wondered—if there might be wedding bells in their future.

"In the fall," Gene admitted shyly when I carried Aunt Zell's beagle in for its booster shots a month after I'd watched him euthanize Junebug. "I guess Archdale did us a favor after all."

"It was good of you to go help her bury the dog," I said, imagining the bittersweetness of the moment. Digging the grave. Laying that poor animal to rest. "Where did y'all put her? In the pasture?" Then I remembered that Marian had a small pet cemetery where her first pony was buried. "Or down by the paddock?"

Hambone yelped as the needle went in and it was a moment before Gene answered. "Under that oak tree at the top of her pasture. We like to ride up there."

"That's a beautiful view," I said, thinking that it was also a romantic view—rolling green pasture that sloped down to thick woods.

. . .

A week later, I found myself enjoying the same view while seated atop one of Marian's mares. I'd driven over that afternoon to ask what she charged for jumping lessons. One of my nieces wanted to learn the proper form and, since her birthday was coming up soon, I thought it might make a great present.

Marian was fuming because all the horses hadn't been exercised and when I showed up in jeans and sneakers, she soon had me booted and in the saddle of a sturdy little dun-colored mare named Cornelia.

She didn't look at all like my idea of a stately Roman matron.

"Her name was Cornmeal when I bought her," said Marian. "Horses and dogs. They know their names and if you want to change it, you have to pick something that sounds similar. Cornelia's maybe a little too elegant but Cornmeal was too much of a put-down."

We spent the next half hour galloping briskly around the pasture. Tuggle, the fox terrier, and Juliet, the new golden retriever, tagged along till Marian blew on a dog whistle strung around her neck and, with a gesture of her arm, sent them to wait for us on the crest of the hill.

"Juliet?" I teased when we pulled up beside them under that big shady oak. "Because the play was where Gene fell for you?"

"And I was so stupid I never noticed him for Paul."

"Don't beat up on yourself," I said. "You weren't the first, you won't be the last."

I glanced around, half expecting to see a stone marker, but the grass was smooth here under the tree. Nor was there any sign of recent digging.

"Where did you and Gene bury Junebug?" I asked.

"Down by the paddock," she said. "Next to Starfire."

I suddenly found myself remembering the apocryphal story of Susanna and the lying elders.

When questioned separately, the first one told Daniel, "We saw her sin under a mastic tree."

"Under an evergreen oak," said the other.

Marian and Gene really needed to get their stories straight.

"Ready for another gallop?" Marian asked, gathering up her reins.

"Not just yet." I hadn't quite finished working it all out, but when I did, I laughed out loud, wondering just what sort of release Gene had maneuvered Paul into signing.

"What?" she asked.

"*What's in a name?*" I quoted happily. "*That which we call a rose, by any other name would smell as sweet,* right, Junebug?"

The golden retriever perked up her ears.

Marian gave me a wary look and her horse moved uneasily beneath her. "What are you talking about?"

"Shakespeare, of course. Juliet took a sleeping potion that, how does it go? . . . *wrought on her the form of death*? Gene gave the dog just enough sedative to put her in a deep sleep and keep her asleep till he could be here with you when she woke up."

Her face paled beneath its tan. "He couldn't bear to let

an animal be killed for spite. You're not going to tell Paul, are you?"

"Tell him what? That you have a new dog? When everyone's heard how much trouble Gene took to find you a dog as near like Junebug as he could?"

She relaxed visibly into the saddle. "Thanks, Deborah."

Down at the stables, an old blue Volvo wagon had pulled into the drive. Both dogs went streaking down the slope, racing to get to Gene Adams first.

Marian cantered after them, her face aglow with quiet happiness.

I chucked Cornelia's reins and we followed more slowly so that Marian would have time to warn Gene that I knew and to assure him their secret was safe with me.

• • •

Except that it wasn't.

The very next day, Paul Archdale waylaid me after court. He stormed into the office I was using and acted ill as a cat with a tail full of sandspurs.

"I guess you and those two lovebirds think all golden retrievers look alike to me," he snarled. He was too angry to accord me the usual courtesy of my robe.

I closed the door and looked at him coldly. "I don't know what you're talking about."

"Marian was in town today and my dog was riding in the back of her truck. Adams never put it down, did he? And you were in on that little farce, too, weren't you? Begging to save it when you knew damn well Adams was just going through the motions to fool me."

"I believe you signed a paper giving him the right to treat the dog as he saw fit," I said, hedging for time.

A worthless ploy. No attorney worth his salt would let a little technicality like that deter him.

"He deliberately misled me." Paul's face was almost beet red beneath his thick white hair. There was nothing handsome about his mouth, now twisted with fury. "By God, I'll have his license and I'll have you up on ethics and I'll damn well see my dog with a bullet through its head before this day's out."

I could only stare at him impotently. While I could truthfully say that I thought Junebug was dead when Gene put her body on the seat of Marian's truck, there was no way I could put my hand on a Bible and swear I still thought she was dead.

Paul was almost bouncing on the balls of his feet in malicious triumph. "Thought you could fool me. Thought I wouldn't know my own dog!"

Well, as a matter of fact, yes. To most people, one golden retriever *does* look pretty much like another. Who'd have guessed that Paul Archdale had taken that much notice of a dog he'd never bonded with?

I thought of Gene Adams hauled up before a professional board of ethics. I pictured the very real possibility of getting censured myself.

And poor old Junebug. Finally free to romp and race and—

Hey, wait a minute here!

"I'm afraid you've made a mistake," I said. "It's not your dog."

"Like hell it's not!"

"No, no," I said, giving him my sweetest smile. "I read the will, remember? You and I are probably the only ones who realize it was probated seventeen years ago. There's no way that's the same dog that old Mrs. Ferncliff left in your care. Marian's dog can't be more than three or four years old. But we'll get an opinion from an outside vet if you like. They can approximate an animal's age. An eighteen-year-old dog would barely be able to hobble across a room. It certainly wouldn't have the stamina to chase after horses all day. I'm sure the trustees over at Duke would be interested in learning just how long the original Junebug's actually been dead. Is this her first replacement or maybe the second or third? If we subpoena your financial records, will we find check stubs or credit card listings for the kennel where you bought them?"

I watched the color drain from his face as our roles reversed and he realized that he was awfully close to starring in his own ethics hearing. Not to mention a possible criminal trial if the Duke trustees did get wind of it and pushed for prosecution. I could almost see him multiplying six thousand dollars a year by eighteen years.

With compound interest.

I myself would need a calculator, but even without one, I knew it wasn't, to use his phrase, chump change.

"You're right," he said at last. "I was mistaken. It's not my dog." The words almost choked him. "I apologize."

As I watched Paul Archdale slink away like the villain in a Possum Creek melodrama, I couldn't help thinking again of good old Shakespeare. An apt phrase for every situation.

Like, *all's well that ends well.*

JAMES CRUMLEY

Born in Three Rivers, Texas, **James Crumley** served three years in the U.S. Army before teaching English as a Visiting Writer at the University of Texas at El Paso and Carnegie Mellon University; he now makes his home in Montana. His detective novels featuring Milo Milodragovitch and C. W. Sughrue, including 1978's *The Last Good Kiss*, are regarded as masterpieces of contemporary crime fiction. Crumley received the Dashiell Hammett Award for Best Literary Crime Novel from the International Association of Crime Writers in 1994.

FIRST MYSTERIOUS PRESS PUBLICATION:
THE MEXICAN TREE DUCK, 1993

COMING AROUND
THE MOUNTAIN

elena sat on the edge of the corn-husk mattress, pulling on the scratchy wool tights she wore against the sharp bite of the morning cold in the narrow, blind canyon. She knew how it would be when the men came back. Even through the fuzzy mist of the infernal soft rain, Helena would see their slickers shining, bright yellow sparks against the mottled green of the hillside, easing their blown, muddy horses down the switchbacks into the hidden valley. The larch had turned golden, gleaming like fool's gold among the dark fir trees, and the bark of the occasional bull pine the loggers had missed glowed darkly like a high-yield vein shot through milky quartz. She would watch and wait. Forever, if necessary. But today she knew the soft rain would blur all the colors into a drifting smudge until she couldn't tell the smoke from the cabin fires from the misty rain as she leaned, elbow deep in bubbling hot water and the hard bite of the lye soap.

Helena paused for a moment after she pulled on the heavy tarred canvas skirt and stepped into her clogs. Her hand darted greedily to the paper-wrapped bundle she had been using as a pillow. Her fingers fumbled nervously at the knot, then she quickly unrolled the bundle. The fine white silk of the wedding dress, a creamy white verging on yellow like ancient ivory, seemed to draw all the light from the dank corners of her small cabin, and, except for a small brown stain on the hem, the dress seemed to glow on the dirty canvas mattress like a ghostly form. Perhaps the ghost of lost happiness, she said to herself. It sounded like the name of a miner's whiskey dream of a glory hole. Helena didn't trust her twisted fingers to touch the material. Instead she knelt beside the mean cot to stroke her cheek against the silk. If she could have purred, she would have.

Quickly she bundled the silk dress, tied new knots, then hid the dress inside the ticking of the corn-shuck mattress. Shaking her skirt as if the tarred canvas were satin, she wrapped her hair in a dirty gray scarf and hustled out to chop kindling wood for her washtub fires. She was the luckiest woman in town.

Of course, when the diggings played out, the women disappeared, so only four other women lived in the mining camp: old Mrs. Beam, whose husband ran the Mercantile; a lovely coolie girl Ben Eastman had bought for a single knuckle-sized nugget over in Oreville; the defrocked preacher's wife, a moonfaced country girl from Illinois; and Pearl, the fat soiled dove who ran a tiny bar cut into the hillside where some lazy miner had abandoned his start on a shaft, built a still, and started the bar with one jug of squeezings of a whiskey so raw a man had to get drunk just to recover from his first drink, two raw yellow pine planks set across two barrels, and a player piano stolen from a bunch of lost Mormons. Helena had come to this tiny place tucked at the end of the box canyon, this place nobody had bothered to name, from San Francisco with Pearl and two other girls. Helena was almost pretty in an exotic, multiracial way — she was the spawn of a high yellow gambler from the Natchez Trace and the daughter of a Japanese seal hunter and a half-

breed California woman—and might have been pretty all
the way through but for her walleye, which destroyed the
symmetry of her long, oval face.

But as she began to split the rounds for kindling, Helena
thought herself the luckiest woman in town. Or if not the
luckiest, the happiest. Certainly happier than Mrs. Beam,
who always looked as if she had a green persimmon stuck
up her bunghole. Or the coolie woman, who was a slave
and who was so tiny that it seemed surely Big Ben Eastman
would split her apart on their four-poster feather bed—Ben
Eastman let other men do his mining; he did his mining
with a sawed-off ten-gauge Remington. And the defrocked
preacher's wife, who followed Adam Dunsmore's shambling,
gambling, gunfighting ass from camp to camp, from financial disaster to disaster, sitting in the bars without a drink,
mooning at him, praying, waiting for the moment his call
to the pulpit returned, which she was sure would happen
any day. And Pearl, poor sodden Pearl. Everybody was happier than Pearl. Her looks had withered into the alcoholic
lard of her face, disappearing like her savings, even her will
to move to the newer strikes up north. She spent her days
sipping the raw whiskey, smoking rotten cheroots, and listening to the one unbroken piano roll as its tinkling notes
drifted like pale smoke in the confines of the blind canyon.

Helena laid her fire carefully under the iron pots, shallow pyramids stacked over coal-oil-soaked sawdust and shav-
ings, then picked up the bucket yoke and hiked stolidly to
the creek to fill the buckets, then walked back, moving
steadily and surely, as she had every day since the diggings
played out and she stopped working on her back.

To be sure, Helena had met Mathieu Van Dorn on her
back in one of the two tiny cribs dug into the abandoned

mine shaft behind the bar. He hadn't known her name—she was just a two-dollar whore to him—but she fell in love with his sturdy Dutchman's body covered by a skin as pale as ivory and white-blond hair. Even polecat drunk, Matt's jaw was firm, his blazing blue eyes steadfast. Helena made a point of finding out his name and not looking him in the eye when he came back several times before he left with the rest of the miners. She thought about him often in the hard days after almost everybody left town and she stopped being a whore and started taking in laundry like some poor Chinaman. But bit by bit some of the miners returned, disappointed with the lack of color in the northern strikes, returned to rebuild the rocker boxes and rewash the tailings more carefully. Helena knew from experience that there would be a long pause while the men washed for dust and before a big company came in with their dirt-eating hydraulic hoses and steam-powered dredges. Helena also knew she had to take advantage of this pause to make enough money to move on before the company came in with their wage slaves, men who seldom had a dollar to spare for clean clothes or two bits for a tip or even a quick smile for an almost pretty girl, a smile that died aborning when they saw her wandering walleye. But she changed her plans the spring day she saw Big Ben Eastman, followed by his China-girl, leading a three-mule pack train down the switchbacks into the canyon. And bringing up the rear, her blue-eyed hope, his blond hair shining in the gray shadows, a half-empty bottle of bonded whiskey hanging from his fingers.

. . .

Matt, ignorant of her new stance and looking for a two-dollar poke, caught up with Helena on the trail back from the creek. She was handcuffed by the heavy buckets at either end of her yoke, and he was full of drunken laughter and seemed to have a dozen rough hands poking and pulling at all her parts, not listening to her at all. But when Helena got back to the washtubs, she set down the buckets, picked up a stick of kindling wood, and went upside his head with a blow that stretched him out like a dead man.

"Holy jumping Jesus, woman!" Matt moaned as he struggled to his knees, holding his left ear together as blood streamed between his fingers. "You fucking two-dollar whore, you damn near took my head off."

"I don't do that no more," she said quietly, then thumped him once more on top of the head to get his attention. "Lemme look at that ear." Matt obediently moved his hand and tilted his head. "Come on up to the cabin, Mathieu, and I'll sew your ear back together."

"How is it you know my name, woman?"

"How is it you don't know mine, mister?"

So they began to court while she poured bonded whiskey over his ear, then helped him drink the rest of the bottle before she picked up the heavy curved canvas needle and thick twine.

Afterward, she patted his rosy cheek and said, "It ain't pretty, but it'll do."

He glanced up from under his blond bangs, a sly smile on his face as he said, "Well, you're pretty and you'll damn sure do. How 'bout a three-dollar poke?"

Helena reached behind her for the kindling stick, held it in front of his face. "You'd look funny, mister, if I knocked the other ear plumb off your block head."

"How about a five-dollar poke?" he asked, smiling as he stroked her hip. The stick slammed against his fingers like a rat trap snapping shut. "Goddammit, woman, you're worse than a drunk redhide nigger with a shotgun with that stick. Just stop it."

"No," Helena said calmly, "you stop it."

And so it went through the spring and summer and into early fall. Matt would leave for weeks at a time with Big Ben Eastman and a couple of Kansas redlegs, then return with bonded whiskey and folding money. But no matter how high Matt raised his offer for just a friendly poke, Helena refused him, refused him even on the night when he broke down drunkenly and asked her to marry him, refused him even the next day when he repeated his offer. "When?" she asked, and he answered, "When I get back from the next job." "Ask me again, then," she said, "ask me again." Matt just nodded, kissed her softly on the lips, and climbed on his horse.

As winter drew closer, and with it the freezing of the small creeks, a man couldn't pan color out of ice or dig it out of the frozen earth. And Helena's laundry business would dry up like last summer's cottonwood leaves.

Then one morning while Helena was buying cornmeal for johnnycakes, she noticed a small note scribbled on the back of a label off an airtight can of peaches: *Wedding dress for sale. Never used. See Mrs. Beam.*

Mrs. Beam had never had much truck with Helena, or any other of the soiled doves for that matter. Her manner had always suggested disapproval. She had taken their money without touching their hands, as if by mere contact she might contract some sordid disease like lust, or charm, or unbridled laughter. Mrs. Beam was a stout woman with a butt as wide as two ax handles, the shoulders of a small bear, and a tiny round head perched on top. Mr. Beam looked like a small child she had adopted, starved, then beaten like a red-

headed stepchild. Mrs. Beam's pinched mouth dropped, outlined by a faint mustache, but when Helena approached the
counter, the note in her hand, Mrs. Beam broke into a mirac-
ulous smile, exposing tiny white teeth like pearls.

"Now, what would you be wanting with a wedding dress,
honey?" Mrs. Beam warbled in a curiously high voice. "You
haven't talked that square-headed Dutchman into changing
his ways, now have you?"

Helena glanced away, turning her bad side to the wall.
"Could I see the dress, please, ma'am?"

"Of course, darling." Mrs. Beam reached under the
counter and brought out a paper bundle. Unwrapped,
stretched out, the long silk dress brightened the small store
as if a stray sunbeam had suddenly filled the canyon. The
heavy stitching at the bodice gleamed like jewels of the first
order. The lace trim at the neckline looked as fragile as spi-
derwebs.

"It's lovely," Helena purred, and without thinking reached
to touch the material with her rough fingers, jerked them
back, then touched her cheek to the front of the skirt, running her skin against it as if the silk were alive. Then Helena noticed the small brown stain near the hem.

"My daughter's," Mrs. Beam said, "my only issue." When
Helena raised an eyebrow, Mrs. Beam continued. "It was
one of those damned blood feuds down on the Arkansas.
Nobody remembered how it started. Just two neighbor families gone insane. Somebody's hog broke into somebody's
corncrib, or somebody's runt stallion topped somebody's
brood mare, or somebody's hound dog ate somebody's favorite fighting rooster. Who knows? But by the time my
Mazie fell in love with Brodie Pike, there was bound to be
a killing over it. I stole the money from Mr. Beam's savings

to buy the silk, nearly ruined my eyesight stitching the dress, gave it to the children and told them to run, run west, start a new life." Mrs. Beam paused.

"My mister caught them over in Carroll County, Missouri, in a stable. The ball he put through Brodie Pike's throat hit Mazie in the eye. The son of a bitch might as well have shot the two of us at the same time.

"We ran west for years, keeping store from one hangtown hole to another." Mrs. Beam ran down like a tired top.

"Why sell it now?" Helena whispered.

"We've run as far away as we can go," Mrs. Beam answered. "Some California mining company bought us out, store and stock. It's time for us to go home—time for Mazie's dress to be worn in love and laughter."

"What would you be wanting for it?"

"Give me one silver dollar, child," she said, "and I'll give you a kiss for luck."

The old woman's dry lips were warm against Helena's cheek. The kiss burned against her cheek as she walked home, her face cool in the damp mist, walked back to her mean cabin to wait through the rain for the return of the men.

■ ■ ■

But the men returned in a heavy, wet snow, the tired horses breaking through the drifts of the switchbacks. Helena had waited through the late summer's rainfall, through a long Indian summer, and the falling and melting of the first two mountain snows, trying to keep her hope alive by unwrapping the dress, touching the silk with her cheek. But she allowed herself to hope no more than once a week. Usually after a quiet drink with fat Pearl, Dunsmore, and his moon-faced wife. Just one.

As the days slipped by toward the sere heart of winter, Helena's hope became as thin as the color in the diggings, and her laundry business dried up like the thin suds of her lye soap. But each day she chopped the wood, carried the water, and waited between the fires, occasionally lifting her face to scan the switchbacks.

Helena heard the horses before she saw them through the thick white light of late afternoon. The two men from bloody Kansas had disappeared as quickly as they had come, and the body of Big Ben Eastman, wrapped in a canvas sheet, rode draped over the pack horse led by the China-girl, as she rode his sorrel as if she had been born to ride the outlaw trail, his twin .44s bundled at her tiny hips. Matt brought up the rear, so drunk he could barely sit his saddle, his right hand holding the handle of a jug of home-made whiskey, his left hand bound in a dirty rag holding the saddle horn, the reins loosely wrapped around the horn. Helena stood in the swirls of heavy snow, but the China-girl went directly to her cabin. And Matt straight to Pearl's.

Helena didn't pause even to douse the fires but walked straight into the cabin, undressed in the raw cold, carefully with her rough hands dug out her only pair of silk stockings and a tattered slip, left over from her days at Pearl's, out of the small trunk she had kept packed for weeks, unwrapped the wedding silk, then quickly dressed. She forced her feet into narrow, high-button shoes, draped her wool coat over her shoulders, then marched through the moving veil of snowflakes to Pearl's.

Nobody noticed when Helena opened the door. The wind hammered at the shutters, the piano tinkled wanly. Pearl stood behind the bar, smoking a twisted cheroot as if that were the sole purpose of her life. Matt and Dunsmore leaned on the bar, sharing the jug. Dunsmore's wife sat forlorn in a far dark corner. Helena slammed the door as hard as she could and slipped the coat off her shoulders. Everyone looked up at once.

"Ask me again," Helena said to Matt's tired, dirty face.

"Now, ain't you something to look at, honey," Matt said, a lopsided grin bright on his stubble-dark face.

"God damn you, ask again," she said.

Matt held up his rag-wrapped hand. "Hell, honey, I ain't hardly dressed for a wedding," he said. "When that shotgun guard took down Ben with a load of horseshoe nails, he took off two of my fingers. I ain't got a ring or a finger to put it on."

"Ask again," she repeated, louder this time.

"If it hadn't been for Bill's China-girl with that little pistol in her purse," he said as if he hadn't heard her, "I'd have been dead with the rest of them."

"Give that preacher-man another drink," Helena said, "and step over here, you damned drunken Dutchman."

"I ain't about to let this piece of trash do nothin' for me," Matt said, his hand on the jug. "And he's about had enough of my whiskey."

The preacher's wife rushed to his side, sobbing and talking in a rush of words. "Adam, marry them. You remember the words. Marry them. You remember."

Dunsmore shoved his wife roughly away from his side. "Marry him?" he said. "I'll bury the son of a bitch. Then dig him up in the spring and sell his body to the Wells Fargo Overland Stage company."

"Damned if you will!" Matt shouted, then dug for the pistol in his coat pocket.

But Dunsmore was faster, his Starr .44 with the trigger tied back out of his cross-draw holster in a flash, the hammer thumbed back and dropped before Matt cleared his pocket. The round caught Matt under the nose. A palm-sized piece of bloody skull landed on the bar. Matt fell to his knees, dead before he hit the floor. But with the last piece of his life, he pulled the trigger, the pistol still in his pocket. The preacher's wife took the round to her breast as if it were a lost child, a spray of heart's blood splashing from the middle of her back, fine droplets soaking into the old ivory of the wedding dress as Helena stood there with a grandly impassive face.

"Oh, Jesus," Dunsmore moaned.

"Don't be calling for Jesus, you bastard," Pearl cursed around the cheroot stub between her teeth as she raised a bung-starter and slammed it into the side of Dunsmore's face so hard that his left eyeball popped out and Helena could hear the dull crunch as his skull caved into his brain. Dunsmore hit the floor as if shot.

"What now?" Helena said quietly.

"Well, honey," Pearl answered, flicking ashes into the skull fragment on the bar, "I been meaning to move out of this shit-hole for a long time now. How about you?"

Helena nodded, slipped into her coat, and stepped into the weather.

. . .

The storm broke just before dusk. The last rays of sunlight glowed golden off the snow and the cold water in the tub where Helena scrubbed lightly at the bloody stains on the wedding dress.

The next morning bloomed clear and cold, sunlight pouring through into the narrow valley as Pearl stopped the two mules, parking her wagon in front of Helena's cabin. Helena stepped out of the cabin, the small trunk on her shoulder, loaded it into the wagon beside the player piano.

"Just a moment," she said to Pearl, then stepped back into the cabin. She came out moments later, the paper-wrapped parcel under her arm.

Inside the Beams' store, Helena set the parcel on the counter and asked for a piece of paper.

"I heard the dress was bloodstained," Mrs. Beam said quietly. "I'm sorry."

"I washed it very carefully," Helena answered, untying the package and spreading the dress out as Mrs. Beam handed her a scrap of paper and a pencil.

"You sure you want to sell the dress?"

"Very sure."

"Even the old stain is gone," Mrs. Beam said as Helena labored over the paper. Two tears dropped from Helena's face onto the silk, stains darker than blood. Then another onto the paper, blurring the words: *For sale wedding dress. Never used.*

M. C. BEATON

M.C. **Beaton**, Scottish by birth, has written seventeen Hamish Macbeth mysteries, beginning with *Death of a Gossip* in 1985, and the BBC has filmed twenty-two one-hour episodes based on the series. Also the author of the Agatha Raisin series, and dozens of Regency romance novels written under a variety of pseudonyms, M. C. Beaton lives in a Cotswold cottage with her husband.

FIRST MYSTERIOUS PRESS PUBLICATION:
DEATH OF A CHARMING MAN, 1994

HANDLE WITH CARE

Jobs were hard to find in the very north of Scotland. Most of the crofters who lived in and around the village of Lochdubh in Sutherland had fallen upon hard times.

So, as often happens in a depression, the women go out to work. And there was always work to be found at the Lochdubh Fish Farm, located only a few miles outside the village. Unfortunately, the owner, Charlie Sneddy, took advantage of the recession by paying rock-bottom wages and expecting the women to work long hours.

Police constable Hamish Macbeth decided one sunny day to walk his dog, Lugs, out to the fish farm. Lugs was partial to smoked salmon, and Hamish knew if he called at the door of the factory where the women were slicing and packing the salmon, they would probably give him some scraps. He also wanted to have a word with Sneddy. He knew there was bad feeling building up against the man. Sneedy had changed in the last two years and had become mean. The women were tired of the low wages and long hours. Any tiny mistake, and money was docked from their meager pay.

Good summer days were rare in the Highlands of Scotland, particularly in Lochdubh, where damp winds from the Atlantic only too often swept rain and sea fog into the village. Hamish had been enjoying a good stretch of crime-free life and he planned to make the most of it by doing what

he did best—very little at all. The call to the fish farm would
serve two purposes: to get tidbits for Lugs and to make sure
that nothing bad was going to happen and he could con-
tinue his lazy days.

He walked along the side of the sea loch, which was as
still as a mirror. His long lanky figure and his flaming-red
hair—for he had, against regulations, gone out without his
cap—were reflected in the still waters of the loch, so that it
looked as if two Hamish Macbeths and two dogs were
strolling in the direction of the fish farm.

"Aye, it's the grand day, Lugs," said Hamish, and two local
children fishing in the loch giggled at the sight of the tall
policeman chatting to his dog. Lugs lolled his tongue out
and looked up at his master with his odd blue eyes.

Hamish saw Angela Brodie, the doctor's wife, walking toward him. He hailed her. "Fine day, Angela."

"It is that. Where are you off to?"

"The fish farm."

"Oh, you've heard."

"Heard what? I was chust going to call in and see if they
had any scraps for Lugs. He aye likes his bit of smoked
salmon."

By the sudden sibilance of Hamish's Highland accent,
Angela guessed that Hamish was worried about circumstances at the fish farm.

"You know Sneddy pays bad wages and makes them work
long hours?"

"That I do, and it hass been bothering me for some time.
Anything new?"

"He's going to celebrate the anniversary of the fish farm
next week, a party for the staff at the Tommel Castle Hotel."

Hamish stared at her in amazement. "I dinnae believe

it! It'll cost the wee man a packet. It's only ten years since he started up the farm. Not a hundred. So what's the problem? The staff'll be glad to see him dipping into his pocket at last."

"Oh, but he's going to get the money out of *them*. In honor of the anniversary, they've to forfeit one-third of their pay for a week."

"He cannae do that! You cannae punish people by paying them less than they're worth chust because it's an anniversary."

"He's doing it, all right, and the message to the staff is that they can like it or lump it, and if they lump it, there's plenty more where they came from. Feeling's running high."

"Thanks, Angela. I'd best be having a word with him."

Hamish went on his way, his pleasure in the glory of the day considerably dimmed.

The factory soon came into view, concrete, squat, and ugly, crouched beside the loch. He went round to the back and through a door which led into a long room where six women slaved at slicing and packaging the salmon after it had been brought in from the smoke shed. Other factories might have machines to slice and pack the salmon, but here it was all done by hand. The strips of smoked salmon were placed on cardboard trays and covered in cling film and then labeled.

There was a chorus of "Hello, Hamish" when the women saw him, but they went on steadily with their work. He waited until the bell rang signaling the lunch hour.

The women gathered round him, patting Lugs. "What's this I hear about the anniversary party?" asked Hamish.

His ears were assailed by a jumbled cacophony of complaint, until a powerful woman, Bridget Macleod, stepped in front to act as spokeswoman. "What can we do about it, Hamish? If we boycott the party or go on strike, the auld scunner says he'll just close the place down."

"I'll have a word with him. Any scraps for Lugs?"

A tall, Gypsy-looking woman, Aileen McPhail, went to her station and scooped up some scraps and put them in a paper bag and was just handing them to Hamish when Charlie Sneddy suddenly appeared in their midst. He was wearing thick rubber-soled shoes and must have crept up on them. He was a small, stooped man with a large nose and small rosebud of a mouth. He had powerful long arms and short bandy legs. He snatched the bag from Aileen and peered inside.

"What's this, lassie?"

"Just a few wee bitties for Hamish's dog," she mumbled.

"That's theft," howled Sneedy. "You know I sell these scraps. Off your wages it comes."

Hamish would not have felt so suddenly frightened had the women screamed and protested, but they stood in a silent group, their eyes as hard as stones, emanating hatred.

"You got it wrong, Sneddy," said Hamish. "I was buying them."

"That'll be three pounds."

"For some tatty edges o' the fish?"

"Aye."

"Let's go into your office," said Hamish. "It iss high time you and I had a talk."

He handed over three pounds. "Thanks," whispered Aileen to his retreating back as Hamish followed Sneddy out of the long shed and through to his office, which was situated in the middle of the complex.

"So what's your beef?" demanded Sneddy, sitting down behind a cheap metal desk.

"Your working practices," said Hamish.

"You can't be getting me on that. I pay the minimum wage."

"What you do is have them working long hours because you claim they haven't met their quota, and you don't pay overtime. They're all that terrified of getting sacked that they let you get away with it. There's not enough women for the smoked salmon packing and so they often have to put in extra hours. Afore this recession, you went by the book. But now you know they're desperate for work, you're taking unfair advantage."

"Havers. You Highlanders are just damn lazy," sneered Sneddy, who came originally from Glasgow.

"Now there's this party, all to the greater glory of Charlie Sneddy, and you're making them pay for it."

"It's right that the staff should put a bit towards the firm that gives them their livelihood."

"I'm here to warn you that you may be in danger."

"And who's going to kill the goose that lays the golden eggs?"

"Brass eggs, mair like," said Hamish bitterly.

Sneddy laughed, comfortably and smugly. "Get out of here. You can't scare me. I let you off this time, you mooching copper. You had no intention of paying for these scraps."

"Remember what I said," said Hamish stiffly.

■ ■ ■

He felt uneasy on the road back to the police station, and as if to harmonize with his mood, long black streamers of cloud, like ghostly fingers, were stretching in from the Atlantic.

He gave Lugs the smoked salmon scraps along with a large bowl of water. Hamish felt restless. But what to do? Perhaps he should call on one of the women after they finished work to see if anything was brewing. Apart from Aileen MacPhail and Bridget Macleod, there was Betty Andrews, a crofter's wife; Jessie Jackson, a widow with three young children; Mary Broad, a thin, anemic-looking girl who supported her mother; and Sally Queen, married to a drunken lout who'd never done a day's work in his life.

None of them could afford to lose their job. He decided to visit Aileen later. But first he would drive up to the Tommel Castle Hotel and see, out of curiosity, just how grand the celebrations were going to be.

■ ■ ■

Mr. Johnston, the hotel manager, welcomed him and invited him into his office for a cup of coffee. Hamish explained the reason for his visit.

"I don't think we'll ever have run such a cheap event," grumbled the manager. "No dinner, just canapés, and punch which is more fruit juice than liquor. Most of the entertainment is a long speech from Sneddy. No band, no dancing, no nothing."

"My, they'll be fit to be tied. Do you know he's docking their wages to pay for the party?"

"Can he do that?"

"I shouldn't think so. Unless the canny miser got them to sign something agreeing to it."

"I think you'll find out he did. His brother's here for the celebration. Harry. Different sort of animal. Very openhanded."

"What does he do?"

"Runs a fish farm down on Loch Fyne. Same business, but I doubt the same practices."

"He with his wife?"

"No, I gather his wife died a couple of years ago. Sneddy's wife left him before he came up here."

"I'm not surprised. I've a bad feeling in my bones about this. You know what we're like up here."

"Highlanders, you mean?"

"Yes, we'll put up with a lot but the passions run dark and deep and one day something nasty is going to erupt at that fish farm."

"Well, if Sneddy gets it, it couldn't happen to a nicer person."

"It's not Sneddy I'm worried about. I'm worried about whoever cracks and hurts him. It would make me fair sick to have to arrest someone who had been driven to it by Sneddy's meanness."

"Let's hope it doesn't happen. Wait here and I'll see if they've a nice bone in the kitchen for Lugs."

. . .

Hamish decided to see if Aileen McPhail was at home.

He knew little about Aileen, only the village gossip that claimed she was a Gypsy who had forsaken life on the road. She had arrived in Lochdubh five years ago and had moved into a broken-down deserted croft house and had done most of the work herself restoring it.

She was at home and invited Hamish in. The cottage kitchen-cum-living room was sparsely furnished. Aileen was in her thirties and attractive in a tanned and weather-beaten way. She had large dark eyes and masses of coarse dark hair. She was wearing men's trousers and a blue shirt knotted at the waist. The shirt was frayed at the collar but with her athletic, slim figure and good bust, she managed to make the outfit look fashionable.

"So what brings you?" asked Aileen. "If it's more salmon, I haven't got any. The security guard checks us out before we go home to make sure we aren't taking any."

"This party," began Hamish. "Did Sneddy get you all to sign anything to agree to the cut in wages?"

"Yes, he did and we all signed." Aileen gave a weary sigh and pushed her hair back from her face. "You know how he is. He didn't threaten us, just somehow implied that if we didn't sign, we may as well start looking for other work." She gave a bitter laugh. "As if there's any other work here."

Hamish frowned. "There must be some way to stop him. Maybe get a tame reporter to write an article. You know, 'Is This the Meanest Man in Scotland?' That kind of thing."

"How would that work? No reporter would want a story where he has to keep on quoting, 'one of my sources at the fish farm said.' We'd all be too frightened to give our names. You know what's been going on, Hamish. Why the sudden worry?" She laughed. "I know. You're fed up because he got three pounds out of you."

"Not that. I'm frightened something might happen to him."

Aileen stared at the stone-flagged floor of her cottage.

"Aileen?"

"What?"

"Something's going on. You know something."

She shrugged. "Just the usual bad feeling. Nobody's going to do anything about it."

"It must be hard for you to end up here, stuck in the job like that."

"I like Lochdubh and I'd be happy enough if the wages were fair."

"No ambitions?"

"You know my biggest ambition, Hamish? To pull the chain."

He looked at her, puzzled.

"I've still got a primitive outdoor toilet. Can't afford to have drains dug. All I want in life is an indoor toilet that flushes. Man, I sometimes think I'd sell my soul for that."

I never really noticed before how attractive she is, thought Hamish. I must be slipping. "Fancy dinner with me one night?" he asked.

"Sorry, Hamish, I've got a fellow."

"Who?"

"Mind your own business, copper."

Probably a married man, thought Hamish gloomily as he made his way back to the police station.

■ ■ ■

Hamish decided to let things lie until after the anniversary party. He would then write a letter to his member of parliament, outlining the working practices at the fish farm, and see if anything could be done.

Nonetheless, when the day of the party arrived, he decided to gate-crash it. There would not be enough in the punch bowls to get anyone drunk, but some of them might be carrying bottles, and tempers, fueled by drink, might flare.

When he arrived, it was to find the employees standing around in the hotel ballroom under a limp banner proclaiming, "Happy Tenth Anniversary." There was no sign of Sneddy.

"Where's the boss?" he asked Bridget, who'd just entered with her fellow workers.

"Don't know and don't care," she said wearily.

Hamish felt a stab of alarm in his stomach. He knew Charlie Sneddy. It was in Sneddy's character to arrive early, to strut around enjoying the power of his little kingdom.

He ran out to the police Land Rover, climbed in, put on the siren, and drove off at a reckless speed round the twisting bends which led to the fish farm. The buildings seemed locked up and deserted. It was still light. It never gets really dark at any time of night during the summer months in the Highlands of Scotland. He walked round the buildings until he came to the shed where the smoked salmon was packed and saw the door standing open.

Hamish went in. He pressed a switch by the door and strips of overhead fluorescent lighting glared down on the shed.

And on what seemed to be a large cling-film-covered object laid out on one of the tables.

Hamish went up to it. Under the cling film, the unlovely features of Charlie Sneddy looked up at him. A label saying HANDLE WITH CARE had been pasted on his chest. Hamish ripped off the cling film and felt the man's neck. There was a faint pulse. Fortunately, they hadn't wrapped him tightly. He took out his phone and called for an ambulance, and then, fighting back a feeling of revulsion, he bent to administer the kiss of life. He noticed that Sneddy's ankles were bound with packaging wire, and from the position of the man's arms, he guessed his wrists were probably bound behind his back as well. He worked away diligently until Sneddy's chest began to rise and fall. His eyes fluttered open. "Don't try to speak," said Hamish.

To his relief, he heard the wail of an ambulance siren in the distance. He found a pair of wire cutters over with some other tools in a corner and cut the wire that bound the man's ankles. Then he gently eased him over and freed his wrists.

Two ambulance men came running in carrying a stretcher. "You're lucky," said one. "We were just leaving a false alarm on the far side of the village when we got the call."

"He'll need oxygen," said Hamish. "Someone tried to asphyxiate him by wrapping him up in cling film. Try to touch as little as possible."

Hamish then phoned police headquarters in Strathbane after phoning the hotel and telling Mr. Johnston what had happened and urging him to keep everyone at the hotel until the police arrived.

■ ■ ■

Weeks and weeks of interviews followed. The six women who worked in the smoked salmon shed insisted they had all finished work and had left together. The security man swore he had locked up after them.

Charlie Sneddy said he had been struck from behind in the corridor outside his office and that's all he remembered. He was turning over the running of the fish farm to his brother and going to go off on a cruise. He said he was sick of the whole business.

And then, by the end of August, as the nights were drawing in, and heather blazed purple on the flanks of the mountains, it seemed as if the attempted murder had never happened. Wages had been raised all round at the fish farm, hours were regular, extra help had been hired, and nobody but Hamish seemed to be interested in who had tried to kill Charlie Sneddy.

When Hamish called at the smoked salmon shed, he was greeted cheerfully enough, but there were no more scraps for Lugs, and Bridget always said they were too busy to speak to him.

A series of burglaries on his beat, which covered Lochdubh and the villages round about, took up his attention and the first frosts of winter had arrived before he could turn his mind back to the case at the fish farm.

He was driving back along the Braikie road one night when he noticed again a new restaurant, called the Highlander. He remembered it used to be, until this year, a dark little pub without much trade. He was hungry and decided to see what the food was like.

The restaurant was busy but he managed to get a corner table. The menu was full of traditional Scottish dishes. He had just decided to have cock-a-leekie soup followed by trout when the waitress put a large glass of malt whiskey in front of him.

"I didn't order that," said Hamish.

"Compliments of the management."

"Is the boss around? Can I have a word with him?"

The waitress left and soon Sam Mackay, the proprietor, joined Hamish. "Thanks for the drink," said Hamish. "But I am not one of those policemen who take free hospitality." Hamish really meant he did not take bribes, although he was well known for mooching teas and coffees.

Sam smiled and said, "Don't worry. You can pay for your meal. We like to treat the police well. You never know when you'll be needing them.

"Having a quiet time? I don't suppose anyone knows or cares who attacked that mean bastard Charlie Sneddy."

"No, that's the difficulty. And his brother's such a good boss that everyone just wants to forget it ever happened."

"I had Harry Sneddy in here a few months back. Nice man."

"Was he alone?"

"No, he had a lady with him."

"Anyone you know?"

"I'd a feeling I'd seen her before. Gypsy-looking type."

Hamish stiffened. "Were they friendly? I mean did you get the idea they were an item?"

"The restaurant was awfully busy. They weren't kissing or canoodling. I really couldn't tell. Enjoy your meal."

"I haven't ordered yet."

Sam took Hamish's order and left.

Aileen McPhail, thought Hamish. And with Harry. It's time I saw that young woman again.

. . .

He was about to head out to the fish farm the next morning when for some reason he decided to have a look at Aileen's cottage. The ground about it was in upheaval and several men were digging trenches.

"What's going on here?" Hamish asked the foreman.

"Putting in the drains," he said. "Connecting up to the water supply."

"Expensive business."

"Aye, it is that. But we're cheaper than most."

Hamish tilted back his cap and scratched his fiery hair. He would not go out to the fish farm. He would wait until

Aileen came home. Better to see her on her own than surrounded by the other women.

. . .

He called several times that evening but it was not until just after nine o'clock that he saw a light in Aileen's kitchen.

He knocked at the door. "Come in," she said reluctantly. "The place is in a mess."

"Getting a toilet put in?" asked Hamish, sitting down in the kitchen and putting his cap on the table.

"Aye and a bathroom, too."

"Where are you getting the money from?"

"None of your business, copper."

"I can find out who's paying the men. It wouldn't be Harry Sneddy by any chance?"

Her face flamed red. "Get out of here."

She stood over him, her fists clenched.

Hamish said sharply, "Sit down, Aileen. I want to tell you a story."

She sat down reluctantly opposite him.

"Sneddy," began Hamish, "that is, Charlie Sneddy, caused a lot of resentment and misery. He was generally hated. Now, you had dinner earlier this year with Harry. What did you talk about? The fish farm? And how it could make double with proper machinery, more staff, and better wages? Who better to run it than Harry? Now, I know that the six of you in the smoked salmon shed were the last to leave for the hotel. Could it have happened like this?

"Harry knocks his brother unconscious and leaves the body in the corridor and tips you off that the deed is done. He takes off for the hotel. With you as the ringleader, you and the rest of the women, fueled by sheer hatred, drag the body into the shed, lift it onto a table, bind his wrists and ankles, and then cover him in cling film. How many more were in on this attempted murder? The security man? You weren't worried about being disturbed. It's a miracle he didn't die."

"Prove it!" Aileen spat at him.

"I'll keep looking. Someone, somewhere is going to crack and then I'll have you."

"And what satisfaction will you get out of it? The fish farm will close. There'll be no work for anyone."

"It was attempted murder," said Hamish. "There iss no excuse for the taking of a life."

"There is in war."

"This wasn't war."

"It was. Now go away."

He left her, hunched over the table.

■ ■ ■

Hamish tried to get proof to back up his suspicions but a wall of silence ringed not only the fish farm but the village of Lochdubh.

Angela Brodie found him one day standing on the beach, moodily skimming stones across the loch.

"Nothing better to do?" she asked.

"Can't get any further with that fish farm business."

"Don't think you will now," said Angela.

"Why's that?"

"The fish farm's been sold."

"What! It wass neffer advertised. Who's bought it?"

"Barry White, the lead singer of Thames." Hamish looked puzzled.

"Top of the charts, Hamish. The women along there are in heaven."

"Why did no one tell me?"

"We've been away and I should think no one in the village wants you to know anything."

"And where's Harry Sneddy gone?"

"Somewhere in South America by now. He sold up the Loch Fyne business as well."

"And Aileen McPhail? Did she go with him?"

"I don't know. I believe she sold her cottage."

. . .

A month later, as the first snows were whitening the mountains above Lochdubh, Hamish received a parcel with a Brazilian stamp. On the outside was a label, HANDLE WITH CARE.

Hamish opened it cautiously. Inside was a pretty little vase of South American design. A slip of paper was sticking out of the top of it. He pulled it out. There was one unsigned message: "I told you I would sell my soul to pull that chain."

JOE R. LANSDALE

Born in East Texas, **Joe R. Lansdale** has worked in an aluminum chair plant, as a garbageman, bouncer, bodyguard, used clothes salesman, rose field hand, truck patch farmer, and janitor, among other occupations. He has written more than two hundred short stories and more than twenty novels in the suspense, horror, and western genres. He has received the British Fantasy Award, the American Mystery Award, and six Bram Stoker Awards from the Horror Writers of America, and is the creator of the Hap Collins/Leonard Pine series, about two tough amateur sleuths in East Texas.

FIRST MYSTERIOUS PRESS PUBLICATION:
MUCHO MOJO, 1994

THE MULE RUSTLERS

It was a blustery San Jacinto day, when leggy black clouds appeared against the pearl-gray sky like tromped-on spiders against tile flooring, that Elliot and James set about rustling the mule.

A week back, James had spotted the critter while out casing the area for a house to burglarize. The burglary idea went down the tubes because there were too many large dogs in the yards, and too many older people sitting in lawn chairs flexing their false teeth amongst concrete lawn ornaments and sprinklers. Most likely they owned guns.

But on the way out of the neighborhood James observed, on a patch of about ten acres with a small pond and lots of trees, the mule. It was average-sized, brown in color, with a touch of white around the nostrils, and it had ears that tracked the countryside like radar instruments.

All of the property was fenced in barb wire, but the gate to the property wasn't any great problem. It was made of hog wire stapled to posts, and there was another wire fastened to it and looped over a creosote corner post. There was a chain and padlock, but that was of no consequence. Wire cutters, and you were in.

The road in front of the property was reasonably traveled, and even as he slowed to check out the hog wire, three cars passed him going in the opposite direction.

James discovered if he drove off the gravel road and turned right on a narrow dirt road and parked to the side, he could walk through another piece of unfenced wooded property and climb over the barb-wire fence at the back of the mule's acreage. Better yet, the fence wasn't too good there, was kinda low, two strands only, and was primarily a line that marked ownership, not a boundary. The mule was in there mostly by her own goodwill.

James put a foot on the low, weak fence and pushed it almost to the ground. It was easy to step over then and he wanted to take the mule immediately, for he could see it browsing through a split in the trees, chomping up grass. It was an old mule, and its ears swung forward and back, but if it was aware of his presence, only the ears seemed to know and failed to send the signal to the critter's brain, or maybe the brain got the signal and didn't care.

James studied the situation. There were plenty of little crop farmers who liked a mule to plow their garden, or wanted one just because mules were cool. So there was a market. As for the job, well, the work would be holding the fence down so the mule could step over, then leading it to the truck. Easy money.

Problem was, James didn't have a truck. He had a Volvo that needed front-end work. It had once been crushed up like an accordion, then straightened somewhat, if not enough. It rattled and occasionally threatened to head off to the right without benefit of having the steering wheel turned.

And the damn thing embarrassed him. His hat touched the roof, and if he went out to the Cattleman's Cafe at the auction barn, he felt like a dork climbing out of it amidst mud-splattered pickups, some of them the size of military assault vehicles.

He had owned a huge Dodge Ram, but had lost it in a card game, and the winner, feeling generous, had swapped titles. The card shark got the Dodge, and James got the goddamn Volvo, worn out with the ceiling cloth dripping, the floor rotted away in spots, and the steering wheel slightly bent where an accident, most likely the one that accordioned the front end, must have thrown some un-seat-belted fella against it. At the top of the steering wheel, in the little rubber tubing wrapped around it, were a couple of teeth marks, souvenirs of that same unfortunate episode. Worse yet, the damn Volvo had been painted yellow, and it wasn't a job to be proud of. Baby-shit-hardened-and-aged-on-a-bedpost yellow.

Bottom line was, the mule couldn't ride in the front seat with him. But his friend Elliot owned both a pickup and a horse trailer.

Elliot had once seen himself as a horseman, but the problem was he never owned but one horse, a pinto, and it died from neglect, and had been on its last legs when Elliot purchased it for too much money. It was the only horse James had seen in Elliot's possession outside of stolen ones passing through his hands, and the only one outside of the one in the movie *Cat Ballou* that could lean against a wall at a forty-five-degree angle.

One morning it kept leaning, stiff as a sixteen-year-old's woody, but without the pulse. Having been there, probably dead, for several days, part of its hide had stuck to the wall and gone liquid and gluish. It took him and Elliot both with a two-by-four and a lot of energy to pry it off the stucco and push it down. They'd hooked it up to a chain by the back legs and dragged it to the center of Elliot's property.

Elliot had inherited his land from his grandfather Clemmons, who hated him. Old Man Clemmons had left him the land, but it was rumored he first salted the twenty-five acres and shit in the well. Sure enough, not much grew there except weeds, but as far as Elliot could tell the well water tasted fine.

According to Elliot, besides the salt and maybe the shit, he was given his grandfather's curse that wished him all life's burdens, none of its joys, and an early death. "He didn't like me much," Elliot was fond of saying when deep in his sauce.

They had coated the deceased pinto with gasoline and set it on fire. It had stunk something awful, and since they were involved with a bottle of Wild Turkey while it burned, it had flamed up and caught the back of Elliot's truck on fire, burning out the rubber truck bed lining. James figured they had just managed to beat it out with their coats moments before the gas tank ignited and blew them over and through the trees, along with the burning pinto's hide and bones.

■ ■ ■

James drove over to Elliot's place after his discovery of the mule. Elliot had grown him a few garden vegetables, mostly chocked with bugs, that he had been pushing from his fruit and vegetable stand next to the road.

James found him trying to sell a half bushel of tomatoes to a tall, moderately attractive blond woman wearing shorts and showing lots of hair on her legs. Short bristly hair like a hog's. James had visions of dropping her in a vat of hot water and scraping that hair off with a knife. Course, he didn't want it hot as hog-scalding water, or she wouldn't be worth much when he got through. He wanted her shaved, not hurt.

Elliot had his brown sweat-stained Stetson pushed up on his head and he was talking the lady up good as he could, considering she was digging through a basket and coming up with some bug-bit tomatoes.

"These are all bit up," she said.

"Bugs attack the good'ns," Elliot said. "Them's the one's you want. These ain't like that crap you get in the store."

"They don't have bugs in them."

"Yeah, but they don't got the flavor these do. You just cut around the spots, and those tomatoes'll taste better than any you ever had."

"That's a crock of shit," the lady said.

"Well now," Elliot said, "that's a matter of opinion."

"It's my opinion you put a few good tomatoes on top of the bug-bit ones," she said. "That's my opinion, and you can keep your tomatoes."

She got in a new red Chevrolet and drove off.

"Good to see you ain't lost your touch," James said.

"Now, these here tomatoes have been goin' pretty fast this morning. Since it's mostly women buyin', I do all right. Fact is that's my first loss. Charm didn't work on her. She's probably a lesbian."

James wanted to call bullshit on that, but right now he wanted Elliot on his side.

"Unless you're doin' so good here you don't need money, I got us a little job."

"You case some spots?" Elliot asked.

"I didn't find nothin' worth doin'. Besides, there's lots of old folks where I was lookin'."

"I don't want no part of them. Always home. Always got dogs and guns."

"Yeah, and lawn gnomes and sprinklers made of wooden animals."

"With the tails that spin and throw water?"

"Yep."

"Kinda like them myself. You know, you picked up some of them things, you could sell them right smart."

"Yeah, well, I got somethin' better."

"Name it."

"Rustlin'."

Elliot worked his mouth a bit. James could see the idea appealed to him. Elliot liked to think of himself as a modern cowboy. "How many head?"

"One."

"One? Hell, that ain't much rustlin'."

"It's a mule. You can get maybe a thousand dollars for one. They're getting rarer, and they're kind of popular now. We rustle it. We could split the money."

Elliot studied on this momentarily. He also liked to think of himself as a respected and experienced thief.

"You know, I know a fella would buy a mule. Let me go up to the house and give him a call."

"It's the same fella I know, ain't it?"

"Yeah," Elliot said.

. . .

Elliot made the call and came out of the bedroom into the living room with good news.

"George wants it right away. He's offerin' us eight hundred."

"I wanted a thousand."

"He's offering eight hundred, he'll sell it for a thousand

or better himself. He said he can't go a thousand. Already got a couple other buys goin' today. It's a deal and it's now."

James considered on that.

"I guess that'll do. We'll need your truck and trailer."

"I figured as much."

"You got any brown shoe polish?"

"Brown shoe polish?"

"That's right," James said.

. . .

The truck was a big four-seater Dodge with a bed big enough to fill, attach a diving board, and call a pool. The Dodge hummed like a sewing machine as it whizzed along on its huge tires. The trailer clattered behind and wove precariously left and right, as if it might pass the truck at any moment. James and Elliot had their windows down, and the cool April wind snapped at the brims of their hats and made the creases in their crowns deeper.

By the time they drove over to the place where the mule was, the smashed spider clouds had begun to twist their legs together and blend into one messy critter that peed sprinkles of rain all over the truck windshield.

They slowed as they passed the gate, then turned right. No cars or people were visible, so Elliot pulled over to the side of the road, got out quick with James carrying a rope. They went through the woods, stepped over the barb-wire fence, and found the mule grazing. They walked right up to it, and Elliot bribed it with an ear of corn from his garden. The mule sniffed at the corn and bit it. As he did, James slipped the rope over its neck, twisted it so that he put a loop over the mule's nose. Doing this, he brushed the mule's ears, and it kicked at the air, spun and kicked again. It took James several minutes to calm it down.

"It's one of them that's touchy about the ears," Elliot said. "Don't touch the ears again."

"I hear that," James said.

They led the mule to the fence. Elliot pushed it almost to the ground with his boot, and James and the mule stepped over. After that, nothing more was required than to lead the mule to the trailer and load it. It did what was expected without a moment's hesitation.

There was some consternation when it came to turning truck and trailer around, but Elliot managed it and they were soon on the road to a rendezvous with eight hundred dollars.

. . .

The place they had to go to meet their buyer, George Taylor, was almost to Tyler, and about sixty miles from where they had nabbed the mule. They often sold stolen material there, and George specialized in livestock and just about anything he could buy quick and sell quicker.

The trailer was not enclosed, and it occurred to James that the mule's owner might pass them, but he doubted the mule would be recognized. They were really hauling ass, and the trailer, with the weight of the old mule to aid it, had slowed in its wobbling but still sounded like a train wreck.

When they were about twenty-five miles away from Taylor's place, James had Elliot pull over. He took the brown shoe polish back to the trailer and, reaching between the bars while Elliot fed the mule corn on the cob, painted the white around the mule's nose brown. It was raining lightly, but he managed the touch-up without having it washed away.

He figured this way Taylor might not notice how old the critter was and not try to talk them down. He had given them a price, but they had dealt with Taylor before and what he offered wasn't always what he wanted to give, and it was rare you talked it up. The trick was to keep him from going down. George knew once they had the mule stolen they'd want to get rid of it, and it would be his plan to start finding problems with the animal and to start lowering his price.

When the mule was painted, they got back in the truck and headed out.

Elliot said, "You are one thinker, James."

"Yes sir," James agreed, "you got to get up pretty goddamned early in the morning to get one over on me. It starts raining hard, it won't wash off. That stuff'll hold."

. . .

When they arrived at Taylor's place, James looked back through the rear truck window and saw the mule with its head lowered, looking at him through sheets of rain. James felt less smart immediately. The brown he had painted on the mule had dried and was darker than the rest of its hide and made it look as if it had dipped its muzzle in a bucket of paint, searching for a carrot on the bottom.

James decided to say nothing to Elliot about this, lest Elliot decide it really wasn't all that necessary to get up early to outsmart him.

Taylor's place was a kind of ranch and junkyard. There were all manner of cars damaged or made thin by the car smasher that Taylor rode with great enthusiasm, wearing a gimme cap with the brim pushed up and his mouth hanging open as if to receive something spoon-fed by a caretaker.

Today, however, the car smasher remained silent near the double-wide where Taylor lived with his bulldog Bullet and his wife, Kay, who was about one ton of woman in a muumuu that might have been made from a circus tent and decorated by children with finger paints. If she owned more than one of these outfits, James was unaware of it. It was possible she had a chest full of them, all the same, folded and ready, with a hole in the center to pull over her head at a moment's notice.

At the back of the place a few cows that looked as if they were ready to be sold for hide and hooves stumbled about. Taylor's station wagon, used to haul a variety of stolen goods, was parked next to the trailer, and next to it was a large red Cadillac with someone at the back of it closing the trunk.

As they drove over the cattle guard and onto the property, the man at the trunk of the Cadillac looked up. He was wearing a blue baseball cap and a blue T-shirt that showed belly at the bottom. He and his belly bounced away from the Caddy, up the steps of the trailer, and inside.

Elliot said, "Who's that?"

"Can't say," James said. "Don't recognize him."

They parked beside the Cadillac, got out, went to the trailer door, and knocked. There was a long pause, then the man with the baseball cap answered the door.

"Yeah," he said.

"We come to see Taylor," Elliot said.

"He ain't here right now," said the man.

"He's expectin' us," James said.

"Say he is?"

"We got a mule to sell him," James said.

"That right?"

"Mrs. Taylor here?" James asked.

"Naw. She ain't. Ain't neither one of them here."

"Where's Bullet?" Elliot asked.

"He don't buy mules, does he?"

"Bullet?" Elliot said.

"Didn't you ask for him?"

"Well, yeah, but not to buy nothin'."

"You boys come on in," came a voice from inside the trailer. "It's all right there, Butch, stand aside. These here boys are wantin' to do some business with George. That's what we're doin'."

Butch stood aside. James and Elliot went inside.

"So is he here?" James asked.

"No. Not just now. But we're expectin' him shortly."

Butch stepped back and leaned against the trailer's kitchen counter, which was stacked with dirty dishes. The place smelled funny. The man who had asked them to come inside was seated on the couch. He was portly, wearing black pants and black shoes with the toes turned up. He had on a big black Hawaiian-style shirt with hula girls in red, blue, and yellow along the bottom. He had greasy black hair combed straight back and tied in a little ponytail. A white short-brimmed hat with a near flat crown was on a coffee table in front of him, along with a can of beer and a white substance in four lines next to a rolled dollar bill. He had his legs crossed and he was playing with the tip of one of his shoes. He had a light growth of beard and he was smiling at them.

"What you boys sellin'?" he asked.

"A mule," James said.

"No shit?"

"That's right," Elliot said. "When's George coming back?"

"Sometime shortly after the Second Coming. But I doubt he'll go with God."

Elliot looked at James. James shrugged, and at that moment he saw past Elliot, and what he saw was Bullet lying on the floor near a doorway to the bedroom, a pool of blood under him. He tried not to let his eyes stay on Bullet long. He said, "Tell you what, boys. I think me and Elliot will come back later, when George is here."

The big man lifted up his Hawaiian shirt and showed him his hairy belly and against it a little flat black automatic pistol. He took the pistol out slowly and put it on his knee and looked at them.

"Naw. He ain't comin' back, and you boys ain't goin' nowhere."

"Aw shit," Elliot said, suddenly getting it. "He ain't no friend of ours. We just come to do business, and if he ain't here to do business, you boys got our blessing. And we'll just leave and not say a word."

Another man came out of the back room. He was naked, and carrying a bowie knife. He was muscular, bug-nosed, with close-cut hair. There was blood on him from thighs to neck. From the back room they heard a moan.

The naked man looked at them, then at the man on the couch.

"Friends of Taylor's," the man on the couch said.

"We ain't," James said. "We hardly know him. We just come to sell a mule."

"A mule, huh," said the naked man. He didn't seem bashful at all. His penis was bloody and stuck to his right leg like some kind of sucker fish. The naked man nodded his head at the open doorway behind him, spoke to the man on the couch. "I've had all of that I want and can take, Viceroy. It's like cutting blubber off a whale."

"You go on and shower," Viceroy said, then smiled, added: "And be sure and wash the parts you don't normally touch."

"Ain't no parts Tim don't touch," Butch said.

"I tell you what," Tim said. "You get in there and go to work, then show me how funny you are. That old woman is hardheaded."

Tim went past Butch, driving the bowie knife into the counter, rattling the dishes.

Viceroy stared at Butch. "Your turn."

"What about you?" Butch said.

"I don't take a turn. Get with it."

Butch put his cap on the counter next to a greasy plate, took off his shirt, pants, underwear, socks, and shoes. He pulled the knife out of the counter and started for the bedroom. He said, "What about these two?"

"Oh, me and them are gonna talk. Any friend of Taylor's is a friend of mine."

"We don't really know him," James said. "We just come to sell a mule."

"Sit down on the floor there, next to the wall, away from the door," Viceroy said, and scratched the side of his cheek with the barrel of the automatic.

A moment later they heard screams from the back room and Butch yelling something, then there was silence, followed shortly by more screams.

"Butch ain't got Tim's touch," Viceroy said. "Tim can skin you and you can walk off before you notice the hide on your back, ass, and legs is missin'. Butch, he's a hacker."

Viceroy leaned forward, took up the dollar bill, and

sucked up a couple lines of the white powder. "Goddamn, that'll do it," he said.

Elliot said, "What is that?"

Viceroy laughed. "Boy, you are a rube, ain't you? Would you believe bakin' soda?"

"Really?" Elliot said.

Viceroy hooted. "No. Not really."

From the bedroom you could hear Butch let out a laugh. "Crackers," he said.

"It's cocaine," James said to Elliot. "I seen it in a movie."

"Good God," Elliot said.

"My, you boys are delicate for a couple of thieves," Viceroy said.

Tim came out of the bathroom, still naked, bouncing his balls with a towel.

"Put some clothes on," Viceroy said. "We don't want to see that."

Tim looked hurt, put on his clothes and adjusted his cap. Viceroy snorted the last two lines of coke. "Damn, that's some good stuff. You can step on that multiple."

"Let me have a snort," Tim said.

"Not right now," Viceroy said.

"How come you get to?" Tim said.

"'Cause I'm the biggest bull in the woods, boy. And you can test that anytime you got the urge."

Tim didn't say anything. He went to the refrigerator, found a beer, popped it, and began to sip.

"I don't think she knows nothing," Tim said. "She wouldn't hold back havin' that done to her for a few thousand dollars. Not for a million."

"I reckon you're right," said Viceroy. "I just don't like

quittin' halfway. You finish a thing, even if it ain't gonna turn out. Ain't that right, boys?"

James and Elliot didn't reply. Viceroy laughed and picked up the beer on the coffee table and took a jolt of it. He said to himself, "Yeah, that's right. You don't do a thing half-ass. You do it all the way. What time is it?"

Tim reached in his pocket and took out a pocket watch. James recognized it as belonging to George Taylor. "It's four."

"All right," Viceroy said, satisfied, and sipped his beer.

. . .

After a time Butch came out of the bedroom bloody and looking tired. "She ain't gonna tell nobody nothin'. She's gone. She couldn't take no more. She'd have known somethin', she'd have told it."

"Guess Taylor didn't tell her," Tim said. "Guess she didn't know nothin'."

"George had more in him than I thought, goin' like that, takin' all that pain and not talkin'," Viceroy said. "I wouldn't have expected it of him."

Tim nodded his head. "When you shot his bulldog, I think he was through. Took the heart right out of him. Wasn't a thing we could do to him then that mattered."

"Money's around here somewhere," Viceroy said.

"He might not have had nothin'," Butch said, walking to the bathroom.

"I think he did," Viceroy said. "I don't think he was brave enough to try and cross me. I think he had the money for the blow, but we double-crossed him too soon. We should have had him put the money on the table, then done what we needed to do. Would have been easier on everybody all the way around, them especially."

"They'd have still been dead," Tim said, drinking the last of his beer, crushing the can.

"But they'd have just been dead. Not hurt a lot, then dead. Old fat gal, that wasn't no easy way to go, and in the end she didn't know nothin'. And Taylor, takin' the knife, then out there in that car in the crusher and us telling him we were gonna run him through, and him still not talkin'."

"Like I said, we killed the bulldog I think he was through. Fat woman wasn't nothin' to him, but he seemed to have a hard-on for that dog. He'd just as soon be crushed. But I still think there might not have been any money. I think maybe they was gonna do what we were gonna do. Double-cross."

"Yeah, but we brought the blow," Viceroy said.

Tim grinned. "Yeah, but was you gonna give it to 'em?"

Viceroy laughed, then his gaze settled lead-heavy on the mule rustlers. "Well, boys, what do you suggest I do with you pickle heads?"

"Just let us go," James said. "Hell, this ain't our business, and we don't want it to be our business. It ain't like Taylor was a relative of ours."

"That's right," Elliot said. "He's cheated us plenty on little deals."

Viceroy was quiet. He looked at Tim. "What do you say?"

Tim pursed his lips and developed the expression of a man looking in the distance for answers. "I sympathize with these boys. I guess we could let 'em go. Give us their word, show us some ID, so they spill any beans we can find them. You know the littlest bit these days and you can find anybody."

"Damn Internet," Viceroy said.

Butch came out of the bathroom, naked, toweling his hair.

"You think we should let 'em go?" Viceroy asked.

Butch looked first at Viceroy and Tim, then at James and Elliot. "Absolutely."

"Get dressed," Viceroy said to Butch, "and we'll let 'em go."

"We won't say a word," Elliot said.

"Sure," Viceroy said. "You look like boys who can be quiet. Don't they?"

"Yeah," Tim said.

"Absolutely," Butch said, tying his shoe.

"Then we'll just go," James said, standing up from his position on the floor, Elliot following suit.

"Not real quick," Viceroy said. "You got a mule, huh?"

James nodded.

"What's he worth?"

"Couple thousand dollars to the right people."

"What about people ain't maybe quite as right?"

"A thousand. Twelve hundred."

"What were you supposed to get?"

"Eight hundred."

"We could do some business, you know."

James didn't say anything. He glanced toward the door where the men had been at work on Mrs. Taylor. He saw the bulldog lying there on the linoleum in its pool of hardened blood, and flowing from the bedroom was fresh blood. The fresh pool flowed around the crusty old pool and bled into the living room of the trailer and died where the patch of carpet near the couch began; the carpet began to slowly absorb it.

James knew these folks weren't going to let them go any-where.

"I think we'll take the mule," Viceroy said. "Though I ain't sure I'm gonna give you any eight hundred dollars."

"We give it to you as a gift," Elliot said. "Just take it, and the trailer it's in, and let us go."

"That's a mighty nice offer," Viceroy said. "Nice, huh, boys?"

"Damn nice," Tim said.

"Absolutely," Butch said. "They could have held out and tried to deal. You don't get much nicer than that."

"And throwing in the trailer too," Tim said. "Now, that's white of 'em."

James took hold of the doorknob, turned it, said, "We'll show him to you."

"Wait a minute," Viceroy said.

"Come on out," James said.

Butch darted across the room, took hold of James's shoul-der. "Hold up."

The door was open now. Rain was really hammering. The mule, its head hung, was visible in the trailer.

"Ain't no need to get wet," Viceroy said.

James had one foot on the steps outside. "You ought to see what you're gettin'."

"It'll do," Viceroy said. "It ain't like we're payin' for it."

Butch tightened his grip on James, and Elliot, seeing how this was going to end up and somehow feeling better about dying out in the open, not eight feet from a deceased bull-dog, a room away from a skinned fat woman, pushed against Butch and stepped out behind James and into the yard.

"Damn," Viceroy said.

"Should I?" Butch said, glancing at Viceroy, touching the gun in his pants.

"Hell, let's look at the mule," Viceroy said.

Viceroy put on his odd hat and they all went out in the rain for a look. Viceroy looked as if he were some sort of escapee from a mental institution, wearing a hubcap. The rain ran off of it and made a curtain of water around his head.

They stood by the trailer staring at the mule. Tim said, "Someone's painted its nose, or it's been dippin' it in shit."

James and Elliot said nothing.

James glanced at the trailer, saw there was no underpinning. He glanced at Elliot, nodded his head slightly. Elliot looked carefully. He had an idea what James meant. They might roll under the trailer and get to the other side and start running. It wasn't worth much. Tim and Butch looked as if they could run fast, and all they had to do was run fast enough to get a clear shot.

"This is a goddamn stupid thing," Butch said, the rain hammering his head. "Us all standing out here in the rain lookin' at a goddamn mule. We could be dry and these two could be—"

A horn honked. Coming up the drive was a black Ford pickup with a camper fastened to the bed.

The truck stopped and a man the shape of a pear with the complexion of a marshmallow, dressed in khakis the color of walnut bark, got out smiling teeth all over the place. He had a rooster under his arm.

He said, "Hey, boys. Where's George?"

"He ain't feelin' so good," Viceroy said.

The man with the rooster saw the gun Viceroy was holding. He said, "You boys plinkin' cans?"

"Somethin' like that," Viceroy said.

"Would you tell George to come out?" the man said.

"He won't come out," Butch said.

The man's smile fell away. "Why not? He knows I'm comin'."

"He's under the weather," Viceroy said.

"Can't we all go inside, it's like being at the bottom of a lake out here."

"Naw. He don't want us in there. Contagious."

"What's he got?"

"You might say a kind of lead poisonin'."

"Well, he wants these here chickens. I got the camper back there full of 'em. They're fightin' chickens. Best damn bunch there is. This'n here, he's special. He's a stud rooster. He ain't fightin' no more. Won his last one. Got a bad shot that put blood in his lungs, but I put his head in my mouth and sucked it out, and he went on to win. Just come back from it and won. I decided to stud him out."

"He's gettin' all wet," Butch said.

"Yeah he is," said the chicken man.

"Let's end this shit," Tim said.

James reached over and pulled the bar on the trailer and the gate came open. He said, "Let's show him to you close-up."

"Not now," Viceroy said, but James was in the trailer now. He took the rope off the trailer rail and tied it around the mule's neck and put a loop over its head, started backing him out.

"That's all right," Viceroy said. "We don't need to see no damn mule."

"He's a good'n," James said when the mule was completely out of the trailer. "A little touchy about the ears."

He turned the mule slightly then, reached up, and grabbed the mule's ears, and it kicked.

The kick was a good one. Both legs shot out and the mule seemed to stand on its front legs like a gymnast that couldn't quite flip over. The shod hooves caught Viceroy in the face and there was a sound like a pound of wet cow shit dropping on a flat rock, and Viceroy's neck turned at a too-far angle and he flew up and fell down.

James bolted, and so did Elliot, slamming into Tim as he went, knocking him down. James hit the ground, rolled under the trailer, scuttled to the other side, Elliot went after him. Butch aimed at the back of Elliot's head and the chicken man said, "Hey, what the hell."

Butch turned and shot the chicken man through the center of the forehead. Chicken man fell and the rooster leaped and squawked, and just for the hell of it, Butch shot the rooster too.

Tim got up cussing. "I'm all muddy."

"Fuck that," Butch said. "They're gettin' away."

Even the mule had bolted, darting across the yard, weaving through the car crusher and a pile of mangled cars. Their last view of it was the tips of its ears over the top of the metallic heap.

Tim ran around the trailer and saw James and Elliot making for a patch of woods in the distance. It was just a little patch that ran along both sides of the creek down there. The land sloped just enough and the rain and wind were hard enough that the shot Tim got off didn't hit James or Elliot. It went past them and smacked a tree.

Tim came back around the trailer and looked at Butch bending over Viceroy, taking his gun, sticking it in his belt.

"He bad?" Tim asked.

"He's dead. Fuckin' neck's broke. If that's bad, he's bad."

"We gonna get them hillbillies?"

"There ain't no hills around here for a billy to live in. They're just the same ole white trash they got everywhere, you idiot."

"Well, this ain't Dallas . . . We gonna chase 'em?"

"What for? Let's get the TV set and go."

"Got a stereo too. I seen it in there. It's a good'n."

"Get that too. I don't think there is no money. I think he was gonna try and sweet-talk Viceroy out of some of that blow. A pay-later deal."

"He damn sure didn't know Viceroy, did he?"

"No, he didn't. But you know what, I ain't gonna miss him."

A moment later the TV and the stereo were loaded in the Cadillac. Then, just for fun, they put the chicken man and Viceroy in the chicken man's truck and used the car crusher on it. As the truck began to crush, chickens squawked momentarily and the tires blew with a sound like mortar fire.

With Viceroy, the chicken man, and the chickens flattened, they slid the truck onto a pile of rusted metal, got in the Cadillac, and drove out of there, Butch at the wheel.

On the way over the cattle guard, Tim said, "You know, we could have sold them chickens."

"My old man always said don't steal or deal in anything you got to feed. I've stuck by that. Fuck them chickens. Fuck that mule."

Tim considered that, decided it was sage advice, the part about not dealing in livestock. He said, "All right."

■ ■ ■

Along the creek James and Elliot crept. The creek was rising and the sound of the rain through the trees was like someone beating tin with a chain.

The land was low and it was holding water. They kept
going and pretty soon they heard a rushing sound. Looking
back, they saw a wall of water surging toward them. The
lake a mile up had overflowed and the creek and all that
rain were causing it to flood.

"Shit," said James.

The water hit them hard and knocked them down, took
their hats. When they managed to stand, the water was knee-
deep and powerful. It kept bowling them over. Soon they
were just flowing with it and logs and limbs were clobber-
ing them at every turn.

They finally got hold of a small tree that had been up-
rooted and hung to that. The water carried them away from
the trees around the creek and out into what had once been
a lowland pasture.

They had gone a fair distance like this when they saw
the mule swimming. Its neck and back were well out of the
water and it held its head as if it were regal and merely
about some sort of entertainment.

Their tree homed in on the mule, and as they passed,
James grabbed the mule's neck and pulled himself onto it.
Elliot got hold of the mule's tail, pulled himself up on its
back where James had settled.

The mule was more frantic now, swimming violently. The
flood slopped suddenly, and James realized this was in fact
where the highway had been cut through what had once
been a fairly large hill. The highway was covered and not
visible, but this was it, and there was a drop-off as the water
flowed over it.

Down they went, and the churning deluge went over them, and they spun that way for a long time, like they were in a washing machine cycle. When they came up, the mule was upside down, feet pointing in the air. Its painted nose sometimes bobbed up and out of the water, but it didn't breathe and it didn't roll over.

James and Elliot clung to its legs and fat belly and washed along like that for about a mile. James said, "I'm through with livestock."

"I hear that," Elliot said.

Then a bolt of lightning, attracted by the mule's upturned, iron-shod hooves, struck them a sizzling, barbecuing strike, so that there was nothing left now but three piles of cooked meat, one with a still visible brown nose and smoking, wilting legs, the other two wearing clothes, hissing smoke from the water, blasting along with the charge of the flood.

LINDSEY DAVIS

Lindsey Davis was born in Birmingham, England, and now lives in London. After taking an English degree at Oxford and working for the civil service for thirteen years, she "ran away to be a writer." Starting with historical romances, Lindsey struggled to make ends meet until she came up with the idea for Marcus Didius Falco, a P.I. working in Rome at the end of the first century A.D. His first appearance was in 1989's *The Silver Pigs*. Since then Lindsey has won the Ellis Peters Historical Dagger for 1999's *Two for the Lions* and Marcus has won the 1999 Sherlock for Best Comic Detective.

FIRST MYSTERIOUS PRESS PUBLICATION:
LAST ACT IN PALMYRA, 1996

BODY ZONE

No Smoking" said a sign on the door. Then, in smaller letters, "XYZ Detection Agency (sole prop, Mr. Grubshaw)."

The black paint on the door had curled into long vertical flakes which revealed a gray undercoat, enhanced by an aluminum sheen, shimmering in patches like fish scales on a harbor wall. The door deterred many prospective clients. When others shyly entered, they were surprised to find the agency's sole prop poised behind his desk smoking a large cigar.

As he set visitors at ease, Mr. Grubshaw would explain the notice by saying that other people's smoke made him cough. This set the surreal tone for the interview.

Sometimes the conversation meandered into questions about the agency's name. Most businesses wanted to catch folk who thumbed the yellow pages in alphabetical order, so they chose titles like the AAAA Cowboys. Mr. Grubshaw claimed his agency was a deliberate front. He wanted to *appear* to be in business, so that Social Services would not force him to accept welfare payments.

"Besides," he would twinkle, " 'XYZ' hasn't put *you* off, has it?"

His new clients would either blush or stare him out stonily. People who ended up in his office had indeed worked through the yellow pages in alphabetical order. They had already approached the AAAA Cowboys; then I Spy Investigations (Ex Met Police: Divorce and Discreet Finance Checks Our Speciality); and Winkies (Suppliers of Personal Protection, Anti-Kidnap Courses available, all our Operatives are versed in Defensive Driving). The other agencies had turned them down. For good reasons.

"I expect you've found," Mr. Grubshaw would comfort these sad clients whom no sensible agency would accept, "the investigation business is awash these days with retired army specials and overweight ex-cops who resigned in a hurry to avoid corruption charges." His clients were unlikely to report the slander. "Useless for anything delicate. Everyone can hear their big boots crashing from half a mile away. None of that here. We work invisibly, we work with finesse."

"So what line were you in before this?" persistent types might venture. Mr. Grubshaw then chuckled and tapped his nose, suggesting that he too had a tough militaristic background which had equipped him not just to seem invisible but to iron his own shirts, operate a submachine gun, and eat worms. Anyone who noticed that he was a sloppily dressed, shambly, middle-aged man with a hole in one sock might doubt it. He had an accent that was just enough north of Watford for him to be seen as an outsider in London, yet not northern enough to be interesting.

To his niece he had once said that he was disbarred from the Tailors' Union after complaints about his taking of inside leg measurements.

"I won't tell that to Auntie Poll," replied the niece.

"No, don't!"

"She already sees you as a social blight," the niece reported, wide-eyed with fake innocence. She was ten, more or less. Mr. Grubshaw had a bad feeling that this was the one named Perdita; while pregnant, her mother had been unhealthily obsessed with Shakespeare's problem plays.

The mother of his niece was the only adult relative who still spoke to him. Married to his city broker youngest brother, she was a woman with more interesting ideas than were good for her. A decent conscience that meant she regularly sent her daughter to check up on Mr. Grubshaw's welfare. The niece welcomed her chance to play with his computer. She was teaching herself how to hack into official databases, which would be fun for her and useful for him.

"Your Aunt Poll," he replied uneasily, "is a vindictive liberal-minded woman who eats organic spinach." Aunt Poll was married to another of his well-heeled brothers.

"Bitter!" retorted the niece. She was a thin, pale child in outsize trainers, with extremely complicated hair-slides like rows of little plastic butterflies in rather lank hair: a normal turn-of-the-millennium mite. Thanks to modern education (and no thanks to the equal opportunities legislation), she would grow into the formidable woman her mother yearned to be; she was already a terrifying ten-year-old. "Pressures of the job getting to him," she added wisely to the computer screen—though she knew (since she had nosily accessed his case records) that Mr. Grubshaw had too few clients for any pressure to apply.

That was why, when a message came from her mother that he had to take his niece to the Millennium Dome, Mr. Grubshaw could not plead the excuse of too much work. Avoiding the outing required too much effort, so he grumpily succumbed. The niece acquired tickets via the Internet. Mr. Grubshaw was bemused to note that she paid using his credit card, without needing to ask him its number or expiry date.

. . .

From Greenwich station, they took the special Dome bus. They had read in the advance literature that it would talk to them, with a recorded message explaining what a good, environmental little bus it was.

"As usual," murmured Mr. Grubshaw, "being *able* to talk does not guarantee talking sense!" In fact the Dome was such a failure as an attraction that only four other people took the bus and the driver did not bother to play the recorded message. "Lovely," said Mr. Grubshaw, "Celebrating a two-thousand-year anniversary but we can't get anybody interested."

They set off through the historical part of Greenwich, bending past the weathered Hawksmoor church, with a tantalizing glimpse of rigging on the *Cutty Sark* tea clipper, before the one-way system took them around the gracious blocks of Sir Christopher Wren's masterpiece, the Royal Naval College—now being refurbished for the local university. To their right lay the architectural perfection of the Queen's House, flanked by the long colonnades of the National Maritime Museum. Through the elegant columns they could see the rising ground of the Royal Park, dominated by the observatory.

"We could jump off this bus now—go and play somewhere real . . ."

"I can't let your mother down."

"Scared!"

"You bet."

Mr. Grubshaw felt ill at ease. Greenwich had its moments. Sometimes fully armed police wearing frogman suits bounced downriver in rubber dinghies to pursue drug-running criminal gangs; but women who witnessed them landing at dawn were interviewed later on TV saying they had just assumed it was a Greenpeace publicity stunt. Greenwich had a gentler environment than neighboring Deptford, where his office was. Deptford had hardly changed in character since Christopher Marlowe was murdered in a drinking house in 1593; now hairdressers were gruesomely slaughtered by their boyfriends, vulnerable youths were pursued and beaten to death by bullies, and on quiet evenings chip shops exploded as a result of gas leaks—or next-door newsagents' shops collapsed in a shower of rubble after being undermined by the builders who were repairing the chip shops.

"Bit of life in Deptford," Mr. Grubshaw commented.

A woman who had seated herself within earshot glared at them. She had a silent, browbeaten husband, but she seemed used to spotting subversiveness. The niece applied the innocent look she wore when she was pretending to be a victim who had been offered sweets by a pedophile; unlike her mother she had no conscience at all. "Can I see it, Uncle?"

"Oh, not here, darling!"

The niece used a beseeching expression and Mr. Grubshaw pretended to give in. He produced something from the pocket of his dirty raincoat, over which he and the girl poured attentively with their heads close together.

"Disgusting!" muttered the stressed woman to her baleful husband, though she seemed to sense that if she reported Mr. Grubshaw as a child molester, she would end up looking a fool.

"Oh, don't start!" begged the husband, but in a mumble as if he half hoped to be misunderstood. He was a well-built fellow looking for a quiet life; she was an evil little baggage who reckoned she ought to run everything, or so Mr. Grubshaw deduced. She probably reported her neighbors for having their motor tax discs out of date.

Turning left at the corner by Greenwich Hospital, the bus lurched badly so the woman who liked disapproving had to grasp at the handrail. A large carrier bag with which she had lumbered herself nearly slipped from her grasp and was rescued by the husband.

"Whoops—come back, Woody!"

What Mr. Grubshaw and his niece were gazing at was a matchbox which contained a dark gray-brown creature half an inch long. This was Mr. Grubshaw's professional assistant. His niece had sensibly suggested that as his business was floundering, he should obtain help. Her mother read detective novels and was currently gobbling up books which featured snooty cats who solved the crimes, inscrutable felines who always knew the vicar had done it. Mr. Grubshaw hated cats. To avoid that, he claimed the lease on his premises did not permit pets. Woody was a compromise. Cheap to keep, and caused no trouble. Letting him out for a walk only involved placing him in a filing tray. There was plenty of rotting wood in the office windows, from which splinters could be yanked to provide bedding and food. If the wood louse died in the matchbox, he was easily replaced too.

"What have you got there?" the angry woman suddenly demanded in a loud, bossy voice.

Mr. Grubshaw glanced at his companion smugly. "Oniscoidea *Armadillidium*, madam."

"A small isopod crustacean found in damp places," smirked the niece.

"Such as my office," her uncle groaned. "Where, regrettably, *Armadillidium* is found in stupendous numbers. One of the oldest creatures on the planet. Some have the capability to roll into armor-plated balls when frightened." He then glanced at the husband as if suggesting there was somebody else who must spend a lot of his time rolled into a ball.

His niece giggled. "It's a wood louse!"

The woman sniffed, to represent her feelings of disgust—and perhaps, her fear that they were playing the fool at her expense.

One of the other passengers left the bus along the route; ordinary passengers could do that. Mr. Grubshaw made a routine professional check of the occupied seats. Apart from the bossy woman and her husband, their only companion now was a neat, mustached man in gray flannel trousers, a white shirt, and a blue blazer with silver buttons. It was oddly formal attire for a visit to the Dome, which must be his destination, as there were no other scheduled stops. This chancer actually flaunted a cravat; he looked as if he spent his time selling scarlet sports cars with dodgy suspension and fiddled mileage clocks.

Approaching the Dome peninsula, through older, poorer districts—all tattooists and tile showrooms—the sky lightened over the River Thames. A toytown plane chugged on the downward flight path to the Docklands Airport. They passed a huge empty gas cylinder, a fantasy spiderweb, then reached the Dome itself. That ought to have been far more fantastic, yet already seemed mundane, like a beached Teflon jellyfish pegged down with a Lilliputian web of wires, apparently just about to disintegrate into a puddle of smelly water. Alongside were silver and blue service towers, conical drums with metal fins, which reminded Mr. Grubshaw of old car air filters. Perhaps the blazered man had come to work on them.

"It's like a rather nasty pustule with a lot of poisoned heads."

"Oh, Uncle! Those are the twelve masts, symbolically representing the hours. Inside we can visit the twelve activity zones under them."

"Representing a very expensive mistake, darling. Maybe it looks wonderful by moonlight, just like the Taj Mahal."

"That's a joke. Do you mean your favorite curry house?"

"It's a joke, all right." Mr. Grubshaw was about to complain that the Dome was an insult to taxpayers, then he remembered that he had failed to pay any tax for several years.

After they negotiated the ticket booths and worked out which way across the bleak forecourt was actually the entrance, a security guard whom he had known previously as a casual burglar hailed them: "Wotcha, Grubby!"

Mr. Grubshaw shot him a furious look, which the guard interpreted as a sign that he was out on surveillance duties for one of his clients, perhaps using the niece as cover. The guard, whose name was Snaky Fibbert, stared suspiciously after the previous entrants—who happened to be the woman from the bus and her husband. "*Bad characters!*" mouthed Mr. Grubshaw to Snaky, before his niece grabbed his hand and dragged him eagerly toward the entrance, singing loudly, "There is nothing like a Dome!"

He wondered how a child so young knew so many songs that had been around years before she was born.

• • •

"Which zones are we after? Learning?"

"No fear! Work?"

"You are joking! Play?"

"I can play by myself."

"What, an unsupervised imagination? We can't have that in post-Thatcherite Britain . . . Money?"

"Yes—that will be a new experience for you, Uncle."

The Millennium coin-minting intrigued them, though caused high indignation when the niece discovered that for a celebration coin with a face value of five pounds her uncle was to be charged ten. "Don't have it. What a rip-off!"

They saw the woman from the bus taking the same stance, to her husband's visible disappointment—so Mr. Grubshaw ostentatiously treated the niece after all, as a gesture of human benevolence. He was wasting his time trying to re-train miseries. The small pinched figure waddled off, trailed by her disconsolate man.

"Can't we for once—" The sad husband's plea petered out. Several decades of sour marriage could be read in that couple. Mr. Grubshaw wondered what they were doing here, but people who fail to communicate do so easily force them-selves into situations where quarrels may occur. Visiting the Dome would be a routine episode, one more day wasted be-cause they lacked any capacity to enjoy life.

"Abortive moments of protest dwindle into depressed compliance—"

"Grubby Grubshaw—modern poet!" mocked the niece.

"Don't be cheeky. If that husband found a dead fly in a jam sandwich, he would just poke it out of the way and say nothing."

Other people did seem to be having a good time. The crowds were sparse; due to small numbers, the Dome was losing money fast. Most people wore anoraks and jogging trousers, although a few dogged elderly ladies were decked out in their smartest skirts and best navy patent shoes. Folk were quiet and well behaved (as was to be expected, given the high entry ticket price) yet they walked through the wide red-floored aisles with an air of determined good nature. People would tolerate much. Where queues for the popular zones existed, they were managed well by watchful stewards who whipped rope barriers into place. The visitors were being kept happy with a good supply of food stalls and lavatories. The place was not sordid; there were plenty of rubbish bins.

"There's plenty of rubbish too!" sneered Mr. Grubshaw's niece. At a supercilious age anyway, she was partaking of zonal experiences with a grim sense of duty and a fierce will to mock. Mr. Grubshaw stayed more relaxed. He hated to let a nannying government get the better of his blood pressure.

The niece, planning for when she possessed a fortune, chose to march into Millennium Jewels and stare at the diamonds. Mr. Grubshaw wandered alone into Faith (by error), where he ducked nervously through "Night Rain—a light space," which he found to be a purple glow, empty except for other people who looked as if they too could not understand it and thought they had come through the wrong door. Exiting hastily, he forged out through a walkway to the open air beyond the rim of the Dome's roof—here was the luxury of natural sensation, rain and the relief of cool fresh air to breathe . . . The fairy-tale, futuristic Docklands with its model trains now seemed substantial and real beyond the grimly unrecycled water of the River Thames.

Returning, he looked for his niece and realized that he had forgotten to wear his watch. The Dome, temple of Time, symbol of the Millennium moment, seemed to contain no clocks. A bored information assistant in a booth deigned to nod, indicating a small, plain electric timepiece; it confirmed that Mr. Grubshaw had a few moments to nip into the gents.

There he encountered a character. He and the niece had already grimaced over the self-conscious zany entertainers who patrolled the aisles among the crowds. They included a woman with a knowing look, who tottered on rickety heels, with a gash of orange lipstick, a bouffant hayrick of hair, and a toy dog pulled behind her on a string; this caricature prostitute was an unlikely addition to a place of "family" entertainment. More acceptable were men on stilts, jugglers, and old-fashioned clowns. Or even the Disneyesque cartoon figures with bloated bodies, monstrous heads and feet, to whom tiny children were led, squealing obligingly with delight (scared to admit they were terrified). A rather good living statue had almost fooled Mr. Grubshaw.

Instant favorites were the Anti-Smile Campaigners. Since Mr. Grubshaw had forgotten his reading glasses as well as his watch, he misread this as the Anti-Simile group and imagined for a wild moment that his intellect had been genuinely challenged. Not so. A disparate group led by a mock vicar, these solemn ones were claiming to be opposed to mirth. At least, thought Mr. Grubshaw, it struck a blow against the constantly grinning puppets in the government, those manipulated wooden men who imagined *they* were manipulating society. As if that were a decent aim in any case.

What he met in the gents was a painted man. He had seen them before, though never at such close quarters. Remarkable creatures, sometimes silver, sometimes midnight blue, for reasons that were not always clear they added to the fun at public events. This one was metallic green; in style a large, paunchy Dickensian clerk, who looked depressed and under the weather financially. He and his costume were sprayed from head to foot with luminescent color. Hair; face; suit with bursting buttons; gloves; long muffler;

shoes; tall hat. All malachite green. He had features, and he moved in an ordinary manner, but the paint gave him an eerie, unreal aspect. Perhaps he could talk, if he was willing to do so, though it seemed best not to intrude by speaking to him. The stillness of his features made him strangely anonymous.

Mr. Grubshaw met the Green Man while they were both washing their hands with recycled water. He put aside wicked curiosity as to whether his companion's personal equipment had been sprayed to match the rest of him . . .

With a shock, he recognized the human being behind the inscrutable color: It was the husband of the misery from the bus. Their eyes met briefly. Mr. Grubshaw was left unnerved—aware that there was more to this man than he had allowed in his first assessment. Perhaps both members of the couple had an eccentric streak. The woman must have been carrying the green clothes and paint spray in that bag she had clutched. Presumably she tolerated—or even encouraged—her husband's public dressing-up.

■　■　■

Returning to his duties as a chaperon, he found the niece waiting, while she cheerfully sang to herself, "Dome, Dome on the range!"

Their timed tickets let them into the Body Zone, two dehumanized pink plastic bulges that were supposed to excite and enthrall. Into the throbbing red coils they glumly went, deafened and disoriented by pulsations of noise. A horse's whinny confused Mr. Grubshaw, before his irritation was taken over by the loudness of the crowd of sperm, teeming and swirling like minnows but making far more racket than the insidiousness of real conception. A suspended eye might have fascinated him if anyone had explained it or shown it working. A digestive tract in working order would have been fun . . . Passing the heart, he noticed a strange smell of old urine and overheated red plastic. That was not part of the official experience; he had rebelled and was using his senses independently.

Suddenly they were outside again, first to join everyone else crying, "Is that it?," then to be led firmly into the extensive area devoted to the pharmaceutical sponsor's work. Beside the operating theater of the future, a woman sneezed violently.

"*That* was the Body?" His niece was scornful. "I saw one silly flea. It wasn't a bit scary. That was *really* disappointing."

"That's life, darling." After all, Mr. Grubshaw thought (privately), you could not expect genuine thrills from a couple of sexless blobs. Many a disappointed woman would agree wholeheartedly—including past clients of his agency who had sought help to combat marital despair. Most wanted to hire contract killers to dispose of their husbands; Mr. Grubshaw passed them on smartly to a solicitor he knew who did divorce work at attractive rates. "So we've laughed at the Body; we'd better have a quick sniff at Mind."

They hated Mind. From the moment spheres of light seemed to chase after them threateningly outside the zone, uncle and niece set themselves against having the nature of their perceptions explored. The brief experience of bombardment with frenetic sound and lurid light in Body had prepared them for mottoes and images rather than brain fodder. They did try to apply their intelligence to the optical illusions, but the niece had seen some of the tricks before and whenever she deigned to stamp on one of the panels that made a display "work," the control turned out to have broken down.

"Due to a technical hitch, you will not be 'seeing the world in new ways' this afternoon . . ."

They were numbed by a statue of a boy who supposedly reminded them that their senses were most alert and questioning in childhood. "What an evil little swine he looks!"

A young woman posed, arms akimbo, beside this crouching pixie with his pointed face and malicious eyes; her male companion took a photograph which would show her definitely not bothering to question the peculiar artifact.

Are humans getting more intelligent? "I can answer that one. Not here! Can we go to the show yet?"

"Not the right time."

They enjoyed Living Island, with its nice sense of irony since it was about a Dying World; they skipped Play; kept talking about Talk but never got there; thought Journey unnecessary.

"They have no idea," marveled Mr. Grubshaw, at his most cynical. "According to the arty sparks who planned this, you can have journeys that are Optimistic, Historic, Legendary, Adventurous. What happened to the kind most people get stuck with? Sheer bloody Miserable?"

The niece shot him an indulgent look and decided to risk Timekeepers, which had a model castle that looked quite imaginative. *Under 12s only. Accompanied by an adult.* "I'm not old enough," Mr. Grubshaw protested, trying to avoid it. So they peered in from the outside and saw there were just slides and other play equipment, with large numbers of tennis balls to shoot at people. A sound track pumped out recordings of panicky voices from characters in some stressful situation, with a doom-laden countdown and noisy explosions; the children playing all ignored it.

Mr. Grubshaw, who had a functional problem on which he had not yet bothered to take medical advice, had to go to the lavatory again. His niece, who knew about taking adults out, waited patiently outside. Inside he found Snaky Fibbert, the security guard, looking shifty. Preferring to ignore bulges in Snaky's pockets which could be other people's wallets, Mr. Grubshaw pretended to think he just looked shifty because he had used the public lavs rather than the staff ones.

"That woman's not what you thought, Grubby," complained the security guard. "She reported some poor con artist; we had to pull him off his patch."

"The lady is by nature down in the mouth, Snaky. What was the scam?"

"Oh, you know how that feller in the old days sold the Eiffel Tower to an American? We have a sad case here who tries to sell the Dome. Blazer, we call him. Mustache and cravat like a gigolo chasing widows on a cruise liner. *'This Dome has to close on the thirty-first of December—I happen to have a private line to the agents . . .'* His problem is that most of the tourists are European and don't go for it, or Japanese and they can't understand him."

"'*Any shrewd investor—like yourself, sir—can snap up share options, but you need to move fast. Let me take your deposit . . .'* The old time-is-of-the-essence ploy! Still, it makes a change from flogging time-share apartments that haven't yet been built—and won't ever be—in lousy Spanish towns."

"Full of runaway British gangsters and their ghastly blond girlfriends!" Snaky completed the description, with the downcast air of one who might have fallen for a salesman, thus using, and losing, the proceeds of his own light-fingered activities. "Anyway, that woman shopped him today."

"Her husband's a green man," reported Mr. Grubshaw noncommittally.

"Oh, that's Pea Soup, then," Snaky answered. "So she's Lois. I never met her, and I only know him when he's painted."

"Funny character."

"Takes all sorts!"

Chortling, Mr. Grubshaw rejoined his niece. Flagging slightly under the effort of admiring devices imposed on them by uncreative minds, they took their chances to see the Millennium Show in the central arena. Told by stewards that they could sit on the terraces, Mr. Grubshaw went instinctively to one that turned out to be designated for senior citizens and persons of impaired mobility. Irritable, he and the niece found another section, where they perched on red plastic chairs, wriggling as the seats in front stuck painfully in their knees.

"Bit squashed. They like to pack them in!" There was nobody else in their section.

Awestruck by the enormous space, they did enjoy the acrobatic show. Neither Mr. Grubshaw nor his niece had any idea what was supposed to be happening, but they watched enthralled as the performers engaged in daring activity at several levels on the vast three-dimensional stage. There was an allegorical narrative—always an excuse for tosh. A story of struggle—the struggle of true spectacle and real technical skill to defeat a banal vision and an ill-conceived narrative. Characters plunged earthward on bungee ropes, then strode magisterially on stilts, while complex props were wheeled about—huge paper flowers and Meccano-like wheels, within which performers were slowly spun while companions twisted stunningly on sky-high trapezes.

Mr. Grubshaw, whose line of work demanded that he notice what he was not supposed to be seeing, found a curious contrast between the fabulous acrobatics and the visible work by ground-based black-clad stagehands. Among them were other distractions—yellow-jerkinned stewards, oblivious to the magical show, who strolled in front of the terraces, looking up at the meek audience as if searching for signs of riot. Then from time to time they ran toward exits with puzzling urgency, while a woman who was hung about with shortwave radios and identity tags marched to and fro.

"Oh, dry ice—smashing! Mind you, my fundament's already frozen." The plastic chairs, no doubt architect-designed, were far from cozy.

Meanwhile the performance continued, like a tribal dance in a TV documentary; it had a powerful sense of legend but constantly left him wondering *what the heck?* Drums throbbed. The lesser characters at ground level performed nightclub jerks and rolled about playing bears like four-year-olds. Celtic instruments zizzed while the principals waved their arms in desperate anguish for uncertain reasons. Towers rose, fireworks blasted from the towers, and a group strangely clad in what seemed to be plastic macs overcame pretty well everyone else, then—like most despots in silly uniforms—looked unsure what to do with the world they had conquered. The prince in pink ("Oh, he's the prince—I thought he was the baddie!") executed breathtaking somersaults almost up against the roof with the princess in yellow ("Oh, the princess! I thought it was the prince"). Finally, backpackers scampered into the arena (apart from a couple in the rear who were too tired to scamper and who walked).

Releasing colored streamers, they were lifted up to form an impressive giant maypole, which evolved thrillingly into a fantastic lampshade fringe where the main characters hung suspended. Noticing the show was over, the audience gave a patter of applause.

"Stunning!" grinned Mr. Grubshaw. "Can we go now? I'm so cold I'm an icicle."

As the person in charge, the niece took the decision that he had had enough. Any moment, it would end in tears. Lying like a parent, she assured him they could go home soon ("I want to go Dome!"). First, she just needed to go through Living Planet, which had a ride in a spaceship and a film; she fixed a meeting place for later and said her uncle ought now to take himself to Rest.

He had been looking forward to Rest. After carefully reading the notice to switch off his mobile phone (he did not own one), he strolled inside. He found a muffled double igloo. More peculiar lighting, in eerie pastel shades, made him anxious. He smelled an unpleasant cheap scent, which must be the refreshing wafts that were supposed to calm the senses. Patterns speckled the ceiling. People became hushed, yet not quite hushed enough, as they tottered to the double banks around the edges where one could sit, loll, or lie down. Lying was the best option, Mr. Grubshaw found, since the sculpted banks had been produced by another set of designers who were strangers to normal human functions. Most of his fellow resters gave up and shuffled out of the zone when they grew tired of sliding off their perches.

He tried to sink into tranquillity.

That failed. Bored, he gazed upward. The double ceiling had grown rather cracked around its central arch. Large pale blue blobs were dotted at roof height. Shifting position, he noticed that the dirty white banks were also marked off at intervals by splodges of orange, like bloodstains. A world without orange would be nice. Nobody else was here now, except one woman stretched out on her back on the top row of a snowbank as if she were asleep.

Music was supposed to suffuse the chamber. *Longplayer*, an original piece, was said to have been started on December 31, 1999, and to be set to last for a thousand years. Unfortunately, the tape broke down during Mr. Grubshaw's visit, so an attendant had to carry in a notice to apologize for the technical hitch. The fact that the notice was ready-printed cast some doubt on the thousand-year claim.

The steward glanced around quickly as she must have been trained to do, searching for trouble. Much was possible; the enclosed space could be a challenge to the young or the brazen. Mr. Grubshaw doubted that much ever happened. He looked for hidden security cameras, but spotted none. The steward left.

I tried to find the Erogenous Zone but failed . . . Still, that was like real life.

Still bored, he thought he would check on Woody. The sleeping woman would never notice. He quietly removed the matchbox from his pocket and inspected his partner. Attracted by the queer mauve lighting, the wood louse clambered frantically against the edge of his box, so Mr. Grubshaw let him out onto the scuffed floor to give his numerous little legs some exercise.

For a short period leopard skin patches moved languidly upon the roof. The light subtly changed to a pinker shade. Mr. Grubshaw despised pink. Still, he despised most things in this place. His failure to be lulled into any feeling of peace was irritating him fiercely. Time to go. He looked for Woody.

Wood lice tend to skulk around. However, they can put on a burst of high speed the moment you take your eyes off them. Turn away to find a flyswat and they scuttle sideways under a cupboard. They have been on earth for many millennia; they know they are at risk of a shoe descending. Hard to squash (though not as tough as wine weevils), even after a nonfatal crushing they are still vulnerable to being deposited down a toilet and summarily drowned. They know this. Woody had a small brain, but generations of armored forebears had imprinted his genes with survival techniques. He understood that if he saw a chance he must scarper. Set down on the zone floor, he was off.

Mr. Grubshaw thought he had retrieved his tiny partner, but it turned out to be a green coat button. He picked it up thoughtfully.

The cool fluorescent igloo was totally silent now. He could feel his own breathing. He half expected to hear snores from the woman asleep. As he glanced toward her, an imperceptible movement caught his eye. *Madam, an escaped wood louse has just run up your skirt* . . . Perhaps not.

Her stillness disturbed him. Maybe it unnerved Woody too, for he had turned away and was slowly descending the bank again. Mr. Grubshaw steeled himself for a rescue attempt. *Excuse me, may I please have my wood louse back?* Since the person was quite motionless, he risked going closer. If she woke suddenly, he would look like a pervert approaching. Best to be bold; stealth would scare her more. He lurched up the misshapen slope and placed Woody's matchbox where the creature could hardly avoid crawling back inside. He kept one eye on the woman, but she never moved.

Closing the matchbox, he stood up. He was ready to ask whether she was all right. That should explain his close proximity.

It was the unhappy woman from the Millennium bus. Lois, implacable wife of Pea Soup. He recognized her belted dark red raincoat and her not-quite-matching shoes. Somewhere she had mislaid both her green-painted husband and their large carrier bag.

Mr. Grubshaw turned to go. He slipped, knocking against the woman. Her arm flopped down. She did not wake. He saw he had a problem.

"Oh dear, Woody."

He could of course have sneaked out and said nothing. It was not in his professional code.

He felt her neck for a pulse, knowing he was unlikely to find one. Marks from a ligature around Lois's neck told the full story. This was no slipping into death through a heart attack. A young girl wandered in to check that nobody was fornicating; Mr. Grubshaw signaled her.

■ ■ ■

Pea Soup was discovered in a cloakroom, trying to spray extra paint on his shirt where a white gap showed behind his missing button. Clutching the hand of his niece, Mr. Grubshaw was present when the man was informed of his wife's death. Pea Soup burst into lavish tears. When Snaky Fibbert and others put to him stern suggestions that he was in fact Lois's murderer, he took it hard. According to him, the green button found in the Rest Zone had just popped off that afternoon; Lois was keeping it to sew back on once they got home.

"Just come clean, sunshine. What did you strangle her with?"

"Nothing! I've got nothing." He did have his green Dickensian muffler though.

"Open-and-shut case," confided a policeman to Mr. Grubshaw, with satisfaction. "I'd like to know why he did it, but we'll soon squeeze it out of him. Our interrogation techniques are very sophisticated. Find your villain and your motive follows." Mr. Grubshaw patiently considered that reversal of the cliché.

Pea Soup's tears became wilder and were disconcertingly genuine. He claimed he and Lois had been inseparable. Constant rowing in public and private was just their way. He protested that, without Lois, his own life was over. And so forth.

Rather than have Social Services called in to care for his niece, which everyone could see would cause family trauma and afflict the child with unwarranted hang-ups, Mr. Grubshaw—though a material witness, finder of the body, and presenter of the green button—was allowed to depart. Snaky Fibbert was deputed to escort them to the exit, as a gesture of Dome courtesy. "Any chance Dome courtesy might extend to a taxi?"

"You're joking! Don't you know what this place costs?"

Mr. Grubshaw's niece made friends with Snaky. She was thrilled by the action and would like to have watched Pea Soup being carried off in a police van. "Wow! That was exciting."

"You had better tell your mother," Mr. Grubshaw instructed nervously. "But don't let Auntie Poll ever hear that I found a dead body when I was supposed to be looking after you."

They were just walking at a smart pace past the Millennium Shop, deciding not to buy any Dome drinks coasters, when Mr. Grubshaw spotted the con man he now knew to be nicknamed Blazer. Every inch a gentleman, Blazer was smoothing his cad's mustache, using long, sensitive fingers. He had a quiet manner and a confident air; he must be looking for a mark who might be made to believe the Dome was a good investment.

Mr. Grubshaw strolled right up to him. "Hello, Blazer!" The con artist managed to look happy at being recognized. Playing suave was his life's work.

Mr. Grubshaw's niece beamed up at him. "What happened to that scarfy thing you had around your neck?" she demanded in a loud voice. A dark flush marred Blazer's almost handsome features. Snaky Fibbert looked intrigued.

The con man's blue coat with its rakish silver buttons was still immaculate, yet one aspect of his neat attire was now not so neat. The white shirt he passed off as hand-stitched, custom-made Savile Row lay open at the neck (a real gent buys his shirts in Jermyn Street). His once pristine cravat was missing.

Mr. Grubshaw beamed; he liked things to end neatly. "I am Mr. Grubshaw, of the XYZ Detection Agency. Where's your neck-choker, Blazer? Not crumpled up and shoved in your pocket, I hope." He turned to Snaky Fibbert, who was starting to follow his logic. "This is the bounder Lois shopped for stalking tourists. He won't have been happy with her over that. She needed a nice Rest after the excitement—but you know that, don't you?" he asked Blazer. "Better get on your radio, Snaky . . ." And to Blazer, he added, "Time's up!"

Blazer did try to make a run for it, but Mr. Grubshaw's niece kicked his ankle with her outsize trainers, tripping him up. "Wrong place, wrong time!" she quipped, already a smart professional.

Snaky picked up the suspect, then picked his pocket smoothly, discovering the hidden cravat that must have strangled Lois. Forensics would sort that. Soon Blazer was being manhandled away.

Mr. Grubshaw and his niece made their own way to the exit. She was very quietly humming the tune whose words went, "Show me the way to go Dome! I'm tired and I want to go to bed . . ." He was looking in the matchbox, to ensure his partner was not slacking.

ROBERT GREER

Robert Greer lives in Denver, where he is a practicing surgical pathologist, research scientist, and professor of pathology and medicine at the University of Colorado Health Sciences Center. His short stories have appeared in numerous national literary magazines and two recent short-story anthologies showcasing western fiction. Bail bondsman C. J. Floyd was introduced in a short story and made his first novel-length appearance in *The Devil's Hatband*. Greer also edits the acclaimed *High Plains Literary Review*, reviews books for National Public Radio, and raises Black Baldy cattle on his ranch near Steamboat Springs, Colorado.

FIRST MYSTERIOUS PRESS PUBLICATION:
THE DEVIL'S HATBAND, 1996

REVISION

Sam Geddes placed the faded "Clerk Wanted, Inquire Within" sign in his liquor store window at just about its usual five-month rotation. Fifteen minutes later Coleman strolled in wearing a navy watch cap and an army field jacket with an 82nd Infantry patch on the right sleeve. A faded, inverted V on the opposite sleeve outlined the site where sergeant's stripes had been. The name COLEMAN jumped out from above the jacket's torn right front pocket. Coleman's face was plain and impassive, but his dark green eyes—eyes that locked in on you and never moved—were like heat-seeking missiles.

"Job still open?" asked Coleman, nodding toward the sign.

Geddes continued what he was doing, attaching bags of corn nuts to a rusty metal display. Out of habit he turned the display around gingerly, but a couple of bags still fell to the floor. Geddes made no effort to pick up the bags. "Depends," he said. "Ever run a cash register?"

"Sure," said Coleman, recognizing that Geddes probably knew that he was lying.

"Know anything about invoicing or balancing accounts?"

"Nope."

"What about taking inventory, ever done that before?"

Coleman shot Geddes an icy stare that quickly turned to a frown. "I just need a job, man. You got one or not?"

Geddes snapped another bag of corn nuts in place, then reached beneath the countertop, pulled out a sheet of paper, and shoved it Coleman's way. "Fill out this application and . . ." Geddes leaned back as Coleman reached for his jacket zipper with only the stub of a right hand. The stub ended with two nubs where five fingers had previously been.

Coleman deftly grabbed the tab with the two nubs and pulled the zipper down in one clean motion. "Don't stare so hard, old man. It's not magic," said Coleman, one nub now extended Geddes's way. He reached across the countertop and gathered up the application. With his left hand, he began filling out the form.

Before the war Coleman had dreamed of becoming a wildlife illustrator. His specialty had been illustrating birds. Not just any bird but diminutives known in the trade as miniatures. He never considered himself an artist, just a man who liked to draw. Back then Coleman made his living painting birds on wallpaper, place mats, even on rolls of paper towels. He had taken his well-worn copy of *A Guide to Field Identification: Birds of North America* with him to Vietnam, sometimes thumbing through the book at night while artillery fire exploded in the distance. After three months in the humid Vietnam jungle the book's binding split. On one casualty-laden night patrol, that culminated in a predawn firefight, he lost most of the pages in a Mekong Delta swamp. By the end of his tour the book's cover was all he had left.

Sam Geddes hired Coleman on a thirty-day trial. Within the week the store's regular charter of winos began to stumble into the store. Caught in twilight stupors from too much cheap fermented grape, they'd ask for "Two Fingers." Coleman took their comments in stride, chalking them up to the caliber of the clientele. During Coleman's second week on the job Geddes learned that Coleman had lost half his platoon and most of his hand in a firefight near Rung Sat; that he had spent the next two months in an army hospital; that after three surgical revisions and two failed skin grafts the hand was as functional as the army could make it; that Coleman had been sent home to California where a team of Stanford University doctors took a shot at repairing the hand; and that when Coleman left Palo Alto and headed east he was left with only a stump and two rudimentary nubs.

Coleman had worked at the store for nearly a month when Sam Geddes looked him in the eye one day and said matter-of-factly, "Let me see you work your hand." Coleman didn't flinch. Spreading his two nubs apart, he picked a pen up from the counter. Half smiling at Geddes, he said, "Hell, according to the army, if I put my mind to it I could go back to drawing again." Then, still holding the pen in his two nubs, an anger engulfed Coleman. He scribbled, "Shit, shit, shit, shit" on a nearby legal pad and shoved it down the counter at Geddes.

Coleman had been on the job for five months when the college boys started coming in. Two fashionably dressed, barely twenty-somethings, who smelled of liquor and expensive cologne. Coleman remembered their first visit well, because the day was blustery, snowy, and bone-chillingly cold. By midafternoon Coleman had found himself fighting near gale-force winds on his trips out of the store to meet the truckers delivering stock for the week. On each new trip outside his wounded hand, partially numb and useless in the cold, would throb with needle sticks of pain. Mostly, though, Coleman remembered it because it was the same day Geddes had said, "Count yourself lucky, Coleman. Not many clerks last past the five-month mark." Geddes had then surprised him with a raise.

At first the college boys appeared only on weekends, Friday or Saturday nights. Then a weekday was added, and then another. Eventually they were in the store shooting the breeze with Geddes three to four times a week. They purchased only wine, the expensive kind, and always cabernet. "Stockbroker's wine," Sam would tell Coleman after their visits.

Geddes and the college boys talked about the fluctuating world market value of the dollar, the Celtics, the cost of sugar futures, and occasionally even the price of corn. At times their conversations lasted for hours, dragging on until time to close. The tall one spoke in a high-pitched monotone, squeaking his words from a wide, oval mouth that dominated his face. He punctuated his sentences with gestures that became almost spastic whenever he talked about power, money, and success.

"Not the minor leagues," Coleman heard him bark to Geddes during one of their extended visits. "Not *your* brand of bootlegger's joy. *I'll* have it all, just you watch." He slammed his fist on the counter, emphasizing his point. "That liquor license of yours, for instance," he continued, pointing to a dusty framed certificate hanging on the wall. "What did it cost?"

"Back when I got it, eight thousand bucks," said Geddes, his voice full of pride.

"For me it would be offered as a courtesy—a gift from the state. Get my drift?"

"Sure," said Geddes, flashing a patronizing smile.

The short one didn't say much, especially if he noticed Coleman hanging around. His aloof edginess reminded Coleman of a couple of the mindless thrill-seekers he had served with in Vietnam. American grunts who far too quickly became accustomed to death and to war. More than once Coleman watched the short one dart around the store like a second-story thief before pouncing on a wine display and carefully examining the bottles one by one.

Coleman swore that the short one could savor the aroma of an unopened bottle of wine by merely leering at the label. After lingering for a while over the bottles he would move on, ready any second, Coleman thought, to ignite and explode. Eventually, his hopscotching had Coleman recalling his sergeant major's words from years before: "Stay out of the way of the nuts over here, Coleman. They're here for the thrill, riding the crest of a wave that just might take you with them straight to the other side of life."

The tall one always paid for the wine, and as the cold gray days of winter lingered, Coleman realized that he had totaled him out at the cash register more times than he cared to count. They never exchanged a single word, and only once did the tall one stare at Coleman's hand. He blinked a look of horror, and from that time on, whenever Coleman rang him out, the tall one always kept his eyes diverted to the floor.

Throughout the winter and into early spring the two college boys continued to regale Geddes with stories about trips to Kenya, Australia, and the Middle East. Dreamlands to a man like Geddes. Places Coleman knew the old man could never hope to see.

"Those boys are sophisticated. They've got life by the tail," said Geddes after one of their three-hour visits.

Coleman gave Geddes a halfhearted nod.

"They've got a program," Geddes continued. "A blueprint

for success. After all, when you come right down to it, life's really no more than a matter of style."

"They're bullshitters, Sam, with too much money and time on their hands," Coleman snapped.

"A little bitter there, aren't we, Coleman? Don't be so quick to judge. They were only kids when you went to Vietnam. Don't blame your loss on them."

"Let's drop it, Sam. Before you say something stupid and have to eat your words. If listening to their daily sermons makes you happy, great. Just don't ask me to join the choir." Coleman walked to the back of the store, shaking his head.

After that visit Coleman didn't see the two college boys for weeks—weeks he spent in a musty corner of the back storeroom secretly attempting to draw once again. The first few days he drew nothing but lines. Lines by the hundreds until they were bold, even-textured, and absolutely straight. Then came lines that intersected, followed by triangles, rectangles, and finally perfectly proportioned squares. He mastered circles and ellipses in a matter of days. Next came the outline of a liquor bottle, then the detail of an old-fashioned cigarette lighter, followed by a miniature drawing of a dead mouse lying in the corner of the room.

Eventually, Coleman added shading to his images. Then he created scores of hastily sketched birds. Finally, he found himself lingering at the shadows of his nature illustrations once again. He was in the storage room making his first real attempt at sketching in the detail of an eagle's wing when Geddes walked in on him late one day.

"Thought you had a shipment to log in," said Geddes.

"I finished most of it. Thought I'd try my hand at drawing again," said Coleman defensively, caught off guard.

"So, you're a lefty now," said Geddes.

"Don't have much choice; only hand that really works."

"Never knew you were an artist."

"I had wanted to be a wildlife illustrator, if that's what you mean."

Geddes shook his head. "Ever seen a major-league pitcher switch throwing arms midcareer?"

"What's your point?" said Coleman, sketching in an outline of feathers on his wing.

"There's a reason for it, for *not* switching arms, I mean," said Geddes. "The caliber of the pitching wouldn't be nearly the same. Stick with the cards you're dealt, Coleman. I always have. Now, how about finishing with that shipment out front?"

Gritting his teeth to check his anger, Coleman watched Geddes leave before he carefully packed up his supplies, moved the easel aside, and slowly started toward the door.

On their next visit Coleman didn't see the college boys come in. He was busy at a register up front. But he suspected they were in the store, because he could hear Geddes complaining loudly, almost boastfully, to someone about a shipment of bad wine.

"Can you imagine? The idiots left three cases of fifty-dollar Bordeaux freezing on a truck for two whole nights. When I got the stuff it was oozing at the cork. Refused to accept it? You bet I did," said Geddes. "The stuff was piss."

Geddes's voice was coming from near the back of the store. Unusual since Geddes and the boys typically held their bull sessions up front in the center of the store. Coleman continued his work at the register, trying to ignore the conversation coming from the back, until the store had emptied of visible customers. He noticed that Geddes had stopped talking, a rarity with the college boys around, and figured the boys had slipped out without buying anything.

"Hey, Sam, bring me up a case of Bud," said Coleman, deciding to stock a nearby fridge.

"I'll get it," came a high-pitched voice from the back.

"Who's back there with you?" asked Coleman, knowing that Geddes never let anyone but employees in the back. When he didn't get an answer, Coleman started toward the back of the store. The tall boy met him halfway up the store's center aisle. Briefly, they stood facing one another, no more than a foot apart.

"Why don't you head back up front and get behind the counter?" said the tall one, grasping Coleman's shoulder, attempting to turn him around.

"Have you lost your mind?" said Coleman, brushing the arm aside.

"Turn your two-fingered self around right now, war hero. I mean it," said the tall boy as he pulled a gun from beneath his coat and jammed it into Coleman's side.

"What gives?" asked Coleman, responding with a half-turn.

"Just head toward the front. This whole thing will be finished real quick."

"If you're here for the money, it's the wrong time of day. Deposit's been made already. Can't be more than a hundred bucks in the till," said Coleman, knowing that close to four thousand dollars was tucked in a wall safe in the back.

When they reached the front, the tall boy motioned for Coleman to get behind the counter.

"We're here for more than money," said the tall one, nervously blinking his eyes.

"Wine. You dipshits want wine," said Coleman.

The short one suddenly came running toward the front. "Keep your mouth shut, Cary. He doesn't need to know any more."

"It won't work," said Coleman.

The tall boy snickered. "Sure it will. And everyone, including the cops, will figure it was your idea. Look at it our way, baby killer. You get to play sucker citizen one last time."

"You're talking too much, Cary. Be quiet," said the short one.

"Where's Sam?" asked Coleman.

Neither boy answered.

Coleman's bad hand felt moist, almost sticky, as he felt for the razor that Sam kept on the plywood shelf below the front counter. Soon he had the razor wedged between his nubs. As his arm burst from beneath the countertop, the tall boy had no time to react. The razor creased the side of his face, opening his cheek like a ripe summer melon. The next instant he was on the floor, bleeding and screaming. Coleman scooped up the dropped gun and chased the short boy to the back of the store. He finally pinned him, razor to his throat, in a corner near an exit where Sam Geddes lay moaning at their feet.

With his good hand Coleman emptied the bullets onto the floor, put the gun in his pocket, and pulled the burglar alarm next to the door. Then with his damaged hand he steadied the razor just below the short one's ear, its blade indenting the boy's tender skin. He slowly moved to face his prey—fierce, dark green eyes locking in on blue eyes that watered. Beads of sweat ran down Coleman's cheeks and he began to shiver—the same way he had shivered the first time he had aimed an M-16 intending to kill a man.

"You sick son of a bitch," he screamed. "You asshole."

He grabbed the short boy by the throat with his good hand, and kneed him into the wall. The boy struggled to free himself, knocking over Coleman's easel in the attempt. The newly painted sketches of brightly colored birds scattered across the floor.

Coleman watched the scene playing out in slow motion as the paintings floated along the floor, their wet paint smearing along the concrete. Still shaking, he slowly lowered his damaged hand. The razor dropped, bouncing to the floor seemingly in rhythm with the wail of approaching sirens. His good hand remained wrapped tightly around the short boy's throat. He squeezed, watching the boy labor to breathe. Then harder, until his fingers went numb and the look in the boy's eyes turned to terror—a terror Coleman hadn't seen since Vietnam.

Finally relaxing his grip, Coleman took a deep breath, blinked back tears, and stared down at his damaged paintings, telling himself that when all of this was over, there would be time to pick up each painting and start again.

CHARLOTTE CARTER

Charlotte Carter now lives in New York City but, like her heroine, Nanette Hayes, has resided in other parts of the world: Canada, North Africa, and France. Equally influenced by the noir films of Robert Mitchum, the crime fiction of Chester Himes, and the bebop stylings of Charlie Parker and Dizzy Gillespie, she introduced her saxophone-playing sleuth in her first novel, *Rhode Island Red*, in 1998.

FIRST MYSTERIOUS PRESS PUBLICATION:
COQ AU VIN, 1999

BIRDBATH

Tuesday, Sept. 2

Andre,

I swore I wasn't going to write to you. And I'm not going to. Instead I'm keeping this notebook for you until you get back. *Until you get back home,* I was about to say.

Where is home for you now? Paris . . . with her? Or here . . . with me? A tough one, eh?

But I said I was going to stop obsessing about that.

Right now there's other stuff to report. Weird shit.

I went to the annual Charlie Parker fest in Tompkins Square Park on Sunday. You remember which park that is, right? The one where I told you there was a full-out riot about ten years ago when they tried to evict all the homeless. I pointed out the apartment where an old boyfriend lived then, and told you about seeing the helicopters from his window that night. And remember how we went and looked at Bird's old apartment building facing the park?

Anyhow, there I am. On the grass in my halter and cut-offs. Sitting on the mangy orange blanket I keep on the floor of the hall closet. Thermos of iced cappuccino. Wishing you were there and trying to stop my mind from wondering where you and the Mrs. are at that moment—picnicking in the country, weekending in Normandy, et cetera. Or just hanging in Paris, reveling in the newness of September.

The concert's okay. Max Roach and other swells in attendance. That deejay from KCR has been playing Parker

■ 313

and Prez for the past seventy-two hours at the station. (I still maintain I'd rather be Bird than Lester. Lester's pain just seems so much uglier than Bird's, irremediable. Neither liquor nor fame could kill it, and even in the silliest sides he cut, there is no trace of lightness in his heart.)

The vibes in the park are pretty nice, low-key. Etta Jones is singing. I'm looking around at the crowd and notice a stunning lady of color in a pair of two-hundred-dollar jeans.

As I'm staring at Miss Thing, who's yammering on her cell phone, a brother in grungy Bermudas passes by her little mat. He stops right next to the beauteous one. I of course think he's about to hit on her. But no. He just stoops down to tie his shoe. Except he hooks her little Kate Spade purse and just keeps right on walking. That's right, he rips her off. And I'm a witness.

By the time I get to my feet and try to catch her attention, he has disappeared into the crowd. Still on the phone, she never even noticed what happened.

The crowd began to swell after that and I lost sight of her. I assume that sooner or later the knockout lady realized her big-name-designer purse was missing. Everywhere you look some girl is toting a fake Kate Spade or Pradda. But undoubtedly this beauty's bag was the real deal. It probably cost three times the amount of cash she was carrying in it.

In a kind of reflex action, I looked down to check on my money belt then. Those things are virtually theftproof, but I swear they can make a woman's hips look like a bag with too much laundry in it. By the way, I blame you, Andre, for my latest potato chip binge.

Don't take this as more obsessing, but I am still a little nuts behind the way we left it when you went back to France.

Don't seem to be able to maintain a regular schedule for anything.

So I find myself doing things I never do: like baking cookies and doing yoga. Yes, yoga. Being a topless dancing star, my old friend Aubrey is always dipping into one fitness fad or another. She's currently proselytizing yoga and I'm her number one convert. Then there is the most un-me bit of all: I've been watching the news every night before I go to bed.

Goddamn if the day after the Parker festivities, Labor Day, I didn't take my evening bath and get into my jams, crank up the air conditioner, and turn on Channel 2.

There were reports on all the ongoing horrors—Kosovo, the stock market, dead kids, such and such'll give you cancer. And then they flash this black-and-white photograph on the screen. It's the purse snatcher from Tompkins Square Park.

I can't believe it at first, but I keep looking at his picture. It's him, all right, but a photo from better days.

Found dead in his apartment up on 135th Street. The cops found him tied to a chair, a screwdriver through his neck. About as bad a way to die as you could imagine.

But there's more. The guy was identified as a drug addict and an unemployed jazz musician.

His name was Richie Rice. I never heard of him and I never heard of the lounge where they say he played once in a while. For that matter, they didn't even say *what* he played.

I was dumbstruck. And not just because he'd been a fellow musician. The thing was, if I had gotten off my butt quicker and blown the whistle on him, he'd probably still be alive. One of the cops at the concert would've cracked him and he'd most likely have spent the night in lockup. Instead, he gets away with a petty offense like purse snatching and the next day he pays for it with his life. Exactly the kind of twist that haunts me. Man, justice can be hard.

The whole thing made me sick at heart. I got no sleep last night and felt like shit all day today.

This afternoon I pulled down my sax and practiced some. A call from Mom interrupted me. No, I haven't blown the whistle on you yet. If she knew you had a wife she'd probably come over there and cap you in one of those faux hip cafés in the Eleventh.

Wednesday, Sept. 3

Better when I woke up this morning. Late afternoon I played at one of our favorite spots, that strip running along Washington Square. I made out okay. The streets were popping. Busy people. Pretty people. Crazy people. Guess I needed a reminder that life goes on. I was beginning to feel better, but couldn't shake Richie Rice's terrible death out of my head completely.

I walked downtown on Sixth to Caesar's, figuring I'd have a drink with Aubrey. She was off, though. I found Justin in the almost empty club. He says they're in that dead spot between end of summer and beginning of fall. So the handful of guys in there boozing were getting something like a private strip show.

Justin says hi and sends a kiss to you. Like always, he plied me with Jack Daniel's and made me laugh.

I had no place to go and neither did he. We got to talking. I told him what had happened at the Bird concert. And more important, what happened to the luckless Richie Rice.

J is my pal. But I know he doesn't share my obsession

with karma and twists of fate. I figured at the very least he will laugh at me for coming unwrapped over a story—tragic though it might be—that involved a total stranger.

He surprised me.

First of all, he knew who Richie Rice was.

Unfathomable! Justin doesn't even know who Wynton Marsalis is. How on earth would he know of an obscure sideman and petty thief?

"Not because of his music," J explains. "Because he used to date Hattie Randall."

"Who?"

"Girl, you don't know who Hattie Randall is? She was David Panama's favorite model. His inspiration."

"David Panama. Oh! Hip fashion designer, right? Hattie Randall is his muse?"

"*Was*. She's yesterday's french fries now. The big designers don't use her much anymore. Richie Rice was her lover two, three years ago. They met doing some video, and for the next year or so they were in all the columns. Two massively beautatious people. Dancing at all the right clubs. Eating at all the right high-end grazing spots. Drugging at all the right parties."

Justin goes off for a minute to settle some dispute between a waitress and a drunk. While he's away I begin to think: Beautatious. Nice word he made up. Model. Muse. Drugs. Could it be possible? Was there ever a twist of fate twisted enough to make it possible: The woman on the little exercise mat at the Bird outing was actually this Hattie Randall?

So into her cell phone conversation that she doesn't see the theft or the thief. And the mangy-looking guy who nicked her purse was none other than her ex-boyfriend, so strung out that he didn't even recognize her.

It can't be, I'm thinking. Not possible.

"J, why don't the fashion people use Hattie Randall anymore? Does she look like shit now?"

"Honey, I should look like that kind of shit. No, she still looks fab. I don't know why they dropped her any more than I know why she dropped Richie. Maybe she was getting too old for the designers. Maybe he was getting too expensive for her."

"Where could I find a picture of her? *Vogue?*"

"Probably not. The big money's going to some new eighteen-year-old by now. But she still does print work. She turns up in the Saks catalog sometimes."

I say okay to a refill on my Jack Daniel's. While he's pouring, it gives me a minute to call up the face of the beautiful woman on the exercise mat. Am I really remembering her accurately, or am I inventing her features? The longer I focus on it, the more convinced I become that not only am I remembering her correctly but I'd seen her somewhere even before that day.

"J, remember the ads they used to do for that malt liquor? There was a billboard in Times Square and—"

"Yes, that was Hattie. She was bending over, wearing a bustier, and there was a tray of drinks balanced on her butt."

I *knew* it. Jeez, I knew it.

Hattie and her ex had indeed been caught up by circumstance, reunited, you could say, by fate. Only they didn't know it.

Thursday, Sept. 4

Went to Jeff's for a lesson today but he wound up talking about Richie Rice for most of the hour. As you might expect, musicians in the city are buzzing with the story.

Maybe to other people the sordid details of Richie's life are mere grist for the gossip mills. I can't look at it that way, though. It still feels too recent, too sad, and somehow too personal.

Jeff says he thinks he once saw Rice, who blew alto, playing in a combo at some Sunday brunch place. He also tells me he heard that Richie had some fair chops once, but after he met "that model" he got real hincty; didn't seem to be interested in anything but designer clothes and designer drugs.

"What I hear," he said, "after she used him up and threw him outta her fancy loft downtown, he lost it."

I wanted to point out how unlikely it was, considering Richie's drug habit, that all the fault in the relationship lay with *that model*. But I knew it was pointless. Jeff was almost old enough to be my grandfather. I wasn't going to change his consciousness.

In the end I decided to say nothing to him about the purse snatching.

After what was supposed to have been my lesson, I walked further uptown to locate the apartment building where Richie Rice had lived. I just wanted to see where he died. He was a stranger to me. Why had I taken him to my heart? Maybe I'm becoming some sort of perv—a death geek. What was next? Would I start trying to get myself invited to executions?

As long as I had the horn with me, I blew for a while down in the subway. I played a movie theme, "The Bad and the Beautiful," not the easiest piece in the world, as you know. I think I did all right by it, though. That one was for Richie and Hattie. I didn't even bother to open the case for tips.

Aubrey has the flu. I went to her place to see if she

needed anything. Justin was there. We clowned a bit, watched a rerun of *Perry Mason*. Then, deciding we should let her get some rest, we split. Riding downtown on the number 1, I asked him, "Who do you have to be to get into one of those Seventh Avenue showrooms?"

. . .

It's right about here, Andre, that I start to hear one of your favorite phrases in my head: *You brought it on yourself, Nanette.*

Oh, guess what? There's a Starbuck's at 125th Street now.

Friday, Sept. 5

Venus. Athena. Helen of Troy. A couple of the girls in David Panama's workshop reminded me of them. Perfectly serene and perfectly formed and standing cool and still as statues while various hands fluttered over and around them—pinning here, wrapping there, draping, cutting, fussing.

Well, these models did have one thing that set them apart from the Greek ladies: They were all black. Actually the colors ranged from eggplant to eggshell, but they were all women of color.

For whatever aesthetic or commercial reasons, David Panama worked exclusively with black models.

I was in my colored woman executive drag: a suit I borrowed from a girlfriend with a real job, my best heels, the high-burnished leather satchel that once belonged to my paternal grandfather.

A completely fabricated story had gotten me this far, I was supposedly a highly placed assistant to the distinguished documentary filmmaker Peter Lefcourt, who was focusing on the fashion industry in his next project. I was scouting, helping him decide which emerging designers to spotlight.

I'd need to observe for an hour or so, maybe talk briefly with Mr. Panama if he was available, chat up a few employees, assess the space in terms of cameras, and so on.

I declined the offers of Evian and green tea and began to roam the loft area, taking bogus notes.

A sassy-looking girl introduced herself to me. She was African, I realized at once, quite pretty but too small to be a model.

"I'm Asia," she said. "David asked me to see if you needed anything."

I assured her that I did not. Except maybe a few minutes of her time.

"Have you been with David for a while?" I asked.

"About four years."

"So you knew Hattie Randall when she was his star."

"Sort of. Oh, here's David now."

"Before he joins us, Asia, why don't you give me your phone number. I'd like to interview you at length."

"Maybe. But let me call you."

I've never had a business card made up. But I had several of the ones they hand out at Caesar's. Justin had designed them. They were tasteful for a strip club—just the name of the place and the phone number. I wrote my name on one of them and handed it to Asia. "Leave a message at this number telling me when we can sit down together."

Mr. Panama, who confessed to being born in suburban Cleveland, did indeed make himself available for a few moments. He was smallish, very well muscled, and not the least bit fey—more like a wiry housebreaker than a dress designer. He graciously answered the dumb questions I put to him about where he went to school and why he loved working with fabric.

"Do you do any modeling yourself?" he asked me. "You should, you know."

"And you're shameless," I replied, grinning. "But I'll try anything once. Do you think I could be the next Hattie Randall?"

I watched the hundred tiny movements of his eyes and mouth.

"There could never be another one of those," Panama said.

"Were the columns right? Did you and Hattie quarrel?"

"Not at all. We adore each other. But she has gone on to other things."

"You still see her, then?" I asked.

"You know how it is in New York. You can live down the block from someone and not run into them for a year."

"Do you mean you and Hattie are neighbors—more or less? You both live in SoHo, don't you?"

He didn't so much nod as blink his eyes winningly.

"I wonder if you remember a handsome musician she was seeing a few years ago. His name was Richie Rice."

"Hmmm. Haven't seen him in ages. Do you know Richie?"

"No. No, I didn't. Just curious. I guess you haven't heard he passed away recently."

"Good Lord, is that true? How awful."

"I'd better let you get back to business, Mr. Panama. Thanks so much for your time. We'll be in touch soon."

Asia escorted me to the elevator. Panama was watching me as I walked away, assessing things. He just might try to contact the famous filmmaker to check me out. If he managed to get hold of the director's production company, he'd get the same information I did: Peter Lefcourt was in the Yucatán.

Panama was clearly no fool. That didn't mean he wasn't a liar. It sure as hell didn't mean he was telling the truth about his parting from Hattie.

I used the long walk back from the showroom to do some thinking. When I reached Third Avenue, I hopped on a bus. Suddenly I felt like having a fried seafood dinner. To get the makings for that—when you're on a budget, that is—you go to Chinatown.

I bought an armload of stuff. Not just jumbo shrimp and scallops and sole. I stopped in at the general store and bought bamboo tongs and kitchen magnets and ginseng soap; I loaded up on all manner of ninety-nine-cent treats.

On my way to the subway I browsed at the sidewalk stands on Canal Street. You can buy just about anything there: from flashlight batteries to the ubiquitous designer bag knockoffs. I did a comic double take when I saw a pseudo Kate Spade, exactly like the one Hattie Randall had lost to Richie that day in the park.

Tuesday, Sept. 9

Justin came through for me again. He didn't know the exact addresses, but he'd asked around and discovered that David Panama and Hattie Randall had lofts on the same block of Greene Street.

First thing Monday, I ripped the dry cleaner's plastic off my black skirt and threw on a tight little top with shiny buttons up the back. I put on my most impenetrable dark glasses, wrapped a multicolor scarf around my head for the sake of insouciance, and set out about eleven in the morning. At the last minute I ditched my backpack and decided to carry my new purse. For luck.

I began the search at one end of the block. Only a couple of the buildings had street doors that weren't locked, so for the most part I was confined to peering into the lobbies to try to read the names on the bells.

At the beautifully kept building just one door in from the southern corner, I thought I could make out the name Randall on one of the mailboxes. I was just about to go looking for a super when one of the building residents called out to me from the window above.

"You're going to Hattie's?" he asked.

Not a moment's hesitation. "Yes."

He disappeared then. A few seconds later the door buzzer went off and I entered. He met me on the first landing.

"You're her sister, right? We met at the Christmas party once?"

"Right. How's it going?"

"I'm glad you came. Nobody quite knows what to do."

"Excuse me?"

"About the break-in. Somebody got into Hattie's loft the other day and trashed it. We called the police but nobody knows where Hattie is."

"Hattie's staying with me for a while. She had an accident."

"Oh my God."

"Would you mind going up with me?"

"Sure. Have you got the key?"

"Yes. I mean no. I got down here and realized I left the keys at home. Did she leave a set with you?"

Luckily the answer was yes. He admitted me to the chaos that had been Hattie's glamorous apartment. Now all smashed porcelain and overturned armoires, bookcases emptied onto the carpet, kitchen cabinets yawning open, mattresses slashed, medicine cabinet torn from the wall.

"It's horrible, isn't it?" he said. "We didn't know what to do."

"Of course you didn't."

"Is she all right?"

Not knowing how to answer that, I gave him a grave look. "All we can do is hope for the best."

He locked up and I headed uptown and west, back to the Garment District.

I guess I had stuck my nose into the Richie-Hattie story initially because I wanted to let her know about their eerie reunion in the park, and maybe because Richie had captured my imagination and I wanted to know the whole story on him.

But now the stakes had shifted. I was fast becoming convinced that the lovers were headed for a final reunion. An eternal one.

I found an acceptable stakeout: the new Starbuck's across from David Panama's showroom. I removed my head wrap, as it was a tad showy for undercover work, and settled in at a front table so that I could keep an eye on the building.

Asia came out around two-thirty. She was moving fast. I gathered my things and followed her.

At the Chase Bank on Sixth Avenue, she went directly to the international transactions window. I watched as she purchased three grand in traveler's checks.

Her next stop was the airline ticket office on Fiftieth Street. From the sidewalk, I could see she was doing business at the KLM desk. She paid with cash.

Somebody was taking a trip. How nice.

It was four o'clock by then and nigh onto impossible to get a cab midtown. Asia hoofed it back to Sixth Avenue and took the F train downtown.

I kept on her. She got on at one end of the car and I scooted down to the other. She got out of the train at the Twenty-third Street station.

Yep. Somebody was blowing the U.S. in a hurry. But I didn't think it was little Asia. My money was on Hattie Randall.

Tatty, Euro-style hotels and B&Bs are springing up around the Flatiron Building faster than you can say Ian Schrager. The one I trailed Asia to is called the Gershwin. Having been a skanky SRO in its former incarnation, it's now the kind of place where the members of your favorite techno music band might stay.

I waited for Asia to take the elevator up and then I took a seat in the lobby and picked up an abandoned copy of W.

Sure enough, within thirty minutes Asia and Hattie were bustling off the elevator. They were out on the street hailing a taxi. I was watching from inside. Asia helped the long-legged beauty into a cab, slammed the door behind her, and then took off at a run.

I whistled up my own cab and told the driver we were going to follow the one ahead.

Hattie's taxi pulled up at the KLM departure gate of Kennedy. She hustled inside the terminal with me on her heels.

"Hattie!" I called.

The fear was visible in her every movement. She nearly tripped over her valise, looked at me in a panic.

"Didn't you lose something recently?" I asked, and flashed my faux Kate Spade.

She gulped air, staring at the bag, transfixed.

"What do you know about Richie's death?" I asked.

Hattie was shaking her head, obviously about to deny any knowledge of Rice's murder. But there was no time to lie.

The shots came from close by. Really close. I saw a man in an ordinary raincoat drop the dark gun and race away.

Hattie was lying on her back, her face blown open.

I wasn't the only one screaming. But I do believe I was the loudest.

. . .

I was caught in a mess. Not just the blood seeping from Hattie Randall's pulpy head. I convinced the police that my only connection with Hattie was that of a fan. I told them I was just asking for her autograph when the shooter struck. But as to why I happened to be at the airport with no luggage, my acting skills failed me. I fumbled out a story about meeting a school friend coming in from New Orleans. The cops didn't buy it and I ended up having to call my friend Detective Leman Sweet of the NYPD. I say we're friends because the language doesn't have a more precise term for our relationship.

When he arrived at last, he did his usual number on me—I'm retarded, stubborn, nosy, arrogant, Satan in a skirt, and my ass is too big. But he was able to save my bacon. The homicide people released me and Leman poured me into his car.

As he drove I gave him the 411 on Hattie and Richie and David Panama, the purse snatch, the drugs, the break-in. I began at the beginning, at the Parker concert, and took him all the way through my follow-that-cab bit from the Gershwin Hotel. By that time we were back in Manhattan.

We scored a couple of Big Macs and a ton of fries at the McDonald's in my nabe, on First Avenue.

"I guess I don't have to tell you who the top priority is now," he said as he tucked into his second burger. "You better find that African chick before the news gets out that Hattie is dead. Obviously Hattie figured the same thing that happened to Rice was going to happen to her if she stuck around. Maybe this Asia got the same fear of God in her now. If she's got any sense, she'll run too."

"What is she running from, though?" I asked. "What are they all running from?"

"Well," he said, "whatever it is, it must mean the world to somebody."

．．．

I was in dreamland when the phone rang. The caller identified himself as Larry. I started to hang up. I didn't know any Larry.

Oh, wait a minute. Yes, I did. He tended bar at Caesar's.

"There's a little fox making a nuisance of herself at the club," he says. "A good-looker with an accent. Seems pretty wigged out. Demanding to see you—*now*. Says she knows you're the heat and she's ready to trade."

I was pulling my jeans on even as I told Larry to sit on her if he had to, but keep her there until I arrived.

"What the fuck, Nan? You're working for the cops?"

I shouted some graphic instructions to him and hung up.

Justin had Asia in his office, door locked. He had a gun out on the desk—just in case, he said. He walked out and left the two of us alone.

"I knew who you were that day in the studio," Asia said

without prompting. "I knew there was no movie—that you were undercover."

I shrugged, saying nothing.

"What do I have to do to get protection?" she cried.

"Talk fast."

"All right. David Panama was being blackmailed. By Richie and Hattie. It's been going on for almost a year. Hattie wasn't a bitch. She could be real sweet to people. But she was used to having her way, used to being number one diva. David had found some new girl and he was going to replace Hattie with her in the new show and in his bed. Hattie was furious.

"It really messed her up. She would stay high for days at a time. David didn't waste any time spreading the word about her. It was like he wanted to destroy her. And she fell right into his trap. She was blowing off jobs, showing up for work wrecked, pissing people off all over the city.

"The thing is, just before Hattie left, she came into some information—something that could destroy *him*. Hattie went into partnership with her old boyfriend Richie. Their affair was finished long ago, but he was still scoring drugs for her.

"The two of them were bleeding David. But he didn't know who was behind it."

"Obviously he found out," I said.

"Yes. He found out."

"So what's the deal? What got Richie and Hattie killed? What is Panama involved in?"

"Don't you know? Isn't that why you're investigating him?"

"If we're going to put him away I have to hear it from you, Asia."

"He owns a piece of one of the big clothing and accessories knockoff operations. That's what Hattie said. He doesn't stop at fake Calvin Kleins, though. His company is financed by organized crime. And sometimes he has the girls bringing things into the country illegally."

"The models, you mean? The African ones."

"Yes."

"What kind of things do they bring in? Drugs? Diamonds?"

"Maybe. She didn't tell me everything."

I nodded sagely. Then I caught her eye and stared harshly at her. "What was your piece of the action?"

"No! I was in on nothing. I didn't know about David. And I didn't know Hattie and Richie were blackmailing him. Not until she phoned me one night and said she was staying in a hotel and needed my help to get out of the country. She begged me.

"I tried to be careful. When David asked if I'd talked to her lately I lied of course. I helped her get it together to take the plane at Kennedy last night but then I . . . I heard it on the news. I called the number you'd given me, and that guy at the bar—Larry—gave me this address. I grabbed a few things and ran over here. Somebody followed Hattie to the airport and killed her. That means they may have seen me helping her. When David finds out he'll kill me too."

She stood suddenly and looked almost threateningly at me. "Look! I didn't do anything wrong and I don't want to die."

"I hear you."

"Will you help me get out? I can go home. David will never get to me in my country. I don't want anything from him. I don't want his money or his secrets. I just want to live."

"All right. But first, didn't Hattie leave you anything?"

"What are you talking about?"

"Don't waste any more time, lady. Either you want to get away from Panama or you don't. What did she leave you with?"

I looked at her, daring her to deny it. Finally she reached into her bag and extracted a manila envelope.

"What's in it?" I asked.

"Photostats of the company books—both versions. And a couple of tapes of Panama with a few people he wouldn't like the law to connect him with."

"Generous of Hattie to give them to you."

Little Asia's wide-eyed look had changed somehow. And in that mellifluous voice of hers there were now iron filings: "What do you care how I came by it? You have it now. Enough to put David out of commission for a long time. Now, get me out of here!" she commanded.

"Hang in there a little bit longer. I've got to bring my supervisor in on this."

My call woke Detective Sweet and he was mad as hell. But only for a few minutes. When I laid out the facts for him he needed no reminder how rapidly his star would be rising on the job.

I opened the bottle of Jack Daniel's that Justin kept on the shelf, poured one for me and one for Asia.

"Okay, sister Asia. He's on the way," I said. "And before he gets here, how about you telling me the truth?"

"I just did."

"I meant the other truth," I said. "If you don't want to come all the way clean with my boss, that's your business. But we're just girlfriends here now. I want the real story and you've only got ten minutes to tell it."

She didn't speak. So I started her off. "Hattie didn't get the blackmail thing going on her own, and God knows Richie didn't. Two people only interested in getting high master- minding a blackmail plot that stumped Panama for months? Oh, please. You were the one behind that. You told Hattie how she could get her revenge on David Panama. It was you who 'came into' the damaging information about him. You who snooped in his office to get the proof he was cooking the books and then recorded him talking to the bad guys. And finally, you that he kicked out of bed for a younger number. How am I doing, Asia?"

"Not so bad."

"Thanks. When Panama traced the blackmail to Richie, his people tortured him until he gave up Hattie. No won- der you busted your ass to help her escape. She'd have given you up in a heartbeat. Sweet little Asia. Maybe you *can* con- vince my boss that you had nothing to do with the scheme."

"I will convince him. Damn right I will, if you don't go opening your mouth about things you can never prove."

I held up my hands in a gesture of surrender. "Hey. Noth- ing in it for me to have you end up like Richie and Hattie. Go home to your country. I assume you've been building up a nice little nest egg back there?"

Asia finished her drink and held the glass out for more. "It's true," she said, "a dollar goes a long way in my village. I'll live like the fat ass royalty."

∎ ∎ ∎

There it is, Andre. I brought it on myself.

Slept all day and way into the evening. Called in Chi- nese food.

The purse snatching I witnessed at the concert wasn't

what it seemed at all. Hattie knew very well that Richie was taking her bag. It must have been the way they passed money, instructions, drugs—whatever. I still don't know how the blackmail scheme worked. Miss Asia never gave that up.

I expect I'll be hearing from Leman soon and he'll tell me all about the bust-up of Panama's operations.

Can't wait for you to read this, Andre. The way I picture it, you're back here with me and it's late at night. I'm taking a long soak in the tub. You finish reading this and after you calm down and realize that no matter how foolishly I acted I'm okay now, you ask me if I want a beer. And then you bring it to me. And you wash my back.

I never watch the late news anymore.

I'll tell you which habit I might keep, though: yoga. It's something you can do all alone. But you don't feel so damn lonely.

BETH SAULNIER

Beth Saulnier is a journalist in Ithaca, New York—
the inspiration for the fictional home of her pro-
tagonist, Alex Bernier. She graduated from Vassar
College in 1990 and has worked at several newspa-
pers. Presently, she is an associate editor of *Cornell
Magazine*, film critic of the *Ithaca Journal*, and co-
host of *Take Two*, a movie-review show on local television.

FIRST MYSTERIOUS PRESS PUBLICATION:
RELIABLE SOURCES, 1999

HIGH MAINTENANCE

here are lots of things a girl can do on a Saturday night in Gabriel, New York. She can, for example, go contra dancing. She can sample a wide variety of lattes. She can seek enlightenment at the local ashram, dodge the lug-head fratboys in the Collegetown bars, or attend a meeting of the Angry Feminists' League. She can, if she wishes, chase a hatha yoga class with a viewing of *Nosferatu*, then shop for organic mesclun at the all-night health food store and sing along with the folkie radio show on the way home.

Truly our cup runneth over.

And on one particular Saturday night in September, this particular girl had yet another social engagement dangled before her snout. It was something called the Bender, and let's face it: The name pretty much says it all.

The Bender is the annual welcome-back party for the students at the Benson University vet college—a bacchanalian blowout too scary even for a boozy newshound such as myself. We're talking horse troughs of stale Budweiser, doggie bowls brimming with noxious punch, latex gloves engorged with Popov vodka. The thing goes on until the sun comes up, at which point everybody stumbles their way to the marsh that passes for the Benson pond and jumps in. Naked.

I decided to give it a pass, which wouldn't have presented much of a problem—except that the Bender was being held in my living room. Or, more accurately, in every crevice of my house, lawn, and driveway. The neighbors were less than thrilled.

The reason that this annual rite of fall had wound up under my roof was fairly straightforward: One of my room-mates is a veterinary radiologist. A very smart, very British, avidly gin-swilling radiologist, to be exact. The story, as I found out later, was that the traditional home of the Ben-der was undergoing emergency flea fumigation, and Emma drew the short straw. So, being wily on top of everything else, she asked me and our third roommate—Steve the or-nithologist—if we'd mind if she hosted a little party. We said of course not, and our address was duly distributed over the vet school listserve. Then somebody let it slip just what the Bender actually entailed, and both Steve and I decided to get the hell out of Dodge and repair to the homes of our respective boyfriends, of which mine is by far the cuter.

That's how I ended up in the apartment of one Detec-tive Brian Cody, drinking yummy Australian cabernet and eating equally yummy lasagna, which we'd managed to stay out of bed long enough to throw together. It took over an hour to cook, but neither of us minded this fact; the casse-role started boiling over right around the time the two of us stopped doing the same, metaphorically speaking.

I'd brought my stuff over, planning to spend the night with malice aforethought—this new level of intimacy being precipitated not so much by my ability to have a mature re-lationship as by the Invasion of the Alcoholic Veterinarians. In addition to a tote bag filled with my clothes, that day's edition of my beloved *Gabriel Monitor*, my contact lens stuff, and some recently acquired birth control pills, I'd brought along my dog, Shakespeare, who's involved in a romance of her own with Cody's mixed-breed pooch.

After dinner, too full even to contemplate a move back to the boudoir, we flopped on the couch for digestion and low-grade snuggling. Cody asked me to hand him the newspaper, and in the spirit of domestic bliss I actually stood up and got it for him.

He took one look at the above-the-fold headline, gave a rather manly sort of groan, and tossed the paper on the coffee table.

"Nice way to treat my deathless prose." I tried poking him in the gut for emphasis, but it was so goddamn muscular it just made my finger hurt. "I spent all day yesterday on that stupid story. Least you could do is pretend you're interested."

"Sorry, baby. I guess this small-time stuff is getting to me. Nothing personal."

"Personal? I *wrote* the damn thing. In my line of work, it doesn't get much more—"

He kissed me for a while, which shut me up quite efficiently. By the time we came up for air, his Irish Catholic guilt had kicked in and he picked up the paper again. We lay there with my head on his chest while he read the story and I kissed him on his extremely white neck. Again with the groaning sound.

"Are you implying," I said into his shoulder, "that chasing down a bunch of hideous sculptures is beneath a highly trained police officer such as yourself?"

"You saying you don't think they're worth finding?"

"I think they look like a high school shop class gone horribly wrong."

"Yeah, well, the chief's having kittens."

"Sure he is. The city paid fifty thousand bucks for those things, and they suck."

The sculptures in question had been commissioned by Common Council as part of its Gabriel Green improvement project; artists had been invited to submit four-part designs to be installed at the corners of the pedestrian mall. The winner was a Bessler College art professor, who proposed a quartet of metal sculptures evoking the Benson bell tower, the main Bessler dorm, the Unitarian Church, and some other tall object whose name escapes me at the moment.

But Gabriel's a tough town, artistically speaking. When the sculptures were unveiled a week previous to the Bender, the mayor himself declared them, quote, "ugly as a pizza-faced Republican." Two days later they were gone—which was a neat trick, considering that they weighed a ton and had been bolted into the concrete by some very burly union members.

Now it was up to Gabriel's finest to track them down, or else; Cody told me he'd never seen this much heat over a case that didn't involve an actual corpse. (This was ironic as the vast majority of Gabrielites would just as soon they stayed lost, thank you very much.) And since Cody was by far the sharpest tack on the force—I'm speaking as a city news reporter here, not as a girlfriend with lust in her heart—the case had fallen smack into his lap.

"So," I said, "are you gonna find them or what?"

"Eventually."

"You don't sound too psyched."

"Look, I know the whole town is going nuts—"

"Around here it doesn't take much."

"No joke. But I gotta tell you, this isn't what I call a *case*. Back in Boston, we . . ."

I stopped listening then, mostly because I was starting to experience a twisty feeling in the gut area. Cody had been talking about Boston a lot lately, and the very idea of him moving back there—some four hundred miles east of yours truly—was making me criminally insane.

"... you want to hear about it?"

"Huh?"

"I said do you want to hear about the Witherbee case?"

"The what?"

"Weren't you even listening?"

I tried to remember what the hell he'd been saying. "Um, sure I was."

"Sure you were." He leaned over and kissed me, either because I'm really cute or because he knew exactly what'd been going through my head. I didn't want to think which.

"So what's the Witherbee case?"

"The Witherbee case was ... Well, you might say it was the one that got away."

"One you never solved?"

"One of a few."

"But this one's the biggie?"

"Yeah. You want a refill?" He drained the dregs of the bottle into my glass, and we repositioned ourselves on opposite ends of the couch, legs intertwined. "So here's the story. Boston Brahmin name of Alicia Witherbee is found murdered in her Beacon Hill town house. Really grisly scene—face bashed in but good. I gotta say, it was one of the most vicious things I've ever seen on the job."

"And that's saying something."

"Yeah. And somehow, seeing it in this rich lady's house, with crystal and paintings and silver all over the place ...

Somehow it made it seem worse than if it just happened on the street."

"So robbery wasn't the point of the thing."

"Huh?"

"None of the expensive stuff was stolen, right?"

He pinned me with his baby greens. "Do you have any idea how sexy it is when you think like a cop?"

"Right back at ya. So am I right?"

"Not exactly. I mean, yeah, the house wasn't that well tossed, but some pretty expensive stuff was missing—a lot of her jewelry, maybe eight grand in cash, a laptop computer, CD player, some handbags that turned out to be worth a grand a pop. Oh, and the perp cleaned out all her fancy lingerie."

"What?"

"Pretty sick, huh? So right away we wonder if it's some thief who's got a thing for ladies' underpants, or else—"

"Or else he wants to shower his girlfriend with somebody else's Skivvies."

"Right. But pretty soon we start going down another road."

"Let me guess—the husband. Assuming she's got one, right?"

"She's got one, all right, but that turns out to be a dead end. First off, the husband was the one who called it in— he was actually on the phone with the vic when the assault happened."

"So he's off the hook?"

"Course not. He was in his office when it happened, but obviously he could've hired somebody to do the job. We looked at him hard, but we never found a thing to connect him to it."

"Motive?"

"Plenty. His wife was a very bad girl."

"Okay, back up. Who was she and what was she into?"

"You sure you're interested in this?"

"It's a hell of a lot better than the goddamn sculptures. Come on, spill."

"All right. Here's the scoop, as you might say." He stretched out until his feet were in my lap. I figured I might as well cultivate the devoted-girlfriend thing, so I started massaging them. Don't tell Gloria Steinem, but I actually enjoy it. "Alicia Harrington Witherbee. Age forty-two. Married, no kids. Daughter of Alistair Harrington, who sat in the state senate for twenty years or so. Real upstanding guy, *Mayflower* descendant and all that goes with it. As Old Boston as you can get. Mighty uptight, from what I saw of him."

"You realize I went to prep school with these creatures."

"Yeah, well, somehow I like you anyway."

"Thanks. So who's Alicia's mom?"

"It's pronounced 'Ah-*lee*-see-ah,' by the way."

"Of course it is. So who was Ah-*lee*-see-ah's mom?"

"Mother's named Patience but is apparently anything but. More like . . . What was that thing you called my ex-wife?"

"High-maintenance."

"Right. I guess that's her in a nutshell. Hosts the kind of society balls you read about in the *Globe* on Sunday."

"And what was the deal with Alicia?"

"She sat on the boards of lots of those blueblood charities."

"Naturally."

"And stole from them."

"*What?*"

"She siphoned off something like three million dollars over the course of five years."

"But why? If she was rolling in it—"

"She wasn't. Her father was, and her husband pulled down six figures, but apparently Alicia wanted some spending money of her own."

"How did she manage it?"

"Don't ask me. Also, don't ask me where the money is. We never found it."

"But somebody was pissed."

"Pissed enough to use her face for batting practice."

"Yikes."

"Yeah. Even the family doctor practically threw up when he ID'd her. Nasty business."

"No kidding."

"And it gets worse. She was also having an affair."

"Busy lady. With who?"

"Some bigwig lawyer who was chairman of the board of one of the charities. A married guy, no less. And yes, we looked at him for the murder, and his wife too. But no dice. And since he was hooked up with one of the places she stole from, we thought maybe he was in on that too. But no dice either, at least as far as we could tell."

"How many cops did you have on this anyway?"

"Dozens. It was what they call a red-ball. Real high-profile, lots of media breathing down our necks. No offense."

"None taken. Murder weapon?"

"Your garden-variety Louisville Slugger. Left at the scene. No prints."

"So who was, you know, the prime suspect?"

"You're not gonna believe it."

"Try me."

"It was the maid."

"You gotta be kidding."

"Nope. They had this woman working for them, not living there but working six days a week. One of seven kids from a tough Irish family in Southie."

"Your old stomping grounds."

"Right."

"You knew them?"

He shook his head. "I'd heard of these guys when I was in high school, but I didn't hang out with them—my dad would've taken a strap to me, frankly. They were trouble."

"And the maid?"

"One Mary Greavey. Three of her brothers belonged to the Shamrocks, and—"

"Please tell me that's not the name of a gang."

"Yep."

"How festive."

"Yeah, well, if you're not one of their own they'd knock you down soon as look at you."

"Oh."

"You might say their idea of being a fine upstanding Irishman is different from mine."

"I like yours better. So why did you suspect the maid?"

"Well, for one thing, a lot of the stuff that was stolen was what you might call . . . You know . . ."

"Girlie."

"Right. A lot of it wasn't just expensive, it was also something a woman might like—jewelry, purses, silk nightgowns. Maybe it wasn't some pervert, or some guy who wanted to give it to his girlfriend. Maybe it was a woman who went . . . shopping."

"Shopping with a baseball bat?"

"Wouldn't be the first time."

"And it also wouldn't be the first time the household help

hated her boss's guts. So what did she have to say for herself?"

"Nothing. She disappeared the day of the murder."

"A-*ha*."

"Went to Logan, used a brand-new passport, and bought a ticket to Dublin. We had Interpol looking for her for months, but she never surfaced."

"So what's the mystery? The maid did it, right?"

"Maybe. But nobody who knew the maid could believe she'd pull something like that. I guess she just wasn't that smart, or that mean either."

"Maybe they were covering for her."

"Could be. But I'm more inclined to think somebody paid her to get lost."

"And why would they do that?"

"Because she was in on it, one way or another. I'm thinking maybe she let the perp in and then looked the other way in exchange for a wad of cash and a trip to the old country."

"Interesting. And this case has been driving you crazy for years?"

He shrugged. "Seems like we should've cracked it."

"Why this one in particular?"

"I don't know. Maybe it sticks in my craw that smashing some lady's head in with a baseball bat should turn out to be the perfect crime. It's just so . . ."

"Inelegant?"

"You sure do have a way with words."

"Okay, so what else? What about the husband?"

"I told you, we never even got close to pinning anything on him."

"But who was he?"

"Investment banker at one of those white-shoe firms downtown. The kind who'll help you turn your million bucks into five, if you're the right type of guy."

"And what type is that?"

"An old-money Protestant from Beacon Hill. Maybe Back Bay if he feels like slumming."

"What'd you think when you interviewed him? Did you get the feeling he was messed up in it somehow?"

"Yep."

"But you didn't trust your instincts?"

"Instincts and no evidence don't get you very far, especially when you're dealing with people like the Harringtons and the Witherbees. Their reach goes up pretty high. These guys go golfing with the governor."

"Jeepers."

"I thought you said you went to school with these people."

"Yeah, well, I never said they actually *spoke* to me. They all thought I was some kind of whacked-out lesbian."

"Hard to picture from where I'm sitting."

"So whatever happened to the husband? He marry somebody else a couple months later?"

"Left town. Said the whole thing was too painful and moved to New York."

"Which probably didn't make him seem any less guilty."

"Right. But we didn't have anything to hold him on, so he went. In the end he had to answer to a higher authority."

"The NYPD?"

"Saint Peter. He died in a car accident a couple of years later. Drove too fast on some Italian highway, and that's all she wrote."

"So what do you think really happened?"

"To the husband? I told you, he—"

"Nah, I mean in general. Who do you think did it?"

"Like I said, I think the husband and the maid were in on it somehow."

"In on it together?"

"Crossed my mind, but I kind of doubt it. Mary Greavey wasn't ugly but she wasn't what you'd call a raving beauty either, and apparently she didn't have so much going on up-stairs. I doubt she'd hold a lot of interest for the likes of Jonathan Witherbee the Third."

"Sure, but maybe he used her. It's the oldest trick in the book, isn't it? He gets her to help him kill his wife, then drops her like a hot potato. And there's nothing she can do about it, 'cause if she comes back to rat on him, she goes to jail too."

"You want to go to bed?"

"I thought we were solving your murder case for you."

"Later."

"You saying you don't want to stay up all night talking about the late Alicia Witherbee?"

"Case's been cold for five years," he said. "I think it can wait until I've had my way with you."

. . .

We finally crawled out of the sack around eleven the next morning. Cody went for a run with the dogs while I whipped up assorted brunchables, and when he got back I hopped in the shower with him on the grounds that it was a sin to waste water.

"So what do you want to do today?" he said as we dug into the stone-cold pancakes. "My Sunday's wide open."

"My first choice would be to flee my house until the coast is clear."

"You really think it was that bad?"

"I'm afraid if I go home I'll find eight drunk vet students in my bed."

"Then I better give you sanctuary."

"I'll try to earn my keep."

"What did you have in mind? I'm more than willing to let you clean my apartment—"

I kicked him under the kitchen table. "If I cleaned the place it'd wind up dirtier than when I started."

"I'd let you cook for me all day."

"How very liberated of you."

"Well, if it was mending you had in mind, you're out of luck. I bring that stuff over to my mom's."

"Hmm . . . Back rub?"

"Sold."

"But first tell me more about the Witherbee case."

"You serious?"

"It's pretty damn fascinating."

"In that case"—he wiggled his eyebrows at me—"you wanna see the file?"

"You seriously have it here?"

"A copy of it, yeah."

"Are you supposed to do that?"

"No."

"Okay, lemme at it." He took off in the direction of the hall closet, and thirty seconds later he was back with one of those document boxes you always see on TV shows about lawyers. "Wowee. Pretty big file."

"Pretty big case."

"And you copied the whole thing? Every page?"

"I was feeling a little obsessive about it at the time. Besides, I needed something to take my mind off the fact that my wife was cheating on me with half the cops in Boston."

"More fun to think about violent death."

"You got that right."

"So what goodies do we have here?"

"You name it. Autopsy report, witness statements, inventory of stolen property, cops' notes—good luck reading those, by the way—household receipts, tax returns, bank statements . . ."

"Think I'll skip the tax returns. Pretty sure I don't want to see the autopsy report either, thanks just the same."

"How about the newspaper clippings?"

"You keep track of that sort of thing?"

"It's always good to stay on top of what the public knows about your case. Common sense."

"Ah." I leafed through the folder, which was in reverse chronological order. The story on the bottom was the breaking news—"Socialite Alicia Witherbee Murdered"—while the ones on top were follow-ups of the "Still No Leads in Witherbee Case" variety. "Who's this Cathy Carlson?"

"Who? Oh, yeah. She was the *Globe*'s cop reporter at the time. Unbelievable pain in the neck. You'd like her."

"Wow. Alicia Witherbee was kind of a tough-looking broad, huh?" I waved the yellowing newspaper at him. "Tough in a patrician sort of way, I mean."

"I'm not sure I get you."

"I don't know. She just seems like the kind of person you wouldn't want to cross. Hard as nails. Always super-duper polite but ready to stick the knife in when you're not looking."

"That's pretty damn accurate, from what I heard."

"Did she have any other enemies?"

"Baby, from what I could tell she didn't have anything *but* enemies. Even her friends weren't what you'd call warm and fuzzy about her, or about anything else for that matter."

"But did anybody have a particular reason to want her dead? I mean, besides the half dozen people you already told me about?"

"Hmm . . . Well, there was a girl who'd been engaged to Witherbee before Alicia met him, and apparently he broke it off and she went overboard about it. Thought she'd been publicly humiliated and wound up having some kind of mental breakdown."

"Now, *that's* high-maintenance for you."

"Yeah. And then there were all the people who ran the charities she stole from. They probably wouldn't have been too sorry to see her go. One of them even went under—place called the Ellis Foundation that ran a little private museum off the Fenway. Had to sell off the art and unload the building to pay off their debts."

"And you're telling me nobody even *suspected* what she was up to until after she was dead?"

"Hardly. She was under investigation for fraud, embezzlement, misappropriation of funds, the whole shebang. But her family had managed to keep it all under wraps for the time being. Pretty powerful folks."

"And you think they would've gotten her off the hook?"

"Not likely. Remember, there were also plenty of big-game people at the charities she bilked, and they wanted her head on a pike."

"Or maybe her face bashed in with a baseball bat."

"You got it. All I'm saying is, her family managed to keep the investigation out of the papers. Everything was being done on the q.t., but I'd bet dollars to doughnuts it all would've hit the fan sooner or later. Probably sooner."

"What if . . ."

"Yeah?"

"Never mind. I was going to say, what if somebody killed her to keep the whole thing quiet, so there wouldn't be a scandal. But there was, obviously. The embezzlement was all over the papers."

"Right. After the murder everything came out. Somebody leaked it to the press, and that was that. Pretty inevitable, if you ask me."

"Maybe whoever killed her didn't know that."

"It's possible, I guess. But—"

"But pretty far-fetched. Okay, what else you got for me?" He handed across another folder, and when I opened it I wished I hadn't. "Yuck. I said icks-nay on the autopsy stuff, okay?"

"That's crime scene."

"Oh." I opened it back up and took another look at the picture. It showed Alicia Harrington Witherbee, dead as the proverbial doornail, splayed out on a floor that looked to be made of some very expensive Italian title. "Is this the kitchen?"

"Bathroom."

"It's *huge.*"

"Looks even bigger in real life."

"Why's she half-dressed?"

"According to the husband, she'd just come home from a meeting and she was changing for a workout with her personal trainer."

"At a gym?"

"They had an exercise room in the basement."

"And did he show up?"

He shook his head. "Said he rang the bell but no one answered, so he left."

"So who called the cops?"

"Like I told you, the husband was supposedly on the phone with her when she was attacked. She'd called him to talk about a dinner party they were hosting, and all of a sudden she screams and drops the cordless and the line goes dead. So the husband calls 911 from his office and goes racing over there but the uniforms beat him to the scene and he goes ballistic."

"Upset because his wife is dead?"

"Really upset, yeah."

"And that didn't make you think he didn't want her that way?"

"There's a hell of a difference between hiring someone to do your dirty work and seeing the result all over your bathroom floor."

"Somebody let him see the body?"

"Got past one of the uniforms, took one look, and lost it. Like I said, it wasn't a pretty sight. Rookie on the scene nearly fainted. *Guy* rookie."

I looked at the picture again. Alicia Witherbee was splayed out on the floor, an oozing red mess where her head used to be. There was plenty of blood covering the fancy tile, a pool so dark red it was almost purple.

"I thought crime scene photos were supposed to be in black and white."

"Progress."

"Lovely."

The color really did make the whole thing way more gruesome; it wasn't like a scene out of an old movie, something long ago and far away, but a death that was real and tragic and absolutely *gross*. Whatever Alicia Witherbee had done, she didn't deserve to wind up like this—diminished and exposed, half-naked on the bathroom floor, her expensive silk blouse open and bloody. Underneath was some equally expensive underwear, also spattered with red. I pictured her shopping for them in New York or Paris or wherever, modeling the silk and lace in the mirror and never imagining that she was going to *die* in them, for Chrissake.

"What's on your mind?"

"Huh?"

"You've got a weird expression on your face."

"You don't want to know."

"Sure I do."

"You really want to hear how quickly your girlfriend can go from cringing at the sight of a corpse to wondering how much her underwear cost?"

"Ouch. Now who's cold-blooded?"

"We women take our lingerie very seriously."

"Apparently so did the killer."

"That is *so* creepy." I flipped through the folder some more, then picked up the list of stolen property. "Clearly these people didn't know the glory that is Filene's Basement. Silver came from Shreve, Crump & Lowe. Some of the jewelry too—and Tiffany's, of course. Bags from Hermès. CD player was Bose. Lingerie was Lise Charmel and La Perla and Rigby & Peller—they make panties for the queen of England, for Chrissake."

"It's kind of sexy to me that you know this."

"Yeah, well, I just know about it. I can't afford to wear it."

"Too bad. I bet you'd look great in—"

"Can I see that crime scene picture again?" He handed it over. "Hmm . . . Are there any from some other angles or something?"

"Bottom of the pile."

"Man, you know, I'd swear there's something that doesn't look right." I laid the photos out on the kitchen table, trying to avoid the minefield of maple syrup spots. "Hey, do you know if Alicia'd lost some weight before she died?"

"Didn't hear anything in particular on that. But she was seeing a personal trainer, so maybe yeah."

"Were all her clothes about the same size?"

"I guess. You can check the inventory of what we found in her closet. Crime scene guys went into overtime."

I flipped through more pages, then looked back at the photos. "Nah, everything's a six or an eight. I suppose she didn't *gain* any weight either, right? But it doesn't make sense . . ."

"What doesn't make sense?"

"Where does it list what clothes she was wearing when she died?"

He looked through another folder. "One cream-colored silk blouse. Label says Ann Taylor. Light pink brassiere and matching underpants. Label says Simon Pearl."

"Simone Pérèle. It's French. Bra alone costs just shy of two hundred bucks."

"Really?"

"Really. Tell me something—how many women detectives did you have on this case?"

"Er . . . that would be none."

"That's what I figured."

"What's your point?"

I held the first photo in front of his nose. "What's wrong with this picture?"

"Um . . . she's dead?"

"That, and . . . her bra doesn't fit."

"How can you tell?"

"The cup is a little too big and the band is a little too tight."

He stared at it for a while. "Looks okay to me."

"See how it's gapping in front? And how her skin is bulging over the part that goes around?"

"So what?"

"So nobody buys a two-hundred-dollar bra that doesn't fit."

"Maybe she ordered the wrong size."

"Listen very carefully. No woman who buys a two-hundred-dollar bra would stand for one that doesn't fit *perfectly*."

"What are you saying?"

"Either that's not Alicia Witherbee's bra," I said. "Or that's not Alicia Witherbee."

▪ ▪ ▪

I have no idea how Cody explained this particular discovery to his old pals at the Boston cop shop, but in the end they followed my advice: Somebody called Simone Pérèle in Paris and found out whether they'd had an order sometime after the murder for the same size, color, and style of underthings that'd been found on the body. They'd had plenty, but only a few were from customers they'd never heard of before. Interpol checked them out, and there she was: Alicia Harrington Witherbee, alive and well and living in the south of France under a very expensive fake passport. Last thing I heard she was fighting extradition.

"She talking?" I said during one of the umpteen dinners out Cody had showered upon me since I solved his most vexing case through my knowledge of fancy underwear.

"No way. She's got five layers of lawyers protecting her flank."

"Didn't your old partner fly over there or something?"

"Yeah, for all the good it did him. He got to meet with her and the suits for an hour, and I guess she was as cold as they come. Said it was a pretty odd experience, though—not often you get to charge the vic with her own murder."

"Or more like Mary Greavey's."

"Exactly."

"They exhume the body yet?"

He nodded. "It's her, all right. Now we know why the husband was so keen on having it cremated. The Harringtons insisted on putting her in the family plot. Good thing they got their way."

"I still don't get how she could've pulled it off."

"Well, she and Mary Greavey were about the same age, same coloring, roughly the same figure—"

"Holy cow. Maybe that's why she hired her in the first place."

His big green eyes got bigger. "You know, I didn't think this could get any uglier. But I wouldn't be surprised."

"But explain one thing to me. How come the switch didn't get caught during the autopsy?"

"Why would it? They only compare dental records and such if there's any question about who the body is. But Alicia Witherbee supposedly died in her own house, wearing her own clothes. She was identified by her husband *and* the family doctor."

"Was he in on it too?"

"Bank records show a tidy cash infusion shortly before the murder. He needed it too—ugly divorce nearly cleaned him out."

"And what about the husband?"

"From what they told me in catechism, I assume he's rotting in hell."

"What I meant was, do you really think his death was an accident? Isn't it a little too neat?"

"You think he faked it too? And he's running around Europe somewhere with—"

"I was thinking more along the lines that Alicia was tying up her loose ends. I mean, look at what she pulled off. Getting rid of hubby would've been a walk in the park."

"You women scare me sometimes."

"We try."

"You know, I try to be liberated and everything, but it's still killing me that I gnawed on this case for five years and you got it in five minutes."

"Let's just say it was out of your area of expertise."

"Did I tell you they found a lot of the stolen goods in her house over there—the jewelry and the handbags and everything? Can you believe she took it with her?"

"Course she did. It wasn't a question of somebody stealing her personal stuff, it was her not being able to part with it all. The fact that it would make Mary Greavey look even more guilty was probably just a fringe benefit."

"But how'd you know she'd call up and order the same damn underwear she'd left on the body?"

"Instinct, I guess. I mean, she must have talked the maid into trying the clothes on, or how else would all the blood-spatter stuff be right? And then to leave those beautiful things all covered in blood, on the body of some Irish maid . . . My guess is getting the brand-new ones wrapped in nice, clean tissue paper would be step one in washing her hands of the whole thing."

"Like I said, you women scare me sometimes."

"So are the Boston cops gonna pin a medal on you?"

Or, I thought with an icky twist of the gut, *are they going to break my little heart and offer you your old job back?*

"Nah. My partner got the credit."

Excellent. "That okay with you?"

"My idea, actually. Plus, it wasn't like I was the one who figured it out. That was your department."

"And Cathy Carlson of the *Boston Globe* gets to break the story, Beacon Hill being a ways out of the *Monitor's* circulation area."

"I'm afraid so."

"So how you gonna make it up to me?"

"Um . . . keep taking you out to decent midpriced restaurants?"

"It's a start."

"But I'm getting the feeling you have other ideas."

"Well, it just so happens," I said, "that there's a lovely little French ensemble I have my eye on . . ."